INTO THE
DARKEST
DAY

BOOKS BY KATE HEWITT

A Mother's Goodbye
Secrets We Keep
Not My Daughter
No Time to Say Goodbye
A Hope for Emily

INTO THE
DARKEST
DAY

KATE HEWITT

Bookouture

Published by Bookouture in 2020

An imprint of Storyfire Ltd.
Carmelite House
50 Victoria Embankment
London EC4Y 0DZ

www.bookouture.com

Copyright © Kate Hewitt, 2020

Kate Hewitt has asserted her right to be identified
as the author of this work.

ISBN: 978-1-83888-510-6
eBook ISBN: 978-1-83888-509-0

This book is a work of fiction. Names, characters, businesses,
organizations, places and events other than those clearly in the
public domain, are either the product of the author's imagination
or are used fictitiously. Any resemblance to actual persons, living or
dead, events or locales is entirely coincidental.

To my old friend Greg Evans, for giving me the germ of the idea for this story, and to Cat and Jim, just because I wanted to dedicate a book to you. Love, K.

PROLOGUE

The street is empty, the city a palette of grays, as she looks out the window and waits. She has been waiting for months, years, her whole life. And she does not know when—or if—the waiting will end.

She understands that promises can't always be kept, and she knows better than to ask or expect words put to paper, not when the whole world has been held in the balance, life itself no more than a dandelion clock in the wind.

Still, she cranes her head to look down the street; the only signs of life she sees now are two raggedy children chasing a cat, and a charwoman lugging her pail. It is late afternoon, the sky a heavy gray, the world dispirited.

It has been three months since the victory in Europe, nearly a month since the war the world over has ended, and yet no one seems able to summon much effort to celebrate, never mind rejoice. Perhaps they are too weary; they have forgotten how to hope.

As she scans the empty street, she does not know if she hopes or not. Her belief feels more certain than that, a hope with a sure foundation, and yet even so she does not know what will happen.

He will come, she thinks.

As the sunlight is leached from the sky, she lets her mind drift. The night at The Berkeley, when they danced and drank champagne. The moment at the stairs to the Underground, and then again in the narrow little hall, when she handed him his coat and the world seemed to tilt as she forgot how to breathe.

Every memory is precious, because she knows that they are all she might have. He has not written since September last year, not one word. Perhaps he is dead. She thinks she would know that; fancifully, she believes she would feel it, but perhaps she wouldn't. Perhaps she'll never know.

The possibility sits inside her like a stone, a lifetime of this. There could be worse things, she tells herself practically, and of course she knows there could be. Far worse. The news has come from Germany, the terrible photographs she can't bear to look at, and yet neither can she make herself look away. Yes, far, far worse than this.

She puts one hand on the cool glass and spreads her fingers wide as a sigh escapes her, a sound of acceptance rather than defeat. Darkness is starting to fall, like a mist creeping in. Not today, then, but perhaps tomorrow.

She will keep waiting. No matter how long, no matter how futile, she will wait.

PART ONE

CHAPTER ONE

ABBY

Abby Reese watched the dust rise from the dirt road in a golden-brown plume, obscuring the car that was causing it, although she knew who was driving. At least, she acknowledged as she stood on the farmhouse's front porch, one hand wrapped around a weathered wooden post, she knew *of* the driver. She'd never met Simon Elliot, and had only heard of him a few weeks ago. Yet now he was almost here, and she had no idea what to expect—a flicker of curiosity was championed by a deeper sense of trepidation, born from experience. Abby didn't like the unexpected.

The dust cloud grew larger as the car continued down the drive, a straight shot of dirt road that Abby knew like her own hand. All thirty-two years of her life had been spent on Willow Tree Orchards, in the southern heartland of Wisconsin, the gateway—or at least one of them—to the state and its many lakes.

She straightened, her hand tightening around the post, fingers pressing into splintered wood. Next to her, her golden retriever Bailey's tail thumped a staccato beat on the weathered boards of the porch, both of them waiting and watching as the car pulled up in front of the farmhouse and the driver cut the engine, leaving a stillness behind like an echo. She couldn't see him through the darkly tinted windows, and she had no idea what he would look like when he opened the door—old or young? Tall or short? All he was to her at this point was a name.

Three weeks ago, Simon Elliot had written her an email through the orchard's website, utterly out of the blue, asking to visit her and her father here in Wisconsin. The only other time she'd communicated with him was two days previous, when he'd sent a confirmation email of his visit, after he'd arrived in Chicago all the way from England. And now he was actually here, to give her—or, really, her father—something that belonged to the family. Something neither of them had even known about, or so her father said.

The car door opened and Abby stepped down from the porch, Bailey trotting at her heels. A smile flirted with her mouth and then slipped away. Nerves danced in her belly, along with a curiosity she couldn't suppress, even though at least part of her wanted to.

"You must be Abby." The man who emerged from the dust-streaked car had floppy brown hair, glasses, and kind eyes—brown and warm, like mahogany, like chocolate. The warmth of his expression had Abby's smile finding its way back. The nerves settled down and her curiosity, although still wary, sharpened just that little bit.

"Yes… and you must be Simon." Obviously. She let out a little laugh, because he was smiling and suddenly this didn't seem as hard as she'd thought it would be. "Welcome to Willow Tree Orchards."

"Thank you. And who is this?" He nodded towards Bailey, who was sticking to Abby's side.

"This is Bailey. You're all right with dogs?" Not that Bailey could do much damage. She was ten years old, a tired, faithful old girl.

"Oh, yes, certainly." Simon bent down to pat Bailey's head before he straightened and looked around, seeming delightfully pleased by everything he saw. "What a beautiful place you have here."

Abby followed his gaze, taking in the familiar sight of fields rolling to a sunny horizon, the apple trees in full, verdant leaf in the distance, the clapboard farmhouse that was a hundred years old and looked it, all under a picture-perfect blue sky. Something settled in her bones, a rightness that she clung to. Yes, this was home. This was good.

"Thank you," she said as she started towards the screen door that led inside the house. "Would you like to come in? I've made lemonade."

"American lemonade?" he asked with a sparkle to his eye, and Abby nodded. What other kind was there? "Marvelous. I'd love some, thank you."

"How long did it take you to drive from Chicago?" she asked as she led him inside, relying on the usual pleasantries to pave the way, at least until she found her social footing.

"Not long at all. An hour and a half, if that. I was expecting it to be longer. You always hear about the great distances in America, everyone taking a trip, give or take a thousand miles."

"Yes, I suppose you do." Not that she'd taken many, or really, any. But that was okay. That had been her choice, made deliberately and definitively, fifteen years ago.

Abby moved down the hallway with its faded runner and the grandfather clock against the wall, still ticking time away after seven decades of standing sentry, to the kitchen at the back of the house—a large, friendly room where she spent a good deal of her time, whether it was with her laptop and paperwork spread out at the old, square table, or standing by the stove, stirring something or other, while Bailey flopped at her feet.

How many evenings had she stood or sat here and watched the sun sink towards the orchards, its golden rays spreading along the backyard like melted butter? How many mornings had she cradled a cup of coffee and watched the mist melt into shreds of fog as the sun burned the last of it away?

Now she took in the view of the backyard, the burgeoning vegetable garden, and then the orchards beyond, their thick green leaves hiding the first small fruits of the season. It was early July, with still over a month to go before the first varieties of apples could be harvested—a busy time of year patrolling the orchards and inspecting the trees for insects or disease, as well as keeping their small farm shop, Abby's own brainchild, running.

She reached for the pitcher of fresh-squeezed lemonade that had been chilling in the fridge and poured them both tall glasses, while Simon stood in the doorway, jangling the keys in his pocket and looking around. "I suppose it's cooler on the front porch," she said. "If you don't mind going back outside?"

"Sounds perfect."

She handed Simon his glass of lemonade and he took a sip, smiling in pleasure at the taste.

"Ah, I've missed this."

"Do you not have lemonade in England?"

"In some places, but lemonade is generally the fizzy drink, not fresh-squeezed. Like Sprite."

"I see." Abby nodded. She'd never known that, but why should she? She hadn't been anywhere in the world but Wisconsin, save for a couple of vacations when she was a child—the ubiquitous trip to Disney, and one golden summer road trip to the Grand Canyon, which felt like a million years ago, sepia-tinted in her mind, frozen forever. "Well, enjoy," she told him as she led the way back outside.

"Your father?" Simon asked carefully as they stepped back onto the front porch, the old boards creaking under their footsteps, Bailey between them. "Is he…?"

"He's in the barn at the moment, inspecting a delivery of pesticide," Abby answered. "Organic," she added. "We do everything sustainably here."

"So I saw on your website." Simon gave her a glinting smile, and she looked away, finding herself just a little bit disconcerted by his easy, rather bookish charm. He looked very British, she decided, in battered cords, a slightly crumpled button-down shirt, and wire-framed glasses.

His accent sounded sophisticated—or what did the British say? Posh. It sounded like something she'd hear on one of the BBC dramas she sometimes watched on Netflix.

"So, will he be coming back soon?" Simon asked as they settled in rocking chairs on the porch, and Bailey sprawled contentedly between them. The day was warm and drowsy, a few bumblebees tumbling lazily through the still air, the scent of honeysuckle that climbed up the side of the house as sweet and heavy as perfume.

"Yes, when he can." Abby injected a note of positivity in her voice that she didn't necessarily feel. The truth was, when Abby had read Simon's first email out to her father, she'd been surprised by his clear reluctance to summon any interest. He'd stated that he didn't need to know about any medal, because the past was in the past, where it belonged. Abby had thought *why can't we live that way then?* but, of course, she hadn't said anything. They were living that way. Sort of.

Still, she hadn't understood her father's obvious reticence. These were different ghosts they were dealing with.

Based on his lack of enthusiasm for Simon's visit, it hadn't surprised her when he'd gone out to the barn right before Simon was meant to arrive. It bordered on rude, but Abby knew it wasn't meant to be, or at least she hoped it wasn't. It was just her father's way of dealing, or not dealing, with something he didn't like.

Abby was well-used to his ways, had learned a tried-and-tested method of handling him that her best friend Shannon said was dysfunctional but Abby preferred to think of as expedient. Besides, Shannon didn't know everything, even though she thought she did. Only Abby and her father did, though they never talked about it. Only she and her father knew how to move carefully around the ghosts that drifted through every room of the house. Only she and her father knew why they were there—what had really happened the day her mother and brother had died.

"I hope he does come," Simon said with another one of his engaging smiles, the kind that crinkled eyes and wrinkled a nose and made Abby feel like smiling back. "It was his father after all, isn't that right?"

"Tom Reese? Yes, he is—*was*—my father's father." Abby shook her head slowly. "Although neither of us know how your grandmother could have ended up with his war medal. My father didn't even know he had been given one in the first place."

"I'm afraid I don't really know why she had it, either. My grandmother didn't tell me that part, at least not exactly, although she gave a few hints."

"It's very strange…"

"But intriguing, don't you think?" Simon leaned forward, his face alight with interest, his brown eyes sparkling behind his glasses.

Abby rolled her glass, damp with condensation, between her palms.

"Yes, I suppose it is." She knew she sounded wary, by the way Simon's smile faltered as his curious gaze scanned her face.

When she'd read Simon's first email, she hadn't known what to think.

Hello, you don't know me, but I know of you—at least a bit! My grandmother Sophie Mather died a few months ago, and she was in possession of your grandfather Tom Reese's Purple Heart medal, awarded during his active service in the second world war. She told me she wanted it returned to "its proper owner".

I've read on your website that your grandfather passed away some time ago, and I'm very sorry for your loss. I presume the proper owner would now be you or your father.

*I'm coming to the United States this summer for an extended
visit, and would love the opportunity to return the medal to
your family.*

Abby had read it all, her mind both blank and spinning.
Sophie Mather? What medal? And a *visit?*

"Do you know anything about your grandfather's war service?"
Simon asked and she looked up, shaking her head.

"No, not really." Not at all, actually. All Abby knew was that
Tom Reese had fought in Europe in the Second World War, come
home to Minnesota, and then moved with his young bride Susan
to Wisconsin. He'd bought Willow Tree Orchards in 1951, and
died when Abby was a toddler, forty years later, a heart attack
when he was seventy-one. Her grandmother had died three years
after that.

Abby didn't remember either of them really at all, save for a few
vague recollections of her granny—a powdered, wrinkled cheek
pressed to hers, and a tin of boiled sweets kept high on a shelf
in the pantry, doled out at special moments. There was only one
portrait of them to go by, hung in the hall, of Tom and Susan's
wedding day, black and white, both of them looking serious and
old-fashioned, even a little bit grim.

And yet, somehow, Simon Elliot's grandmother back in Britain
had been in possession of Tom Reese's war medal. There had to
be a reason.

"It was clearly very important to her," Simon said after a
moment. "*He* was. The tone in her voice, the way she talked about
him—they clearly had a friendship of some sort."

Abby shifted in her seat, the rocking chair giving a protesting
creak. "I really don't know anything about it. I'm sorry…"

"He never mentioned my grandmother?" Simon asked,
sounding both earnest and disappointed. "Sophie Mather? Not
even in passing?"

"Not that I know of. But, as I said in the email, he died when I was a very young child. I don't remember him at all. Maybe my father…" She stopped, not wanting to give him more hope than was warranted. She doubted very much that her father wanted to stroll down memory lane with Simon Elliot.

"Don't be sorry." Simon glanced out at the rolling lawns that led to the main road, everything lush and green this time of year, before the heat of the summer dried the grass out and turned it brown. "It's so beautiful here, and I've always loved the States. I spent a year here after university, in Pennsylvania. I absolutely loved it."

"What were you doing?"

"It was a teaching program for new graduates. I taught history to a bunch of students in inner-city Philadelphia."

"Goodness. That sounds challenging."

"Yes, but wonderful too." He cocked his head. "What about you? Have you traveled?"

"Not at all." She tried to lighten her response with a smile. "I've been to a few places in America, but basically I've stayed here my whole life, helping on the farm."

"You must like it, then."

"Yes, I do." She spoke firmly—maybe too firmly. Abby turned her head to gaze out towards the barns, their red-painted sides weathered and peeling under the bright summer sun. She squinted, trying to make out the familiar, slightly stooped figure of her father coming across the yard, but she didn't see him. "Should I get my dad?" she asked. "You'll want to meet him, and I suppose the medal belongs to him, really. He was my grandfather's only child."

"Yes, I suppose it does. But I don't want to trouble him—"

"It's no trouble. I'm sure he wants to meet you." Abby hoped she sounded more convincing than she felt. "And see the medal, of course," she added.

"All right." Simon's gaze scanned her face, seeming to look for clues. Was he wondering why she wasn't more interested, more engaged?

Abby smiled back at him, trying to convey a level of interest she wasn't sure she felt, and she knew her father didn't.

Sometimes the past was better buried.

SIMON

Simon watched Abby walk across the yard, towards the barn. The dog had raised her head as Abby had gone down the steps, and then dropped it down again with a tired sigh. A nuthatch trilled from its branch in the giant willow in front of the house that must have given the orchard its name. Simon recognized it as the orchard's emblem on its website.

He sat back in the rocking chair, taking a sip of lemonade as he tried to figure out what felt just a bit off about the whole situation. Abby Reese didn't seem particularly interested in the Purple Heart, and Simon suspected her father was even less. He hadn't been expecting unbridled enthusiasm, not like he felt, perhaps, but *something*.

Instead, despite the bright beauty of the day, he felt a tangible sense of sorrow hanging over the whole house like an invisible mist, and emanating from Abby herself. He saw it in her dark eyes, her uncertain smile, the careful way she spoke. And he wondered.

Of course everyone had sorrows in their life, as well as regrets. He had his fair share of both, and they could cripple him if he let them. But the Purple Heart medal was seventy-five years old. All the people involved were dead, Tom Reese for nearly thirty years. Why would his family not want to know?

Or maybe he was presuming, taking a natural reticence and making it into something bigger. Maybe David Reese would come striding onto the porch, shake his hand, and exclaim over the medal resting in its little box in his pocket.

Simon patted his trouser leg to make sure it was still there, and then he slid his phone and checked the screen for messages, although he knew better than to expect any. He saw that his message to Maggie, sent from Chicago with a picture of the Sears Tower from his hotel window, had been read, but not responded to. Par for the course, and sadly he didn't blame her.

A noise in the distance had him looking up, and as he slid his phone back into his pocket, he saw Abby coming back across the yard, followed by a tall, rangy man with a full head of gray hair and a craggy, weathered face. He wasn't smiling.

Simon stood up as they approached; he felt weirdly nervous. David Reese had to be six three at least, a loose-limbed man with a sense of restrained power in the way his arms swung at his sides, his long strides. He didn't look angry, but he didn't look friendly, either.

Abby gave them both a fleeting smile. "Dad, this is Simon Elliot. Simon, this is my father David Reese."

David gave a nod as way of hello, and Simon smiled back.

"Pleased to meet you, sir." He had no idea where the "sir" came from, only that with a man like David Reese it felt right, and David didn't question it.

"Shall I get you some lemonade, Dad?" Abby asked. Her voice had an over-bright quality that Simon didn't understand.

"All right."

As Abby went into the house, David lowered himself into a rocking chair, giving the dog's head a gentle pat before resting his large, callused hands on his thighs. He gave Simon a level look. "I'm sorry you came all this way, son. I'm not sure what I can tell you about these things." His voice was a low rumble, and he seemed a man sparing with words. Simon tried to resist the urge to overcompensate, to crack jokes and keep things light and breezy, as was his usual nervous habit. He sensed in this case it would be a futile effort.

"I realize that, but perhaps I can tell you some things," he said with what he hoped was an easy smile. "If you're interested."

"Not sure what the point is, bringing all this up now. Won't make much difference to anything, and, as far as I'm concerned, the past is the past. Gone."

"True... but wouldn't you like to know why my grandmother had your father's Purple Heart?"

David shrugged. "You don't know, do you?"

"No, but I'd like to find out."

David made no reply, and Simon felt as if he'd said the wrong thing.

"At least, you must want it back," he added with a little laugh.

"If it's here and you have it, I suppose, but I don't see the point in anything else." David shifted in his chair, and Simon thought he was going to say something else, but then he didn't. The silence felt clumsy, and he struggled to know how to fill it.

This was all decidedly odd. David Reese's reticence was far more ingrained than he'd expected; it almost felt hostile, although maybe that was just the man himself. His attitude made Simon more curious, even as he felt a desire to hand over the medal and hightail it out of Willow Tree Orchards as soon as he could. Then Abby came back onto the porch.

"Here you go, Dad." She gave him the glass of lemonade and then took her own, leaning against the porch railing as they both waited for Simon to speak.

Simon met her gaze before hers flitted away. She was, he couldn't help but notice, very pretty, in a quiet sort of way. Thick, dark hair caught back in a ponytail, lovely dark eyes. A sense of contained stillness about her. Was it sorrow? Or maybe just shyness? She didn't seem nervous, though. Just reserved.

"So, why don't I tell you what I know?" he said when the silence had stretched to several seconds, and threatened to become something seriously awkward. He tried to summon something of the cheerful tone he'd had with Abby earlier, but it was starting to feel forced.

Unsurprisingly, David didn't respond, but Abby raised her eyebrows expectantly, giving him a little smile. *Lovely smile, too.*

Simon pushed the thought away as he began. "My grandmother Sophie Mather lived in London during the war. I think that's where she must have met your father, Tom Reese." He directed this towards David, but then glanced at Abby, who nodded encouragingly. "I don't know the nature of their relationship, of course, but it seemed... close. My grandmother certainly spoke fondly of him before she died. She seemed to have seen quite a bit of him."

"My father never mentioned her to me." David moved his implacable gaze from the distance to Simon. "Not one word." The reticence must have run in the family.

"My grandmother never said anything to me either, or my mother, until she was diagnosed with terminal cancer last year," he agreed. Not that his grandmother had had many opportunities to share such details; her relationship with her daughter, and her daughter's family, had been complicated and often fraught. "These things... they're difficult to speak about, aren't they? The war, I mean, and all that happened then. My grandmother hardly ever mentioned it."

"There's a reason for that." David's tone was flat.

"What *did* she say about Grandad?" Abby asked. Simon could tell she was trying to pitch her tone somewhere between cheerful and cautious, and it wavered between the two.

Her father shot her a quelling look that brought a faint flush to her cheeks. Abby had to be thirty years old, at least. What was she doing, living at home, under her father's thumb? Or was he imagining the unhealthy dynamic, reading too much into a single look?

Simon directed his reply to David. "Not all that much, to be honest. Just that he was an American soldier stationed near London before D-Day, and they'd become... friends. She said they'd parted badly and he'd given her his medal as a keepsake. She felt it was time to give it back." He paused. "She also said she should have given it back a long time ago, and she hoped that he could forgive her." Another pause as he let that information sink in. "She gave me the address of your place. She said she'd lost touch with your father right after the war, but she told me she looked him up on the internet. She was surprisingly savvy, that way." If Simon had been hoping for a small smile at that, he didn't get one. He felt ridiculous, as if he were in a play, pretending this was a fun, friendly conversation when it was anything but. David wasn't overtly hostile, not exactly, but close enough. "She wanted him—or his descendants—to have the medal back." He looked between Abby and David, trying to gage Abby's mood. Was she interested in the medal, despite her father's determined lack of interest? "Do you... do you want to see it?"

David rose from the rocking chair with a creak of both joints and rockers. "I don't need to see it."

"Dad," Abby protested quietly. "What's the harm—"

"I already knew he was wounded."

Abby's eyes widened. "You never told me that—"

"There was never any reason to. He didn't like talking about it, and it wasn't too serious, anyway." He turned to Simon. "I don't mean to be rude, but I'm not interested in digging up the past, finding out what my father had to do with your grandmother. He was happily married to my mother for forty years. He made his life here. No good will ever come of poking around in the past, digging up things people don't want to talk about." He nodded towards Simon as he thrust his barely touched glass of lemonade onto the porch railing. "I appreciate your interest and concern, and I thank you for your time, going out of your way to bring back this medal, but this is the end of it," he stated, and then, giving the dog one last pat, he stepped off the porch and started walking back towards the barn.

ABBY

Wow. That had gone even worse than Abby could have possibly expected, which was saying something. She felt herself flush as the ensuing silence stretched and stretched between them. Simon looked bemused, staring after her father's retreating back. Bailey lifted her head, looking between them, and then pressed her head against Abby's knee, as she so often did when she sensed tension.

"I'm sorry," Abby said at last as she fondled Bailey's ears, her gaze lowered. "I know what it sounded like, but he really doesn't mean to be rude."

Simon turned to her, eyebrows raised, a wry smile quirking his mouth. "Are you sure about that?"

"It's just... he doesn't like talking about the past." Which was rather obvious.

Simon nodded and sighed. "No, I'm the one who's sorry. I don't mean to cause trouble." He smiled ruefully. "But I have, haven't I? For whatever reason, your father does not want this medal back, or for anyone to talk about Tom Reese."

"It doesn't have to be such a mystery," Abby felt compelled to say, although she wasn't sure why. Maybe it *was* a mystery. "It's just... my father doesn't like anything to change."

"But this wouldn't change things, would it? If anything happened, it was almost eighty years ago. Surely it couldn't matter now."

"I know." She gazed at her father's retreating back as he headed into the barn, noting his heavy tread, his stooped shoulders, before dropping into the seat he'd just left. "It might change his opinion of his father, I suppose, if he got up to something…" She trailed off, unsure what she was implying, especially of Simon's grandmother. The truth was, she had no idea why her father was so reluctant to receive the medal, or know about Simon's grandmother. Was it just his natural reticence to talk about the past, or something deeper?

"Got up to something?" Simon repeated, sounding skeptical. "It's true he might have had a wartime romance, years before he was married. That hardly seems scandalous." Simon sounded gently incredulous, and Abby shrugged again, spreading her hands in a gesture of helpless apology.

"Honestly, I don't know."

"Do *you* want to see it?"

She blinked, a little startled. "The medal?"

"It belongs to your family. I need to give it back, whether you want it or not. It was my grandmother's wish."

"All right." Bailey flopped on the floor again as Abby held out her hand and Simon reached into his pocket. Abby's breath caught as he gently, and almost reverently, opened a little box and then deposited the little heart with its faded purple ribbon into her palm.

"The Purple Heart," he stated, his tone solemn. "Awarded to men wounded in combat. That's George Washington on the front."

"Yes…"

"Oldest medal in American history," Simon continued. "Awarded to members of the military who were wounded or killed in combat, and nowadays also anyone wounded or killed in a terrorist attack."

Abby turned the battered little heart over, to read the inscription on the other side. *For Military Merit Thomas Reese.* The heart felt strangely heavy resting in the palm of her hand, laden with significance. "It couldn't… it couldn't be some other Tom Reese, could it?" she asked suddenly. "I know my dad said my grandfather was wounded, but maybe he still has his medal somewhere, and this is a different one. It's a common name."

"And yet my grandmother had this address? There's a photo of your grandparents on the website. She sounded very certain, when I spoke to her."

"Do you think she really saw our website?"

"I'm sure of it. Granny was quite internet-savvy, right up until the end. Wouldn't go anywhere without her iPad. I used to play Candy Crush with her."

Abby smiled faintly. "She sounds like a character."

"She was. I wish I knew her better. My mother had a… tumultuous… relationship with her. They were both emotional people." He grimaced slightly. "So we didn't see her—or that side of the family—very often. And my mother died before my grandmother, about ten years ago." He stopped suddenly, as if he'd said enough. Too much, maybe.

Abby searched his face and saw a certain blankness come into his eyes before he looked away.

"Families can be tricky," she said, which was a gross understatement, really.

"Yes."

"I'm sorry for your loss." The words could have been rote, but Abby meant them genuinely. Losing family was hard, a grief that went on and on, without end. She knew that all too well.

"Thank you." Simon nodded his acknowledgment before leaning forward to peer at the medal still resting in the palm of her hand. "Aren't you at least a little intrigued?" he asked, lowering his voice conspiratorially, although her father was far away, back in the barn. "About what might have happened between your grandfather and my grandmother, during the war? Some tragic romance? Or maybe something completely different and surprising? Wouldn't it be… fun… to find out?"

She looked up, meeting his friendly, open gaze, the blankness gone, replaced by a glint of interest that made some sort of strange feeling shoot through her, a little bolt of electricity that felt entirely unexpected. Unfamiliar, even—or at least forgotten. It flashed through her, jolting her awake, and she had the urge to shake her head, as if to clear it.

"What do you think happened?" she asked. "You said you spoke to your grandmother about it?"

"Yes, before she died a few months ago." He sighed as he relaxed back into his chair and Abby did the same, the medal still in her hand. "She didn't say much more than I've already told you, but there was a certain tone to her voice… I could tell she'd held him in affection, that she felt some sort of regret about what had—or hadn't—happened between them. She said she hoped he could forgive her, after all. So they must have had some sort of relationship, and she must have felt she'd done something wrong."

"It sounds as if she didn't know he had died."

"I don't know whether she did or not. I would have assumed so, considering how long ago it happened, but who can say? Maybe she felt returning the medal to his family would atone for something."

"Maybe." Abby's fingers closed around the medal, the small ridges digging into her fingers. "It's all very strange, isn't it? I'm sorry we can't give you more information."

"That's all right." Simon smiled wryly. "Perhaps something will come to mind? I'm staying in the area for a few weeks, if you think of anything."

"You are?" Abby looked at him in surprise. Although he'd said he was staying in America for a few weeks, she hadn't thought the whole time would be in Wisconsin.

"Yes, I've rented a little cabin on Lake Geneva, about twenty minutes from here. I'm a history teacher, and I've got six weeks of summer break." His smile was wide and easy as he scanned her face, trying to gage her reaction. "I couldn't think of a better place to spend it while I work on my book."

"Your book?"

"I'm hoping to write a book about wartime romances between British women and American GIs. There's another couple nearby, in Genoa City, who said they would be happy for me to interview—"

"They're alive?"

"No, but their children are. So if you do remember any more details…" Simon trailed off with seemingly deliberate casualness, his eyebrows raised.

Abby looked down at the medal and swallowed. For some reason, it felt different, knowing Simon would be nearby, that he was writing a book. She suspected her father wouldn't be happy with either. "Of course, but I'm afraid I don't think I will."

"You have my email address anyway. Would you mind if I gave you my mobile number? Or cell, as you Yanks call it?" He smiled teasingly and she forced herself not to look away. He wasn't *flirting*. He was just being friendly. But it still felt strange. She couldn't remember the last time anyone had flirted with her, at least anyone she'd consider attractive. And she did, Abby realized, consider Simon, with his floppy hair and kind eyes, attractive.

"Sure," she said, and he held out his phone so Abby could type her contact details into it. "My father might come around," she said as Simon prepared to leave. She didn't actually think he would, but she felt she had to say it, and she realized she was reluctant to have such a final farewell. What if she never saw Simon again? She probably wouldn't. "He might remember something."

"I hope so. I wish I'd asked my grandmother for more details, but it made her so sad to talk about it. One of life's big regrets maybe, eh?" The smile he gave her was touched with sorrow, and Abby found she couldn't reply. Yes, life certainly had regrets, big ones. "Thank you for the lemonade, and your hospitality," he finished more formally. "And perhaps I'll see you again?"

"Yes, perhaps." Abby didn't say anything more as she stood up, and Simon walked to his car. He waved from the driver's seat, and the dust kicked up, just as it had before, as the car headed back down the long dirt drive, from where it had come.

CHAPTER TWO

London

January 1944

The American troops first started arriving in Britain in January 1942, but the Mather family did not meet any directly until two years later.

The Mathers had, by then, had what some might have called "a good war". They had no sons who lay beyond rescue on the ash-strewn, bombarded shores of Dunkirk, or to fear might fall from the sky in a smoke-plumed arrow of fire. Their house had not been bombed in those dark, endless nights of the Blitz, although its foundation had been said to be weakened by a nearby blast, and a large crack now bisected the kitchen ceiling. None of their relatives had been killed; a nephew was serving in the Pacific, but, by all accounts, was still alive, and a cousin had been invalided out in 1943. The closest casualty was their neighbor's boy, who had died at sea during the Norwegian Campaign in 1941, and a friend of the family who had died in an air raid, hit by flying rubble as she'd run for the shelter in the back garden.

Their two daughters, Sophie and Lily, eighteen and sixteen when war was declared in 1939, occupied themselves industriously throughout—Sophie had become a secretary for the War Office, and Lily a Wren in the Casualties Section of the Naval Office. Sophie had volunteered as soon as she could, eager to get involved in the excitement, and Lily had been conscripted in 1941, when she was eighteen.

Their mother, Carol Mather, was prominent in the local Women's Voluntary Service, and she had been both delighted and determined to plow over tulips and azaleas to make room for a Victory garden behind their small semi-detached house in Clapham, to sew and knit and bake as much as she could, and to champion every cause, from hats and mittens for evacuees to serving tea to bombed-out citizens from mobile canteens, graciously officious with a large metal urn and a great number of rather stale buns. Carol reveled in the can-do opportunities the war presented women, although she was never so imprudent as to articulate it quite like that.

In January 1944, with the Americans firmly ensconced in their country and preparing for an invasion of Europe, for the Mathers, the end of the war seemed, if not precisely in sight, then at least flickering dimly on the horizon, a hope one could almost hold onto.

After nearly five years of relentless war and threat of invasion, of deprivation and death, of the long, lonely wail of the air-raid siren cutting through a clear night and one out of every four spent in clammy cellars or dingy shelters, of ration books and bacon and butter once considered enough for a day now meant to last a week, of dodging craters in pavements and walking past buildings that looked like broken teeth, the Mathers, like everyone else in the country, were desperately tired of war.

"I've invited two American boys to dinner," Carol informed the family one evening, early in that cold, dark month, as they were having their usual bedtime cup of weak tea while the wireless played classical music after the latest nine o'clock news broadcast—a mixture of dour reporting and desperate hope. "They're coming here on Sunday, after church."

"Americans?" Sophie paused with her cup halfway to her carmine-red lips, her ash-blond head cocked at an angle. "Where on earth did you meet them, Mother?"

"The vicar asked me to have them over. He's taken an interest in some soldiers who have been billeted nearby until they're shipped to a proper base. He's invited a few to church, and asked me to have them for dinner, after. The poor boys are feeling lonely, as they might do. They could all use a good square meal, I should think."

Sophie rolled her eyes. "As if one can be found."

"Home cooking," Carol informed her older daughter, with a touch of severity. "That's what I mean, Sophie, whatever I manage to serve. Home cooking and decent company."

Lily watched her sister's expression turn milkily bland. As much as she couldn't resist a sharp retort, Sophie, Lily knew, would not risk the possibility of soldiers—and American ones at that—not coming to the house. Their presence would be something different; it held the promise of adventure, or at least of change. At the very least, a decent meal for everyone, since their mother would want to impress.

Her sister lowered her eyes over her teacup, now all meek docility. "What shall we serve them?"

Carol pursed her lips thoughtfully. "I was thinking I'd see if the butcher had an ox cheek. He usually can find one for me."

Lily knew her mother went to great pains to keep on the right side of their butcher, Mr. Allen. It meant that he sometimes "found" ox cheeks and tongue and other non-rationed cuts of meat—ones they would have all turned their noses up at before the war—for the Mather family. While others were thickening their meat stews with porridge oats, Carol was braising a cow's tongue in red wine.

"A barley soup to start, and an apple crumble for dessert. There are still some apples from the summer." Carol smiled in satisfaction before taking another sip of her tea. Clearly it had all been decided.

Later, after she'd helped her mother with the washing up, both of them standing at the sink, working in companionable silence in the creaking, night-time quiet of the house, Lily found her sister upstairs in their bedroom, her head craned out the window as she smoked a cigarette. At least the lights were off, in accordance with blackout regulations, the pale light from a half-moon filtering in through the window and bathing the small room, with its matching twin beds and bureaus, in silver.

"What do you think to the Yanks, then?" Sophie asked. She leaned her head back against the window as she inhaled deeply, regarding Lily out of sleepily narrowed eyes.

Lily shook her head. "You know Mother doesn't like you smoking." Carol thought it was common, even though many young women smoked these days, at least when they could get cigarettes. Lily didn't smoke; she didn't know how, and she didn't want to, anyway.

Sophie rolled her eyes. "Don't be such a bore, Lily, please. Do you suppose you could manage that for a moment?" There was a note of teasing affection to her sister's voice that kept her words from being an insult.

"I know I'm a bore," Lily replied with a small smile as she reached for her nightgown, tucked under her pillow. Her breath came out in a puff of frosty air, and she saw ice on the inside of the windowpanes. "Could you please close that window before you freeze us to death?"

"I'm almost done." Sophie took another drag of her cigarette, which Lily suspected was one of those cheap, evil-smelling Spanish Shawls rather than from a pack of Player's or Dunhill's. Their mother would almost certainly smell it, just as Lily knew she would, as they all often did, and turn a rueful eye to Sophie's minor misdemeanor.

Perhaps it was her sister's irrepressible good humor, or maybe the fact that she made fun of herself as much as anyone else, but neither of her parents, nor Lily herself, ever took Sophie to task for the streak of wildness that ran through her like a tongue of fire. So far it had never singed anyone; it almost felt like a theory rather than a reality, a possibility rather than a promise. Sophie, Lily thought, was a good girl at heart—or perhaps she was wild at heart and a good girl on the outside. Either way, she didn't get up to too much, although Lily suspected she wanted to. Still, she never dared.

"The Americans," Sophie said now, almost dreamily, turning her cigarette over between her fingers. "Do you know, I've never actually met one of the doughboys properly?"

"Haven't you?" Lily slipped out of her dress and into her nightgown as quickly as she could. Wherever the cold air touched her bared flesh, goosebumps rippled in its wake. Sophie, lying half out the window, in only her blouse and skirt, seemed indifferent to the freezing temperature.

"I've seen them, of course. They're everywhere nowadays, swaggering about, aren't they? I've danced with one or two, but it never went anywhere. They *can* be forward." She giggled, then turned her bright hazel eyes on her sister. "Have you met one?" She didn't wait for Lily to respond before she answered her own question. "Of course you haven't. Who *do* you meet, at the Admiralty, besides some stuffy old generals snoring away at their desks?"

"There aren't any generals in the navy," Lily reminded her sister. It was hardly the first time she'd said such a thing. "And, in any case, it's mainly women in the Casualties Section."

"It's mainly women everywhere," Sophie answered dismissively. She flicked her cigarette butt out the window, a glimmer of orange against the endless dark of the blackout.

"Sophie," Lily said in gentle reproof.

"There hasn't been an air raid in over a week."

"That doesn't mean there couldn't be one tonight." There had been talk about the Germans launching another bombing campaign, now that the Allies were giving Berlin a beating. It had been fairly quiet for months, but no one ever knew what next hardship or tragedy lay ahead. The future felt like a minefield, littered with dashed hopes, and, worse, dreams that might never be realized.

Sophie rose from the windowsill and Lily moved to close the curtains, staring out at the night sky for a moment, a thousand stars glittering and twinkling amidst all the black, making everything seem wonderfully serene, frosty and still, like Christmas, although that had passed nearly a fortnight ago, a scant celebration with no Christmas tree to be found, although her mother had saved enough coupons to make a Christmas cake.

If she closed her eyes and breathed in deep, she could almost be lulled to sleep by that false yet alluring sense of tranquility, peace on earth, even though there was anything but.

Already she could imagine how the still silence would be punctured by that awful insistent whine that rose in volume and frequency until it was followed by far, far worse sounds—the loud buzzing drone of planes flying low over the city, and then the thud and crackle of bombs falling as the night sky lit up like an inferno, impossible to take in, to believe it was real.

Lily shut the window and drew the blackout curtains tightly across, closing out another night. "Let's go to bed," she said firmly and Sophie sighed and stretched languorously before flicking on a lamp, bathing the room in a warm, yellow glow.

"I bet you wouldn't even know what to do with an American soldier if you met him," she tossed over her shoulder as she started to undress.

"I wouldn't know what to do with a British one, either," Lily quipped.

Sophie started to unbutton her blouse. "You need a boyfriend, Lil. A proper boyfriend."

"As do you, it seems." Lily slipped beneath the covers of her bed, wincing at how icy the sheets were. She tucked up her legs and curled her toes, fighting to keep hold of what little warmth she had.

"Don't I ever," Sophie drawled. Neither of them had ever had a proper boyfriend. Lily hadn't so much as said boo to a boy, and while Sophie had had plenty of admirers, she seemed content to preen and pet, flirt and fawn for only a brief while before she dropped them flat. *He has bad breath*, she'd tell Lily. *Or his ears stick out, it makes him look like a monkey.* Or, the most damning of all: *I discovered he is simply too deadly dull.*

Lily wondered if it would be different for Sophie with an American. Would a GI catch her interest for more than a moment? Long enough to last? It seemed unlikely, and in any case, she doubted their mother would approve of an American courting one of her daughters.

"Maybe *I* need an American," Sophie stated, clearly thinking along the same lines. She glanced in the mirror, pouting dramatically at her reflection before she turned away with a laugh, unable to take even herself seriously. "You know what they say about them, don't you?"

"Got any gum, chum?" Lily guessed. Although she'd never talked properly to any American soldiers, she'd seen them in the street and sometimes in the dance halls, when she'd accompanied Sophie, and stumbled her way through a jitterbug or two, before her partner inevitably found a woman who was more adept. Standing on the sidelines, sipping a glass of lukewarm lemonade, she couldn't help but notice their smart uniforms and hear their brash accents, and see how free they were with cigarettes and chewing gum and wide, white smiles.

"No, not that," Sophie said as she stripped off her blouse and skirt, dropping them carelessly onto a chair and standing before Lily, unabashed, in nothing but her brassiere and slip. How, Lily wondered, was she not freezing? "They say they're overpaid, oversexed, and over here." She giggled before shrugging out of her underclothes and then grabbed her nightgown and pulled it over her head.

"I wouldn't know anything about any of that," Lily said.

"Oh, don't sound so *prim*." Sophie turned off the light and jumped into bed, the mattress springs protesting at her actions.

"I can't help it," Lily returned with a little laugh. "I am prim."

"Maybe you just haven't met anyone interesting yet," Sophie answered mischievously, her covers drawn up to her chin. "Perhaps you need to meet a GI—*properly*." She imbued the innocent word with a melodramatic lasciviousness that made Lily smile, despite her tiredness.

"Perhaps," she agreed, rolling over onto her side to present her back to her sister, not that she could see it in the dark, or if she could, that it would keep her from talking.

"Imagine having a GI as a boyfriend," Sophie mused. "They've got ever so much money. Heaps and heaps."

"And they live in America," Lily pointed out. "Which is rather far away."

"I wouldn't mind living in America."

"Wouldn't you?" Lily couldn't imagine living so far from her parents and Clapham, all that she knew and held dear. Yet, for a second, she imagined a GI—blond, brash, so typically American—favoring her with his smile. Asking her to dance, or to take a walk…

Inwardly, she laughed at her herself, and the vague daydream she couldn't hold onto for long. Even her fantasies felt tame.

"No, I certainly wouldn't mind," Sophie declared. "I'd live like Marlene Dietrich or Joan Fontaine. Neither of them was born in America, you know." Sophie was a devout reader of *Picturegoer*—something else their mother disapproved of, and would throw into the fire if she caught sight of it.

"I doubt most Americans live like movie stars."

"They live better than us." There was no bitterness to Sophie's voice, only plain statement of fact. She sighed, a soft gust of sound in the darkness. "I'm so bloody *tired* of this war. It's gone on and on and on, and it's made a ruin of the best years of our lives."

Lily stayed silent, because there was nothing to say. She was tired of the war; everyone was tired of the war—of the bombed-out buildings, the grimy streets, the lack of food or fun or frippery, the dispiriting news on the wireless day after day after day, the fear and death that hounded everyone, kept at their heels. Of course they were all tired of the bloody war.

"And it's not even as if I've been able to do anything exciting," Sophie continued. "I know there are girls doing properly exciting, important things, not just taking dictation and typing letters for some pompous fool, while that old trout Mrs. Simmons polices our every move. It's *dire*."

"All war work is important," Lily protested quietly. For eight hours a day, all she did was type letters, too, but she believed they were important. Not essential to the war effort, perhaps, but a ministry of compassion to those the war had sacrificed. She *had* to believe that, otherwise what was the point? "Anyway, it might be over soon," she added, without any real optimism.

"Yes, thanks to the GIs." Lily heard the creak of springs and the slide of covers as Sophie turned over on her side. "What do you think they're like?"

Lily knew Sophie meant the two soldiers coming to dinner, rather than the entire American army. "I have no idea." She pictured two bland, blank-faced soldiers, dummies rather than men, and then she pictured Gregory Peck or Gary Cooper in uniform. Neither were real.

"I hope they're handsome."

"They probably will be." Most American soldiers seemed handsome, with their bright uniforms, their faces radiating health and good eating, and most of life spent away from bombs and rationing and war.

"Good," Sophie said with satisfaction, and snuggled down under the covers. "I just might snag myself a proper American boyfriend, then."

"Then maybe you'll smoke better cigarettes than those awful Spanish Shawls," Lily said as she closed her eyes, more than ready for sleep. She had an early start tomorrow—as she always did—having to take the Tube to the Admiralty; it was unreliable on the best of days, and often she ended up having to hope for a bus, or simply walk.

"Yes." Sophie laughed softly to herself, seeming altogether pleased by the notion. "Yes, then I won't have to smoke those wretched Shawls."

CHAPTER THREE

On Sunday morning, the little house on Holmside Road was dusted and polished to a determined if well-worn shine, and the kitchen was full of tantalizing smells of braised ox cheek and apple crumble.

Carol was a briskly efficient mistress of the kitchen; she had the potatoes peeled, the beef in the oven and the crumble cooling on the kitchen table before they headed out to the morning service at Holy Trinity Church, where she'd gone every Sunday of her married life. Sophie and Lily went with her, as did their father, Richard; church attendance had never been a matter of negotiation in the Mather family.

Lily didn't mind the service; she enjoyed the hymns, as well as the sense of something sacred, seeming closer there, yet still out of reach, a hope of something greater than anything she'd experienced so far. She also appreciated an hour of quiet.

Sophie didn't mind it, either, as far as Lily could tell, restless though she tended to be. Church provided an opportunity to dress up and, more importantly, to flirt, at least with one's eyes, and Sophie liked to flirt with every possible man. Not that there were any eligible ones in the dim and dusty nave of the church. Still, she'd give the balding, middle-aged shopkeeper with his hat in his lap a coy smile and then look away, causing him to blush and look confused. Lily watched it all with a bemused resignation; she knew it was just entertainment for Sophie, rather than anything meaningful or malicious.

That morning, however, there were far better prospects for flirtation. Two GIs were crammed into the back pew, looking far too big for it, their broad shoulders brushing, their smart army-green uniforms standing out amidst the sober Sunday coats and dark suits and dresses.

"Our Americans," Sophie whispered with a meaningful nod.

Lily did not reply. She did, however, slide a quick, questioning glance at the two men as she reached for her hymnal; the servicemen were tall, one broader and blonder than the other, the epitome of what Lily thought of when it came to American GIs, with his wheat-colored hair, blue eyes, and quick, cocky grin as he caught her eye.

She looked away quickly, blushing. She hadn't been able to see much of the other man, only that he was a bit shorter and darker, but still impressive and somehow alarming in his physique.

All through the service, Lily felt a burning awareness of the two men that was quite at odds with her usual, sensible self. Sophie felt the same, she knew, although perhaps with a bit more insouciance; she looked towards the back pew enough times to make their mother give her a quelling look, which Sophie ignored. Lily kept her eyes firmly to the front of the church, and listened to the sermon with more earnest attention than she had in some time.

At the end of the service, there was a shuffle of feet and hymnals as people began to move towards the doors; the weather was icy, even inside the church, and no one was minded to stay to chat. The two American servicemen stood by their pew, caps in hands, seeming unsure where to go or who to look for.

Carol approached them with her usual firm manner. "How lovely to meet you both. I'm so glad the vicar invited you along. I'm Mrs. Mather, and you're coming home with us for Sunday dinner."

Lily hung back, watching as the blond one smiled readily, shaking her mother's hand, and then her father's, and then Sophie's. He came to her last, his smile as wide for her as it had been for everyone else. Too shy to do more than stammer some sort of hello, she felt his strong hand close around her fingers as he said his name—Second Lieutenant Tom Reese—and then the second man was being introduced.

"This is Staff Sergeant Matthew Lawson, but he's a quiet one," Tom said with a laugh. "You won't get much out of him, I'm afraid."

Everyone shook hands all over again, while Lily gave Matthew Lawson a quick, considering look. His smile was just as ready as Tom's, but seemed contained somehow, the look in his dark eyes strangely watchful. His hand was cool as he touched Lily's briefly, and then they were all heading outside into the wintry day, the sky hanging grayly over the city like a damp shroud, the air icy and still.

Sophie had managed to position herself next to Tom, just as Lily had known she would. Of the two men, Second Lieutenant Tom Reese was certainly the more attractive, as well as the more obviously American, with his blond good looks and his easy manner, his loose, long-legged stride and his slightly loud laugh. He was exactly what Lily might have expected of a GI, and that made him seem both comfortable and intriguing.

As for Matthew Lawson... he seemed far more mysterious, although Lily thought perhaps he was just shy. He spoke very little, and his guarded gaze moved silently from one person to the next. His skin was sallow, his eyes a deep brown, his hair just as dark, brushed back from a high forehead. Next to Tom's blond radiance, he seemed even darker, but Lily admired the determined set of his jaw, the quiet containment she sensed from him that felt like strength, at least to her.

It was a ten-minute walk across Clapham Common back to Holmside Road, past the four big guns stationed there that Lily didn't like to look at, and the neat rows of the community allotment that part of the Common had been given over to.

Lily hung back while Carol marched ahead, and Sophie's tinkling laugh rang out among the stark, leafless trees as she and Tom chatted easily.

Her father, Lily saw, tried to engage Matthew in conversation, but didn't seem to make much headway and eventually walked ahead with his wife, leaving Lily a few steps behind the strange soldier.

Feeling strangely reckless, her heart beating hard, she quickened her steps until he was obliged to fall into step next to her. They walked in silence for a few minutes, the only sound Sophie's bright voice and Tom Reese's rumbling responses from in front of them, with the occasional burst of laughter, making Lily think of a raucous birdcall.

"Where are you from in America?" she finally worked up the courage to ask, her voice a bit breathless.

"New York." His voice was clipped, the simple answer spoken carefully, as if he parted with every word with both consideration and reluctance.

"I don't know anything about America, besides that it's big." Lily flushed at how stupid she sounded. Surely she could do better than that. "New York… you mean the city, I suppose?"

"Yes."

"Have you seen the Statue of Liberty? And the Empire State Building?"

"Yes." His manner wasn't unfriendly precisely, but neither did it invite further conversation, and, in any case, Lily couldn't think of anything more to say than what she already had, pitiful though it had been. She didn't know anything else about New York, or even America. Her paltry effort had fallen to the ground, unheeded. They walked the rest of the way in silence.

Back at the house, Carol set everything in motion, bringing dishes out of the oven while Lily helped. Richard stoked the fire before sitting down in front of it, and Sophie fetched the two men cups of tea, her voice carrying throughout the downstairs.

"We would offer you sherry, but we haven't seen any in years," she said with a laugh. "Do you even drink sherry in America? Or is it all whiskey and gin?"

"Sophie," Richard admonished, but there was a smile in his voice.

"I believe my mother drinks it, ma'am," Tom said as he took his cup of tea.

"Ma'am!" Sophie threw her head back with a throaty laugh. "You mustn't call me that. I feel about a hundred years old."

"You don't look it," Tom answered chivalrously, and Sophie laughed again, batting her eyelashes with such deliberate coquetry that no one could take her seriously, and all the men smiled.

In the kitchen, Carol pursed her lips, but her eyes twinkled. Lily concentrated on scraping off bits of browned potato from the pan, shooting occasional glances into the sitting room, feeling as if exotic creatures had landed there.

Soon enough, they were all sat down, with Carol dishing out bowls of soup as a first course, and a way to fill manly stomachs, before the meat was served. Then Richard was carving thin slivers of ox cheek, hoping to make the remaining meat last the week.

Tom enthused about the food and filled his plate; Lily saw Carol eye the heaps of food only slightly askance, but, of course, she said nothing. The two Americans would eat more food than the whole family normally had in nearly a week, Lily suspected, and not even realize it.

The conversation came and went in fits and starts, with Sophie and Tom leading the charge. It was clear that Sophie had marked Tom Reese for herself, in the way she poured his wine, and leaned closer to him as she spoke. Carol watched the pair in sharp-eyed quiet; Lily had the sense that her mother was not entirely impressed with Tom Reese, although she couldn't say why. He certainly seemed charming enough to her, and if he was brash, well, that was because he was American, surely. Already Lily knew he belonged to Sophie.

And as for Matthew Lawson…? Lily snuck another quick look at his saturnine features, his neutral expression, and thought he belonged to no one. Although, she concluded upon another hurried glance, she couldn't decide if he was gloomy or merely contained. He was certainly quiet.

"So when did you arrive in this country, Lieutenant?" Carol asked brightly, and Tom answered, while Matthew cut his meat—he'd only taken one thin sliver, while Tom had asked for three—into small pieces.

"Only a few weeks ago, ma'am. We're greenhorns. The 82nd has been fighting in Sicily since April '43, but we're a new division just shipped over." Tom smiled, flashing his teeth. "We were in training back in Louisiana for two years, and now we're ready for some action." He glanced at Matthew, whose expression was bland. "Although Matthew here didn't join the 82nd until we were on the ship. I don't know where he's been." He let out a laugh, which seemed too loud in the small dining room.

"The 82nd?" Sophie queried, looking between them both.

"82nd Airborne," Tom explained. "We're paratroopers. When the time comes, we'll parachute into Europe." He gave her what Lily supposed was meant to be a mysterious smile. "Can't say more than that, though." Lily doubted he knew much more than that.

"Goodness." Sophie looked delightfully impressed. "And how long do you think you'll be in London?"

"No one knows." Tom shrugged. "A few months, I should think, although perhaps not in London. There's talk about moving somewhere up north for more training, but we're still waiting for our orders."

"And what do you think to our country?" Carol asked. "Although I fear it is sadly diminished in these difficult times."

Tom and Matthew exchanged looks, but neither spoke.

Sophie let out another pealing laugh. "Oh, go on and say what you really think, Lieutenant, Sergeant," she said as her eyes danced and she looked at each of them in turn. "It's all rather dreadful, isn't it? Dark and rainy and so horribly shabby nowadays."

"Sophie." This time there was no smile in Richard's voice. "We are a country at war."

"Indeed you are, sir," Tom said earnestly as he leaned over his plate. He'd eaten everything. "And we don't forget it. We know we're not seeing your country at its best, and that the houses aren't painted bright as a new penny because your factories aren't making paint—they're making planes. Your gardens and parks aren't as pretty because they're needed for vegetables, and your cars look old because the British are building tanks. We know all that, sir."

A resounding silence fell like a thunderclap over the table, and Carol and Richard exchanged inscrutable looks. Sophie pressed her fingers to her lips, her eyes alight.

"Well," Richard finally said. "Indeed."

"We were warned that the beer would be warm," Tom continued with the same earnest look that made Lily's parents glance at one another again. "But, to tell you the truth, I don't find it so bad."

"Heavens, Lieutenant, if all you have to worry about is warm beer, I shouldn't be too concerned," Sophie teased. "Really, we'll start to think you Americans are all a bunch of complainers."

"Not at all," Tom replied with a gallant smile. Carol and Richard watched on, bemused, while Matthew continued to eat, his gaze lowered. "I love this country, or at least what I've seen of it so far. Although, I admit, there's a bit more rain than we get back in Minnesota, but I don't mind."

"And it hasn't even been that rainy," Sophie answered as she took a sip of wine; Richard had opened a bottle for the occasion.

"Hasn't it?" Tom's smile was aimed just at her as he reached for his own glass. "Then I guess I'll be in for it when it does start to pour."

"Won't you just?" Sophie replied, keeping his gaze, and Lily wondered how her sister managed to flirt so outrageously whilst talking about the weather.

Richard cleared his throat.

"Sergeant, you've only had one slice of meat," he remarked. "Would you care for another?"

"No thank you, sir. This is sufficient." Matthew spoke crisply, each word spoken with careful precision, as if formed and then cut off, and a look of curiosity rippled across Richard's face as he observed the younger man.

"Where did you say you were from?"

There was the slightest of pauses, like a drawn breath. "New York."

"I see." Richard sounded nonplussed, and Lily wondered at it. What did her father know about New York, or any part of America? Yet she knew there was something about Matthew Lawson that seemed the tiniest bit odd, something just slightly *off*.

Was it his careful, clipped voice, or his intentionally restrained manner? The way his dark eyes gave nothing away, while watching everything? He seemed a man determined to keep himself in check, utterly opposite to his garrulous companion. They were certainly an unlikely pair.

"So how did you two meet up?" Sophie asked, nodding at both the soldiers, seeming to have the same thought as Lily. "Was it on the ship?"

Tom glanced at Matthew, who, as usual, remained silent. "Yes, we were bunkmates. And then I promised my mother I'd go to church while I was here, and the pastor of your church asked me along, and Matthew said he'd come as well, so here we are."

"That's very good of you, Lieutenant," Carol said with a thawed approval. "It's important to keep up good habits, even in the midst of a war."

"So it is, ma'am."

They retired to the sitting room after the meal, and Lily and Sophie cleared the table while Carol made coffee.

"Thank you for the dinner," Tom said as she came into the sitting room with a tray of cups and saucers. "It's mighty kind of you, especially when we're so far from home, and, as we say in the army, it was some real good chow."

Carol laughed a little at this; she seemed to have warmed slightly to Tom, despite his rather forward manner. "It is the least we can do," she said as she handed him a cup of coffee.

They sat in the sitting room, with cups and saucers balanced on their knees, talking about the weather and the war and then the various sights of London the GIs might wish to see.

Tom and Sophie kept the conversation going, but, despite their bright efforts, it trickled out after a while and eventually Richard turned the wireless on.

The men drank their coffees and then stood to say their goodbyes.

"We're on leave next weekend," Tom said as he fixed his cap on his head, his words clearly directed at Sophie. They were in the front hall, with Richard's hand on the front door. "Perhaps you young ladies would care to show us some of London's sights? I've heard about the dancing at The Berkeley Hotel, and wanted to give it a whirl."

Carol opened her mouth and then shut it. Richard took his hand off the door, looking surprised, and Matthew spoke not at all.

"Oh, we'd *love* to," Sophie practically purred. "Wouldn't we, Lily?"

Lily, who had said less even than Matthew all afternoon, merely nodded. She didn't know how she felt about going dancing with the two servicemen, but she also knew their mother would not allow Sophie to go on her own, never mind that she was twenty-three years old. As far as Carol was concerned, her two daughters were still girls who needed protecting, and perhaps restraining.

"That's settled, then. Shall we pick you up at seven?" Tom glanced at Richard, for form's sake, who nodded rather stiffly. Moments later, they were gone.

That evening, after supper, while Richard and Carol listened to the wireless in the front room, Lily perched on the edge of her bed, while Sophie groaned at the lack of dancing frocks in the little wardrobe they shared.

"I've got nothing, Lily, *nothing*. Damn this war and the ridiculous clothing rations. As if I want to wear some horrid utility dress to go dancing with a GI."

"Everyone's in the same boat," Lily pointed out. No one had had new dresses in years, save for the far too sensible utility clothing they had to make do with, or else mend something old. She pulled her cardigan tighter around her; the room was freezing and she'd rather be downstairs with her parents, sitting in front of the fire and listening to George Formby, but as usual Sophie had compelled her to stay.

"Weren't they divine?" Sophie said as she closed the door of the wardrobe, dresses—or lack thereof—forgotten for a moment.

"Don't you mean *he*?" Lily returned a bit tartly. "I don't think you looked at Sergeant Lawson once."

"Oh, but *you* did. I saw you sneaking glances, you sly thing! Don't pretend you don't fancy him, because I know you do."

"I don't *know* him," Lily answered, but she could feel herself blush and chose to say nothing more.

"He is a quiet one," Sophie agreed. She ran her fingers through her hair to fluff it as she studied her reflection in the small, speckled mirror over the chest of drawers. "Do you think Tom fancies me?"

Tom, it was, now? "Of course he does." Sophie wasn't film-star beautiful, but she was striking, with her large eyes and lips, her strong jaw and her ash-blond hair. She wore her confidence like beauty, which seemed even better. Next to her, Lily had always felt like a pale shadow—mousy hair, brown eyes to Sophie's hazel, slimmer in the hip and bust, and a full three inches shorter. Quieter too, and certainly shyer, although Sophie had always said she had a nice smile. When Lily practiced in the mirror, she wasn't sure it was anything special.

"Yes, I rather think he does." Sophie's gaze rested on her reflection as her lips curved in a knowing, catlike smile. "Did you *smell* him, Lily? Didn't he smell heavenly?"

Lily let out an incredulous laugh. "No, of course I didn't smell him."

"He wears aftershave. Why won't British men wear it? And the faintest hint of cigarette smoke… mmm." Sophie licked her lips and Lily smiled and shook her head. She suspected Sophie was all talk—or at least mostly. When had her sister had opportunity to get up to much?

Besides, there was something innocent, even naïve, about her jokes, her good humor, her determination to shock and to titillate. Something inexperienced and a little clumsy, despite her desire to seem the opposite, and even in her own inexperience, Lily thought she could recognize that.

"You know what they say, don't you?" Sophie said, her eyes dancing as she continued to regard herself in the mirror, seeming to like what she saw.

"What do they say?" Lily asked, her eyebrows raised, ready for her sister to try to shock.

"It's about the new utility underwear." Sophie turned to face her sister, her hands on her hips, her eyes sparkling with mischief. "One Yank and it's off!"

"Oh, *Sophie*." Lily gave a muffled laugh, before she shook her head and rose from the bed, determined now to join her parents in the sitting room.

The sound of Sophie's delighted laughter followed her all the way downstairs, until it was drowned out by the wireless.

CHAPTER FOUR

ABBY

"It's you again!"

Abby looked up from the gas tank of her pickup truck that she was filling to see Simon Elliot smiling at her with an expression of such cheerful good humor that she had to smile back.

"Oh… hello," she said. She'd been thinking about Simon since he'd left Willow Tree three days ago, and feeling a little guilty for how poorly he'd been treated. To come all the way from England and be given nothing more than ten minutes of their time and a glass of lemonade. Abby had cringed in embarrassment at the thought.

Why hadn't she asked more questions? Why hadn't she seemed more interested? Because she *was* interested; it was far more interesting, not to mention easier, to think about her grandfather's past than her own. Her father, however, clearly felt differently, and had seemed to consider the whole matter closed as soon as Simon had left, with Abby reluctant to bring it all up again.

She wasn't used to rocking the boat. She'd learned, over the last fifteen years, to glide upon untroubled waters, never mind what lurked darkly below. Their treatment of Simon had pricked her conscience, however, and, she had been willing to acknowledge she wanted to see him again.

"I was thinking, Dad," she'd ventured cautiously that evening as they'd dug into macaroni and cheese at the kitchen table, breaking their habitual mealtime silence, "that maybe we should invite Simon Elliot to dinner."

"What?" Her father had looked up with a frown, bushy eyebrows drawn together.

"He's staying in the area for a few weeks, and he's gone to so much trouble."

"Has he?"

"To bring the medal back." She'd left it on top of her father's dresser, but unsurprisingly he hadn't mentioned it. "Aren't you glad to have it again?"

"I didn't know I didn't have it before," David had returned.

"But you know Grandad was wounded?"

David had shrugged. "I didn't think about a medal. Like I said, he didn't talk about it."

Abby had decided to try a different tack. "We don't have to talk about all that with Simon, if you really don't want to. I'm just thinking about being neighborly. Saying thank you, because the medal does belong to us—to you—and it's part of our history. It's right and good to have it back."

David had heaved a sigh as he sat back in his chair, which was as much of an acknowledgment of her point as he was likely to give. Abby knew her father disliked the thought of not seeming neighborly. No matter how taciturn he could be, he always helped out when one of the local farmers was having trouble; he plowed their elderly neighbor Sue's driveway every time it snowed, and he donated baskets of apples to the local elementary school's harvest fair every fall.

He wasn't a cold or hard man, just a tired and sad one. Sometimes Abby had to remind herself of that; at other times, it was far too evident.

"I suppose we could," he'd finally said, his reluctance clear in every syllable, and Abby had felt a rush of relief—as well as excitement, at the prospect of seeing Simon again.

"Thanks, Dad," she'd said quietly. "I'll call him and ask."

Except three days had gone by and she'd never quite managed to work up the courage to do just that, stupidly enough, and now he was here at the gas station, grinning at her with so much enthusiasm, a quart of milk dangling from his fingers, his other arm wrapped around a red box of Lucky Charms.

"It's my secret weakness," he told her as his gaze followed hers to the box of cereal. "Sugary American cereal. Delicious."

"Magically delicious," Abby quipped, and Simon laughed.

"Yes," he agreed. "Yes."

Abby shook her head a little, wondering how he had so much zest for life. He was positively brimming with it, seeming to greet everything with the kind of interest and joy that she couldn't remember the last time she'd felt, if ever. It was infectious, but it was also a bit overwhelming. How did he keep it up? Why wasn't he exhausted?

"I'm glad I've run into you," she said a bit stiltedly, knowing that now was her obvious opportunity. "I felt badly for how quickly you left the other day. I think the whole medal thing took my Dad by surprise…"

"No, no," Simon assured her. "It was fine. And the lemonade was fantastic."

"Even so," she continued, "I wondered if you'd like to come to dinner? It won't be anything special. Nothing like Lucky Charms." She smiled, and he quickly returned it, which made her smile more. "But it would be nice to hear a little bit more about your grandmother…" She trailed off, waiting for his response, which seemed to take a second.

"Yes," Simon said, as if he had to startle himself awake. "Yes. I would like that very much. Just tell me when."

"Tomorrow night?" Abby suggested, thinking that would hopefully be enough time for her dad to adjust to the idea. "Around six?"

"I'll be there."

"Great." Abby nodded, and Simon nodded back, and then she laughed and gestured to her truck. "I guess I'll finish here."

"Right," he said. "Okay." And, after another semi-awkward moment, he took himself off, and Abby watched out of the corner of her eye as he headed for the rental car parked by the convenience store.

She let out a shaky breath as she finished pumping the gas. What was *wrong* with her? She was thirty-two years old and she was acting as if she were sixteen. All she'd done was ask him to dinner, not even anything remotely like a date, and yet her knees felt weak, her hands shaky, as she put the nozzle back in its holder. She really needed to get a grip.

Or maybe just some experience. Thirty-two years old and she'd had a handful of mediocre dates since she'd hit thirty, and not many more before that. Certainly nothing she could call a proper relationship. Abby knew how pathetic that was, especially considering the dates had all been fairly awful—setups by Shannon with guys from Milwaukee or Chicago, and only one that she'd been willing to see more than once.

One had had a nervous laugh and damp hands; another had been completely silent; a third had put his hand on her knee while they'd been sipping their first glass of wine. Mike, an accountant from Milwaukee, had made it to three dates before they'd both accepted there just wasn't much there. Abby had been relieved to agree to end it, even though it had barely begun, and she'd been in no hurry to go on another date since—not that she'd had many opportunities.

Ashford was a small place, a close-knit community, and besides Shannon, who had moved back after her high-flying job in Chicago had gone bust, most people her age had moved away for jobs. What was more, everyone here knew her history, or at least some of it, and they understood that some essential part of her remained frozen in time from fifteen years ago, and nothing had thawed her yet. Most likely, nothing would.

Fighting the discouragement that came over her like a drizzle, Abby forced the thoughts away and climbed into her truck. It was another beautiful summer's day, baking hot but with a breeze, the sky a blue so bright and hard, it hurt her eyes, the rippling fields and meadows flashing by as she headed back out of town towards the orchard.

She drove past the long, straight driveway that led to the farmhouse, taking the next left and pulling into the gravel parking lot of the Willow Tree Gift Shop.

Housed in one of the old barns, the shop had been Abby's brainchild ten years ago, and felt like her baby now. It had grown from offering a few apple-related products to having an organic line of soaps and perfumes, locally made jellies and jams, and a variety of handcrafted gifts and other items. It had been featured in the local paper, as well as magazines in Chicago, and although it would never be a huge money-maker, Abby loved every bit of it.

She stepped into the shop, smiling at Tina, the part-time manager they'd hired four years ago whom she counted as a close friend. She ran the shop pretty much single-handedly, and Abby took the shifts she couldn't do and managed the inventory and dealing with their suppliers.

"How are things?" she asked as she picked up one of their new products, a green, apple-scented candle, and gave an appreciative sniff.

"Quiet, but not too quiet," Tina replied. "Summer can be slow when it's not the weekend. Too hot."

Abby nodded. Fall and winter were their busiest times, when the baskets of apples outside the shop, and the free cider tastings and bags of hot, sugary donuts, enticed people inside. Summer weekends brought tourists from the cities, but the average summer weekday was hot and slow.

She picked up a soap dish made from a local pottery place and ran her fingers along the silky-smooth clay. "How is this new range selling?"

Tina shrugged. "Okay, but I think it might be more of a Christmas item."

"Right." The profit margin for the shop was narrow, something her dad was always reminding her of. He preferred to stick with what he knew—apples, day in and day out, and nothing else. No change. No surprises. Abby put the soap dish down. "There's a local quilter who wants to collaborate with us," she said. "She sent me an email the other day. The quilts would be expensive—a couple hundred dollars each, but they're beautiful—handmade, good quality. Real artistic pieces." Abby had loved one with a colorful starburst pattern; the needlework had been exquisite.

Tina simply nodded, looking cautious, waiting for more.

"I thought we could take one or two, see how it goes. What do you think?"

Tina frowned. "I don't know. Locals wouldn't buy them, would they? Anyone who wants a quilt around here makes their own."

"Yes, but tourists…"

"It's a lot of money for a bedspread."

"I know." And it was a lot more than anything they'd sold in the shop before. Her father, Abby knew, wouldn't approve, not that she'd mentioned it to him. Still, she knew what he'd say. Too much risk. Too much money, laying out hundreds of dollars for a couple of quilts that no one in their right mind would buy. "Still, it might be worth a try," Abby said firmly. "Just one or two, to see." She had dreams for this shop, dreams that felt small and yet still seemed too big. Both Tina and her father were far more cautious, which was saying something, considering how cautious she was generally. Yet the shop felt like the one thing in her life that had gone right, that could still go somewhere, if she let it. She loved coming up with new ideas for it—and, more than that, she needed to. She needed some part of her life to feel exciting, or even just possible.

"So, what is this I hear about some Brit visiting you?" Tina asked, putting her elbows on the counter as she leaned forward, her flyaway white hair pulled back into a bun, her round, smiling face alight with interest. Clearly it was far more interesting to gossip than talk shop.

Abby rolled her eyes good-naturedly. "How did you hear about him?"

"He's renting from a friend of mine, Pete Holmwood, out by the lake. And he's shopped in town. He bought organic coffee at the Pick 'n Save." Tina raised her eyebrows. "Fancy. Everyone's wondering about him."

"Of course they are." With a population of fifteen hundred, Ashford residents always recognized one more, especially if he had a British accent and bought organic, drove a rental car and asked lots of questions. Marked as different in a dozen ways.

"Well?" Tina prompted. "Give me the lowdown."

"There isn't much to say." Abby hesitated, knowing her father wouldn't want their business bandied about, but, in this case, what harm could it really do? Whatever might have happened between Tom Reese and Sophie Mather had ended seventy years ago or more. "His grandmother had a medal of my grandfather's from the second world war, and he wanted to return it to us."

"Really?" Tina looked intrigued, more than either Abby or her father had been, and she regretted admitting this much, even though she told herself again that it didn't really matter, despite how reluctant her father had seemed about the whole thing. "Why did she have it? Did they have some wartime romance?" She let out a dreamy sigh. "How romantic would that be?"

"I don't know if they did or not. Apparently my grandad never mentioned it, and my dad doesn't want to, either." Abby gave her what she hoped was a meaningful look. Tina knew how taciturn her father could be, just as everyone in Ashford did.

"Does this Englishman know anything more?"

"Not really." Abby hesitated, then, because she wanted to feel as if she had *something* of a life, she added, "But maybe he'll tell us more. He's coming to dinner tomorrow night."

"Ooh." Tina clasped her hands together, looking far more thrilled than Abby wanted her to be. Soon, all of Ashford would be talking about Abby Reese and her Englishman.

"It's not a date," she warned her friend. "Just a thank you, for coming all this way."

"Right. But the real question is, do you think he's good-looking?"

Abby thought about Simon's floppy hair, his hazel eyes, his wiry frame and the way he made her smile. "I suppose," she said, trying to sound nonchalant, even indifferent, but the belly laugh that Tina let out told her she'd failed.

By five-thirty the next evening, everything was ready. The lasagne—Abby had decided not to go overboard with anything fancy—was bubbling away in the oven, and the garlic bread was ready to go in. The table was set, and she'd bought a gallon of Breyers mint chocolate chip ice cream for dessert, feeling that baking a cake would be a step too far. She didn't want to seem eager.

She *wasn't* eager, she reminded herself. This really was just a simple thank you. Neighborly politeness, nothing more.

David came into the house at quarter to six, giving the set table a rather baleful look before heading upstairs to wash.

Abby ran her fingers through her hair and checked her reflection in the hall mirror—she wore her dark brown hair in its usual braid down her back, and she'd exchanged her workday clothes of T-shirt and shorts for a denim skirt and sleeveless top. Was it too much? Was she trying too hard? She had no idea. She'd long ago lost the ability to judge these kinds of things.

Shannon kept wanting her to have a makeover, dye her hair or wear something racy, but Abby just wasn't interested. "You have the soul of a sixty-year-old," her friend had said, shaking her head, and Abby had just smiled. It was easier to laugh it off than think about why she was that way, and how she didn't think she'd ever change.

The doorbell rang, and Bailey's paws skittered across the floor as she matched Abby's quick pace to discover who had come calling.

"Hello!" Simon beamed at her from behind a ridiculously large bouquet of brown-eyed Susans. "Aren't these marvelous? We don't have them in the UK, but I've always loved them. They look so *friendly.* "

"Yes, they do, don't they?" Abby took the flowers, brushing her nose against their velvety brown centers as Simon bent down to give Bailey a pat. "Thank you so much. What kind of flowers do you have in England?"

"Oh, your run-of-the-mill roses," Simon said in such a deliberately dismissive voice that Abby had to smile. "Lilies. Lilac. Bluebells. All very boring stuff."

"I doubt that." Back in the kitchen, Abby reached for one of the dusty crystal vases kept in a high cabinet and rarely used. She gave it a quick wipe down before filling it with water. "So, what have you been up to over the last few days?"

"Not much, really. Recovering from jet lag, relaxing by the lake."

Abby put the flowers in the middle of the table as Simon leaned back against the counter, folding his arms. He wore another button-down shirt, this one in pale blue, and a pair of faded jeans. Abby wondered if British men never wore shorts. Even though it was evening, the kitchen felt stuffy and hot, especially with the oven on.

"And what about your book?"

"Ah, yes. My book." Simon made a comical grimace. "To tell you the truth, I'm not sure how much material I have. I'm afraid I might have gone on a bit of a wild goose chase with this, and I'm starting to wonder if it leads anywhere." For a second, Abby saw something under his wry, laughing tone, something surprisingly bleak, but it was gone in an instant.

"I'm sorry we couldn't help you more."

"Not your fault. I simply hoped for more than there was, or at least was known, and I'm not sure there is."

"What about the other couple, in Genoa City? You mentioned their kids wanted to talk to you?"

"Yes, there's that, but, from all accounts, there's not much mystery to it. A happily-ever-after, the end. Still, I'm going to see them on the weekend."

Abby checked the lasagne, bubbling away, and then put the garlic bread in the oven. "Do you really think there's some mystery to this medal?" she asked, glad her father was upstairs and couldn't hear.

"I don't know," Simon said slowly. "I sort of think there is, especially because of your father's reaction."

She glanced at him, and saw he was looking straight and steadily at her, and she felt that same strange shivery sensation she'd felt before, like an invisible fingertip was trailing up her arm. Ridiculous.

"Why would my grandfather give Sophie his medal?" Abby wondered aloud. "As a keepsake, a way to remember him?"

"Perhaps."

"That doesn't seem too mysterious. If they had a wartime romance, it obviously didn't last, but perhaps they parted on good terms."

"Then why would my grandmother say she hoped he could forgive her?"

Abby paused, considering. "Maybe he asked her to come to America with him and she said no?"

"Perhaps, but it felt like something more than that. Like… a grievance."

Abby cocked her head as she gave him a smile. It felt the tiniest bit like flirting. "Are you sure that's just not wishful thinking on your part? Making more of a mystery than there was? More of a drama, so you can write a book about it?"

"Perhaps," Simon acknowledged with a laugh. "I'm usually happy to have my imagination run away with me."

"Well, it *is* interesting."

"Your father hasn't said anything more, I suppose?"

Abby raised her eyebrows. "What do you think?"

Simon laughed his acknowledgment. "Right. He does seem strangely reluctant."

"He's like that about everything. I wouldn't read too much into it."

"You seem… used to dealing with him."

Abby tensed at that, but then made herself relax as she shrugged and went to take the lasagne out of the oven. "We get along."

They both fell silent as they heard David's familiar, heavy tread on the stair.

"I think everything's just about ready," Abby murmured.

David came into the kitchen, giving Simon a nod before he sat down at the head of the table. Abby placed the lasagne in the middle, and gestured for Simon to take the opposite end.

"So how long have you had this place?" he asked as he put his napkin on his lap, and David gave him the briefest of rundowns on the orchard's history—how Tom moved from Minnesota after the war and bought it in the fifties, starting from scratch as a going concern, changing it from dairy to apples.

"He didn't want to stay in Minnesota? With his family?"

"Seems not." David's voice was flat.

Abby felt a slight tension tauten the air and decided a subject change was a good idea. "What about your grandmother?" she asked as she started serving the lasagne. "Did she live in London her whole life?"

"She lived there during the war, and then married my grandfather, William Elliot, in 1948. He was a pilot during the war, and a solicitor after. They moved to Surrey, just south of London, in the fifties, and then, after he died, she retired to Devon, on the coast."

"And the first you ever heard of us was when your grandmother mentioned the medal a few months ago?"

"Yes. And my parents hadn't heard of it either—as I said before, my mother died a few years ago, so I was never able to ask her, but my dad hadn't the foggiest. Strange, isn't it?" He gave David an easy smile that the older man grudgingly returned.

"Not so strange," he said after a moment, his voice gruff. "Like you said, most people didn't want to talk about the war. It was a hard time, best forgotten. People wanted to move on, look to the future."

"That's true." Simon nodded his agreement. "My grandmother didn't say much about the war at all, at least as far as I can remember. I know she worked in the War Office as a secretary, but she didn't seem to rate it very highly. She always said she didn't do much for the war other than type letters for fusty old men."

A silence fell over the table as they started to eat. Abby wished she could think of something interesting or witty to say, but her mind felt as if it had been wiped clean, and her father seemed only interested in eating. Simon seemed game enough, his expression as alert as ever, but Abby suspected he would tire of them both soon. They had to seem like the most boring people on the planet.

Sure enough, her father excused himself before dessert, saying he had work to do, which was both a relief and a disappointment.

Abby wished he'd try, just a little, even as she was glad he was gone. Maybe now she could talk to Simon properly.

SIMON

As soon as David Reese left the room, Simon felt as if he could breathe easier. The man was like a dark cloud hovering over everything. He wondered how Abby stood it. She seemed to relax as well, he noticed, as he rose to help her clear the table.

"So you've never left the orchard," he said musingly as she rinsed plates and handed them to him to stack in the dishwasher. It felt companionable to work together, finding their rhythm. Rinse, pass over, stack. "But have you ever wanted to?"

A plate nearly slipped from Abby's hands and Simon deftly caught it, giving her a quick smile. So that had touched a nerve. He'd thought it might.

"Not really," she said as she turned back to the sink. "Otherwise I would have."

"There are loads of reasons for staying in the same place."

"Did you?"

Simon grinned to acknowledge the parry and thrust. "It seems like your father isn't the only person in the Reese family who doesn't like talking about themselves."

"It's just there's not much to say." Abby let out a little laugh, or tried to. "Honestly. I'm very dull. I've been thinking about that all evening, how very boring I must seem to you. I haven't gone anywhere, or done anything, except live and work on this orchard, which is actually fine, if a bit dull to the outsider."

"Not at all," Simon assured her. "But have you wanted to go somewhere?" He chose to press. "Anywhere, ever? That's the real question."

"Maybe, a long time ago." Abby's voice had a faraway quality that Simon wondered at. "But I grew out of it."

"Is it something you have to grow out of?"

"My life is here." She spoke firmly. "And it always will be. I'm very happy with that."

Was that a warning, Simon wondered, not to get too close? He was just being friendly, but occasionally he felt himself veer into flirting, which was weird, since he hadn't dated anyone in years, and he generally wasn't a flirtatious kind of guy. Yet Abby intrigued him. He liked her—or at least he wanted to, if she would let him. Maybe it was her reserve that fascinated him; it felt safe. She wouldn't blow up on him. She wouldn't start shrieking about how something was all his fault. Yes, he had emotional baggage, just as she seemed to have hers.

Suppressing the inevitable sigh, Simon turned back to her. "Well, you don't seem boring to me. Not boring at all." He held her gaze for a moment longer than necessary, noticing her blush, liking it.

All right, yes, he was definitely flirting. So what? It felt good. It didn't have to make him feel guilty, to think about home, about Maggie, and how she still hadn't responded to his message. He was a free man. Unfortunately.

Abby turned back to the sink, shaking her head a little. He'd hardly done anything, yet Simon wondered if already he'd pushed her too far.

ABBY

Why couldn't she handle this? Abby wondered as she continued to rinse plates. This was all so *new*, so different from her dependable days, her empty nights. Besides Shannon and Tina, she had few friends, and most of them were older, or married, or living somewhere far away. Her life was quiet—a deliberate choice she'd made at just seventeen, the only atonement she could offer, and the only thing from that time that she didn't regret. But it left her woefully unprepared for moments like this one—a little light flirting over dirty dishes as a violet twilight settled softly over the fields outside, and the cicadas started up in a noisy hum.

"You didn't actually say," she said as she closed the dishwasher and then went to get the ice cream. "Whether you stayed put or not, I mean."

"No, I didn't stay." For a second, Simon's voice dropped its usual good humor and irrepressible energy. He sounded strangely bleak.

The gallon of ice cream in her hands, Abby turned to look at him. He seemed lost in thought, but as he caught her gaze he perked up, giving her a quick smile that for once didn't reach his eyes.

"Childhood in Lincolnshire, university in Nottingham, and then on to Cambridge, where I teach sixth form. I've been around, although I've never gone anywhere too far."

"Don't forget your year in Philadelphia."

"True."

They took their bowls of ice cream out to the back porch, Bailey following them hopefully, although Abby regretted the decision when she realized the only place to sit was on the old bench swing, which seemed a little too cozy.

Simon solved the problem by plonking himself down on the back steps, and Abby did likewise, with Bailey planted between them. Dusk was settling on the fields and orchards in a purple blanket, the air still warm and drowsy from a day under the baking sun. An owl hooted in the distance, audible over the determined chirping of the cicadas. A perfect summer night.

Abby took a bite of ice cream, savoring the sweet, creamy coldness of it.

Simon gave a sigh of appreciation. "Delicious."

"Straight out of the freezer."

He glanced at her. "I can see why you'd stay here. It seems pretty perfect to me."

It felt like an apology of sorts, for pushing her earlier. Not that he had all that much. It just felt that way to Abby, because she'd become so private.

She didn't know what to say in response—there was so much that was both right and wrong with his statement—so she just popped another bite of ice cream into her mouth and savored the taste, along with the peaceful silence.

"So, will you work on your book?" she asked after she'd swallowed it down. "That's why you came, right?"

"I'll do my best." He propped his elbows on his knees. "Did you know seventy thousand British women married GIs after the war? That's quite a number."

"I didn't know that."

"Makes me wonder why it didn't work out between Sophie and Tom."

"You don't even know if they had a romance," Abby pointed out, even though she'd been the one to suggest it earlier.

"I think they did. Come on, don't you? What else could it have been?"

Abby considered the point. "I suppose," she said at last. "There must have been something there."

"So why do you think your dad is so reluctant to know more?"

She shook her head. "He's not," she said as firmly as she could. The last thing she wanted was for Simon to start poking and prying into their lives, or trying to figure out what made them tick—she so quiet, her dad so grumpy. "Not in the way you mean. He's just like that, about everything."

"I don't believe you."

She turned to him, startled, her mouth dropping open. "What…"

"I don't believe you," Simon repeated, smiling, almost sounding flirtatious. *Again.* "It's more than that. Yes, I get it, he's reluctant. He's your standard taciturn farmer, man of few words, salt of the earth, et cetera, et cetera."

"Wow." Abby shook her head, smiling a little. "How many clichés can you use?"

"I'm not trying to imply your father is a cliché—"

"Really?" she returned lightly. It felt good to challenge him, to tease, like stretching an old muscle she'd forgotten she had.

"All right, maybe I am." Simon grinned, unabashed. "He seems a bit that way to me. But, at the same time, he seems more. Like he's hiding something. I think he is."

Abby's stomach tightened at this assertion. "You mean about my grandfather?"

"Yes."

"All right, Sherlock." She shook her head, trying to laugh it off.

"Tell me you're not curious."

Abby hesitated, staring out at the darkening night. *Was* she curious? For a moment, her instinctive caution wavered. For a second, she truly wondered. What had happened, seventy-odd years ago? Could it possibly matter to anyone now? To her?

"I don't know," she said slowly. "Will knowing what happened make much difference, all these years later?"

"It could. You know the phrase—'those who forget history are doomed to repeat it'?"

Abby rolled her eyes. "Isn't that meant to apply to wars and genocides and things like that?"

"And failed romances, and personal regrets." A touch of sorrowful whimsy colored his voice, like the tug of a thread, leading to an unraveling.

Abby bent down to stroke Bailey, sliding her fingers along her silky ears as the darkness settled softly over them.

"If your grandmother and my grandfather had stayed together, neither of us would be here," she said slowly. "So I'm kind of glad they didn't."

"So am I." The throb of sincerity in Simon's voice made Abby keep her gaze on her dog.

Were they flirting again? Why couldn't she tell?

Simon cleared his throat. "What was your grandmother like, anyway? The woman Tom Reese *did* marry?"

"I'm afraid I don't really remember her. There's a picture of them in the hall, though. Their wedding photo. I'll show it to you, if you like."

"All right." That seemed like a signal for Simon to leave, which Abby hadn't meant, but he'd finished his ice cream and so he stood up, and she started to do likewise, half-wishing the evening wasn't coming to an end.

Simon reached down with one hand to help her up, and, after a second's pause, Abby took it. His palm slid across hers, warm and dry, and she felt ridiculous for reacting to it. She really needed to get a social life. The next time Shannon wanted to set her up, she'd say yes. Even if it was to some bozo from Milwaukee whose laugh would be too loud, or who would bore her senseless talking about the stock exchange or fantasy football.

She dumped their bowls in the sink before leading Simon to the front hallway, and the photo of Tom and Susan Reese hanging by the stairs. It was black and white and they were both unsmiling, the way people seemed to be for photos back then. Tom was in a dark suit, Susan in a relatively plain white dress, belted at the waist. Though they stood next to each other, they weren't touching.

Simon leaned closer to study it intently, his hair flopping forward. He raked it back with one long-fingered hand as he squinted at the photo.

"Where was it taken?"

"Um… a registry office in Milwaukee, I think."

He turned to look at her in surprise. "Not in Minnesota? Not in a church?"

Abby shrugged, startled by the question, one she'd never considered before. "I don't know. I don't think so." She searched her memory. "I think it was a small wedding. No family. There's only that one photo, and no one ever talked about Grandad's family back in Minnesota, anyway."

"How did they meet?"

Abby cast her mind over what little family history she knew. Life began and ended with Willow Tree Orchards; no one had ever really talked about anything before. Her mother's family was from Chicago, and there was only her elderly grandmother left, in a nursing home with dementia. As for the Reeses…

"I don't know," Abby confessed. "I know my grandfather came from Minnesota, but I don't know where my granny came from, and I never met either of their families."

"Don't you think that's a bit odd?"

"Is it?" She felt a little defensive. "How many people know their whole family tree? Besides, it's not as if we've had lots of opportunity to go visiting. We live on a working orchard. It's an around-the-clock job—"

"Surely it's not like livestock, though," Simon countered gently. "Where you have to milk the cows every morning, or whatever?" He let out a laugh. "Not that I know the first thing about any of it. I'm a city boy, through and through."

Abby turned back to the photo. She tried to remember her grandmother, but she had only the vaguest wisp of a recollection—a woman in an apron, her hair in a bun. Or was she imagining even that? "I don't know," she said again. She stared at her grandfather's face. Was she imagining the bleak set to his eyes, his jaw, the way he looked at the camera as if he were challenging it? Was there a mystery here, after all? And, if so, was it one she wanted to discover?

"Look, why don't you come with me?" Simon asked, and Abby turned to him.

"Come with you?" she repeated blankly. "Where?"

"To the Bryants, the family in Genoa City. I'm interviewing them on Saturday. You're a local, you could be a help. And it might be interesting…"

Abby had no idea how she could help Simon conduct an interview, and while the family's life story could be interesting, it had no relevance to her. And yet, all the same, she found herself nodding. Smiling, even, because he'd asked, and she knew she wanted to see him again.

"All right," she said as her smile widened. "I could go with you."

CHAPTER FIVE

January 1944

The Berkeley Hotel was a grand edifice on the corner of Berkeley Street and Piccadilly, its golden stone façade making it one of the most elegant buildings Lily had ever been in. The sound of a swing orchestra spilled out from its open doors as Tom took Sophie's arm and headed inside, with Lily and Matthew behind.

Lily had been anxious all week for this evening, fretting about what to wear, what to say, how to be. As she'd suspected, Sophie and Tom had paired off the moment they'd all left the house. By the time they were halfway down Holmside Road, Sophie had her arm in Tom's, while Lily and Matthew trailed silently behind, both of them struggling to find anything to say. At least Lily was. Perhaps Matthew simply didn't care.

They couldn't talk much on the Tube, with the press of people and the noisy rattling of the car, but as soon as they emerged from the station, London's nightlife hidden and seething beneath a veil of blackout darkness, Tom was all jaunty assuredness.

"The Berkeley is the place to be," he informed them all as they came into the foyer and a girl in a black dress took their coats with a simpering smile.

Bereft of her coat, Lily felt her dress's plainness acutely. Sophie had magicked up a dancing frock from the paltry depths of the wardrobe—or, more accurately, from one of the girls at the War

Office. It was a shimmering, silvery thing that bared her shoulders and floated as she moved. A bit dated, but lovely.

Lily, on the other hand, was in a far more sensible dress she'd worn every year of the war at Christmas. It was dark green taffeta, its modest skirt and square neckline as appropriate for church as a dance hall. Its only concession to the occasion was a bow knot at the neck.

Tom whistled appreciatively as Sophie did a little twirl in her silver dress, tossing her head back and laughing. She was radiant, sparkling like a star, while Lily felt as drab as a sparrow; she was wearing less makeup than the coat-check girl.

She glanced at Matthew, who had his hands in his trouser pockets and was looking completely disinterested in anything going on.

And so much *was*—women in beautiful dresses, men in uniform, everyone chatting and laughing and tossing back drinks like something out of a radio play. Lily had never seen so many Americans, of all different types and ranks, a sea of army green and khaki brown and navy blue, everyone looking as if they were born to be there, the women coquettish, the men swaggering.

"We're only a hop, skip, and a jump from General Eisenhower's headquarters," Tom explained as he put his arm around Sophie and they headed into the ballroom, where a full orchestra was playing a lively tune and the dance floor was packed. "This really is the place to be."

It certainly seemed like it. Lily's eyes nearly popped at the sight of so many elegantly clad women and dapper men jitterbugging on the dance floor, a far cry from the shabbier dance halls nearer to home that she and Sophie had gone to, where the press of bodies lent a smell of boiled wool and stale sweat to the air, and the only drink on offer was watery beer or weak lemonade.

Tom found them a table on the edge of the dance floor, and they all crowded onto the velvet banquette while he went in search of drinks.

Sophie gazed around the crowded room with greedy delight, even as she already began to adopt an air of worldly self-assurance, resting her elbow on the back of her seat, her chin tilted at a haughty angle, as if she had been to a thousand places like this before, when Lily knew very well that she hadn't.

"Champagne?" Sophie exclaimed when Tom came back, triumphantly brandishing a bottle. "You *darling*. I haven't had so much as a sip of champagne in *years*. How ever did you manage it?"

Tom rubbed two fingers together as he gave Sophie a brazen wink. "If you know the right people, all it takes is a little lettuce."

Sophie wrinkled her nose. "Lettuce?"

"Money," Tom answered with a laugh as he poured them all fizzing glasses. "Don't you watch any American movies?"

Sophie's eyes danced as she took a sip of her champagne. "You're going to have to teach me all the American slang," she said. "I'm sure it will become the rage here once you boys have won the war for us."

"Sophie," Lily interjected, stung by the remark, and Sophie shrugged one bare shoulder.

"What? Everyone knows it's true."

Lily pressed her lips together. *Not the boys who gave their lives for this war*, she thought but couldn't work up the nerve to say it with Tom and Matthew there. She thought of the letters she wrote, day after day, dozen after dozen. *Dear So-and-so, It is my painful duty to inform you that your son, Sergeant X, has been reported Missing believed Killed as the result of operations…* Those faceless men had certainly done their part in winning this awful war. She reached for her glass of champagne but found she couldn't take a sip.

"Oh Lily, don't be such a bore," Sophie exclaimed. "You're not, really. I know you're thinking of all those poor boys, but I didn't mean them. You know I didn't."

"What poor boys?" Matthew asked.

"Oh, Lily's job. It's wretched, worse than mine."

"It isn't—"

Sophie leaned over the table, lowering her voice to a melo-dramatic hush. "She writes letters to the families who have sons who have been killed in action. Sons or husbands or brothers. Every day, all day. Can you even imagine? Nothing but death. At least I get to type up lists of ammunition and battle plans and permissions for leave." She let out a rather sharp laugh and tossed back her champagne.

"It isn't wretched," Lily stated with dignity, and she caught Matthew's eye. He didn't smile, but somehow she felt as if he had.

"Let's dance." Sophie had finished her champagne and Tom sprang up from his seat to take her hand.

Lily watched them head to the dance floor in a blur of silver and army green, and the silence that fell on the table felt like a raincloud, or perhaps a thunderclap. Lily sneaked a glance at Matthew and saw him staring at the blur of motion on the dance floor, his face expressionless, one hand resting flat on the table. Any sense of a smile had vanished completely. The evening, she feared, was going to be interminable.

"Do you dance much?" she asked, simply to break the heavy silence, only to realize it might sound as if she were fishing for an invitation from him. "I'm afraid I don't."

"Nor do I." Matthew glanced at her, his lips twitching in what could almost be called a smile. "I'm what Lieutenant Reese would call a dead hoofer."

The wry glimmer in his dark eyes made Lily's heart give a strange squeeze. "A dead hoofer?"

"Two left feet."

"Ah. Well, I suppose that's what I am, as well. I try, but I really can't manage it. If you asked me to dance, I'm sure you'd regret it, or at least your feet would."

"Ah, well." Matthew gave a nod, his eyes still glinting with wry humor. "There are more important things in life than dancing."

"I'm not sure everyone out there would agree." She cocked her head towards the dance floor. "But I don't mind not being able to, honestly." Even though she realized she would have liked him to have asked.

He smiled then, the tiniest thing, but it felt like a spark had leapt across the table from him to her, as if she'd caught it in her bare hands. "I know you don't," he said.

The warmth in his voice surprised and thrilled her, and, discomfited, Lily reached for her champagne, simply to have something to do with her hands. The bubbles tickled her nose and made her cough.

"I haven't had champagne in years," she said as she put the glass back down. "I forgot how funny it is."

He looked at her with a strangely penetrating gaze, his eyes so very dark, the irises nearly the same color as the pupils. "Has it been very hard here?" he asked. "During the war?"

"Not as hard as some have it, I'm sure." Lily was always conscious that she shouldn't complain, not when others had lost homes, or lives. "We haven't been bombed out, and we haven't lost anyone close to us yet. Mother says we're very fortunate, really." She sounded like such a *child*, she thought with a wince. How was it that her sister could seem so effortlessly sophisticated, and meanwhile she sounded as if she were about six? "What about you? I don't suppose the war has affected you much yet, in New York."

"No," he agreed after a brief, heightened pause. "Not in New York."

"Of course, now that you're here..." With an uneasy ripple of awareness, she realized how one day, perhaps even one day soon, both Matthew and Tom would be right in the action, on the front lines, fighting for their lives, as well as for victory. One day they might be the names mentioned in one of the letters she wrote. *Dear So-and-so...*

Except, of course, they weren't in the navy. It would be some other nameless girl, some American girl in a strange city somewhere, who would sit in front of a typewriter, her fingers poised over the keys. *It is my painful duty to inform you...*

"Are you scared?" she blurted. "When you think about fighting?"

"No." The answer was so swift and stony that Lily blinked.

"Are you scared when you're caught in a raid?" Matthew countered, and she shrugged uncertainly.

"Sometimes, but usually it doesn't feel quite real. It's almost as if I'm watching a film, or a newsreel. I wonder if that's the only way we can survive it—by feeling as if it's not actually happening to us."

Matthew was silent for a long moment, his fingers rotating the stem of his coupe of untouched champagne. "At some point," he said finally, "you will have to accept that it is real."

There was no real censure to his voice, but Lily felt it all the same. Why had she sounded so... so *vacuous*, as if the war hadn't really affected her, as if she wasn't bothered at all by all the tragedy and violence around her, by the letters she wrote every day?

Words crowded in her throat, crammed in her mouth, unspoken revelations about how she couldn't keep from imagining the faceless men whose letters she wrote, the men who had drowned in cold, empty seas, or died in the burning carcasses of torpedoed ships. How she lay in bed awake at night and pictured their terrible last moments, wondered if, when the end finally came, they'd been scared or sad or simply accepting? Had it *hurt*?

She wanted to tell Matthew how, in those sleepless moments, she felt a silent scream building in her chest, a howl of fury and fear and hopelessness, as the wooden tray on her desk filled with freshly typed letters every day, and yet there were always, *always* more to type.

And each one belonged to a person—a young man who had lived and loved, who had come down with colds and maybe kissed a girl; a boy who had hugged his mother. How could that be? How could that possibly *be*?

Staring at his implacable expression, dark eyebrows drawn over darker eyes, she wanted to share so much, and yet she struggled to say anything at all.

"Yes," she finally mumbled. "I suppose you're right."

The silence stretched on again, painful this time. It was horribly apparent they had nothing to say to one another—or, at least, Sergeant Lawson had nothing to say to her, and she couldn't even blame him. Somehow she hadn't been able to convey anything of how she really felt—how *much* she felt.

Lily reached for her champagne once more, only to put it down, afraid she might cough again and embarrass herself further.

"So you write letters," Matthew said after a moment. "What division?"

"I'm a Wren. That's the Women's Royal Naval Service—I work in the Admiralty."

"And do you do as your sister said? Typing letters all day, every day, to the families of the servicemen who have been killed?"

"Or missing in action. Yes."

Something flickered in Matthew's eyes as he looked at her. "That must be terribly sad."

Lily thought of all she'd wanted to say earlier, and still couldn't. "Sometimes," she said quietly, and looked away. "But it's not as bad for me as it is for them," she added after a moment, struggling to form her thoughts into words. "For the men, I mean, and for the families." She turned back to him; he looked as inscrutable as ever. "It must be horrible, to receive one of those letters. To… to *know*."

She'd imagined it many times—a woman in a housedress, or perhaps a young wife, a baby in her arms, taking the thin envelope, reading the impersonal typescript, the scant sentences. Lily tried, foolishly, she knew, to imbue each letter she wrote with some kind of warmth, a silent prayer said over the impersonal words that were always the same.

"Of course," she added when Matthew had not said anything, "they receive letters from the soldiers themselves. Did you know that? Every soldier writes a letter that will be sent in case he dies."

"Yes, I know." His voice was toneless, his gaze somewhere off to the left. "I've written one myself, actually."

"Oh." Childishly, tears sprang to her eyes. She was making such a dreadful ninny of herself. "Of course you did," she whispered and then looked down at her lap.

The music ended and the orchestra struck up another lively tune. Lily looked up to try to catch a glimpse of her sister; Sophie was a good dancer, but Lily didn't think she'd ever jitterbugged as wildly as this before, heels kicking up and skirts flying. Lily couldn't see her in the crowd of dancers, and with the silence like a heavy blanket over the table, she muttered an excuse and blindly made her way out of the ballroom to find the ladies'.

The room was thankfully empty, and Lily spent a moment taking deep breaths as she dabbed her eyes, feeling both ridiculous and terribly sad. She'd been nervous about this evening, but everything felt so much worse than she'd expected. Why did Matthew Lawson have to be so quiet? Why did he have to make her feel so stupid? Except he wasn't really; he'd been quite kind, in his way. She'd managed to make herself feel stupid all on her own.

She drew a shuddering breath as the door swung open and three women sallied in, clearly in high spirits, chatting and laughing as they reached for lipsticks and started primping in front of the large gilt-edged mirror.

Lily angled her face away from them, but not quickly enough.

"Oh, you poor chicken!" A woman lowered her lipstick as she surveyed Lily's bright eyes and trembling chin. "Has some dreadful Yank broken your heart?" She laughed raucously at this, taking any sympathy from her words, and Lily forced her chin up, her face heating. Was nowhere in this wretched hotel safe?

"No one has broken my heart," she stated firmly.

"Just give him time," the woman warned and, leaning towards the mirror, she puckered her lips.

"Don't mind her, duck," one of her companions said with a kindlier smile. "She's three sheets to the wind already." She patted Lily's shoulder. "Chin up, love. Most likely, he's not worth it."

"If he's American, he is," the drunk woman stated. "For the cigarettes alone." She narrowed her eyes as she outlined her lips in carmine red.

"I don't smoke," Lily said, which caused another eruption of laughter.

"Look, have a nip of this." To her shock, the kindly woman took a silver flask from her handbag and gave it to Lily. Her numb fingers closed around it automatically. "It'll keep your spirits up."

Lily had no intention of drinking whatever was in the flask, but then she recalled Matthew Lawson's flat voice, his blank look, and recklessly she unscrewed the top and took a large gulp of the stuff, only to sputter and cough half of it out, causing even more laughter.

The alcohol burned its way down her throat to her stomach, where it lit a warm fire of purpose and determination. She would not make a ninny of herself in front of Matthew Lawson, or anyone else, and she would not let him make her feel like one, either.

"There you go, darling," the drunk woman called out encouragingly. "Go get him."

Lily thrust the flask back at its owner and, with her head held high, she strode out of the ladies', back to the ballroom.

CHAPTER SIX

When Lily returned to the table, Sophie and Tom were sitting with Matthew. Sophie was, rather shockingly, on Tom's lap, another coupe of champagne in her hand, laughing at something he'd said. If the woman in the ladies' was three sheets to the wind, Lily thought with foreboding, then her sister was at least two.

"Get a load of this, Lily," she called out.

Lily glanced at Matthew, who was staring at the table, but he lifted his head when she sat down, and the searching look he gave her made her blush and look away, because she didn't understand it at all.

"That's what you say, isn't it?" Sophie continued teasingly as she twisted around to face Tom. "Get a load of this?" She put on a horribly twangy American accent that made Tom boom with laughter.

"Sure it is, honey."

Sophie reached into Tom's jacket and plucked out a little brown booklet. She turned back to Lily, a cigarette dangling from her fingers, and not a Spanish Shawl. "All that codswallop Tom was saying at Sunday lunch?" she told her. "It's all from this book." She waved it in front of Lily, who gazed at it blankly. "Listen to this." Sophie straightened, Tom's arm snug around her waist, and said in a loud, carrying voice, "'Don't be a show-off. The British dislike bragging and showing off. American wages and American soldier's pay are the highest in the world. When payday comes, it would be sound practice to learn to spend your money according to British standards.'" She tossed the book down on the table. "I hope you don't take that bit to heart," she told Tom as she nestled closer. "Because I've heard about all the wonderful things you can get from your army shops—nylons and chocolate and these lovely, lovely cigarettes."

Tom gave her a squeeze. "Anything you want, baby."

Lily couldn't bear to look at them. There was something so smug about the way Lieutenant Reese had his arm around Sophie's waist, and the glitter in her sister's eyes seemed dangerous. If their mother could see Sophie, she'd be utterly appalled.

And yet, Lily acknowledged, Sophie wasn't acting any differently than a hundred women in this very ballroom—or a thousand, a million, in London. Women who flirted and danced, who managed to snag a GI, who seized their moments when they could, whether it was up against a brick wall or in the narrow bunk of an air-raid shelter. Lily had seen it before and averted her eyes from the sight of twined bodies moving sinuously together under the cover of darkness, or merely a thin blanket.

Her mother talked darkly of loose women of low morals, of the mysterious and bitter ends they invariably came to. And yet that was the reality of the terrifying world they now lived in—perhaps a single night of snatched pleasure was all anyone could hope for, all anybody could dare to get.

It is my painful duty to inform you...

What pleasure had those poor boys had?

"And listen to this," Sophie continued as she snatched the book up once more. "'You will be naturally interested in getting to know your opposite number, the British soldier, the "Tommy" you have heard and read about. You can understand that two actions on your part will slow up the friendship—swiping his girl, and not appreciating what his army has been up against. Yes, and rubbing it in that you are better paid than he is.'" Sophie threw her head back and laughed. "You're not rubbing it in, are you, Tom?" She made it sound dirty.

"Who, me?" Tom made a face of exaggerated innocence before he caught Matthew's eye; the other man, Lily saw, was scowling now. "What's gotten you looking so down in the dumps?" he demanded. He nodded, a bit dismissively, to Lily. "Why don't you go dance with her?"

Matthew smiled tightly; there was nothing friendly about it. "I'm not a jive bender like you." He made it sound like an insult.

"So why don't you give it a whirl? She looks like she'd like a spin around the floor."

Lily sat frozen in her seat, mortified by the exchange.

"Yes, go on, Lil," Sophie said. "Go bebop." She'd put on the American accent again, and both she and Tom laughed far too loudly at her supposed witticism.

Lily glanced at Matthew, who had risen from his chair.

"Shall we?" he said, without any particular enthusiasm. He held out his hand, leaving Lily no choice but to take it.

Out on the dance floor, they were surrounded by jitterbugging couples, moving with such swift assurance their limbs were nothing more than a blur of motion.

"I'm really not a good dancer," Lily said, feeling she had to remind him.

"My feet have been warned." He put one hand on her waist, warm and firm, and Lily put her hand on his shoulder.

While couples flew and spun around them, they managed a simple box step.

"I'm sorry about Tom," Matthew said after a moment. "He's a bit high-spirited. I don't think he means any harm."

"Neither does Sophie."

"A good match, then."

"Or a very bad one. They'll egg each other on."

Matthew raised his eyebrows. "Would that be so bad?"

"I don't know," Lily admitted. What was she so afraid of, when it came to Sophie? When it came to herself? "I don't really have enough experience to say," she admitted, then blushed.

"Experience?"

"Of life. Of… romance." She blushed even more, amazed she'd said such a thing. She never would have, if she hadn't had that slug of whatever it was in the flask, still burning in her belly.

Matthew seemed unfazed by her confession. "That's no bad thing."

"Isn't it?"

"Better to wait for the right person than waste your hopes on someone wrong."

What was he saying…? Lily glanced up at Matthew's face, shocked to realize just how close he was. He wasn't handsome in the hale and hearty way of Tom Reese, the way she expected all Americans to be, but there was something compelling about his dark looks, his sense of quiet containment. She only wished she knew what he was thinking, how he felt.

"Am I terribly boring to you?" she blurted, emboldened further. "Do I seem like such a…" She swallowed painfully. "A little girl?"

Matthew glanced down at her, his dark eyes narrowed. "How old are you?"

"Twenty-one."

"I'm only two years older than you."

"Are you?" She'd thought him much older, perhaps near thirty. "I feel as if everything I've said tonight has been a bit stupid and foolish."

"Not at all." He nodded back towards the table. "You're a font of wisdom in comparison."

Her lips twitched at that. She realized she liked the way he spoke—so clearly and precisely, choosing each word before deciding to speak it, as if each one mattered. She liked a lot of things about him. "Your standards must be rather low, then," she teased, and he raised his eyebrows.

"Not at all. Quite the contrary."

The firmness of his words thrilled her, and she had to look away. "You may not be a—a jive bender," she told him. "But you are certainly no dead hoofer."

"When it comes to the box step, no," he agreed. "My mother taught me when I was young."

Lily could picture it—the wireless playing a waltz, an elegant woman with upswept hair, dark like Matthew's, leading him around a little sitting room, a gentle look on her face.

"She'd be proud to see you now," she said.

Something flashed across his face, like a lightning streak of pain. Jolted, Lily felt as if she'd said something clumsy or wrong, and she started to stammer an uncertain apology, only to be cut off by Matthew's quiet voice.

"I hope she would be," he said, and then the music ended, and he was leading her back to the table, and Lily felt as if she'd spoiled it—if there had even been anything to spoil.

Tom had bought a bottle of wine—no more lettuce for champagne, it seemed—Lily saw as she took her seat, but at least Sophie wasn't on his lap anymore.

She glanced at her watch and saw it was after nine; their parents expected them home by ten, although Lily suspected her sister would not come willingly, as most of The Berkeley's patrons would be dancing half the night away.

"So, what do you Yanks do for fun?" Sophie asked as she lit yet another cigarette.

"Whatever we can," Tom returned. "You'll have to come to Rainbow Corner with us and see what it's all about."

Lily had seen Rainbow Corner—the club for GIs run by the American Red Cross on Shaftesbury Avenue that offered a slice of

American life to homesick servicemen. She'd also seen the queues of her countrymen outside, snaking around the corner, desperate to get inside and sample its delights.

"Oh, will you take us there?" Sophie asked. "Wouldn't I have to have my name on a list?"

"I think I can manage it."

Lily wondered if he could. Tom Reese seemed full of swagger and brash talk, and his wallet was certainly bulging with money, but he was only a second lieutenant, after all, and he couldn't be much older than Matthew's twenty-three, if that. Yet her sister had clearly decided to cast her lot with him; she'd shown more affection to Lieutenant Tom Reese than any other man Lily had seen her with before, and she couldn't help but let it worry her. Where would it lead?

The music was still thumping and Lily's head ached. Her mouth tasted stale from the alcohol she'd drunk, and the room had become stuffy with the smell of sweat and cigarettes. She realized just how badly she wanted to go home.

She sank back into her chair as Sophie led Tom back onto the dance floor. It felt as if the evening would never end.

"I'm sorry you're not enjoying yourself," Matthew remarked as he glanced at her. He hadn't drunk anything, Lily noticed, and he looked as coolly unflappable as always.

She made a grimace of apology. "I'm sorry. I have enjoyed myself, it's just it's getting late and I'm tired. I'm afraid I've never been much of one for parties."

"Nor have I."

"Did you go to many, in New York?" Her only image of the city was what she'd seen on a newsreel, but she pictured fancy cars and movie stars, endless parties and dances.

"No." He paused. "I only moved to New York in 1939, when I was eighteen. I'm not from there."

"Oh? Where are you from, then?"

Another pause, this one longer and more considering. "A small town. You wouldn't have heard of it."

Lily sensed something repressed about his tone, and decided not to ask anything more.

Matthew seemed content to be silent, and Lily realized she didn't mind. It was enough simply to sit at the same table, watching the dancers blur by, knowing they were in agreement about much of the evening.

Eventually, Sophie and Tom came stumbling back to the table, and then drank more wine, and flirted outrageously, before, finally, at nearly eleven, Lily was at last able to pry her sister away.

Outside, the air was sharp and cold, and an icy fog lay over the darkened city. Despite the late hour, there were plenty of people about, cabs gliding through the dark streets like predatory shadows, and people linking arms as they made their stumbling way to the Tube station, singing drunkenly. *"I'll be seeing you in all the old familiar places that this heart of mine embraces…"*

There was a feeling of bonhomie that Lily couldn't help but enjoy, despite the awkwardness of the occasion. Sophie and Tom had their arms wrapped around one another, her head leaning against his shoulder. Meanwhile, Matthew walked a sensible two feet away from Lily, and both of their heads were tucked low. She dreaded the inevitably awkward moment of farewell, and when it came, it was just as she'd feared.

At the steps down to the station, Sophie turned to Tom and twined her arms around him. While a few GIs nearby whistled and catcalled, the pair kissed, and Matthew and Lily stood mutely and waited, neither of them looking at the embracing pair, or each other.

Then, when she least expected it, Lily caught Matthew's eye and he gave her the glimmer of a smile—a wry quirk of his lips that suggested a shared joke, a lovely secret. As Tom and Sophie broke apart, Lily felt herself smiling back, her heart lifting improbably, buoyed inside her.

As the train rattled back towards Clapham, Sophie's gaiety drained out of her like champagne from a bottle. She leaned against a pole, her face pale, her lipstick blood red and slightly smeared, seeming to sink into herself the farther they traveled.

"I don't think Mother will be too cross," Lily said by way of encouragement. "We're not that late, and she knows tonight was something special."

"I don't care about Mother," Sophie answered, and turned away to stare out the window at the blackness of the tunnel they were trundling through.

As it happened, Carol Mather *was* cross, but only a little. "What if there had been an air raid?" she demanded as Sophie and Lily took their coats off in the hall. "We wouldn't have known if you'd got to safety. We would have been worried to death."

"Surely not to death," Sophie tossed back, and Carol pressed her lips together. "Besides, The Berkeley has its own shelter. We'd have been as safe as houses."

Carol harrumphed but left it at that; the hot-water bottles she offered them for their beds felt like a peace offering.

Upstairs in their bedroom, with the blackout curtain drawn tightly across and the water bottles warming their beds, Lily slipped off the dark green dress that had seemed frumpy next to Sophie's silver frock.

"You and Lieutenant Reese certainly got on," she remarked as Sophie unpinned her hair.

"Oh, don't sound so stuffy," she returned, and yawned. "He's all right."

"I'm not being stuffy," Lily objected, knowing she could have been a good deal stuffier. "You think he's just all right?"

Sophie shrugged and sat down to unroll her stockings. "He's going to leave, isn't he? Tom said they were only in London for a short while, until they're transferred to a base somewhere."

"They could still come to London on leave."

"There's a hundred willing girls for every GI," Sophie answered with another shrug. She sounded more matter-of-fact than despondent.

Lily frowned, surprised by her sister's sudden low mood. "He was certainly taken with you," she persisted.

"Perhaps, but even so…" Sophie paused, a stocking in one hand, her gaze resting on some distant shore. "He'll be over there soon enough, won't he? Fighting for victory. And, meanwhile, I'm here, taking dictation from an—an old fart!"

"Sophie—"

"It's true, isn't it?" Sophie's voice was fierce as she turned to face her. "It's all true. Every day, I sit in a stuffy office and type boring letters, while some smarmy old coot smacks my bottom and tells me what a 'fine gel' I am. I can't *stand* it, Lily. I can't stand another minute of it."

Lily stared at her sister in wordless shock. She'd never heard her sound so impassioned, or so despairing. "But you're doing your bit—"

"If that's my bit, I don't want to do it! Look what else I read in that silly little book." Sophie reached for her handbag and yanked out the little book of Tom's that he'd carelessly given her. "'A British woman officer or non-commissioned officer can—and often does—give orders to a man private. The men obey smartly and know it is no shame. For British women have proven themselves in this way. They have stuck to their posts near burning ammunition dumps, delivered messages afoot after their motorcycles have been blasted from under them.'" Sophie's voice trembled, but she kept reading, her voice full of an angry determination. "'They have pulled aviators from burning planes. They have died at the gun posts and, as they have fallen, another girl has stepped directly into the position and carried on. There is not a single record of any British woman in uniformed service quitting her post or failing in her duty under fire. Now you understand why British soldiers respect the women in uniform. They have won the right to the utmost respect. When you see a girl in khaki or air-force blue with a bit of ribbon on her tunic—remember she didn't get it for knitting more socks than anyone else in Ipswich.'"

Sophie tossed the book onto the top of the bureau, her face full of a loathing Lily didn't understand. "What have I done to be worthy of such respect, Lily? I haven't even knit any socks." She let out a humorless laugh as she stripped off her silver dress and flung it carelessly to the floor.

"Not everyone can be a hero," Lily said quietly. Sophie had been requisitioned by the War Office thanks to the secretarial course she'd completed when she was seventeen; there was no shame in it, none at all.

While Sophie fumed silently, Lily picked up her dress and hung it on the back of a chair. If it belonged to one of the girls at the War Office, she'd want it back in good nick.

"I don't need to be a hero," Sophie said at last. "I just want to feel *useful*. If a bomb flattened me tomorrow, it wouldn't matter in the least."

Lily stared at her, horrified. "It would matter to me—"

"I don't mean to people. I mean to the war. I'm not doing anything, Lily. Not one thing I can be proud of, and I don't think I ever will." Pulling her nightgown over her head, Sophie slipped under the covers of her bed and turned her back to Lily, the conversation clearly over.

Lily undressed in silence and then got into her own bed. Despite the welcome warmth of the hot-water bottle, the bed sheets were freezing. She closed her eyes, her mind spinning a little from the alcohol, Sophie's surprising and desperate vitriol, the whole evening. Yet the last thing she thought of before sleep claimed her was Matthew Lawson's funny little smile as they'd said goodbye.

CHAPTER SEVEN

ABBY

Abby stood on the porch as Simon came up the dusty drive in his rental car, one hand waving out the window as he pulled up in front of the farmhouse.

She hadn't told her dad where she was going today; she didn't usually and, in any case, he was out in the orchard spraying all afternoon, and it had seemed easier not to say anything. She'd given Bailey her morning walk and was meant to be balancing the farm's books and getting ahead on the publicity for the harvest weekend they held every year, but she could work this evening, and it wasn't pressing anyway.

Simon turned off the engine and climbed out of the car, smiling at her in a way that made her stomach give a little leap. She never did stuff like this. Never went anywhere much, and certainly not with a man she found attractive. Because, yes, she was willing to admit she found Simon Elliot attractive, which was why she felt so nervous now, even though she knew she shouldn't be. This didn't have to be a big deal. She'd told Shannon it wasn't, when her friend had called her asking about "her Englishman".

"He's not mine," Abby had protested, but Shannon wasn't having it.

"Not according to the Ashford grapevine. First dinner, now a date?"

How, Abby wondered, did everyone know everything in this town? She could guess how it had happened—Simon had mentioned something to Betty at the Citgo Station, and she'd passed it onto her husband Merv, who worked at the hardware store. He'd told Shannon's mother, who stocked shelves there part-time, and there they were.

"It's really not a date."

"You are going out alone with a man of similar age to you. For you, that's a date. That's practically *marriage*."

Abby had been able to hear the smile in Shannon's voice, but the remark had stung just the tiniest bit. Yes, for *her*, because her life was so small and boring. Not for anyone else.

"You know what I mean," Shannon had said, her tone gentler, and Abby knew she'd picked up on that fraction of a second of silence.

"I'm really not thinking of it that way," she'd said, except she knew she was. Sort of.

Even now she was trying to tell herself that this didn't mean anything, that she wasn't sure she wanted it to. She and Simon were from different continents, different worlds. It wasn't like this could go anywhere, if "it" even started at all, which it probably wouldn't.

Yet, despite all those warnings and caveats, she couldn't deny it felt—*fun*—to be spending the day with someone. To not know exactly, down to the minute, how the hours would pass. To feel that little leap in her belly and prod it curiously.

"Are you ready?" Simon asked, smiling up at her.

"Yes, I think so." She turned back to the house to get her purse, not that she'd even need it, before closing the door and coming down the steps.

Simon looked exactly the same, his hair ruffled from the window, his eyes glinting hazel. A few freckles had come out on his nose, thanks to the summer sun.

"Do you always wear a button-down shirt?" Abby asked, and he laughed.

"Pretty much. I'm terribly boring, aren't I?"

"No, I just wondered." She smiled, before getting into the passenger seat, telling herself not to be so nervous. The last thing she wanted was Simon to pick up on it. "So who are the Bryants, exactly?" she asked as he headed back down the drive, the dust billowing out behind them. "And what do you know about them?"

"Not much, really." Simon flexed his hands on the steering wheel as he shot her another quick smile, eyes crinkling, the whole gamut. Abby's stomach leapt again. "I came across them when I was doing an internet search on Tom Reese. I searched something like Wisconsin GIs and stumbled on Douglas Bryant. He'd written a memoir that he'd had published with a small press some years ago, although I've yet to get my hands on a copy. He served in the artillery, came to the UK in '43. That's about all I know."

"And he married a British woman?"

"Yes, a nurse named Stella from Wolverhampton. They came back here. And that's it, as far as I know." He turned to give her a wry grimace. "Doesn't seem like there's much mystery or drama, but it will be interesting to hear their perspective on the war. And, who knows? Perhaps it will shed some light on your grandfather's situation somehow."

"Maybe," Abby said doubtfully. She couldn't see how two strangers would tell her anything about Tom Reese, but she supposed learning a little more about the war could be interesting. And, truthfully, she just wanted to spend an afternoon away from Willow Tree, with Simon.

She gazed out the window at the farms flashing by, big red barns in yellow-green fields, the landscape of her life. So familiar, if she closed her eyes, she could see it all perfectly, down to every last detail—the split in the fence post, the weathered billboard for the Tristan Crist Magic Theatre in Lake Geneva, the farmhouse with two dusty pickup trucks in the drive and an American flag on the front porch. She knew it all. She'd lived it all, hadn't lived anything else.

Why did she feel the tiniest bit restless, even bored by it, now?

She couldn't let herself be bored. She didn't have that freedom, that right.

Abby pressed her hand against the window for a moment, a way to anchor herself, and Simon glanced at her again.

"Shall I roll down the windows? Get some fresh air?"

"All right."

He pressed a button and the windows came down, the warm breeze rolling over her like a wave. She put one hand to her hair in its usual braid, wisps flying around her face.

"I'm going to look like a total mess by the time we get there."

"You look lovely."

The sincerity in his voice would make her blush if she let it, but Abby didn't respond. She turned back to the window, looking out at the view she knew so well, letting the details soak right into her.

It was only twenty minutes to Genoa City, a town of about three thousand. Simon followed the satnav on his phone to a modest ranch house on the outskirts of the town, with a neat yard and a minivan in the driveway.

"So, we're seeing Helen Wegman, the Bryants' daughter, married to Ralph," he briefed her as he turned off the engine and rolled up the windows. "They're in their early seventies—retired, spent all their lives here in Genoa City."

"Sounds familiar."

Simon flashed her a quick, commiserating smile. "Do you feel like you're looking into your future?"

Abby glanced at the little house. Her whole life in Ashford, alone? This, and nothing more? There was no reason to think why not, and yet she had to suppress a sudden visceral shudder at the thought. "Not quite," she said. "Not yet."

"Good."

Abby decided there was no need to unpack that statement as they got out of the car and headed up to the house.

Helen Wegman answered the door as soon as Simon had rung the bell.

"You must be Simon. You look English." She gave them both wide smiles. "And you are…?"

"Abby Reese. And I'm not English." She smiled back. "A genuine Wisconsinite, from over near Ashford."

"Well, welcome both of you." Helen stepped aside so they could come into the small living room; Abby took in a three-piece suite in blue corduroy and a lot of family photos. "Ralph had to run some errands, but he'll be back shortly. I've gotten some old mementoes and things out—I thought you might want to have a look." She turned to Simon. "You said you're writing a book…?"

"Hoping to." He smiled wryly. "I only just started, but I'm gathering information, so anything you could tell us about your parents' romance during the war…"

"Well, they did like to talk about it," Helen said with a laugh. "Love at first sight, they said it was."

"How did they meet?"

"Oh, that's quite a story, let me tell you. But, first, can I get you something to drink? Eat?"

Simon glanced questioningly at Abby, who shrugged back.

"Yes, thanks, that would be lovely."

"Oh, your accent!" Helen laughed and shook her head. "You sound like something on one of those British dramas. I've got lemonade…"

"I love lemonade," Simon declared, and Abby smiled.

"American lemonade," she reminded him quietly as Helen bustled back to the kitchen, and Simon gave her a quick, laughing look.

"But of course."

They settled onto the sofa, sitting on each end, and glanced at the various memorabilia Helen had got out—a wedding photo, a worn and faded ration book, a war medal. Simon picked up the photograph and studied it. Abby leaned over so she could have a look.

"Why did everyone in the 1940s look so glamorous?" she asked as she gazed at the picture of the woman with her dark hair done up in a French roll. The man wore his army uniform, his hair slicked back with pomade. They were both wearing wide smiles, looking happy and full of life, rather different from the subdued looks of her own grandparents in their wedding photo.

"I think it was the lipstick," Simon remarked thoughtfully. "And the hair. Makes it all seem very stylish."

"You can't even tell if she's wearing lipstick," Abby protested. "It's a black and white photo."

"Don't you think? Her lips look so dark. If this were a color photo, they'd be bright red, I'd bet."

"Maybe. Did women have lipstick during the war? Weren't things like that difficult to get hold of?"

"Everything was, or so it seems, but people found ways to make do. I read in a book somewhere that women used boot polish for mascara and beetroot for lipstick."

"Goodness." Abby couldn't imagine it; she never wore makeup, not even a slick of lip gloss or hint of concealer. There usually wasn't any point, and she hadn't even thought of it for today.

"'Beauty is a Duty', I believe the phrase was," Simon remarked.

"That sounds a bit sexist."

"I suppose everything was a bit sexist back then, but that was the amazing thing about the war—it gave women the opportunity to do things they never were able to before."

"That sounds like another book."

Simon smiled at her. "Maybe it is."

"Here we are," Helen announced as she came into the room with a tray of lemonade and the ubiquitous cheese platter—a

seeming necessity when entertaining in Wisconsin. She distributed the drinks as Simon and Abby murmured their thanks,
and then she settled herself in an armchair opposite them before
nodding at the photo Simon had put back on the table. "That's
my parents. Douglas and Stella Bryant."

"They look like a lovely couple."

"They were." She smiled fondly. "And so in love, right till the
end." Laughing self-consciously, she dabbed at her eyes. "That's
what you want, isn't it? For your marriage?"

Abby glanced at Simon, who had a strangely serious look on
his face, something close to sadness. Looking at him, she felt
jolted, as if she'd missed the last step in a staircase.

"I would think so," she said when he didn't seem as if he was
going to respond. "Although, I must admit, I don't have any
experience, myself."

"Oh…" Helen glanced between the two of them with confusion. "You're not…"

"No, no," Abby said quickly. "I only met Simon last week.
He's researching my grandfather as well, who fought in the war."
She could feel herself speaking too quickly. "So how did your
parents meet?"

"Sorry, I just assumed…" Helen shook her head and then
sat back, settling herself more comfortably in her armchair. "It's
such a sweet story. My dad was sent to England in 1943, before
the D-Day invasion. He was in the artillery, kicking his heels up
somewhere in the Midlands before being mobilized. From the
stories he told, you'd think it was a party every day. Dances, going
to the pictures… he was a good-looking man, as you can see, and
although he never said it quite so bluntly, I think he could have
had his pick of women."

"I've heard it was tough on the poor Tommies," Simon said
with a small smile. He had recovered his usual relaxed and engag-

ing manner. "The GIs had everything—smart uniforms, more money, cigarettes, chewing gum."

"Yes, I suppose they did. Although my mother always said she fell for his smile."

"I'm sure she did." Simon nodded towards the photo. "He had a good one."

"Anyway, they met at a dance put on by the American Red Cross, in Wolverhampton. They used to do that for the soldiers—they'd been away from home for months, or sometimes even years, and they got homesick. They had all sorts of things to help them feel more at home. I remember my dad used to tell me about Rainbow Corner in London, where he went when he was on leave. It had everything—a movie theater, a barber's, a corner drugstore, an endless supply of Coca-Colas." She smiled. "I'd have liked to have seen it. In any case, my mother wasn't going to go to this dance—she wasn't much of one for things like that, but her friend dragged her along. My father knew how to cut up a rug for sure—he was on the floor with a different girl for every dance. They couldn't have been more different."

"So what happened?" Abby asked, genuinely curious.

"My mother caught my father's eye. Not with anything she'd done—she was standing against the wall, wishing she could go home! But my father liked the look of her, and he asked her to dance. She decided she liked his smile and so she said yes. They danced every dance together after that, even though my mother had two left feet. And the rest, they say, is history." Helen sat back, satisfied.

"That's lovely." Simon nodded towards the war medal on the coffee table—the same kind of Purple Heart that was now in her father's bedroom. "That was his?"

"Yes, he was shot in the shoulder during the Normandy landings. Put him out of action for two months. He was so annoyed he got shot, but he was proud too. Always liked to tell the story."

Which was about as different from her grandfather as could be, Abby thought, who had never talked about it and given away his medal besides. "What about your mother?" she asked. "She didn't mind moving all the way to America?"

"No, she'd lost both her parents in the war, and she didn't have any siblings. I think she was more than glad to go. Dad's family took her in, and they stayed right here in Genoa City their whole lives."

They chatted a bit more, and Simon gamely took a cracker and an orange cube of cheddar cheese from the platter, but there wasn't much more to learn, and there was certainly no mystery. Still, it was interesting to hear about Helen's memories of her parents' experiences during the war, and it made Abby wonder even more about her grandfather… and Sophie Mather.

"Maybe she had family who could tell you more," Abby said when they'd said their goodbyes to the Wegmans. Ralph had come in for the last few minutes, shaking their hands and seeming pleased they'd come.

"I know she did," Simon answered as he opened the passenger door for her. Abby felt strangely pleased that he knew immediately whom she'd been talking about. "She had parents, of course, and a sister, Lily—I believe her name was—although I think they lost touch a long time ago, maybe even right after the war. At least, I think that's what Mum said. She met her once, when she was a little girl, but I think Lily died a while ago, I don't know how or why, or whether she had family." He shook his head helplessly as he slid into the driver's seat.

"Why do you think she and Sophie lost touch?"

Simon spread his hands. "I don't know that, either. I think there was a lot of personality in the family—my grandmother, as well as my mother." He paused, as if he were going to say more. "They were very dramatic, emotional people." A tension had crept into his voice, his mouth tightening, his eyes narrowing.

"Well, you know what they say," Abby said, only semi-joking as Simon started the car, "dysfunctional families are ones with people in them."

"Right." He managed a small smile before seeming to shake off his dark mood, the way a dog shook off water. "Anyway, looking back, I don't suppose you realize at the time that you've lost touch with someone. You just see them less and less, a gradual slipping away. I think that's how it might have been for my grandmother and her sister."

"So you never met Lily."

"No, not that I can remember." He considered for a moment. "I'm quite sure I didn't."

Simon started to reverse out of the driveway, and Abby waved to the Wegmans, who were still standing on the front doorstep.

"And when you're a child," he continued ruminatively, "you don't think about the adults in your life having lives of their own, do you? They're just part of the backdrop—weekend visits, slipping you a sweet or a fiver. When I was older, I asked my grandmother a bit about the war—I did my thesis in university on the Mass Observation Project, and I wanted her input."

"The Mass—what? What was that?"

"People were encouraged to keep diaries during the war, to record their thoughts and feelings as well as what they got up to, and then send them to a national review. It's a fascinating glimpse into what life really was like back then. I wrote about whether the diaries were an accurate reflection of wartime life, or if people were writing down what they thought others wanted to read. Anyway, I asked Granny about it, but she didn't have much to say, at least that was personal. She'd talk about rationing or the Anderson shelter in their back garden, but it all seemed pretty removed from what she was experiencing or feeling. And she didn't mention Tom Reese until shortly before her death." He shrugged. "Your father is right in that, I think. There are some things people just don't want to talk about. I would have asked more, but it felt invasive."

"I can understand that." Abby knew she certainly wasn't one to press anyone about anything. And yet the result was a vacuum of knowledge, a yawning ignorance, and one that she felt now more than ever.

Lily and Sophie. Two sisters, eighty years ago, and somehow her grandfather had been involved. How? Why? What had he needed to forgive Sophie Mather for?

"Do you have to get back?" Simon asked. "Or would you like to grab some lunch?" They were driving through Genoa City's main drag, a friendly-looking street with a variety of brick and clapboard buildings on either side, looking as if it had fallen straight out of the 1950s. Simon nodded towards an old neon sign above a small diner. "That place looks like it could have been around in the Bryants' time."

"Yes, something out of that Rainbow Corner Helen mentioned."

"So are you all right to stay out a bit longer?"

Abby hesitated, caught between temptation and a niggling anxiety. Would her father come back to the house for lunch and notice she was missing? Would he care? She was thirty-two years old. She didn't need to answer to him for absolutely everything. She just felt like she did, an endless atonement for the way she'd once failed.

"Yes, although I should get back fairly soon to let Bailey out," she said at last. "But another hour can't hurt."

Faye's Diner was nearly empty when they walked through the door, a waitress behind the counter pouring coffee for a lone customer at a table in the back.

Simon slid into a red vinyl booth in the window with an expression of delight.

"This place is amazing. I'd say it's retro, but I don't think it's ever changed. It's *vintage*."

"Hopefully the food isn't," Abby quipped as she took one of the slightly greasy laminated menus that had been stuck between the salt and pepper shakers and perused the usual offerings— all-day breakfast, burgers and hotdogs, club sandwiches and fries.

"The food looks *delicious*," Simon declared. "I'm going to eat my body weight in French fries."

Abby laughed at his air of intent. "I am not," she assured him and he pretended to look crestfallen.

The waitress came to take their orders, and she asked for a club sandwich, while Simon was as good as his word and asked for a large order of French fries, along with a cheeseburger.

"They seemed like a sweet couple, didn't they?" Abby remarked once the waitress had gone.

"Douglas and Stella? They did. I'm sure I could include lots of lovely tidbits for this book I have yet to write."

"But you will write it, won't you?" Abby asked. Something about his tone made her think he doubted himself.

Simon shrugged. "To be honest, I'm feeling more interested in the mystery of my grandmother and your grandfather than writing about a load of other couples." He paused. "Your father's reticence made it seem even more like a mystery to me. I know you don't think he's hiding something, but if he was… what would it be?"

Abby glanced out the window at the sleepy main street of the little town. The heat was radiating up from the black tarmac in visible waves, and not a soul was in sight. "Honestly, I have no idea. I think he just doesn't like anyone digging into his past, getting personal." And neither did she.

"Was he close with his father? I know you don't remember him, but did you ever get a sense of their relationship?"

"Not really. They were both farmers, strong, silent types." She smiled wryly. "Salt of the earth, like you said." And yet again she felt that sense of yawning ignorance, this time about her own family. Why didn't she know more? Did most people know their grandparents' stories? Why had Tom Reese left Minnesota, and never seemed to return—at least not that Abby knew about?

The questions kept piling up, yet maybe there was less mystery there than Abby suspected, or Simon wanted there to be. After all, people did just slip away. Days and years passed and you realized how far you'd drifted along the currents of time. Wasn't life just like that?

Or maybe there was a mystery, a secret, even. Then, the question was, did Abby want to discover what it was?

SIMON

Simon watched Abby as she sipped her drink, her expression pensive and a little bit sad. A wisp of dark hair had fallen across her cheek and he had the rather absurd urge to lean over and tuck it behind her ear. He wouldn't, of course.

"What about your immediate family?" he asked, and he didn't miss the way Abby tensed just a little, before she made herself relax as she turned back to look at them.

"What about them?"

"It's just you and your dad…?" he prompted, waiting for the response she seemed reluctant to give.

"Yes." A pause while Simon waited some more, for there was clearly something to be said. Abby didn't seem to want to say it, though.

"Has it always been that way?" he asked gently.

"No." She sighed and pushed her drink away a little. "My mom and brother died in a car accident fifteen years ago, when I was seventeen."

"Oh, Abby." Simon almost reached over to touch her hand, but there was something so prickly and restive about her that he didn't. She folded her arms and looked out the window. "I'm so sorry."

"Thank you. It… it was a tough time."

Which had to be a massive understatement. "Is that why you've stayed?" he asked, and Abby turned back to look at him.

"What do you mean?" she asked sharply, too sharply.

"Sorry… I just meant because your father would have been alone. Running the orchard by himself…"

"Oh." She seemed to relax, her shoulders rounding a little. "Yes, I suppose that's why. But, like I said before, if I'd wanted to go, I would have." She seemed to be saying that as much for her benefit as for his, a need to remind herself of it. To believe it.

"And where would you have gone?" he asked lightly.

"What?" She frowned and then reached for her drink again. "I had a place at University of Wisconsin Madison." She spoke dismissively, as if it hadn't mattered. "I wanted to major in German—how ridiculous is that?"

"It's not ridiculous."

"I'm not sure what I would have done with a degree in German. I think I chose it just because I liked my high school German teacher. I did study the Second World War, a little, as part of it. Not that it helps with any of this."

"It's always hard to give up a dream." What would Abby have been like, Simon wondered, if her mother and brother hadn't died? If she'd gone to university? Maybe she would have moved away, lived in a city, had a more normal and varied life. Although who was he to say her life wasn't normal, or that she had regrets, just because he did?

"It wasn't so much about losing a dream as gaining perspective," Abby said slowly. "My mother and brother's deaths—they made me realize what was important. I never felt like I was giving up anything, just making the choice I needed to at that time."

"And wanted to?"

Something flashed across her face and was gone. She lifted her chin an inch or two. "Yes."

Their food came then, which was probably a good thing. Simon dug into his cheeseburger and they ate in silence for a few moments as the unspoken tension their conversation had created trickled away. He wasn't even sure why he'd pushed—did he really want to involve himself in another person's emotional mess? He had enough of his own.

"What about you?" Abby finally asked. "Did you always want to be a history teacher?"

"Yes." Simon put his half-eaten burger down and took a sip of his lemonade. "It runs in my family. Everyone's an academic. University lecturers, though. I chickened out and went for the easy option." He hoped he didn't sound bitter when he said that. Simon, the disappointment of the family, or so his mother had said often enough, when she'd been in one of her moods.

"You didn't want to be like everyone else?"

"I didn't have the brains, or the work ethic, to be honest." He shrugged. "I have two older sisters who are absolutely fierce. One's a professor of Women's Studies, the other of Sociology. They both terrify me a little."

Abby smiled a little at that. "And your parents?"

"Dad's retired now, but he was chair of the mathematics department at the University of Lincoln. *That* gene skipped me completely. Mum was an assistant lecturer of Norse mythology, of all things." Which had suited her, because she'd been like some tempestuous Nordic goddess herself, perhaps Freya, goddess of love and war, sorcery and death.

Abby sat back. "That sounds like quite a family."

"Yes." Talking about his family made him think of Maggie, and how she still hadn't texted him, even though he'd sent her a video on WhatsApp of his tiny cabin by the lake, with a jokey narrative, longing for her just to smile at something he'd said. He'd also asked her if she wanted him to bring back anything American—"A whole suitcase of Hershey's, sweetheart. Whatever you like."

All of it was too little, too late, Simon knew. He hadn't even told her he was going to the States for several weeks until he was practically on the plane, a fact that made everything in him cringe and squirm in shame, as if snakes were writhing under his skin, in his gut.

Perhaps that was why he wanted there to be a mystery to discover, because it would justify him coming here for so long. Then it would be less about running away, and more about going *to*.

But maybe there was no mystery, at least not a big one. Maybe they'd just been friends or sweethearts and it had fizzled out. That's all it probably was, and yet here he was, digging, digging, trying to justify coming all this way... and for what?

Just so he could avoid what was unraveling back at home, what had unraveled a long time ago?

"I've discovered something," Simon said after a moment, feeling he needed to tell Abby, and wanting to get away from his own desperately circling thoughts.

"Discovered...?" Abby looked more trapped than curious. Was she hiding something, or was he just paranoid, because he knew he was? He could have told her about Maggie, but he hadn't, and the truth was, he had no intention of doing so. He wanted to keep his complications back home. "What is it about?"

"Tom Reese."

"Oh." A look of naked relief passed over her face. So she *was* hiding something, even if just her own reticence. Like father, like daughter. Why were they so reluctant to share anything? Of course, he was too, so he could hardly point the finger. "Okay..."

"I looked up his Purple Heart medal online. There's a Hall of Honor thing—you type in a name and it gives you all the information about the person and why they received the medal, or at least as much as is known." He gave a grimace of apology. "Sorry if I was prying. I was just curious, especially after your dad seemed so reluctant to talk about it."

"That's okay. If it's online, it's there for anyone to see, isn't it?"

"I suppose."

"So what did you find out?"

"He was in the 82nd Airborne, which was a unit of paratroopers who parachuted into Normandy behind enemy lines on D-Day. He was wounded in Belgium, in December 1944, during the Battle of the Bulge."

"Oh." Abby let out an embarrassed laugh. "I don't actually know about any of that, really."

"Didn't you say you studied the Second World War?" Simon teased, and she laughed again.

"That was years ago. I've forgotten it all now."

"I don't know if it's important, anyway, in terms of your family. It was a surprise attack by the Germans, who had amassed a huge amount, or 'bulge,' of troops and weaponry, in Belgium, to prevent the Allies from advancing into Germany. There were a lot of casualties."

The waitress came back to check on them, and Abby gave her a fleeting smile of thanks before turning back to Simon. "So what do you think?" she asked. "It doesn't tell you much more about your grandmother, does it? Or even much more about my grandfather, really."

"I just wonder," Simon said slowly, "why it was such a secret in your family. His Purple Heart. You heard Helen—most people were proud of those medals. It meant they'd fought for their country, and they'd paid a price. And if he received it during that operation… it meant he'd been fighting on the front lines for months. I did a little research on the 82nd Airborne, and although they had some leave in the middle, they saw all the major battles.

It was seriously tough stuff. Crack troops and all that, and your grandfather was part of it. Wouldn't he have been proud?"

Abby held his gaze for a moment before looking away. "When you talk about him," she said slowly, "it feels as if you're talking about someone else. A stranger, not a relative. You could be talking about Douglas Bryant, or anyone, really. Not my grandfather. Not that I even remember him, but… all I've known, all I've related him to, is the orchard. The land."

"So are you curious?" he asked, because he heard a tremor of wonder in her voice. At least he hoped he did.

"I'm afraid to be curious," Abby admitted with a sigh. "As ridiculous as that probably sounds. My dad and I… we have a complicated relationship. You've probably realized that."

"It was a bit noticeable." Simon smiled, trying to lighten the mood, but Abby still looked unhappy, and he didn't like it. "Because of your mother and brother dying?" he guessed.

"That's part of it," she answered after a moment. She turned to look out the window again, and Simon had the sense she didn't want him to see the expression on her face.

He was silent for a moment, wondering how much to press. How much he wanted to. He usually avoided the messy, emotional stuff, kept it light and charming. Easy. But something about Abby's sadness tugged at him, made him want to help.

"Could you… could you tell me why?" he asked gently.

ABBY

The question was spoken so kindly, so sympathetically, that Abby felt her eyes film with tears. No, she was not going to cry. She swallowed dryly and then took a sip of her Coke.

"It's all a bit difficult," she said, thankful that she'd managed to stem the threat of tears. She turned to look at him. "It's been such a nice day. I don't want to go into all of that and ruin it."

"Would it ruin it?"

She felt a prickle of annoyance, one emotion piling on top of another. He was starting to sound as if he were her therapist. "Yes, it would, actually. I know you mean well, but I really don't want to go into all that right now. Let's focus on Sophie and Tom."

Simon blinked, and Abby felt as if she'd slapped him. Then he summoned a smile, even if it looked a little rusty. "Okay. Message received. Sorry."

She shrugged, half in apology, half in acceptance, and Simon picked up his cheeseburger. They ate in silence for a few minutes, and Abby felt she'd ruined the day anyway. Her memories had.

At moments like this, she felt as if she were living under a huge, looming shadow, or a thousand-pound weight, every day a struggle. Then she told herself to stop being so melodramatic. She had a good life. She liked the work she did for the orchard, the way she'd developed the little shop. She lived in a lovely house in a beautiful place, and she had some good friends and a father whom she knew loved her, deep down, in spite of everything. Plus she had a wonderful dog. That was a lot, wasn't it?

It was enough.

Abby looked out the window again, and saw the color had been leached from the sky, so it was bone-white, the world seeming muted under its lack of light. A summer storm was forecast for that evening, the kind with heavy purple clouds and neon forks of lightning, the rain pounding on the tin roof of the barn, streaming down the windows.

Why *couldn't* she allow herself to be more curious about Sophie and Tom? Why did everything between her and her dad have to be a dead end, a closed door? Why couldn't this little mystery draw them together, as they picked at the threads and unraveled it together? Instead, it felt like yet another thing forcing them apart.

As she considered it, her thoughts roamed further, recklessly now. What if Tom Reese and Sophie Mather had had a wartime romance, a dramatic, star-crossed love affair, even? What if Sophie had done something terrible that had haunted her for the rest of her life? And what if finding out would be a way to put their own ghosts to rest?

For the first time, Abby felt a true flicker of curiosity, a tempting whisper of "what if".

Why hadn't Sophie and Tom found their happy ending? Heaven knew she wanted someone to.

"There's a trunk with some of my grandfather's things in the attic," she told Simon with an impulsive recklessness that was so unlike her. "At least, I think there is. I could have a look through it, if you wanted. See if there's anything in there that relates to all this."

Simon's eyes lit up. "I don't want to ruffle any feathers…"

"I don't have to tell my dad I'm doing it."

He frowned. "Maybe you should."

Abby shook her head, knowing that was impossible. "It's better if I don't."

"I'm sorry." Lightly, barely a brush of his fingertips, Simon touched her hand. "I hope maybe you can tell me about it sometime."

Abby could only nod.

A few hours later, as late-afternoon sunlight slanted through the windows of the empty rooms of the farmhouse, she walked slowly upstairs. Her father was still out spraying; he hadn't missed her at all, and, bizarrely, that made her feel as sad as it did relieved.

Bailey, at least, had greeted her with enthusiasm when she'd come in the house, tail wagging, head pressing against her leg as soon as she opened the door. Abby had smiled and stroked her soft head; sometimes Bailey felt almost human in her understanding, her gentle affection.

Now, the stairs creaked under her careful steps as she turned the corner and walked past her father's bedroom, a guest bedroom that was never used, her own bedroom, and then the fourth bedroom whose door remained shut. Luke's room—still with its football pennants tacked to the walls, the navy bedspread pulled tight across the single bed. Neither of them ever went in there; she'd closed the door fifteen years ago and, as far as she knew, neither of them had ever opened it again. Everything in there had to be covered with dust.

She hesitated at the narrow door leading to an equally narrow set of stairs that went to the attic of the old farmhouse, the drafty unused storage space they'd never really needed, except to keep the memories at bay, out of sight, if not out of mind.

Taking a steadying breath, Abby opened the door. The stairs were covered in cobwebs—she hadn't come up here since last January, when she'd brought their decorations back up after another quiet Christmas. She'd shoved the box of ornaments by the top of the stairs and hurried back down again. Now the creak of her steps felt abnormally loud in her ears.

She wasn't doing anything wrong, but she felt as if she was. She wasn't actually sure if her grandfather's stuff was even up there; she had a vague memory of an old leather-banded trunk that she'd been told not to open as a child, and she suspected it held her grandparents' memorabilia, but maybe it didn't. And even if it did, she had no idea whether the stuff inside went all the way back to the war.

At the top of the stairs, Abby flicked on the light switch, and the single bulb's weak glow barely penetrated the shadowy space, with its stacks of plastic crates and cardboard boxes. Nearer the stairs and easiest to access were the things they actually used—Christmas decorations, a box of winter clothes, three dozen canning jars.

Farther back, everything became more ambiguous, dangerous. Unmarked boxes of old school books and report cards, photographs, picture frames. A plastic crate of baby clothes that surely hadn't been opened in nearly thirty years. Another one of dresses, her mother's Sunday clothes. Abby had been the one to pack up her mother's things; her father hadn't wanted to throw anything away. He hadn't wanted to look at it, either.

And neither did Abby now—she averted her eyes from a box of high heels, another one of sheet music, a dusty tennis racket and a pair of skis—things she wasn't ready to look at, and didn't think she ever would be. Normally when she came up here, she grabbed whatever she was looking for and hurried downstairs again, keeping her head tucked low. She didn't move among the shadows, courting ghosts.

Yet now she was, picking her way through the uneven stacks, breathing in dust and regret, trying to ignore both the cobwebs and the memories. At the very far end of the room, behind a tottering pile of plastic crates and tucked under the eaves, she finally found what she'd been looking for. An old trunk, banded with worn leather, just as she'd remembered, its lock rusted and broken. She didn't know whether anything of interest to Simon would be inside, and she felt reluctant to open and disturb the memories within, whatever they were.

What was she really doing up here, anyway? What was the *point*?

Abby glanced around at all the boxes and bags, the trunks and crates, the memories packed up and tucked away, an inner life she tried never to access, and yet where had it left her?

I'm happy, she told herself, and then wondered why she'd had to say it.

She knelt in front of the trunk, running her hands over its ridged lid. Then she opened it—or tried to. It resisted at first, nothing budging, making her wonder if it actually was locked, even though she could see it wasn't.

Another tug, having to mean it this time, and then, finally, with a protesting creak, the lid lifted.

A sheet of tissue paper had been lain across the top, and she removed it carefully, laying it to one side, so she could put it back later. Underneath, she found things she would have expected— her grandmother's wedding dress, folded and yellowed with age; her father's baby shoes, the leather now speckled and cracked. There was an album of photos she'd never seen before, most of them dating from the fifties, when Tom Reese had been getting Willow Orchards going. He stood with his wife Susan in front of a dozen skinny saplings.

There was nothing, as far as Abby could see, about the war, and she wasn't even surprised. Why would her grandfather keep something from a time he hadn't wanted to talk about?

She lifted up the wedding dress to see what was beneath—a pair of men's dress shoes, a checkbook from a savings and loan company that must have closed its doors fifty years ago—and then felt her fingers close around something silky and yet hard, its edges cutting into her skin through the fabric that it was wrapped in.

Abby took it out carefully, her heart turning over even though she didn't know what she held. It was small and oddly shaped, fitting in the palm of her hand. Slowly, she unwrapped the handkerchief—a square of slippery silk in dark navy—and then blinked down at the object revealed.

It was an ornate cross with an eagle overlaid, hanging from a blue ribbon bordered with red and white trim. A war medal— another one—different from the Purple Heart Sophie Mather had had. Why had her grandfather kept one while he'd given another away?

She turned it over, and then blinked again at what was inscribed there. *For Distinguished Service, May 1945, Awarded to Master Sergeant Matthew Lawson, 82nd Airborne.*

Who, Abby wondered, was Matthew Lawson, and why had her grandfather had his medal?

CHAPTER EIGHT

January 1944

Lily worked in an office that was little more than a broom cupboard, in a forgotten corner of the Old Admiralty on Horse Guards, not far away from the bombproof Citadel of command where the real decisions were being taken, orders being carried out, a sense of urgency tautening the very air.

The typing pool of the Casualties Section felt like another world entirely, another war. The section was staffed by three girls, overseen by the determined Miss Challis, all of whom typed letters to families whose sons or husbands had been killed or presumed missing in action. Day after day, hour after hour, Lily and her two colleagues typed the same words, the same sentiments, for one faceless soldier after another.

On a good day—if it could be called such a thing—she might type fifty or sixty letters. Miss Challis was emphatic that the letters be perfect, with no mistakes or smears of ink, the paper crisp, not crumpled.

"This letter will be kept," she told the girls severely, more than once. "It might be read many times, by many different people. It would be a sign of grossest disrespect not to have it in the most excellent condition."

While Lily agreed with her in theory, she did not think the letter informing a family of their loved one's demise would necessarily be kept. She was not sure she would wish to keep such a thing.

She imagined a heartbroken mother tossing it despairingly into the fire, or a wife ripping it into a thousand tiny pieces. She pictured it splotched with tears, or crumpled up and then smoothed out, as someone scanned it yet again, futilely hoping for a different message this time, as if the words on the page might rearrange themselves, or perhaps they'd just missed out a crucial *not*. Not missing in action. Not killed. As if they sent letters to say such things.

She'd envisioned faceless strangers receiving the letters so many times, she felt as if an army of mourners lived in her head. Sometimes she thought she could hear their muffled weeping, a constant litany of sorrow, the backdrop to her workday, her whole life.

Miss Challis had warned them that writing such letters could make some girls "nervy". She said it was important they kept their chins up, and held onto their courage. The way she said it, Lily thought it sounded as if they were on the front lines, battling Germans rather than offering up ghosts to the bereaved.

Yet she understood what her supervisor meant, because some days she felt as if she'd rather do anything, *anything* than type another letter, saying that someone was dead. Some days, when she saw the stack of notices and names piling up in the wooden tray on her desk, she felt like either screaming or putting her hands over her ears, to stop the sobbing she knew she only heard in her head.

She knew better than to say any of this to anyone. Clara, one of the girls she'd worked with, had been transferred to another department because she'd started to become weepy and anxious during work. Miss Challis had been briskly sympathetic, but afterwards she'd given Lily and the other girl Iris another one of her chin-up lectures, insisting that what they did for the war effort was just as important as the girls in the factory making fighter planes, or any of the other many jobs women found themselves doing now that it was wartime.

"Not *quite* as important," Iris, a girl with a beaky nose and a constant sniff, had answered, rolling her eyes. She nodded towards the overfull tray on her own desk. "After all, the war is over for these poor blighters."

It was an unsettling thought. For eight hours a day, as she sat at her desk and typed, a sliver of weak sunlight filtering through the room's one small, high window, Lily felt as if the war was actually over.

Then she emerged, squinting like a mole, into the frantic rush of central London, men in uniform everywhere, hoardings plastered with posters commanding her to "Work to Win" and to "Stamp Out Black Markets" and she realized it wasn't over at all. It was all around her, surging and seething.

Whenever Miss Challis wasn't present, Iris complained about the monotonous drudgery of typing such depressing letters, but she did it with an acerbic wit that both troubled and amused Lily in turns.

Sometimes she'd read out the addresses on the letters and make all sorts of suppositions—"Nether Wallop, Hampshire—can you imagine living in such a place? I bet they thought *they* were going to give Hitler a beating. Too bad for this chap it didn't turn out that way. He should have lived in *Greater* Wallop."

Lily would smile, and then feel guilty for doing so, even though it could be such a *relief* to have a bit of fun, even if it was at the expense of the poor soldiers whose letters they typed.

"They're dead, Lily," Iris had said when she'd expressed this once. "They don't care."

"I know, but..."

Iris had rolled her eyes and sniffed—again—and Lily fell silent. Perhaps it didn't matter as much as she feared it did.

Although she didn't particularly enjoy her work, she'd heard of some jobs her friends from school had been conscripted for—shining men's boots, or scrubbing latrines, or sweeping streets—and she counted herself fortunate, thanks to a strong set of O Levels and a reference from her head teacher about how diligent she was. Having to put up with Iris' constant sniff was probably the worst thing about it, really.

Yet sometimes, in the midst of the drudgery of typing letters, Lily felt a flicker of longing. It was never to do something exciting as Sophie seemed to wish to, but rather simply to be where people were alive and life happened. The few minutes of idle chat with Iris and Mabel, the new girl, was the only conversation she had all day, and it was far from sparkling. Sometimes, as she ate her sandwich made from the National Loaf, with the thinnest scraping of margarine and a teaspoonful of potted meat, listening to Iris sniff, she wished she could talk and listen to someone who was alive, hear their opinions, maybe even laugh a little.

One evening, a little over a week since the night at The Berkeley, she headed up Whitehall, night having fallen hours ago, the city swathed in an impenetrable darkness that was alleviated neither by stars nor moon, as thick cloud covered the sky.

They'd had three air raids in the last week, nights spent in the cold and cramped Anderson shelter in the back of the muddy garden while the world around them buzzed and screamed and crackled; they'd emerged each time blinking in the gloom of the night, the sky still reddened like a wound, the air full of the acrid smell of burning. No one on their street had been hurt, but a house the next street over had had a direct hit, and a mother and baby had been killed in their beds.

"You would think, after all this time, they would know to go to the shelter," Carol had said with a shake of her head, and then made a Woolton pie and taken it over to the woman's sister, who now had care of the two older children, along with her own three.

Lily hurried up the road, her head tucked low, weaving in and out of the other pedestrians who were just as eager as her to get home. The night at The Berkeley, with its champagne and dancing and laughter, felt like a lifetime ago, or a dream, so different from the days in the office, evenings at home with a cup of tea and the wireless, and then the raids. Sometimes she felt as if it hadn't happened at all, or if it had, it had only happened to Sophie.

Her sister had resented Tom Reese's silence, had been offended and purposefully indifferent in turns, her moods as lightning quick as ever. As for Matthew Lawson… his silence didn't surprise Lily at all.

By the time she made it back to Holmside Road, after enduring a twenty-minute wait to be pressed into the train car like a sardine wedged into its tiny tin, it was after six o'clock, and she was weary and footsore—her shoes were giving out and they didn't have the clothing coupons to buy another pair—and a light, icy rain had started falling, drenching her in drizzle.

"*Lily*." Carol greeted her at the door, her expression so animated, Lily felt an odd lurch of uncertain hope—what could possibly make her mother look so bright? What good news might have happened that she hadn't heard about? "Come, look what Sergeant Lawson has brought."

"Sergeant Lawson…" Lily unwrapped her scarf as she stepped into the sitting room, staring in surprise at the sight of Matthew Lawson standing by the fire, smart and serious in his uniform, his cap in his hands.

"Good day, Miss Mather. Or I suppose I should say good evening."

"Good evening." Lily's head felt as if it were full of cotton wool. It would be rude to ask him what he was doing here, but what *was* he doing here? There hadn't been a peep from either Matthew or Tom since the night at The Berkeley, something which had put Sophie decidedly out of sorts.

Lily had been subjected every night to her sister's chameleon-like ruminations about Tom's silence—one evening he simply must be too busy, another he'd gone off Sophie, and yet another she didn't care anyway because he was a bit dull—"corn-fed farm boy, really. He didn't even know what Big Ben was. Can you imagine?"

Lily had simply assumed the evening was a one-off, two American soldiers amusing themselves in the city, before they were called to duty, or, more likely, to someone else more suitable who caught their fancy. Lily had no illusions about her own allure, or even, for that matter, Sophie's. They were two rather simple, middle-class girls, brought up strictly, without the worldly experience a thousand other London girls might have, no matter how Sophie liked to pretend and put on airs.

Yet here was Sergeant Lawson, and Lily couldn't think what to say. "What have you brought, Sergeant Lawson?" she asked, and Carol nodded towards the kitchen.

"Come see."

So Lily did, with Matthew following behind, as silent as ever. The table was full of food—more food than Lily could remember ever seeing during wartime. There were tins of pears and peaches and Spam, a net bag of oranges, and several bars of Hershey's chocolate. And even more than that, as her incredulous gaze scanned the table—a whole tinned ham, a slab of bacon, a pat of butter. Lily's mouth watered at the sight of it all.

"You didn't have to—"

"I assured him he didn't, of course," Carol said quickly. "But he wanted to say thank you, for Sunday dinner."

"I should have brought it before. I'm ashamed to say neither Lieutenant Reese nor I thought of it at the time."

"But you thought of it now," Carol said firmly. "And we are very appreciative, I assure you. We shall share with all the neighbors."

Immediately, Lily saw the food disappearing; of course her mother would insist they share. She wouldn't have it otherwise, but she had the absurd urge to gobble it up right then and there—she'd just spied a pot of strawberry jam amidst all the bounty.

"I was just telling Sergeant Lawson he must stay for a cup of tea," Carol said. "I'll put the kettle on—why don't you take him to the front room, Lily?"

Lily murmured her assent as she shed her coat and walked slowly into the front room, surprised when her mother shut the door to the kitchen, giving them at least a semblance of privacy. Neither her father nor Sophie were home yet, although they would be soon.

"That was so very kind of you," Lily said, wishing she had more words. "Really very kind."

"It was no trouble." Matthew's lips twisted. "We're swimming in the stuff, to tell you the truth. It almost feels…" He paused, a hard look coming over his face that Lily didn't understand. "Wrong."

"But at least you're sharing it with us," she said with a small smile. "Not everyone would."

Matthew gave a brief nod. "Truly, I am glad to do it."

"What have you been up to this last week?" Lily asked, trying to sound mildly flirtatious and feeling she failed. "Or should I not ask, because it's all hush-hush?" She could not manage Sophie's light, laughing tone at all. She sounded far too earnest.

"Just the usual. Drills and more drills. They want to keep us busy and not just kicking our heels. But we'll be posted somewhere soon—things are a bit of a shambles right now, with so many divisions coming in at once, but I expect they'll sort us out in the next week or so."

"Are you bored, with the waiting? Or would you rather keep on waiting?"

Matthew cocked his head, considering her question.

"I don't know which is worse," Lily continued a bit breathlessly. "Waiting for the worst to happen, or when it really does."

"Has the worst happened to you, Lily?" His voice was gentle, but she bit her lip guiltily anyway.

"No, it hasn't, not yet, anyway." She gave a little laugh, wanting to lighten the mood, to see him smile. "But it might, if my mother gives the strawberry jam away to someone on our street."

Matthew laughed, a quick huff of sound that delighted her because she knew instinctively how rare it was. "Now that would be a tragedy. But at least you'd still have the Spam."

"I'll tell you a secret," Lily said, hardly able to believe she was teasing, even flirting. "I hate Spam."

Matthew raised his eyebrows. "No!"

"Truly."

"Should I take it back, then?" His eyes seemed to sparkle.

"No, Sophie likes it," Lily said generously. "She can have it."

Matthew laughed again and put his hands in his trouser pockets. Lily grinned, and he smiled back, and she didn't think she'd ever felt so happy. And they'd been talking about *Spam*.

"I don't think we'll be here too much longer," Matthew said after a moment, his voice serious once more. "All things considered."

Lily bit her lip. "It's really going to happen, then."

Matthew nodded, understanding her meaning. "Yes, it will." Briefly, the hard look came over Matthew's face again. "But as to when, I have no idea. No one does. *That* is certainly hush-hush, and needs to be."

"I don't suppose it will be during winter, at any rate."

"No."

Carol bustled in with the tea tray, and Lily stepped away from Matthew, even though they hadn't been standing very close. "Do you write to your family, Sergeant Lawson?" Carol asked as she set it down and began pouring. "They must be worried about you, so far away."

"I write them," Matthew answered briefly.

"And are they much reassured, that you are well looked after in our country?"

"I hope so." There was something strangely bleak about his tone.

"Lily, why don't you give Sergeant Lawson his tea?" With a rather officious manner, Carol handed the cup and saucer to her daughter, although she could have just as easily given it to their guest himself.

Lily handed the cup to Matthew, his fingers brushing hers as he took it. She risked a glance upwards, and his lips gave that lovely quirk she remembered from the night at The Berkeley, sending her heart lurching—and tea slopping over the cup onto her fingers.

"Oh…." She yanked her hand away, resisting the urge to put her burned fingers in her mouth like a child. "I'm so sorry. How clumsy of me."

"Not at all. It was my fault."

Carol gave them both a sideways glance and smiled, saying nothing.

"Hell-*o*!" Sophie sang out as the front door opened. She appeared in the doorway, her hazel eyes widening as she caught sight of them all taking tea. "Sergeant Lawson, what a delightful surprise." Her gaze scanned the room, looking for the person who wasn't there.

"I'm afraid I've come on my own. Lieutenant Reese was otherwise occupied."

"Oh, well, never mind," Sophie said airily. "It's lovely to see you, all the same."

Despite her bright manner, Lily could tell her sister was disappointed, although she took great pains—perhaps too many—not to show it, exclaiming over the bounty in the kitchen, and then accepting a cup of tea from their mother, before sitting on the arm of the sofa, one leg swinging jauntily, in a way Carol wouldn't normally allow. In light of their guest, she said nothing.

"This was jolly generous of you," Sophie said with a nod towards the kitchen. "Did you feel badly because Lieutenant Reese ate so much of our Sunday lunch?"

"*Sophie.*"

"Well, he did," Sophie answered with a laugh. "I suspect he's used to life on the farm, when there's meat and milk aplenty. How *is* Lieutenant Reese, Sergeant Lawson?" Her bright gaze met Matthew's with unflinching directness. "Kicking his heels, I imagine, as the 82nd Airborne waits to be moved?"

"They keep us busy."

"Not too busy, though, I'm sure."

"Busy enough."

Matthew met Sophie's gaze without a waver, and in his unyielding stare Lily sensed a command for her sister to drop the subject. Thankfully, she did.

"Ah, well." Sophie rose from the sofa. "These air raids have made everything frightfully dull these days, anyway. Never mind dancing, I can't get a wink of sleep."

"I imagine some don't find them dull," Matthew said with an intensity that felt like a reprimand, worse somehow because of how quiet he sounded.

Sophie turned to look at him, a flush starting in her cheeks.

"No, I don't suppose they do," she said after a moment, and Matthew rose from his seat.

"I'm afraid I must go. Duty calls, as ever."

"Thank you again, Sergeant Lawson, you've been so kind—"

Matthew waved Carol's words aside, and she nodded towards Lily.

"Fetch the sergeant's coat for him, Lily—"

Her mother seemed determined to afford them every opportunity to talk alone.

Lily went into the hall and Matthew followed her, while Carol took the tea tray back to the kitchen, bidding Sophie help her.

The hallway felt quiet and confined as Lily took Matthew's coat from the stand.

"Thank you," she said yet again as she handed it to him and he put his arms through the sleeves. She breathed in the scent of his aftershave, something sharp and clean. Sophie had been right: American soldiers did smell heavenly.

"I told you, it was no trouble." He turned to face her, close enough so his arm brushed her shoulder, and at that brief, tantalizing contact, Lily felt as if her heart had leapt into her throat.

She stood as if paralyzed, unable to utter a word, as Matthew gazed down at her, his face startlingly close, and Lily heard the clatter of dishes from the kitchen.

"Perhaps I shall see you again," he suggested quietly.

"That would be…" She couldn't finish the sentence. Her senses were swimming.

"It would have to be soon, I think. We're leaving soon."

"Do you know where?"

"Not yet. They keep everything under wraps for as long as they can. Just in case…"

"Of course."

"It's wretched, this war." His voice was so low, she strained to hear it, even though she was stood right next to him. "In so many ways."

She heard a throb of intensity in his voice and her hand fluttered by her side; she wanted to touch his sleeve but couldn't quite dare. "It is," she whispered. "For so many… I know I'm one of the lucky ones." She didn't know why she felt the need to say that, only that she did. "I don't forget it."

"No, I don't suppose you do."

For a second, Lily thought he might touch her cheek, she could almost feel his fingers there, dry and cool, but then he didn't. They remained standing close together for a moment, the only sound in the enclosed space that of their breathing. There were so many things Lily wanted to say, so many important and intimate things about war and life and hope and sadness, and yet she couldn't manage one.

Matthew stepped back, towards the door.

"Until then," he said, and then, with a gust of cold, damp air from the open door, he was gone.

Lily pressed her hands to her flaming cheeks.

"Well." Sophie appeared in the hallway, hands on her hips, lips pursed. "*Someone's* taken a shine to you."

"He was just being kind." Lily turned around, dropping her hands from her face, and Sophie let out a laugh.

"Look at you blush!"

"Don't, Sophie—" Lily felt, quite suddenly, that she could not take her sister's light-hearted teasing right now. Not about this.

Sophie's expression softened. "I'm not making fun, honestly, Lil. You lucky thing, snagging a GI."

"I *haven't*," Lily protested. She felt ridiculously near tears; it seemed wrong, to joke about something that seemed almost sacred. She didn't want to *snag* Matthew Lawson. She wasn't looking for nylons or cigarettes or a good time on the dance floor. She didn't care about any of that.

"Oh, but you have," Sophie assured her with a wink. "He's so clearly smitten. Although, I have to say, there's something a bit... odd about Sergeant Lawson, don't you think? Just the tiniest bit queer?" She frowned in reflection. "It's not that he's awkward or anything like that, but he's so *quiet*. Yet not because he doesn't have anything to say. Did you hear how he took me to task over the remark I made about the air raids?" She gave a little shrug. "I know it was rather thoughtless, but still, he seemed so furious, in his understated way."

"He feels things," Lily said, the words inadequate yet the sentiment one she meant utterly. She sensed it from him—a depth of emotion he kept hidden, reined in, just as she did, a current of feeling that ran through both of them. Or was she being fanciful, thinking they were alike in any way at all?

"Yes, I rather think he does," Sophie agreed seriously, before her face split into a smile and she gave Lily a friendly little push. "He certainly feels things for *you*."

"Girls." Carol's voice was full of good humor. "Come and set the table. Your father will be home any minute."

Still smiling, Sophie went, and Lily followed. Her heart felt as if it were fizzing now. Was Matthew smitten? Or not even smitten, because that was like snagging—she didn't want or care about that sort of absurd pedantry—but did he *feel* something, the way she did? That would be enough for her. It would be more than enough. It would be everything.

CHAPTER NINE

Two days later, Lily was wriggling into her nightgown after a dinner of cottage pie and lovely tinned pears from Matthew's hamper for dessert, followed by their usual cup of tea during the nine o'clock news. The Allies were bombing Berlin despite the poor weather, and in response the Nazis were giving London a remembered taste of the Blitz.

There had been an air raid last night, and the Mathers had stayed in the Anderson shelter at the bottom of the garden until four in the morning. Lily hoped there wouldn't be another raid tonight, thanks to the blessed fog. Although it seemed both sides, in desperation, were flying anyway, no matter what the weather.

"Sophie, what on earth are you doing?"

While Lily had been hurrying into her nightgown, bare feet freezing on the floor, her sister was frowning into the mirror as she dabbed beetroot juice onto her lips. Her last lipstick had given out a week ago, much to her annoyance.

"What does it look like I'm doing?" Sophie said as she smacked her lips together. "I'm going out."

"Going out?" Lily stared at her blankly. "But it's nearly ten o'clock at night."

"So?"

"But…" Lily shook her head slowly. The house was dark, her parents in bed, everything locked up and shuttered tight. How could her sister be going *out*? "Where are you going?" she asked finally.

Sophie tossed a mischievous look over her shoulder, hazel eyes glinting. "To see the lovely Lieutenant Reese, of course."

"What? Where?"

"We're meeting at that pub by the Common. The Queen's Something."

"The Queen's Head? But you haven't even talked to him—"

"I sent him a note. He'd told me he was billeted on Broxash Road, with the Darbys. You know that family, the one with the girl with the spotty chin? She was a year below us in school, quite deadly dull."

"I don't remember…"

"I'm not surprised, she was that boring. Anyway, it was all easy enough to do." Sophie spoke so insouciantly, as if she did this sort of thing all the time.

"But…" Lily's head was spinning at this unexpected news. "Did he write a note back?"

"No." Sophie shrugged, seeming deliberately careless. "But I didn't think he would. There was hardly enough time, and anyway…" She paused, and Lily knew she was thinking of their mother, and her undoubted disapproval of such forward schemes. "I just asked him to meet me at the pub at ten."

"But it will close by half ten," Lily protested. "If not before." Since the bombing had started again, evening hours of any establishment had been erratic, doors sometimes shutting at teatime if the bombing was bad or the beer ran out.

Sophie lifted one shoulder. "So?"

"Sophie…" Lily hesitated, in awe of her sister's sheer brazenness, as well as nervous about her edgy mood. She seemed both sharp and fragile, her careless tone and shrugs hiding a seething urgency underneath that threatened to seep out, bubble over. "Don't you think it's a bit… forward… of you? To invite him out like that, on your own? Mother wouldn't—"

"I don't care about Mother." Sophie's face hardened before she turned back to her reflection. "We've got to make the most of every opportunity, Lily." She reached for her compact, giving her face the lightest dusting of precious face powder. "Who knows how long any of us will be here?"

"The war won't go on forever."

"Neither will we."

"But…" Lily watched as Sophie changed her sensible utility-issued work shoes for a pair of impractical heels she'd had before the war, the leather well-worn but serviceable. She could hardly believe her sister was actually planning to sneak out of the house to meet a man. She'd never done such a thing before, at least not to Lily's knowledge.

Despite Sophie's wildness, her air of mischief and her ability to shock, Lily had always felt a shared sense of innocence with her sister—they were two well-brought-up girls, raised by stern but loving parents, church every Sunday, bed at ten o'clock, teatime and evenings by the wireless and sedate walks in the Common. That was their life, not this.

It was comforting, in a way, to know there were lines even Sophie would not dare to cross, and yet here she was, striding right over them, just as she had that night at The Berkeley. It was as if she was slipping into a role and deciding it was who she really was.

"What will Lieutenant Reese think?" she wondered out loud. Would he be disapproving, or think he had reason to believe Sophie was one of *those* girls, the kind who melted into the shadows with a soldier, so all you could hear was their low laughter and, worse—far worse—their animal sounds of pleasure?

Lily knew it happened. It happened all the time. War made people reckless, and desperate, and bold. But surely that kind of behavior had nothing to do with them.

"Oh, Lily, don't be such a *child*," Sophie exclaimed as she dabbed a bit of "Evening in Paris" perfume on her wrists and behind her ears. "I'm twenty-three years old, for heaven's sake. Most girls my age are married with a baby or three by now. All I'm doing is meeting an acquaintance at the local. It's hardly the act of some brazen harlot." She rolled her eyes, inviting Lily to share the absurdity of it, and she tried.

"I know that. It's just… you've never done it before."

"There's always a first time, isn't there?"

"If Mother knew…"

Sophie turned to her, eyes flashing. "But she won't, will she?"

"I'm not going to tell her," Lily exclaimed with affront.

Sophie gave her a quick, dazzling smile as she leaned forward to pat Lily's cheek. "I know you wouldn't. You're a darling, really. Honestly, Lily, you ought to try it."

Lily's eyes widened. "Sneaking out?"

"Living a little. You're so frightened half the time, unable to say boo to a goose, but I know there's more to you than that. There has to be."

Lily tried to smile; she didn't want Sophie to see how her words had hurt her. "Does there?"

"One day you'll discover just how brave you are," Sophie said with a laugh. "I'm sure of it." She turned away to give her reflection one last satisfied glance before her lips pursed and her eyes flashed again. "I know you think I'm being reckless, but I need to *do* something, Lily. I can't wait this war out for another minute, hoping something will happen to me."

"But, Sophie, what do you *want* to happen?"

"Something. Anything." Sophie turned from the mirror and went to the window, the blackout curtain drawn across the night sky. She raised one hand towards the heavy, dark material, and for a tense second Lily thought she might pull it open, just because she could. "Aren't you tired of the waiting? We're sitting out the war at our *typewriters*, Lily."

"As are a thousand other girls," Lily returned. "Ten thousand." She wouldn't be ashamed of what she did. "Besides," she pointed out as reasonably as she could, "meeting Lieutenant Reese at the pub is hardly some sort of act of wartime bravery."

"It's an act of something," Sophie returned fiercely. "At least I'm doing something. *Feeling* something. I don't care if it gets me in trouble. Right now I don't care if it gets me killed."

"*Sophie.*"

"I mean it." Sophie turned to face her, a wild glitter in her eyes, her whole body seeming to vibrate with the force of her emotion. She looked strange and fierce and frighteningly beautiful. "Don't you dare try to stop me."

"How could I?" Lily shook her head slowly. "But what if there's an air raid? You'll be caught out…"

"Then I'll go to one of the Tube station shelters."

"But Mother and Father will realize you're not home then."

Sophie hesitated for a fraction of a second before she gave another shrug. "Then that's what happens."

"They'll be angry."

"What can they do? I'm not a child, and I won't be treated like one." Sophie tossed her head. "Anyway, there was already an air raid last night."

"You know that doesn't mean anything."

"I don't care." Despite her declarations that she was not a child, Sophie was starting to sound petulant.

Lily sank onto her bed, knowing there was nothing she could do.

"I just want to have fun, Lily," Sophie insisted, her mood making one of its lightning shifts as she reached out her hands to catch Lily's own. "Is that so much to ask? Everything is so dreary, so dull. I just want to live a little." She squeezed Lily's hands, her eyes wide, her voice wheedling.

"I know you do." Lily tried to smile. Really, Sophie wasn't getting up to much at all. It just felt like it, with the secrecy, the ferocity of her feeling, and even the dullness of their lives. "Be careful, will you?" she said as she gave her sister's hands a squeeze back.

"Of course I will."

Sophie slipped her hands from Lily's and hurried out of the room, closing the door behind her with a soft click. Lily strained her ears to hear the telltale creak on the stairs, but her sister was impressively quiet. Lily couldn't even hear the front door open and shut, and she knew her parents, tucked in their beds, wouldn't either. They wouldn't dream of Sophie slipping out like this.

With a sigh, Lily got into bed. Her worry for her sister was shadowed by something more revealing—a twinge of envy. Sophie had said she'd discover how brave she was one day, but it certainly hadn't happened yet. Why couldn't she be as daring as her sister? What if she'd sent a postcard to Matthew Lawson's billet? Not that she knew where he was, but Sophie might. She could be the one meeting him at the pub, or going for a late-night walk in the Common. She could be having an adventure, learning to live a little, after all.

But Lily hadn't even thought of any of it. None of it had ever—not once—so much as crossed her mind, a delicious flicker of "what if". It annoyed her that it hadn't occurred to her, as much as that she hadn't actually done it. Could she not even *think* of something daring to do?

Even now that she had, Lily knew she wouldn't be so bold. She hadn't even asked Matthew to set a time when he'd said he hoped he saw her again, and now maybe she never would, despite what he'd suggested. *Perhaps I shall see you again?* Had he meant it, or had it just been a pleasantry, a way to end a conversation? She could have found out, asked him when he next had leave. She could have smiled and batted her eyes and given him a knowing look… or, heavens, just *smiled*. Perhaps that would have been enough.

Lily let out a groan, cursing her own cowardice. She wasn't brave, and she never had been, not like Sophie. It had been Sophie who had waded into the deeper water while Lily had splashed in the shallows, on their summer trips to Brighton. Sophie who had accepted the dare to stick out her tongue at one of the boys at school, or throw a snowball at the milk float one icy winter. Sophie who had come downstairs in bright red lipstick when she was fourteen, and her mother hadn't made her wash it off, even though Lily knew she hadn't liked it one bit.

But those were all just childish pranks, and Sophie was no longer a child. She was a woman, determined to live out her own destiny, and, right now, for better or worse, that seemed to include Lieutenant Tom Reese.

Still, Lily told herself as she plumped her pillow, it wasn't as if Sophie was being truly outrageous. She was simply slipping out to the pub. It wasn't a big to-do at all. And yet, when she recalled that manic glitter in her sister's eye, Lily suspected that, in some strange way, tonight had the power to change everything.

She tried to wait up for Sophie's return, and managed to well after the pub had closed, but at some point after midnight Lily fell asleep, only to wake to the dreaded and far too familiar wail of the air-raid siren, its rising and falling sound as plaintive and distressing as a woman's heartbroken cry.

She rose and dressed with hurried, automatic movements, the room a sea of black all around her as she fumbled for her dress and thrust her legs into the heavy lisle stockings she wore for work. She couldn't even see Sophie's bed, but she sensed her sister's absence, and as she went to the door, she ran her hand along the length of the mattress, only to find it cold and empty as she'd expected, yet even so her stomach clenched in fear.

"Sophie? Lily?" Her mother's disembodied voice called out to her in the darkness.

"I'm here." Even if her sister wasn't. Her parents clearly hadn't realized that yet.

Silently, the only light a flickering candle her father held, they all headed downstairs in single file, her mother first, followed by her father, and then her. Then out to the back garden, the siren still wailing, the air frigid and damp, the muddy ground squelching beneath their feet as they trod the well-worn path to the shelter.

Four years ago, when they'd first erected the Anderson shelter, and the government had distributed a little booklet about how to make it comfortable, they'd all approached the exercise with something almost like enthusiasm, or at least a determination not to let the constant raids get them down.

Lily's father had built metal bunks, and her mother had stuffed mattresses and sewn sleeping bags. She'd even kept a few books and games out there to while away the time, until they'd become damp and moldy.

Yet sometime in the intervening years, enthusiasm had given way to grim endurance. As night after night had passed with droning planes and thudding bombs, as smoke-filled dawns broke with the charred smell of destruction, the once-familiar landscape now cratered and littered with rubble, women standing in the streets clutching their babies, looking blank-eyed and dazed, any sense of optimistic purpose had drained away.

Now no one spoke as they filed into the cramped shelter, the sleeping bags icy, a smell of mildew hanging in the air, everyone anticipating another uncomfortable and mostly sleepless night. In the distance, they heard the thuds of the first bombs falling, none close enough yet to be too worrisome, yet somewhere, Lily knew, someone's house was being hit, someone's life was being destroyed. *Please God, not Sophie's.*

Once, after a particularly brutal raid, she had walked past a bombed house and trod on a mud-splattered book; when she'd bent down, she'd seen it was a wedding album with photos carefully pasted on its stiff cardboard pages, and the sight of it had made her want to cry. Lily had picked it up and given it to her mother, to give to someone at the WVS, but who knew whether it had found its way to its owner, or if there had been anyone left who still treasured it.

Lily shut down the door of the shelter as Carol blew out the candle and Richard lit the lantern they kept there. In its paltry light, Carol's eyes narrowed. "Where's Sophie?" Her voice was sharp.

Richard's eyes widened as he looked around the small, gloomy space, realizing for the first time that their oldest daughter was not present.

"She's out," Lily said. Her voice sounded thin.

"*Out?*"

"She went out." Lily didn't know how much more she should say.

Her father stared at her blankly, while Carol looked utterly incredulous. "When?"

A whistling sound split the air, and everyone tensed, eyes wide as they waited for it to land. The thud was enough to shake the corrugated-iron sides of the shelter, and the lantern Richard had set between the bunks flickered and then steadied.

"She's out in this?" Carol's voice wavered.

Another thud sounded nearer then, followed by a crash. The lantern flickered and went out.

"Dear God," Carol whispered in the dark. "Dear *God.*"

Richard fumbled with the lantern and lit it again. In the dim, wavering glow, everyone's faces looked like pale, frightened moons.

"She'll be all right," Lily said, her voice just as thin as before, although she'd meant to sound bracing. "She'll go to the Underground station. Loads of people do…"

"And do you remember when a bomb fell on the line, and broke through to Balham station? Two hundred people sleeping on the platforms were drowned."

Lily looked down at her lap, biting her lips, saying nothing.

"Where is she, Lily?" Carol sounded as scolding as she had when Lily was a little girl. Her lips were pursed tightly. "Because it is clear to me that you know where she went, and who with."

"She went to meet Lieutenant Reese," Lily whispered. There was no question of keeping it secret any longer.

"Lieutenant Reese!" Carol's lips tightened further, drawn up like the strings of a purse. "I should have known."

"They were just going to the pub, the one by the Common. Just for a drink."

"It is one o'clock in the morning," Carol returned. "They have certainly not been at the pub all this time."

"She's a grown woman, Carol," Richard said quietly. "Twenty-three last October. She's bound to…" He trailed off as another whistling hummed through the air, followed by a thud close enough for them to hear the sound of breaking glass.

"I know she's a grown woman," Carol snapped. "But grown women can, and should, act with dignity and self-respect."

"It was just the pub," Lily said a bit desperately.

"The pub shut three hours before the bombing started," Carol cut across her. "Who knows where she is now!"

A silence descended on the cramped space, interspersed with the whistling and thuds of the bombs raining down outside. At least they didn't sound so close now, but who knew where the next one would land.

"She'll be all right," Richard said, laying a clumsy hand on his wife's arm. "We can't wrap her in cotton wool all her life—"

"I hardly want to do *that*."

"Lieutenant Reese seemed like a good lad," Richard persisted. "He meant well."

"Did he?"

Another silence fell, this one suffocating. The bombs continued, a symphony of thuds in the distance that they were all trying to ignore.

"Let's get some sleep," Richard said finally. "We all have work in the morning."

Lily stretched out on her bunk, cringing at the cold, damp sleeping bag and trying not to shiver. Richard had turned off the lantern and the darkness was so impenetrable, she could not see her own hand in front of her face. She felt as if she were entombed, as if the earth on top of the shelter was pressing down on her. It was hard to breathe, and she tried to concentrate on each breath she took, evenly in, evenly out, doing her best not to think about Sophie or where she might be.

She'd had to repeat this little exercise every night she'd spent in the dark and damp little shelter. She'd managed to hide her panic from her family, but she'd always dreaded the time inside the shelter, more even than the bombs whistling outside. She hated not being able to see, despised the way the walls felt as if they were coming closer, bathing her body in an icy sweat that had nothing to do with the chilled air or the damp sleeping bag. In the silence, her breathing sounded ragged, and images of Sophie caught out, the bombs falling around her, kept flashing through her mind.

"Do be quiet, Lily," Carol said crossly.

Lily pressed her lips together and turned on her side. Another thud rattled the sides of the shelter. She didn't sleep.

The long, flat sound of the all-clear rousted them from an unsettled doze at six o'clock in the morning. It was still dark outside, the clouds floating in shreds across a scarred and livid sky. The smell of smoke clung to everything, along with another, indefinable smell of destruction that Lily didn't like to think about too closely. Sophie was still gone.

In silence, they headed back to the house, Richard to inspect for damage and Carol to make tea. Lily stood uncertainly in the kitchen as her mother filled the kettle.

"She'll be back," she said, needing to convince both herself and her mother.

Carol did not reply. The back she presented to Lily was rigid with both anxiety and affront.

If something happened to Sophie, Lily realized in that moment, it would be her fault. Never mind that Sophie had been determined to go out, or that Lily had tried to stop her, or that she was the younger one. It would still be her fault, and she realized she accepted that.

She might be younger, quieter, shyer, but she was more responsible. She always had been, just as Sophie had always been braver. It was the way they had worked, from the time they'd been little girls in pinafores to now. Perhaps it would never change.

The three of them were just sitting down to their morning oatmeal and tea when the front door opened and Sophie's voice sang out merrily, as if she were coming in from a day at work rather than a night on the street.

"Hell-*o*!"

Relief shot through Lily even as she tensed at the sound of Sophie's jolly voice, while Carol rose from the table.

"Where," she asked, her voice both shaking and cold, "have you been?"

Sophie stopped in the doorway of the kitchen, taking in her mother's fury, her father's silence. Lily saw that her hair was in disarray, her makeup smeared. Even worse, beneath her open coat, her blouse was buttoned up wrong. She wondered if her mother noticed.

"I was caught by the air raid," Sophie said. "I spent the night in the Clapham Common Tube station. It was ever so fun, actually. Everyone was singing! It felt like a party." She laughed, but no one else did. No one else even smiled.

"You snuck out to see that Lieutenant Reese?" Carol said.

Sophie darted a look at Lily, who gave a grimace of apology.

"*That* Lieutenant Reese?" Sophie raised her eyebrows. "What have you got against him?"

"He seemed a bit fast to me."

"Fast! Just because he's American, I suppose? Except it can't be that, because you were fond enough of Sergeant Lawson when he brought that hamper by, weren't you? Pushing him and Lily together. It *was* rather obvious, Mother."

Carol seemed to swell in front of them, her face flushed with outrage. "Sergeant Lawson has clearly been brought up well—"

"So has Tom," Sophie flashed. "You've only gone against him because I met him last night."

"Any decent boy wouldn't—"

"He's not a boy, he's a man," Sophie cut across her mother, her voice hard. "A perfectly nice, grown-up man, and I'm a woman. I earn a respectable wage, and I do my duty for this wretched war. I can live as I like." Each sentence felt like a grenade being hurled into the room, a line being drawn in the sand. There would be no going back to the way things had been—two girls laying the table, cups of tea by the wireless, everything predictable and stodgy and safe. A family together. Their whole way of life was at risk, everything she longed to keep hold of, and Lily couldn't stand it. Everything else could be ruined—every house on Holmside Road, every letter of condolence in the wooden tray at work—but not this. *Not this.*

"If you really mean that," Carol said coldly, "then—"

"Don't," Lily cried. "*Don't*. It was just an evening out. You went to the pub, didn't you, Sophie?"

Sophie managed to look both contemptuous and relieved by Lily's intervention. "Of course I did. I had a shandy and learned all about Tom's family back in Minnesota. They're dairy farmers, but he'd rather do something with apples. Not that you *care*." This flung at Carol, who compressed her lips and said nothing.

"Let's not fall out," Lily begged. "None of it matters. We're all safe and sound, not even a window broken." She glanced at her father for confirmation, who nodded emphatically.

"Not so much as a crack this time. Not a single one."

"Please," Lily said more quietly.

A silence stretched on tautly while Sophie and Carol glared at each other. Then Carol nodded once, a jerk of her head more than anything else.

"There's still some tea left in the pot," she said, and turned to the stove to fetch her oldest daughter some oatmeal.

CHAPTER TEN

ABBY

Abby held onto Matthew Lawson's medal for a whole day before she decided to tell Simon about it. She'd wanted to ask her dad about it first, but he'd been so quiet and she hadn't wanted to admit she'd gone digging in the attic, which she feared he'd see as some sort of betrayal. She doubted he'd tell her anything about it, anyway.

She'd thought about putting it back, tucking it in its handkerchief in the bottom of the trunk and forgetting all about it, but somehow that didn't feel right, either. Who *was* Matthew Lawson—and what had he had to do with her grandfather?

Yet what if telling Simon opened up a Pandora's box of emotions and memories that made things even worse between her and her father? Could they even be worse?

Abby called Simon. "I've found something," she said after he'd answered his cell phone in his usual cheery way. "It might be nothing…"

"And it might not. What is it?"

"A medal. Another one, not a Purple Heart, though. But this one doesn't belong to my grandfather."

Simon was silent for a moment, as he absorbed this news. "Who does it belong to?" he finally asked.

"Someone called Matthew Lawson—Master Sergeant."

"You haven't heard of him before?"

"No, never. Have you?"

"Not a thing." Simon paused. "I don't suppose you've asked your dad?" There was no censure in his voice, just a wry acknowledgment of the complexity of that relationship.

"No, I haven't." Abby managed a shaky laugh. "And, to be honest, I don't think I will. I know it seems weird, but that's just how it is."

"It's no weirder than what goes in any other family." Simon was silent for a moment. "Look," he said finally, "why don't you bring it over?"

"Over…" she repeated slowly. "Where?"

"My little cabin at the lake. It's a beautiful day, and I'm sitting right here looking at all this loveliness by myself. Bring it over and we can have a think about it all, maybe over a picnic? I've got plenty of food that needs to be eaten, and if you felt like bringing some lemonade, well, I wouldn't say no."

"Oh…" A smile spread over Abby's face as she realized how much she liked that idea.

"That is, if you can get away? I know you must be busy with everything."

"It's okay." Tina was covering the shop, and balancing the books could wait. Again. "I'd love to come," she said, and she heard the smile in Simon's voice as he responded.

"Brilliant. I'll give you the address for your phone. Bring Bailey, if you like."

An hour later, Abby was driving towards Lake Geneva, a thermos of fresh lemonade in the backseat, along with some homemade chocolate chip cookies she'd baked the day before, and the medal wrapped in the old silk handkerchief. She'd left Bailey at home, sprawled by the stove, looking like all she wanted was a nice, long snooze.

The sun was shining and the day was baking hot, and nerves jangled in her stomach, along with an undeniable sense of excitement. This almost felt like a date. Maybe it was one. Maybe she could be crazy enough to consider it one, to act like it. Shannon would want her to. She imagined her friend's exaggerated mic-drop moment. *He invited you for a picnic? And you brought lemonade? When are you sending out the wedding announcements?*

Abby was still smiling as she spotted the sign for Holmwood Farm and turned up the dirt road, then parked the car by an old, weathered barn. The place had been easy to find, right off Route 12, between Big Foot Beach State Park and the town of Lake Geneva—a prime piece of property that developers would no doubt love to get their hands on, if the dairy farmer ever decided to sell up.

She got her things out of the back and then headed across the grass to the small cabin, little more than a glorified shed with a tacked-on porch, that was only a dozen or so feet from the edge of the lake.

She paused as she gazed at the lake shimmering beneath a cloudless sky, blue glinting under blue. In the distance, a motorboat skimmed along the water, and if she swam out past this little inlet, she knew she'd be able to see the large floats and cordoned-off areas of the town's Riviera Beach, where her mom used to take her when she was little. Her and Luke, splashing, playing Marco Polo, lying on the little beach, their legs dusted with sand…

Abby clamped down on that thought before she could let it take root, even though she knew that, of course, it already had. All the old memories were there in her mind already, burrowed deep. She just couldn't let them spring up. Take over. Because she was afraid of what might happen if she did.

"You made it." Simon came out onto the little porch of his cabin, resting his hands on the railing as he smiled his welcome. "What do you think of my palace?"

"It's amazing. Prime real estate, right here."

"I know, right? Though somehow I don't think Andrew Holmwood is going to sell to Wisconsin's next water park."

"No?" Abby met Simon's dancing gaze, her mouth tugging upwards as it always seemed to do in his presence. His happiness, his joy, felt infectious. Easy. "His family's probably been here for a hundred years."

"A hundred and fifty."

She laughed, and he nodded towards the thermos and Tupperware in her arms. "What have you brought me?"

"Cookies and lemonade."

"You *angel*." Grinning, he liberated her parcels from her, taking them inside.

The medal was in her shoulder bag, still wrapped in its handkerchief.

Abby followed him inside—the cabin was simplicity itself, a corner carved off as a kitchen, a folding table with two chairs, and a double bed in the corner. The best thing about it was the large window overlooking the lake.

"It's rather basic, but it does the job," Simon said. "Are you hungry? I've made chicken salad sandwiches."

"That sounds perfect."

"Why don't we go outside? It seems criminal to stay a second in here with a day like this one." Simon gathered up all their provisions and they headed back out.

The shoreline of the lake was a strip of scrubby sand and not much more, the water shallow and clear, looking almost golden in the sunlight, the colors of everything—the sky, the lake, the trees—so bright and pure it hurt Abby's eyes, even as it made her want to stare and stare, take it all in.

"How do you cope with these summers?" Simon asked as he spread out a blanket for them to sit on. "I mean, day after day of the most gorgeous weather. How do you not talk about it all the time, just exclaiming over how amazing it is?"

"Isn't that what you Brits do? Talk about the weather?"

"Only because it's so miserable." He sat down, then patted the space next to him. "Now show me this medal."

Shyly, as if she were offering him a treasure—and perhaps she was—Abby took the wrapped medal from her bag and handed it over as she sat down. Simon unwrapped it with the reverence it seemed to deserve, studying it carefully, holding the heft of it in his hand.

"Wow," he said quietly.

"I have no idea why my grandfather had it."

"Or why my grandmother had his Purple Heart. It's a case of musical medals."

She gave a small smile. "Yes, maybe."

Simon turned to look at her, his expression serious, the medal resting in the palm of his hand. "You know this is a different kettle of fish, though, don't you?"

"What do you mean?"

"This is a Distinguished Service Cross. They didn't hand those out like candy. Not, of course," he added quickly, "that they did that with Purple Hearts. But to put it into perspective... they gave out over a million Purple Hearts to soldiers wounded or killed during the Second World War, and just five thousand Distinguished Service Crosses, for acts of extraordinary bravery."

Abby leaned back on her hands as she considered the differential. "Wow."

"So how did your grandfather get Sergeant Matthew Lawson's?" Simon wondered out loud.

Abby shrugged, smiling. "Like I said, I have no idea."

"Take a guess, though." Simon wrapped the medal back in the handkerchief and placed it on the blanket between them. He leaned back, his hands nearly touching hers. "What do we know?" he mused out loud.

"That Tom Reese was in the 82nd Airborne, and he was wounded in Belgium in December 1944."

"And Matthew Lawson?"

"Was also in the 82nd Airborne, and did something very brave a little while later?"

"Yes, he must have. So they must have known each other."

"I suppose, considering one had the other's medal. But where does your grandmother fit into this?"

"She was in love with them both? Or perhaps both of them were in love with her." Simon's eyes twinkled as he glanced at her. "She was quite a looker, in her day. Very glamorous."

"You're a bit of a romantic, aren't you?" Abby teased, only for Simon to look at her seriously, making her heart stutter.

"I like to think I am."

Abby looked away; she couldn't think what else to do. She stared blindly at the tranquil surface of the lake, wishing moments like this didn't discomfit her quite so much. She was a grown-up, for heaven's sake. She should be able to handle a little light flirting.

"Why," Simon asked after a moment, "do I keep sensing something sad from you? Is it because of your mother and brother? I would understand if it was that, of course. But… am I wrong in feeling like it's something different, or maybe just more?"

Abby blinked, her gaze still firmly on the lake. "I'm not sad."

"No, you're right, not sad, not exactly. But…" Simon paused, weighing his words. "You don't seem entirely happy."

She forced herself to look at him. "I thought we were talking about Matthew Lawson."

"Can't we talk about each other too?"

"Then tell me something about you. When you ask me these questions…" She took a quick, raggedy sort of breath. "I'm not used to it. I don't like talking about it. It feels… it feels like peeling back my skin."

"Ouch."

"I know." She managed a small smile. Simon returned it, his eyes so gentle. She could fall in love with him, Abby realized with a jolt. She had so little experience of men, of life, that she could fall right in love with the first decent guy who walked up to her. Who was kind. The thought was completely alarming.

"You want to know something about me?" Simon mused out loud. "All right, then." He paused, his gaze on the tranquil surface of the lake. In the distance, Abby heard the buzz of a motorboat. "I'm divorced."

SIMON

Abby didn't move, but Simon felt her surprise, a palpable thing, a substance between them, creating a barrier, just as he'd known it would.

"Oh," she said after a moment. Did she sound disappointed? Why wouldn't she be, if something was happening between them, which Simon was sort of starting to hope there was, even in this very early stage? No one wanted to deal with that kind of messy emotional baggage unless they had to. "What happened?"

Where even to begin? His failings or hers? One had begat the other, he supposed.

"The easy answer is that my wife left me. She had an affair with the handyman who was working on our house. But…" He let out a breath. "The long answer is, I wasn't very good at marriage." He winced at how he'd phrased it, because that made him sound like some philandering jerk, and he may have been many things, but he hadn't been that. "I was very young when I got married. Twenty-two, and I wasn't much good with the emotional stuff. I think it had to do with the way my mother was… she could be incredibly volatile, her emotions up and down in a matter of seconds. My way of dealing with that was to shut down, in a way. I became remote, at least when things got intense. Emotionally unavailable, was how my ex-wife put it, and I came to realize she had a point." Because emotion, intensity, had scared him. Still did, which maybe was why he liked Abby—because, like him, she was contained. He kept it light and she kept it back. They were surprisingly similar, even if they showed it in different ways.

"You were emotionally unavailable?" Abby's eyebrows rose. "Because, I have to say, you certainly seem pretty in touch with your emotions now."

Simon gave a soft huff of laughter. "On the surface, maybe. But, yes, I do hope I've learned something from everything that happened."

"I feel like I'm the emotionally unavailable one," she said, meaning it, Simon thought, as a bit of a joke, but it made them sound like a couple and he could tell she realized that as she looked away quickly.

"Maybe that's why I'm attracted to you," he returned before he had time to think it through.

Abby jerked back to face him, her eyes widening, and belatedly Simon realized what he'd said. He'd been following the train of his thoughts without meaning to verbalize it out loud.

"That was *not* the best time to say that," he admitted in a slightly strangled voice.

"You're blushing."

He forced a laugh. "I'm embarrassed." Here he was, talking about the breakdown of his marriage, his failure as a husband, and he'd just told this lovely woman that he was attracted to her. Really smooth. Really great timing.

Abby simply stared at him, and recklessly deciding he might as well go the distance, Simon leaned forward and kissed her.

ABBY

The feel of Simon's lips on hers, cool and soft, was the equivalent of putting her finger in an electric socket and having no idea what might happen. Every sense suddenly sprang to buzzing, panicked life. *Where did that come from?* Lips on lips, so *close.* She'd forgotten what it felt like.

Abby hadn't been kissed for two years. She'd gone through most of her twenties with barely a smack or a buss, and actually it had been okay. Mostly. Yes, she'd had some yearning and loneliness like any normal woman, but she'd kept herself busy with the orchard and the shop and keeping the home front going. She hadn't wanted the emotional mess of a romantic relationship.

But now she resented the yawning lack of experience, the emotional emptiness of an entire decade, when she felt as if she had to remember how to kiss by reading an instruction manual, her brain telling her body what to do.

Eyes, close. Lips, open, but not too wide. But she didn't want to breathe into his mouth, that would be gross, surely. What if she passed out from holding her breath? How did she *do* this?

And then, suddenly, she remembered; it was really just like riding a bike, except a thousand times nicer.

Simon's hand cupped her cheek and she leaned into him as his lips moved gently over hers and her eyes fluttered closed and it felt entirely natural and right.

It lasted a couple of seconds, if that, and then it was over.

Simon eased back with a self-conscious smile and worried eyes. Abby's breath came out in a rush; she'd been holding it after all.

"Well, then." His gaze moved over her face, as if checking for injuries. Was she okay with the kiss? his slightly anxious expression seemed to be asking. Yes, Abby realized, she was, even though she had no idea what it meant, if anything. It had just been a kiss, after all. "So." He smiled, seeming content with whatever he saw in her face. "Why would someone give up a Distinguished Service Cross… unless he'd died?"

Abby had the urge to shake her head to clear it. They were talking about Matthew Lawson again, but she was still reliving those three seconds of wonder. But surely it was better to move on… the last thing either of them wanted was an analysis of what had just happened.

"Do you think he died?" she asked, doing her best to seem normal, as if a simple little kiss hadn't blown her world apart, which it shouldn't have.

Simon considered her question for a moment. "We could look it up, I think. They have a registry online for DSCs, like they do for the Purple Heart."

"So we could find out?"

"It depends on how much is recorded. Usually there's at least some reference to what the Cross was awarded for, as well as birth and death dates of the recipient."

Abby hesitated, wondering again how her father would feel about any of this, and then she nodded. This wasn't even about Tom Reese anymore; it was about the mysterious Matthew Lawson, whom her dad most likely had never heard about. It was about a mystery that was drawing her and Simon together, never mind what her father thought. She didn't need to think about him now. She didn't want to. "Okay, she said. "Why not?"

Simon slid his phone out of his pocket. It only took a few seconds for a registry of names of DSC recipients, some accompanied by photos, to appear on the phone screen. A minute or so passed as he scrolled through the names, and then he sucked in his breath.

"Here he is."

Abby leaned forward, her arm brushing his shoulder. The little bit of contact felt weirdly natural now; there was both an ease and a heightened awareness between them, thanks to that kiss. Abby didn't know how the two states could co-exist, only that they did, at least in her. She had no idea how Simon felt. He'd been *married*, after all. She hadn't fully processed that, or what it meant. They were in different stratospheres experience-wise.

Simon clicked on Matthew Lawson's name; there was no accompanying photo. The information was brief, and mostly what they already knew. Simon read it aloud: "Awarded for Actions during WWII. Service: Army. Rank: Master Sergeant. Regiment: 508th. Division: 82nd Airborne. Citation: The President of The United States of America, authorized by Act of Congress... yes, yes... for extraordinary heroism in connection with military operations against an armed enemy..." He lowered his phone to look at Abby. "It's just the usual patter."

"So no more information?" She realized she was disappointed.

"There's something, look." He showed her the screen. "Born in 1921, date of death unknown." He frowned. "So does that mean he died during the war, or that he didn't and they lost track of him over the years?"

"If he died in action, surely it would be noted?"

"Yes, I rather think it would. Which means Lawson was most likely alive when he gave his DSC to your grandfather."

"Maybe he didn't give it," Abby thought out loud.

Simon turned to her, eyebrows raised. "You think your grandfather nicked it?"

"No, not necessarily. Maybe Matthew Lawson lost it, and my grandfather found it."

"Why wouldn't he return it, then?"

"I don't know," Abby admitted. "Obviously. But anything could have happened. Maybe he tried."

"Possibly." Simon slid his phone back into his pocket. "Although he could have sent it to a centralized office somewhere and had it forwarded on. It seems odd he would have kept it, if he meant to return it to him. I could dig a bit more, most likely. There might be a Facebook group or something online for veterans of the 82nd Airborne. Someone might even still be alive who remembers him."

"They'd have to be a hundred years old."

"Yes, but it's not impossible."

She let out a little laugh. "This has really whet your appetite, hasn't it? Even more than Sophie Mather and Tom Reese."

Simon smiled self-consciously. "Somehow it feels like more of a mystery. A Distinguished Service Cross, hidden away all these years. Aren't you curious?"

"Yes, a bit." Abby straightened, wrapping her arms around her knees as she hugged them to her chest. "Do you think they were friends?"

"It seems likely, but who knows?"

"And what about your grandmother?"

"I feel like she must have been involved in some way, considering she had Tom's medal, but I can't figure out how."

"It all feels so far away, from this." Abby nodded to the lake, the sunshine. "But it really happened. It was important to the people involved. It seems so strange."

"It does."

They looked at each other for a moment, and, with a flutter of nerves, Abby wondered if he would kiss her again. She wondered if she wanted him to, and thought she did, even if it felt scary, like leaping wildly into the unknown. The question was moot, because he didn't.

"Maybe you'll show me around Willow Tree one of these days?" he said instead. "I'd like to see it, if your dad doesn't mind."

"I don't think he would." She smiled wryly. "He's not some ogre, you know. He's just a cautious man."

"I know." Simon grimaced wryly. "But I'm not sure he's taken a liking to me."

"More what you're doing, perhaps." Maybe she should tell her dad about the Cross. It seemed silly to be so secretive about it, like she'd been a little girl digging through her parents' drawers, when it really wasn't like that. She had every right to look into her ancestry, find out something that had happened before her father was born, something that couldn't possibly matter to anyone now. She wished she didn't feel guilty, but it was an emotion she'd got used to long ago, especially when it came to her dad.

"Why don't we have our picnic?" Simon suggested. "I'm starving."

Abby nodded, relieved to be on easy ground. And it was easy, to eat sandwiches and chat about nothing in particular; she offered up some trivia about Wisconsin, and told him her favorite apple among the varieties they grew, as well as a little bit about the gift shop. In return, Simon explained why he loved history, and how inexplicable cricket was, and how he'd never been waterskiing but wanted to try.

By the time Abby was packing up a few hours later, she was pleasantly sleepy and sunburned, content in a way she hadn't been in a long time. They'd made a plan for Simon to come to the farm for lunch the day after next, and she'd give him a tour.

"And meanwhile I'll try to look up some information about this Matthew Lawson," he told her. "And Tom Reese, for that matter. See what I can find."

He didn't kiss her when they said goodbye, and Abby had to sternly tell herself that she didn't mind. One kiss did not a relationship make. Even she, in her woeful inexperience, knew that.

Besides, the Holmwoods had come out of their farmhouse to say hello, and it would have been awkward to do anything but wave. It probably would have been awkward anyway. There would be time later, if that was what she actually wanted.

She was still lost in a pleasantly vague daydream about Simon kissing her as she showed him the apple orchard, the bright green leaves hiding them from view like something out of a frothy romance novel, as she pulled up in front of the farmhouse, and then climbed the porch steps to let herself in. The screen door had just closed behind her with a satisfying slap when she heard her father's voice.

He was standing in the kitchen doorway; after coming in from the bright sunlight, he loomed up like a dark, hulking shadow, and she tensed, because she knew she'd been here before. When he spoke, his voice was both defeated and angry, a sorrowful growl of despair.

"What the hell have you been up to, Abby?"

CHAPTER ELEVEN

February 1944

Lily clutched her handbag to her chest as she stood by the front gate and stared up at the unassuming house on Keildon Road, just a short walk away from her own home. It was where Matthew was billeted, and she had decided to stop by after work even though she wasn't expected. Even though it wasn't at all like her to do something so unprompted, so forward and bold.

She'd got the address from Sophie, after that taut morning encounter, when her sister had seemed so blithe, her blouse buttoned wrong, her eyes alight.

Richard's bewilderment and Carol's pursed-lip silence hadn't dented Sophie's optimism at all. She'd seemed incandescent as she hurried upstairs to change into her clothes for work. Lily had followed her, full of trepidation, as well as an undeniably avid curiosity.

"What happened?" she'd asked as Sophie wriggled out of her skirt.

"What do you mean, what happened?"

"Did Lieutenant Reese meet you at the pub?"

"Lieutenant Reese, Lieutenant Reese." Sophie had laughed, a little wildly. "I think you can call him Tom by now, Lily." She gave her reflection a quick, smug smile. "Yes, I most certainly think you can call him Tom."

"Your blouse is buttoned up wrong," Lily had blurted. If she'd expected her sister to be embarrassed by this fact, she was disappointed. Sophie's smug smile had just curved wider.

"So it is," she'd agreed, and started to unbutton it, a challenge glinting in her eyes. She was reveling in whatever had happened last night, Lily realized. Reveling in her freedom and her power, her experience and her allure. She'd practically shone with it; it radiated from her fingertips, and Lily had felt, quite suddenly, a deep, penetrating pang of envy.

"Did you have a nice time?" she'd asked, feeling the question was inadequate, even ridiculous.

Sophie had slipped out of her blouse with a shrug. "We most certainly did."

Her tone had made Lily want to know every detail, even as she already knew she wouldn't ask anything more. "I don't think Mother noticed about your blouse," she'd said instead.

Sophie had tossed her head as she caught her reflection again, her gaze lingering on her own smile. "So what if she did?"

"Sophie—" Lily had begun, although she wasn't sure what she could say.

"I told you, Lily, I don't *care*." Sophie had let out another wild laugh, full of joy. "I don't care," she'd said again, her tone triumphant. "I really don't."

Lily had stared at her uncertainly. "What did you and Lieu— Tom get up to, then?" she'd asked, even though she'd already told herself she didn't want to know any details.

"We went to the pub, of course."

"But after… The air raid didn't start till after midnight, Sophie, and the pub would have closed by ten. What were you doing during all that time?" Although Lily hadn't been sure she wanted to know.

Sophie had turned back to face her, blouse unbuttoned, hands on her hips. "Do you really want to know?" she'd asked with a catlike smile.

Lily knew then that she really didn't. "Do you care for him, then?" she'd asked.

Sophie's smile had dropped as she'd gazed thoughtfully at her sister. "Do you know, Lily," she'd said slowly, "I actually think I do."

"And… will you see him again?" She'd thought of Matthew, standing so close to her in the hall, asking her the same question. Why, oh why, had she been such a ninny about it? Why couldn't she just have said *yes, two o'clock on Sunday, we'll go for a walk?*

"He's taking me to Rainbow Corner on Friday," Sophie had said as she began to button up a fresh blouse.

"Oh." Lily couldn't keep the disappointment from swooping emptily in her stomach. No double date this time, then. That much was obvious.

"Are you missing your little sergeant?" Sophie had teased. "He *is* a dark one. Do you know, Tom doesn't really know him at all? I asked about him for you, but he hadn't much to say. Only that he'd met him on the boat over, and the good sergeant never says much. Keeps himself to himself, and talks a bit funny too—have you noticed? Almost as if he's some sort of lisp he's trying to hide."

"He doesn't have a *lisp*," Lily had returned fiercely. "Far from it. He speaks very clearly. Very precisely."

"Exactly. He's *too* precise, don't you think? As if he's trying too hard. Anyway, Tom thinks he's a bit queer. He wouldn't call him his friend, certainly. I'm not sure he even really likes him." She had spoken matter-of-factly, but Lily had still been stung.

"I'm not at all certain that Sergeant Lawson would call Lieutenant Reese his friend either," she had retorted, but Sophie had only hooted with laughter.

"Listen to you! I've got your back up, haven't I? Well, I'm only trying to give you fair warning. Tom said he's often missing at times when he shouldn't be, but, for some reason, no one seems to bat an eye. And he doesn't have any real friends, except for a bloke named Guy, who's just the same."

"Tom sounds envious."

"Envious?" Sophie had let out a scornful laugh. "Of what?" It was so obvious that Sophie thought Tom Reese was the better man, the better catch. Lily's chest had burned with the effrontery of it. Tom Reese, she suspected, was all brash swagger and shallow charm. Nothing he'd done or said so far convinced her otherwise, but she was sure Matthew was different. He had to be.

"Does Tom know where Matthew is billeted?" she'd asked recklessly.

"Ooh! Are you going to see him, then? Send him a postcard?" Her sister had sounded amused, which had made Lily feel as if she could almost hate her. It was a new and shocking feeling; she loved Sophie, she always had. Her high spirits kept them all buoyed up when life was so low. She was laughter and fun and light-hearted simplicity. But, right now, Lily's fists were clenched and she had to take a breath before she spoke levelly.

"I might."

"Oh, don't be cross." In typical Sophie style, her sister's mood had changed and she dropped to her knees in front of her and laid her head in her lap as if she were a child. "I'm sorry, Lily, I really am. I'm acting like a cow when I shouldn't be. It's just I'm so happy."

Lily didn't know why being happy would make one act like a cow, but she'd forborne saying so. "I'm pleased you're happy."

"Are you?" Sophie had twisted her head to look up at her. "Are you, really?"

"Yes, of course I am. Truly." Although Lily knew she was still worried, about so many things. "Do be careful, Sophie," she'd said quietly. "Lieutenant Reese—Tom—he's going to go away, isn't he?"

"He'll come back on leave."

"Did he say so?"

"And so what if he doesn't?" Sophie had scrambled up to her feet. "Not everyone is looking for a wedding ring, you know."

"Even so," Lily had said quietly. "I don't want you to get hurt."

Sophie had grabbed her utility skirt from the wardrobe and thrust her legs into it. "Perhaps I just want a good time." She'd sounded defiant, and Lily suspected her sister was trying to convince herself as much as her.

"Then do be careful," she'd repeated. "Don't let him break your heart, or…" *Get you into trouble.* She couldn't say it. She didn't even like thinking it. She could not imagine what their mother's response to *that* would be.

"Don't worry about me, Lily," Sophie had stated rather loftily. "I can take care of myself, you know." She'd grabbed her hairbrush and started yanking it through her mussed hair. "And don't worry, I'll get you the address for your sergeant."

He's not mine, Lily had almost said, but then didn't. Perhaps he was hers, if just a little bit. Two days later, Sophie had handed her a slip of paper with a smile; she'd been out to Rainbow Corner with Tom and she was fizzing from it.

"You should have seen all the things they had there, Lily! Endless supply of just *everything*. I tried Coca-Cola. It tickled my nose! Oh, it made me laugh."

Lily had thought of how she'd felt the same when she'd drunk champagne. She'd smiled and patted her sister's hand, genuinely glad for her happiness, and she'd put the slip of paper in the pocket of her dress where she felt its promising weight all day.

And now she was here, under a darkening sky, knowing she should hurry home—there had been another raid last night—and yet so wanting to be daring. Wanting to do something, just the way Sophie had said—to seize life and what it had to offer, no matter how little or fleeting.

The house was small and unassuming, brick-fronted, the blackout curtains drawn across every window. Lily took a deep breath and started forward. With her gloved fingers clenched tightly, she rapped on the front door and then waited, shivering a little in the cold, still air. It was a clear night, a silver crescent of moon slender in the sky. She waited, sensing the emptiness within. It shouldn't have surprised her that Matthew wasn't home; he might be on leave, or on an operation, or at the base. He could be anywhere.

But what about the family he was living with? She'd been prepared to stammer out an explanation of who she was here to see to whoever came to the door, but it remained closed, the house clearly empty.

Lily waited another minute before she started to turn to go back down the path, stopping after just a step. She couldn't leave it at that. To work up all this courage only to walk away at the first hurdle…? She glanced again at the house, but, of course, she couldn't see any lights inside, thanks to the blackout curtains. Still, it *felt* empty.

Then she noticed a wooden gate at the side of the house that no doubt led to the back garden. Hardly daring to believe she was considering it—she didn't *do* things like this—Lily walked towards the gate. It was latched, but when she stood on her tiptoes, she was able to work the latch from the other side. A bit of back and forth and it slid free, pinching Lily's fingers in the process, but she didn't care.

She glanced around, but no one was about, and even if there was, they wouldn't be able to see her. Everything was swathed in deep, blackout darkness. Holding her breath, she pushed the gate, and it swung open with a shudder and creak.

The narrow alley that ran the length of the house was darker still, and the paving stones were slick under Lily's shoes. There was a faint smell of drains and when she pressed one hand against the brick wall to steady herself, she felt damp seep through her gloves.

What was she *doing* here? What could she possibly hope to find? Yet she kept walking, feeling her way along the wall, having no real idea why, only that she needed to do something, just as Sophie had.

The narrow alleyway emerged into the back garden, exactly like just about every other on the street, or Holmside Road, for that matter. A rectangle of muddy grass—it hadn't been turned into a Victory garden, which was a bit surprising—and a back door that led into the kitchen. There was no blackout curtain, but the room was dark.

By the pale light of the slender moon, Lily was just about able to make out the bulky shapes of furniture—a table, two chairs, a sink, a range cooker, and a larder cupboard.

She turned away from the door, gazing blankly at the dark garden. There was no Anderson shelter, just an expanse of muddy grass, everything seeming unlived and unloved in a way she didn't understand. Surely there should be a washing line, or a vegetable patch— or *something*. There was nothing.

There was no reason for her to hang about here, and it would look decidedly odd if Matthew came home and found her skulking about the back garden. Lily knew she would never be able to explain it, and her cheeks heated simply at the thought of having to do so. She needed to leave, immediately, before she was discovered by Matthew or a nosy neighbor.

She'd just started back to the alley alongside the house when she heard a noise coming from the opposite side of the garden— the sound of something alive, although she couldn't have said what it was. Blinking through the gloom, she made out a rickety little shed against the garden wall.

Lily hesitated, her heart starting to pound. The horrid absurdity of the situation struck her forcefully—really, what had she been thinking, coming here like this, skulking about in the garden, looking for clues like some schoolgirl detective? And yet somehow, despite that, she found herself turning around and walking slowly towards the shed.

The sound came again, like a soft sigh, almost a moan. A strange sound, especially to come from a dilapidated little shed, that looked as if it should hold firewood or coal, perhaps a rusty bicycle or two.

Lily reached for the latch. It slipped out easily, and the door swung open. She stepped into the darkness, breathing in a sweetish animal scent. Rustling sounded all around her, and she heard the strange sigh again—it was a cooing, she realized. The shed was full of birds. They rustled again, louder, making her want to step back, yet she stood still.

By the pale sliver of moonlight, she was able to make them out—at least a dozen, all in wicker cages. They rustled and cooed and clucked, disturbed by her presence.

It wasn't entirely out of place for someone to keep birds, Lily knew, although she'd thought pigeons had been requisitioned for the war effort years ago. Then she noticed that each of the birds had a small metal canister attached to one of their legs. These had to be carrier pigeons, meant to send messages into occupied Europe. She'd heard about such things, but only vaguely, and now, curious in spite of every instinct telling her to walk away, she reached into the cage closest to her and unfastened the metal tube from the bird's leg.

It took a moment of fussing, and the bird tried to peck her hand, but for a reason she couldn't articulate, Lily was determined. She unscrewed the lid of the tube and withdrew the paper folded tightly inside. She had to step outside the shed and hold the paper up to the moonlight to read it, but when she was able to make out the words—only just—her heart felt as if it had dropped right out of her chest. The message was in German.

At least, she thought it was German. The only German she'd seen was in newsreels about Hitler, but she thought she recognized the style, and some of the words. *Der. Sind. Heer.*

She stared at the message, desperately trying to think of a suitable reason why Matthew Lawson would have carrier pigeons in his shed, with messages in German attached to their legs.

A noise sounded from somewhere at the front of the house, the squeak of a gate, and Lily jumped. She darted back into the shed and, with shaking fingers, tied the canister back onto the pigeon's leg; it pecked her hand, causing a hole in her glove, but she couldn't care about that.

She'd had no time to roll up and replace the message, so she slipped it into her pocket, where it seemed to pulse in awful accusation. *A message in German.* What if someone found it? What on earth would they think?

What did *she* think?

She knew many Germans living in England had been classified as enemy aliens. They'd been rounded up at the start of the war, many of them Jews, and sent to internment camps as far away as the Isle of Man, although the public outcry since then had had the majority of them released. Still, people were afraid of spies, seemed to see them everywhere.

She thought of the posters she'd seen on her way to work, or by the Underground—"Zipp it! Careless Talk Costs Lives!" or "Bits of Careless Talk Are Pieced Together By The Enemy" with a picture of a jigsaw map of Europe and a hand moving the pieces with an awful swastika ring. Some people said there were hundreds—thousands of spies, all through the country, listening, watching, waiting for the right moment.

Another noise sounded from somewhere in the street, and Lily knew she couldn't stay here a moment longer. She hurried out of the shed, her legs watery, her hands shaking as she latched the door. Her mind was buzzing, a haze of thoughts she couldn't bear to discern. Messages in German. The empty house. Matthew's clipped, precise voice. The way Tom Reese had said he was strange, even mysterious, joining the regiment later than everyone else… She had to get out of here.

She walked as quickly as she could towards the alleyway, slipping on the damp paving stones and nearly falling. When she threw one hand out to the wall to steady herself, she scraped her wrist hard across the brick. Her breath was coming in ragged gasps, her heart thudding so hard it hurt.

Somehow she made it to the end of the alleyway, and, standing on her tiptoes, she did her best to force the latch's bolt back in, but she couldn't manage it. Lily let out a desperate, disbelieving cry, wondering if she should just leave the gate unlatched. Would Matthew even notice? *If he was a spy, he would.*

Finally the bolt slid through, and Lily let out a near-sob of relief. She whirled around, intending to sprint towards the street and safe towards home, when she caught sight of the figure at the front gate, one hand about to open it. Even in the dark, she knew who it was; she recognized the straight bearing, the set of his shoulders, and the cap on his head.

"Hello," Matthew said in his familiar, clipped voice. He sounded surprised, and why shouldn't he be? "Is that you, Lily?"

CHAPTER TWELVE

Lily stared at Matthew and suddenly had the absurd urge to laugh wildly. How could this be happening? Why had she come here, why had she sneaked into the back garden, and why, oh why, had she opened the door of that wretched shed? All of it had been so very, very unlike her. She was sedate, safe, and deadly dull. *Deadly...* Her hand slipped into the pocket of her coat and clenched around that terrible slip of paper.

Matthew opened the gate and started walking towards her. Lily found she couldn't move.

"Is everything all right?" he asked. "What are you doing here?"

"I came to see you. I wanted to thank you for the hamper..." The words came thoughtlessly, her voice high and thin.

Matthew stood before her, frowning slightly, his dark brows drawn together, his eyes so fathomless. She'd once thought his dark looks handsome, but now they almost frightened her. He seemed utterly unknowable.

"You've already thanked me for the hamper, Lily. You didn't need to do it again."

Oh heaven help her, did he sound as if he knew? Surely he must suspect.

Lily shook her head, a mechanical back and forth. "And... I wanted to ask if you'd like to take a walk on the Common. Before you're sent away. You'd said something before."

Matthew's eyebrow rose as the smallest of smiles quirked his mouth. "Yes, I did and that would indeed be very pleasant, but it is a bit dark, yes?"

That precise voice... the very careful way he spoke every word... was he hiding an accent, a German one? It suddenly seemed almost obvious. No one spoke the way he did, choosing each word with such deliberate care.

"Yes, it is dark. I meant on the weekend, perhaps, if you have the time off."

"I'm afraid I do not." He studied her while Lily tried to look normal, friendly even, a smile skirting her lips and then sliding away. "You're bleeding," Matthew said, gesturing to her hand.

Lily glanced down to see where she'd scraped her wrist against the brick. A few drops of blood had welled up and started to drip towards her cuff. "It's nothing—"

"You should have a dressing." His tone brooked no argument. "If you come inside, I can see to it."

"Really, you don't have to—" she began, but Matthew shook his head.

"Nonsense. It is no trouble." He moved towards the door and, after a tense second of awful indecision, she followed, not knowing what else she could do. To refuse would invite suspicion.

And really, Lily told herself as Matthew unlocked the door, perhaps she was overreacting, because of all the posters and paranoia. There had to be some explanation for the pigeons, the message in German. He was in the army, after all, the U.S. Army. How could he possibly be a spy? It seemed ridiculous, and yet...

Matthew opened the door and stepped aside so she could enter first. The hallway was dark and smelled a bit musty, a bit unlived in. There were no coats on the stand, no umbrellas leaning by the door.

Matthew closed the door and gestured towards the kitchen in the back of the house. "Why don't you come through?"

Lily walked back towards the kitchen she'd glimpsed in shadowy darkness from the back door. She stood in the entrance of the small room while Matthew moved past her to draw the blackout curtains across and then turn on the lights.

"You're shivering," he remarked. "You must be freezing."

"It's so cold out."

"Why don't I make you a cup of tea? Or would you rather have coffee?"

Lily stared at him miserably. He looked so concerned, an almost tender look in his dark eyes—or was she imagining it? Had she imagined everything—the brief intimacy she'd felt with him, the connection, the kindness? *The danger?* "Tea, please," she managed.

Matthew stoked the fire in the range and then went to the sink to fill the kettle. Lily watched his brisk, efficient movements, too overwhelmed even to think.

"Why is the house so empty?" she finally asked. "Who lives here?"

"Just me, I'm afraid." He gave her a small, fleeting smile. "The family who lived here evacuated to Somerset, to be with the wife's sister. The husband is fighting. The British army requisitioned it, and then gave it to us."

"Oh." So he lived here on his own, free to do as he liked. She slipped her hand into her coat pocket and fingered the piece of paper.

Matthew put the kettle on top of the range.

"Let's see to your wrist," he said as he turned to her.

Wordlessly, Lily held her arm out.

Matthew turned her wrist over with gentle hands and inspected the scratch. It wasn't deep, but it had drawn enough blood to need to be dressed. His fingers were lean and long as they moved over her wrist. Piano player's hands, she thought irrelevantly.

Carol had insisted both she and Sophie have lessons when they were children. Sophie hadn't practiced and Lily had been as good as tone-deaf, banging diligently on the keys until Carol had put a stop to the whole thing.

Now Lily wondered if Matthew played the piano. She imagined him seated in front of one, his long fingers rippling over the keys. He'd told her how he'd danced with his mother, and she thought he must like music. But what sort of man *was* he? The sort who could be a spy? What else was she meant to think? Who would have a message in German, attached to the leg of a carrier pigeon?

"It's not too bad," Matthew said. "But I'll put some salve on it."

He was still holding her hand in his own as she looked up at him. His face was close, and his dark eyes seemed liquid, as if she could drown in them. For a second, Lily felt as if the whole world had fallen away, and she didn't know whether it was from fear or longing.

"I'll fetch it," Matthew murmured and, releasing her hand, he left the room.

Lily let out a shuddering breath and clutched her wrist with her other hand, as if it were broken. She had half a mind to run out of the house, and yet the other half was telling herself not to be so utterly ridiculous.

What would Sophie do, if she were here? Lily knew the answer immediately. She would flirt and laugh and try to winkle out information from Matthew, just in case he really was a spy. She would find it all the most tremendous fun, thrilled that she was finally doing something exciting for the war, that something interesting was happening to her. She might even be disappointed if Matthew turned out *not* to be a spy.

Why couldn't Lily be like her?

"Here we are." Matthew came back into the kitchen, brandishing a bottle of brown glass. He smiled, his eyes crinkling, his expression so very gentle. It made Lily feel like bursting into tears. She couldn't stand him being kind right now. She really couldn't, not when she thought he might be a spy, and she should hate him for it.

"Thank you," she managed in little more than a hoarse whisper, and she held her arm out again, as Matthew took the stopper out and then dipped a finger into the salve before holding Lily's hand and rubbing the cream gently into the abrasion.

It was such a simple act, and yet it made Lily catch her breath. The feel of his fingers on her skin was mesmerizing, electrifying. She felt as if she could curl up and go to sleep, and yet at the same time she was more awake than she'd ever been. How was that possible? *How could he be a spy?*

"Does it hurt?" Matthew asked, and she looked up, only to find his face close to hers once more, his gaze seeming to pull her in. His fingers tensed on her wrist and for a second—a lifetime—everything felt suspended, endless, the world slowing down and speeding up at the same time, so Lily was aware of the beat of her blood, the tick of the clock, the catch of Matthew's breath—

Then he released her hand and stepped away.

"The tea," he said, and Lily realized the kettle had started to whistle.

She closed her eyes.

Matthew made the tea while Lily simply stood there. She knew she should make some chitchat, or at least herself useful, but simply standing there and breathing felt like all she was capable of. Her wrist had started to throb, and she didn't know whether it was from the graze or Matthew's gentle attentions.

"I forgot the dressing," he said, and left the kitchen for a moment, to return with a length of gauze.

"Where did you get that?" Lily asked. "We haven't seen gauze dressings since the start of the war."

"There's plenty, at the base." He gestured for her to hold out her hand yet again, and then wrapped the dressing around it, tucking it neatly. "There you go. Now come and warm up with a cup of tea."

Lily sat down at the table, wrapping her hands around the cup Matthew gave her for warmth. He sat opposite her, smiling faintly.

"Better?"

She smiled back, the curve of her lips taking effort. "Yes."

The quiet kitchen felt like a world away from everything else—the Casualties Section, Holmside Road, the war. Right now, the night still and silent all around them, the only sound the occasional clank or crackle from the range, Lily felt as if they could be the only two people alive. The only ones left.

"You remind me of my little sister," Matthew said unexpectedly. He cocked his head to one side, his smile still faint but in place.

"Do I?"

"Yes. She was quiet and shy, until you came to know her. Then she could be very playful, a little performer. I think perhaps you are a little like that."

Lily's gaze swept downwards as pleasure unfurled inside her. "I think I've always been a bit shy."

"Compared to some, perhaps." She knew he was talking about Sophie. "But when it matters… I think you would not be. I think you would be bold. Brave."

It was a compliment, but for some reason it didn't feel right to say thank you. "What is your sister's name?" she asked instead.

The slightest of pauses, like a held breath. "Gertie."

"And she is back in America? In New York?"

"Not in New York. Only I went there."

"When did you last see her?"

Another pause, this one slightly longer. "November 10th," he finally said. "1938."

She looked at him, startled. "Before you left for New York?"

"It took me a while to get there."

"And you haven't been back home?"

"No, alas. It was not possible, and then I enlisted in 1942."

1942? Then why hadn't he joined the regiment earlier? Lily knew she wouldn't ask. She didn't want to pry, and was afraid a question might reveal something she didn't want to know. "You must miss her, then," she said. She pictured a young girl, dark like Matthew, with quiet eyes and a playful smile.

"Yes. I miss all my family."

"You haven't seen any of them?"

"My father is dead, but, no, I have not seen the rest. Not my mother, not my sister, not my two little brothers." He let out a little sigh, as if he were laying a burden down. "But one day, I hope I will. When we win this war."

He wasn't a spy, Lily thought with a rush of relieved conviction as she looked at him, saw the grief in his eyes, in the grim set of both his lips and shoulders. He couldn't be. Not with the way he talked about his family, the war.

"I'm sorry," she murmured. "I can't imagine not seeing my family for so long."

"But you can, I think." He smiled sadly at her. "I think you can imagine too much, perhaps."

Lily stared at him, both moved and discomfited. It was as if he could see into her head, as if he knew all the terrible thoughts she had about the dead seamen she wrote about, how she pictured their deaths and their families and the lives that would now never go on, their little moments of joy, their last ones of agony. "How…" she began, and then couldn't finish.

"You feel things," Matthew said. "I see it in your eyes." He let out a little, embarrassed laugh and shook his head. "I'm being sent up north in a few days," he said. "Perhaps that is why I am allowing myself to say such sentimental things."

"Up north?" She stared at him in surprise, even though it wasn't unexpected.

"Yes. So we will not be able to take that walk, I am afraid." He smiled wryly. "But perhaps I could walk you home?"

Lily stared at him, unable to make sense of the whole, strange evening. The pigeons… the message still in her pocket… Matthew's smile. None of it made sense. A few minutes ago she'd had the absurd notion that if she followed him into this house he might actually hurt her. Now she was near tears at the thought he was leaving.

"Lily?" he prompted gently.

"Y-y—yes, of course." She rose from the table. "Thank you, Sergeant."

"Please, call me Matthew."

"Yes, of course," she said again. "Matthew."

Lily waited while Matthew locked the house, and then they were walking in silence down Keildon Road, towards home. The street was near-empty, the only light from the sliver of moon. Neither of them spoke, but it didn't matter.

Then, out of nowhere, the sound of the air-raid siren split the still air, rising in a familiar moan. Lily froze; she'd never been caught out on the street like this before. She'd always been at home, or at work, where everyone could pile in to the purpose-built shelter. A few times she'd been close to the Underground and gone there, but now they were in the middle of a residential street, with nowhere at all to hide. Lily met the panicked gaze of a woman across the road; she was holding the hand of a boy who couldn't be more than six, both of them frozen in place.

"What do we do?" Lily asked, as much of herself as to Matthew.

Before he could reply, the air was full of droning, louder than the siren, louder than Lily had ever heard before. It filled her head and throbbed in her ears; she felt it thrum through her chest. It was as if she was being consumed by the noise, as if it had taken over her body.

She looked up, her mouth dropping open at the sight of a German Messerschmitt flying so low she could see the markings on its side, and the silhouette of the pilot in the cockpit. It took her breath away; it was all so *real*, so tangible, far more than a distant sound or far-off speck that the planes usually were, when she was safe in a shelter or the Underground.

She watched as the bomb was released elegantly from the plane's underbelly and then Matthew yanked on her arm hard enough to make her cry out as he pulled her towards the only possible shelter nearby, the doorway of a house with a small porch overhang.

Lily fell against the doorway as Matthew completely covered her body with his. The air was full of noise and smoke—crackles and thuds, the whine of the plane and the breaking of glass, all of it loud enough to make her eardrums throb and her chest hurt.

Matthew had pressed his body closely against hers, so even through their heavy coats she could feel the joining of his limbs, the beating of his heart. It was the most intimate she'd ever been with anyone, his arms wrapped around her, her face buried in the curve of his neck, her eyes tightly closed as the world dissolved into a destructive whirlwind around them.

His body jolted and she realized he must have been hit by some flying debris—she prayed it was no more than that.

The raid seemed to go on and on, the screaming of the planes and the awful thuds of the bombs, until Lily thought they would surely die, they would *have* to die, because no one could endure this and live.

Then, suddenly, it was silent, as if the planes had simply disappeared, as if it had been a nightmare and she'd woken up.

Lily lifted her head from Matthew's shoulder, blinking in the red-hazed gloom of a shattered world.

"Are you hurt?" she asked, and her voice sounded muted and faraway, as if she were talking underwater, the way she and Sophie used to do on those seaside holidays, having tea parties as they sat cross-legged on the sandy bottom. She realized the noise of the bombing must have damaged her hearing, hopefully only temporarily.

"I'm fine." He eased away from her, his face grave. There was plaster dust sprinkled through his hair, and a bloody cut on one cheek. His coat was torn.

"Are you sure—"

"It's nothing." He turned to survey the street, and that's when Lily saw the extent of the damage. The house immediately opposite had suffered a direct hit; it was nothing but wreckage now, practically flattened, timbers protruding from the rubble like giant matchsticks, items visible amidst the rubble—the leg of a chair, the door of a wardrobe, a single cup.

Lily had seen plenty of bomb damage before; she walked past bombed-out buildings every day, had delivered cups of tea to neighbors who had suffered some damage. Yet she'd never seen anything as immediate, as overwhelming, as this, with the stench of it still in her nostrils, a haze of smoke hovering over the destruction.

Then her gaze moved from the destroyed house to the woman she'd locked gazes with before Matthew had pulled her into the doorway. She was standing in the middle of the street, staring sightlessly at her son, who was sprawled at her feet.

Lily caught sight of his head first; his eyes closed, his lips slightly pursed, like a baby sleeping. Then her gaze moved lower and she saw that beneath his middle he was nothing but a mess of blood and guts and bone. Her stomach heaved at the sight. He was most certainly dead.

"She needs help," she said, nodding to the woman. Her voice still sounded faraway.

Somehow, she found the strength to walk across the street on wobbly legs; the air was thick was smoke and her chest hurt every time she breathed in, and her ears were ringing painfully.

"Let me help you," she said to the woman, who turned her blank gaze towards Lily. "Come with me to get warm, have a cup of tea." As if such things would make a difference, but what more could she offer? The woman couldn't stay here. It wasn't safe. At any moment more buildings could collapse, another raid could start.

"My son... Teddy..." The woman swallowed convulsively. "I can't just leave him here."

Lily glanced at Matthew, who had followed her into the street, and a silent conversation passed between them, as clear as if they'd both spoken out loud and come to an agreement. He would take care of the boy; she would help the woman.

"I'll get someone," he said. "The police, or an ambulance. He'll be taken care of, I promise."

The poor boy didn't need an ambulance, but Lily knew Matthew would find someone to take his broken body from the street. She put her arm around the woman's shoulders and drew her away from her son. The woman moved stiffly, jerkily, clearly still in shock.

"Come with me," Lily said softly. "We'll get you warm. Sergeant Lawson will take care of your boy."

The woman nodded and let Lily lead her away like a child, her hand in hers as they walked down the street, past more bombed-out buildings, the few people wandering around as if they couldn't believe how quickly it had all happened. A fire engine screamed down a nearby street. Lily felt as if the world had ended, and yet somehow it was still going on. It didn't make any sense.

Ten minutes later, they were back at Holmside Road, which thankfully looked as if it hadn't suffered any damage.

Carol opened the door, her face tight with anxiety, before relief crashed over as she caught sight of Lily. Then she took one look at the blank-faced woman next to her before giving a quick nod.

"Tea," she said. "And brandy. Come inside."

In the kitchen, the woman collapsed into a chair, and it wasn't until Carol had pressed a cup of hot tea laced heavily with brandy into her hands that she began to sob, her body shuddering with the force of it, the reality of her son's death finally penetrating.

"What happened?" Carol asked in a low voice as she patted the woman's shoulder and Sophie looked on from the doorway, her arms folded.

Lily felt as if she could collapse. She leaned against the table instead, the edge digging into her hip, a reminder that she was here, that she'd survived.

"We were caught in the raid…" she said numbly. The world still felt muted. "She was across the street. Her son… he couldn't be more than six…" Lily's breath caught and she felt the urge to sob the same as the woman, but she swallowed it back. This wasn't her grief.

"You poor thing." Carol leaned over to give Lily's shoulder a quick squeeze. "Such a shock."

"I'm all right—"

"Sophie, make your sister a cup of tea," Carol barked.

Sophie, looked at her mother, clearly surprised by her sharp tone.

"She's had a shock," Carol continued. "And she's been ever so brave. You did the right thing, Lily, bringing her here. It'll be all right, love." She gave the woman's back another pat. "It'll be all right."

Sophie slunk to the table and poured Lily a cup of tea from the big brown pot. As Lily met her sister's gaze, she saw her eyes narrow, and in that moment she realized something intangible had shifted between all of them again.

Sophie was no longer the favored child, the laughing girl, who, despite, or perhaps because of, her high spirits, could do no wrong. Thanks to her evening with Tom Reese, thanks to Lily's actions tonight, something had started to change, roles reversed, or at least forever altered. And as she thrust a cup of tea into Lily's hands, it was clear Sophie knew it.

"*We*," she said softly, so only Lily could hear, as she poured a splash of milk into her cup. "I wonder who you were with, Lily Mather."

CHAPTER THIRTEEN

ABBY

"Abby?"

Abby closed the door slowly, her heart thudding. Memories tumbled through her mind of a moment like this one—fifteen years ago, her father in the doorway just as he was now, a look of naked grief and disbelieving despair on his face as she'd watched him turn into an old man.

What have you done, Abby?

That was all he'd said. He hadn't waited for an answer, not that she'd had the courage to give one. He'd simply turned around and shuffled into the kitchen. He hadn't said a word to her for an endless, agonizing week.

But that was then, and now was completely different. She'd hadn't been *up* to anything. Her father couldn't be angry that she'd spent the afternoon with Simon. She was a grown woman, after all, perfectly entitled to a private life.

Abby took a deep breath and let it out slowly. "I don't know what you mean, Dad."

"I mean the trunk upstairs in the attic that has clearly been opened."

What? Abby blinked at him through the gloom of the hallway. How had he known she'd opened the trunk? She'd put everything back exactly as she'd found it, and in any case her dad never went up to the attic. Never revisited all the memories and ghosts that resided there. She was the one who fetched the Christmas decorations or canning jars, who scurried up and down and tried not to look at anything too closely.

Goodness, but they were a sorry pair, ducking away from the past, trying to forget the truth even as it dominated their lives. Abby was so very tired of it.

"You went up to the attic?" she asked.

"You don't deny it," he said flatly.

"No, I can't. I wouldn't. I mean, I'm not going to *lie* about it."

"Why did you?"

"I was curious about Grandad." Abby tried to lighten her voice. "Does that have to be such a big deal?" She managed a smile as she walked towards her father. He didn't move from the doorway and she slipped past him into the kitchen, Bailey following her, determined to lend some sort of normalcy to this situation.

David turned around slowly. "It's a big deal because you knew my feelings about it. I didn't want the past all dug up. I told you so."

"Because there's something to hide?"

"Because I don't want it!" David's voice rose. "Even if it doesn't make sense to you, why can't you respect that?"

Abby cringed, not at her father's angry tone, but the despair and grief she saw on his face. Guilt corroded her insides, reminded her of all she had to make up for—would always have to make up for, no matter how hard or long she tried. "I'm sorry, Dad. I just… I don't understand why this is such a big thing. Grandad's been gone for thirty years. Whatever happened, whatever he did, surely it doesn't matter anymore?"

"It matters to me." David heaved a heavy sigh. "Memories matter, Abby. The way you think of someone, what you know about them, how they live on. Surely you can appreciate that? Especially when they're all you have."

"I know that," she said quietly. Of course she knew that. She could never forget it. Her mother and brother were frozen forever in time, forty-five and fifteen. She sank into a chair at the kitchen table, and Bailey immediately put her head on her knee, her liquid brown eyes gazing up at her unblinkingly. "But I didn't realize your memories of Grandad were…" She paused, her thoughts so tangled. "Complicated."

"It wasn't complicated, what I asked," David returned flatly. "To drop it."

Abby kept her gaze on Bailey, her hands sliding almost mechanically over her fur. Of course she'd known this was painful for her father. He'd made it plenty clear, and she'd kept her meetings with Simon secret for a reason. She'd tried to hide that she'd gone into the attic at all. Guilt, her constant companion, pressed even closer. "I'm sorry," she said after a long, tense moment. "I didn't mean to upset you."

"Why can't you just leave it alone?" He sounded weary, which was worse than if he'd stayed furious.

"Why can't you tell me?" The challenge was unexpected for both of them. Abby never challenged her father. She managed him, it was true, with careful, gentle handling, but she didn't oppose or question him. Yet now, for a reason she couldn't quite fathom, she was. "Why can't you tell me whatever it is you're hiding about Grandad?" she asked, trying to keep her voice reasonable. Gentle. "Is it something about the war? Something you don't want people to know? Who is Matthew Lawson?" The questions spilled out of her, surprising them both.

David's face darkened as he shook his head, a vehement back and forth that reminded Abby of an angry bear. "I don't want to talk about this, Abby."

"I know you don't, but it's my family too. Don't I have a right to—"

"No." The word was flatly spoken, an absolute. When it came to their family, she didn't have any rights, period. She'd lost them.

"That's not fair," Abby said quietly, her voice so low she half-hoped her father hadn't heard her.

"Not fair?" he repeated. "Do we really want to talk about what's not fair?"

"*Dad*." The word caught in her throat. She couldn't bear him to dredge up *that*.

"Please, Abby." The anger drained away, leaving her father looking like a broken man, his shoulders slumped, his voice faltering. "I know it doesn't make sense to you, and it's all old history, but... I can't stand the thought of that guy writing our family's history in a book. Poking and prying into private matters."

"He wouldn't have to put in a book," Abby said quietly. "And even if you told me, I wouldn't necessarily tell him. Not if you didn't want me to." Although she hadn't exactly respected her father's wishes in this matter so far.

"It's not worth knowing." David slumped into the chair opposite her, and detecting a mood as ever, Bailey moved her head from Abby's knee to her father's. With a sad smile, he stroked her head. "Remember when we got this old girl?"

"Yes." Her father had brought Bailey home one spring day, a golden fluffball of fur, after their old sheepdog Sam had died. Abby had been delighted with the puppy, who seemed less of a working dog than the loving companion they both needed—and still did. "She's been a good friend."

"Yes." David's gnarled hand rested on top of Bailey's head. "I'm sorry," he said after a moment, and Abby tensed in surprise. Her father never apologized. "I know I seem unreasonable. But this is painful for me. I don't... I don't want it dredged up. Any of it. I know it may not seem important to you, but... some things are better left unknown."

Abby's throat felt tight. The deep sadness, and even grief, in her father's voice made her eyes sting. "I'm sorry, Dad. I didn't mean to upset you."

"I know you didn't." But she had. With a sigh, he heaved himself up from the table. "Let's just leave it," he said, and Abby felt as if that were the catchphrase of their lives. Leave everything behind, never talk about it, and yet still it loomed, forefront and center of their lives.

David didn't wait for her reply, and Abby watched miserably as he shuffled out of the room. She listened to the sound of the front door close—a soft, despairing click, rather than an angry slam—and she brushed at her eyes impatiently.

This was why she never lost patience with her father, never left Willow Tree. Instead of being coldly furious, he became pathetically broken. And it was her fault. She knew she had to make peace with that somehow—Shannon had told her many times, a therapist she'd seen briefly had told her repeatedly, she knew it in her bones—but conversations like this one had the old, awful guilt rearing up, taking over. *It's my fault he's like this. My fault our family is broken.*

Abby took a deep breath and tried to focus. Mechanically, she went to the fridge to take something out for dinner. Her mind felt frozen as she started chopping an onion, her eyes smarting from the activity, which was better than crying because she felt so frustrated, so despairing, so *sad*.

Fifteen years. Fifteen years she'd lived with her dad, lived with the guilt. Found happiness in small but significant ways, yes, thank goodness. Shannon. The shop. Harvest festivals and summer fairs, chatting with customers, having dinner with a few friends. Bailey. She'd made a life, but she knew, at some basic heart level, she hadn't been truly happy, not deep down, in a contented, settled sort of way. She'd always been looking for something.

And you think you've found that with Simon?

The scoffing voice in her head almost seemed audible, a silent, sneering echo that reverberated through the room. Abby paused, knife in midair. Was *that* what was going on here? She was clinging to some pathetic romantic fantasy that belonged in a romcom or a frothy novel, not real life? Simon might have kissed her, but she barely knew him, and in any case, he was going back to England—when? A few weeks, he'd said. She was being *ridiculous*.

She'd let her interest in Simon guide her actions, make her dig into her grandfather's past even though she'd known—she'd absolutely known—that her father was reluctant. More than reluctant, even. Whatever secret her father was protecting—and Abby could not even begin to imagine what it was—it wasn't her right to dig it up and expose it to the light, to cause him more pain than she already had.

Abby resumed chopping the onion, determined now, her movements swift and purposeful. When Simon came, she'd tell him he needed to stop his research into her family, and the mysterious Matthew Lawson. She didn't want to know who he was, or why Tom Reese had his medal, and Sophie Mather had his. She didn't need to know any of it. She didn't even want to, anymore. It didn't matter. She could choose for it not to.

She pushed the pile of chopped onion aside, her eyes still stinging. She took a deep breath and willed herself to feel calmer. After a few moments, she did.

Two days later, Abby stood on the front porch, just as she had a little over a week ago, watching Simon's rental car come down the dirt road. The air was full of the sweet smell of freshly mown grass, reminding her of sunny summer afternoons a lifetime ago, when she and Luke had lain in the backyard, staring up at a cloudless sky, while their mother churned ice cream on the back porch.

Thinking back on it now, it sounded almost ludicrous—like something out of *The Waltons*, and yet it had happened, many times. Snowy Christmases, sledding on the big hill out back, catching fireflies on the front porch, a childhood's worth of a Norman Rockwell painting that she hadn't even appreciated. It had been real, all of it, even if it felt like a fantasy now, sepia-tinted, a montage of poignant moments set to sentimental music.

Simon pulled up in front of the house and came out of the car with an easy smile that reminded Abby of that closeness they'd had the day before yesterday, when they'd lain on a blanket by the lake and he'd kissed her. Forty-eight hours later, it still made her insides give a shivery little dance that she tried to suppress, because things were different now.

He bounded up the stairs with a wide smile, and when he leaned forward to greet her, she froze, not knowing what he meant to do, only for them to bump noses awkwardly and a bit painfully.

"Sorry," Simon said with a laugh as he rubbed his nose. "I only meant to kiss your cheek."

Abby muttered something unintelligible, and fussed with Bailey for a few seconds to avoid looking at him. "So are you ready for the grand tour?" she asked a bit too brightly, to cover her embarrassment. She suspected Simon saw right through her.

"Yes, absolutely." He glanced around in silent enquiry, and Abby answered the question he didn't ask.

"He's out today, getting some supplies in Milwaukee."

"Right."

"He's not scary, you know," she added.

"He is, a little bit, you have to admit." Simon cocked his head, his gaze sweeping speculatively over her.

"He doesn't mean to be," Abby said quietly. She thought of the way her father had shuffled out of the kitchen after their argument, an old man broken by memories. No, he wasn't scary, not to her. Just sad, which made it so much worse.

"I think you really believe that—"

"That sounds so patronizing," Abby returned, her voice sharpening, surprising them both, but she still felt raw from the argument. "I *know* it. Don't act as if you know my father better than I do, Simon, because, trust me, you don't."

Her words seemed to reverberate between them, like the echo of a slap.

Simon blinked once, twice.

"Noted," he said softly.

Abby flushed. "I'm sorry. I didn't mean to sound quite so aggressive."

"I know you didn't." He smiled. "I'm the one who's overstepped."

On that uncertain and somewhat sour note, they started the tour of the farm. Abby breathed in the scent of mown grass again as they headed across the front yard to the main barn, Bailey trotting faithfully beside them.

Now that they were talking, Abby realized there wasn't all that much to see—the barn, the trees, the shop.

"That's the tree the farm's named after," she said, nodding towards the large willow with its fronded, drooping branches in front of the house. "I suppose that's obvious."

"It's lovely." Simon paused to give the tree in the center of the front yard his full attention. "How old is it?"

"Seventy years or so? I think my grandfather planted it when he first bought the farm." Willow trees only lived seventy or eighty years total, Abby knew. She didn't like to think about losing the farm's emblem, the end of an era, worryingly symbolic.

As they resumed walking towards the barn, she tried to think of a friendly way to tell Simon that she didn't want him digging into Matthew Lawson or Tom Reese's pasts anymore. It had been so clear a decision after talking to her father, but now she felt full of uneasy doubts. Was it too bossy, to ask him to stop? It wasn't as if Matthew Lawson was a relative of hers. Would she be the one overstepping?

She shelved the conversation for later as they stepped into the cool dimness of the barn and she began to show him around—the cider press, the cold atmosphere storage. She handed Simon an apple from the storage and laughed when his eyes widened at how crisp it tasted, despite being a year old.

"We used to have refrigerated storage, but we moved to controlled atmosphere a couple years ago. Keeps the apples very fresh-tasting."

"And you make cider?" he asked, nodding towards the press and the stacks of fermenting apples.

"Yes, but it's more of a sideline, for the farm shop. We mainly sell apples to supermarkets through Wisconsin and Illinois."

They strolled through an orchard of Comstocks, and she explained about the "June-drop", when the trees naturally shed fruit, and then how they had to thin again in July, to make sure the apples remaining were healthy and of a good size.

"Do you love it?" he asked seriously as they paused beneath the sheltering branches of a tree, and Bailey flopped at their feet for a rest. "Do you love what you do?"

He looked so serious that Abby paused. "Yes," she said at last. "I do. I really do." She meant it absolutely, but it still felt too simple an answer for what she knew was a complicated question, a complicated life. Yes, she loved it, but as Simon already suspected, she'd never really had the opportunity to choose anything else—college at Wisconsin State, studying a language she'd once loved, a career in a city. Old dreams that had barely begun to take shape before she'd abandoned them for other ones formed by duty and grief.

"Abby." Simon's voice had gentled, and when she turned to look at him, he was smiling in a sleepy way that made her mouth dry. She knew that look, even if she'd never actually seen it before. She felt its response in herself.

Simon reached for her hand, and it was easy to let him take it, let him pull her towards him so their bodies brushed and their mouths touched, and, yes, they were kissing again, and it felt even better than last time.

Abby leaned back against a tree, the leafy branches a canopy overhead, the bark hard against her back. Yet, after just a few seconds, she felt her brain going into hyperdrive. *What does this mean? Is Simon serious?*

The answers came hard and fast—*It means nothing! Of course he isn't. This is a fling, you idiot, that's all.* And Abby had no experience whatsoever of flings. Simon, she realized as she started to tense, had to know that.

He broke the kiss first, a slight frown gathered between his brows as he gazed down at her. "All right?" he asked gently, and for some reason that annoyed her, as if he knew she was fragile, as if she needed handling after just one simple kiss.

"I'm fine," she replied, a touch aggressively. "Why wouldn't I be?"

"Honestly? Because you seemed... a bit removed, towards the end."

"You could tell?"

A smile curved his mouth. "Yes, I could, actually. You went stiff as a board, Abby, which generally isn't a good sign when you're kissing someone."

"Ah." She managed a laugh. "Sorry. I suppose I was wondering what this is." She gestured to the small space between them. "Not to turn all serious on you, but you are going back to England soon, and I'm... I'm not a fling kind of person, if that's what you had in mind."

He raised his eyebrows, tucking his hands into the pockets of his trousers as he rocked back on his heels. "And you think I am?"

"I have no idea what you are."

He flinched slightly, and she realized she'd hurt him with her words. Simon, who seemed so light-hearted, so easy-going, had a woundedness of his own. She forgot that, because of his carefree friendliness. But he was divorced, after all. He'd said he was emotionally unavailable, even if she'd never seen that herself.

"I don't mean that unkindly," she said. "It's just that we barely know each other. And if you're thinking of an actual relationship, considering the distance, I can't see it going anywhere."

Simon was silent, and Abby wished she hadn't said anything.

Why had she? She'd been enjoying it all—the flirting, the kiss, the feeling of expectation, that something was finally happening to her. Why did she have to go and ruin it before it had barely begun? And yet, even so, she didn't regret stating the obvious; maybe they both needed reminding.

"I must confess I hadn't thought through things as much as that," Simon said finally. "I like you. I wanted to kiss you. That's about as far as I'd got, to be honest."

"Okay." She tried to keep her expression neutral. It shouldn't hurt her, that his mind hadn't leapfrogged ahead the way hers had. Most people's probably didn't, or maybe here was the emotional reserve he'd told her about. "Well, this is probably a good time to tell you that I don't want you digging into Matthew Lawson or Tom Reese anymore." Actually, it probably wasn't a good time at all. It seemed she was in self-destruct mode now, but she couldn't help it. She had a weird urge to push him away, as strongly as if she'd placed her hands flat on his chest and shoved. This was all getting a bit too much, a bit too close.

"You don't?" Simon looked surprised, more surprised than Abby had expected him to be. Surely he'd understood her reluctance all along, even though she'd brought him the medal?

"No, I don't. I spoke to my father after I came back from the lake, and he was pretty upset. He really doesn't want either of us digging into either of their histories, and he definitely doesn't want you to write a book."

"And he has the final word?" Simon's voice wasn't cool, but almost.

"It's his family."

"It's my family, too." Simon's eyes had narrowed, and Abby lifted her chin.

"I respect his wishes, and I hope you will, too."

Simon stared at her for a long moment while Abby waited, her heart starting to thud. She didn't like the look on his face, and already their kiss felt like a million years ago.

"I'm sorry, Abby," he finally said quietly. "But I can't do that."

SIMON

"What?" Abby blinked at him, mouth agape, and Simon tried for a conciliatory smile. He hadn't meant to sound so obdurate, and he didn't know how their conversation had driven downhill so quickly, but somehow they were here, both of them feeling aggressive, shoulders back, chins lifted, any memory of a kiss evaporated.

"I'm not willing to let this go," he said, as gently as he could. "It affects my family, as well. It's my history as much as yours."

"How? It's my grandfather—"

"And my grandmother."

"You don't even know if your grandmother knew this Matthew Lawson—"

"Actually, I do."

She stared at him for a moment, looking even more flummoxed. Her face was flushed, her hazel eyes glittering, a strand of dark hair stuck to her cheek. She swiped it away with an impatient hand. "What are you talking about?"

"I rang my sister the other day, after I saw you. Eleanor, she's a bit obsessed with our genealogy, although she's done research on my father's side rather than my mother's. The Irish side."

He smiled, but Abby just stared at him, and so, resolutely, he continued. "I asked her to look through some boxes of photos and memorabilia, stuff that's been kept in her loft since my grandmother died, when she took command of it all. It took some digging, but she found a photo. She sent it to me—I can show it to you." He reached for his phone and swiped the screen, scrolling through his emails to find the relevant one. "Here."

He handed her the phone, and Abby took it without a word. She gazed down at the photo that had mesmerized Simon when he'd first seen it—two men in 82nd Airborne uniforms, standing before the front door of a terraced house, shoulders back, a determined yet haunted look in their eyes.

"It was dated June 1944. Right before D-Day." He paused. "The back of the photo had their names and the place where the photo was taken, in my grandmother's handwriting—Lieutenant Tom Reese and Sergeant Matthew Lawson, Holmside Road."

She stared at the photo for another moment—Tom so blond and assured, his small smile a little cocky despite the fear in his eyes, while Matthew was dark-haired and eyed, the expression on his face so serious, it had unsettled Simon a bit. The two men couldn't have been more different, and it had made him wonder all the more how they were connected.

Finally Abby looked up. "Why didn't you tell me?" It wasn't quite an accusation, but almost, and Simon understood why, just as he'd known, on some level, why he hadn't told her right away. Because he'd feared this very reaction, because he could feel their relationship already becoming complicated, and that scared him. Because part of him preferred Abby when she was quiet and reserved, and it was his choice whether to wake her up or not.

"I was planning to today," he said. "And I just have."

"You know what I mean."

Were they *arguing*? Something prickled in Simon, something old and remembered. He hated arguments. He hated confrontation. Had dreaded it as a child, when it felt like an explosion that came out of nowhere, and he'd still loathed it later, when it had been more reasoned and understandable. The result was he'd done his best to avoid it whenever he could. Much easier simply to smile, offer a light laugh, defuse any tension by pretending it wasn't there.

Yet all afternoon Abby had been sharp, unsheathing claws he hadn't realized she'd had, making little digs that were becoming harder and harder to ignore even as he'd tried to.

"I suppose," he said after a moment, "I didn't want you to get skittish on me."

"Skittish? I'm not a *horse*."

They really were arguing. "I'm sorry. Wrong word."

Abby looked down at the photo again and then thrust the phone back at Simon. "I mean what I said. This has to stop."

He didn't think she was just talking about his research. "Abby, I understand why you want to protect your father—"

"You really don't."

"Then tell me?"

She stared at him hard, and for a second he thought she'd say—what? He had no idea, but he knew there was *something* there, something hidden, something dark and painful that she needed to say but wouldn't.

"All I'm asking, Simon, is for you to stop researching my family. I think that's a reasonable request."

"Matthew Lawson is not your family," he returned quietly.

She jerked back a little at that, as if he'd hurt her. He hadn't meant to, but he knew he wasn't going to back down. For her sake as well as his. As well as history's.

"I know you may find this hard to believe, but I'm saying this because I care about you. And I don't think dropping this simply because your father said so is the right thing to do—"

"And you think you have the right to decide what's best for me? To make decisions for me, as if I'm a child?"

"No, of course not. But this is about my family too, my history, and I don't want to leave it here." He thought about telling her what else he'd found—the group on Facebook for veterans of the 82nd Airborne and their families, the message he'd sent to a veteran named Guy Wessel, who had written back saying he remembered Matthew Lawson very well. He lived in a senior living facility outside Minneapolis and had invited Simon to visit him. He hadn't said any of that to Abby yet because he'd been afraid it might be too much for her to take in. Now he knew it was.

She stared at him for another long moment. "So you're refusing," she said flatly.

Simon could feel himself start to shut down. It was an instinctive response, like an animal retreating into its shell, a door closing firmly shut. A part of him went dark even as he kept his voice light. "I don't think we need to put it quite like that," he said with a little smile. "Let's just think about this sensibly—"

"I don't need to think about it at all," she snapped. "I asked you to stop doing something and you won't. That's the end of it now." Her meaning was clear, as were her actions, as she strode away from him, back to the farmhouse, Bailey clambering up to follow her at a trot, the leafy green branches of the apple trees soon swallowing them both up so Simon was left alone.

CHAPTER FOURTEEN

March 1944

In the days after the air raid, Lily walked around in a daze, her mind a welter of indecision. One moment she was certain she should report Matthew to the proper authorities, show the paper she'd tucked in the back of her underwear drawer, and let those in charge take care of the matter. The next moment she told herself to stop being so silly, of *course* Matthew wasn't some sort of spy, and she should destroy the slip of paper and simply get on with things.

She thought of trying to translate the few words on the paper, as if that might make a difference, but she didn't know any German speakers, and she was afraid to ask for a German dictionary from the library, if they even had one, in case it aroused suspicion. Who wanted to know German these days? Then once again she'd tell herself to stop being so ridiculous.

Then she'd walk past one of the posters by the Underground, and see the stern warnings about careless talk costing lives, "Tell Nobody—Not Even Her", and a shudder of apprehension went through her, and she knew she had to do something.

"Do you think there are many spies in London?" she asked Iris during their lunch break. Iris was prising apart her sandwich and licking off the potted meat, something Lily found revolting, especially when it was accompanied by one of her drippy sniffs.

"Spies? You mean Germans?"

"Yes, what other kind would there be?"

"Oh, I'm sure there are heaps," Iris said in the lofty tone of someone who liked to think they knew what they were talking about. "Ever so many. One *hears* things, doesn't one?"

"Hears things? What do you mean?"

"Well, one only has to look at the posters," Iris said with a shrug. "A single word and—boom! A plane goes up."

"Yes, but that's just to scare us, surely." Lily was quickly realizing that, as usual, Iris knew no more than she did. She just liked to talk as if she did. "It doesn't mean anything."

"They wouldn't put all the posters up if they didn't have reason, would they?"

"I suppose, but surely they're just being cautious."

"Why are you asking, anyway?" Iris leaned forward, her eyes alight. "Do you suspect someone? I've always wondered about Miss Challis."

"Miss Challis!" Lily gave a huff of disbelieving laughter as she quickly checked to see if their supervisor was listening. "Oh Iris, don't be absurd."

"She's so *keen*. It's obviously a cover." Iris let out a hoot of laughter before she licked her bread again. "So who do you suspect?"

"No one," Lily returned sharply. "I was just wondering."

"Back to work, girls," Miss Challis called out, and Iris gave Lily a laughing look before turning back to her typewriter with a sniff.

A few days ago, the HMS *Spartan* had been sunk by a Henschel Hs 293 glide bomb, with a loss of five officers and forty-one enlisted men. Their trays were full, and there was no time to worry about spies.

As the days passed without her acting, Lily feared her indecision might cost someone something—who even knew what or how much? If Matthew was passing on information from the 82nd Airborne… she pictured the poster Iris had mentioned, of a man shaking hands and wishing a pilot good luck for tomorrow, and then, below, the plane going up in flames. What if her silence caused something like that to happen? What if the letters filling her tray every day were actually her fault?

It was too hideous a thought to contemplate.

But then she reminded herself that Matthew might not be doing anything of the sort. There could be a perfectly reasonable explanation for the pigeons, the note in German. The last thing she wanted to do was get him into trouble, or waste precious time and manpower investigating someone who was perfectly innocent. There *had* to be a reason for it all. It was just that Lily couldn't think what it was.

But then it was too late to do anything, because she came home from work one evening just a few days after the raid, to find both Tom Reese and Matthew Lawson on the doorstep, looking very smart in their dress uniforms.

"They're here to say goodbye," Sophie cried in a voice whose gaiety sounded almost manic. Lily had barely spoken to her sister since the raid; lost in her own circling, worrying thoughts, she hadn't paid much attention to Sophie's huffy silence. "I said we simply must have a photo." She brandished their father's Selfix that usually only came out on holidays.

"Oh, I see." Lily glanced at Matthew, who was looking at her in concern. "Are you leaving right away?"

"In the morning," Tom said. "Up to Lincolnshire until the invasion."

"But they'll be back to visit, won't you?" Sophie turned to Tom with a bright smile. "You promised to take me to The Berkeley again, you know."

"And I will, of course I will," Tom rejoined as he jangled some change in his pocket. "Wouldn't miss it for the world." He smiled at Sophie, who smiled back, and Lily looked at Matthew, who said nothing.

So this was it, then. They were going. Perhaps they'd return, perhaps they wouldn't. Lily knew it wouldn't be the same, and she'd missed the opportunity to tell someone about the pigeons, the paper. She felt a treacherous relief, that it was out of her hands.

Then she remembered Matthew telling her he thought she'd be brave when it mattered. Now she knew she wouldn't be.

"Do be careful," she said, and Sophie called out for them to stand in front of the door. Lily watched them take their places, Matthew looking so very grave, and she felt a cry catch at her throat. This was *goodbye*. It felt too awful, too final. There was still so much she wanted to say, and it had nothing to do with that wretched little piece of paper.

The picture was taken and Carol and Richard came out to say their farewells, and Lily stood on the side and felt as if it were all happening to someone else. She met Matthew's gaze and he smiled at her, and she tried to smile back but found she couldn't.

And then they were leaving, with another round of shaking hands and a chorus of farewells, and through it all Lily found she could barely speak at all.

"I hope I see you again," Matthew said, as he pressed her cold fingers against his own. "I'll come back on leave, if... if you want me to?" His dark gaze moved over her face as if looking for answers.

"Yes," Lily managed, and did not say anything more, although words—so many words—crowded in her throat and lodged in her mouth. *Are you a spy? Do you care for me? Be safe. No matter who or what you are, I don't want one of those awful letters to be written about you.*

Then they were gone, swallowed up by the darkness of blackout London, and Lily stared after them disconsolately, hardly able to believe she'd stayed so silent.

Sophie flounced inside, edgy and restless, picking up a little vase on the hall table and then putting it down again with a clatter, before twitching away to the fireplace, and then flopping onto the sofa with a long, drawn-out sigh. Carol gave her a reproving look and went into the kitchen. Lily followed.

"Do you think Tom will visit you?" Lily asked as they were washing up after dinner. She meant it as a peace offering, a way to bridge the stilted silence that had emerged between them since the raid.

"Would you rather he didn't?" Sophie retorted, thrusting a soapy plate at her so hard Lily nearly dropped it.

"Of course I wouldn't."

"Are you quite certain about that, Lily? Because sometimes I think you want the exciting things only to happen to you."

This was so unfair, and so patently untrue, that all Lily could do was stare.

"Oh, I don't mean it," Sophie cried. "I know I don't. I'm just so *afraid*, Lily. Tom… he'll be parachuting down behind enemy lines. Can you even imagine? And he's so brave, I know he'll be right in the thick of the action. Sometimes I wish I were a man." She spoke so savagely that Lily simply blinked. "Instead we just have to wait and wait and *wait*," Sophie said in disgust as she picked up another plate. "And pour tea and say 'chin up, duck' and be so *stupid*. I can't stand it. I really can't." She threw Lily a sudden, despairing look. "Do you know I envied you, being caught in the raid? Helping someone? I haven't done a *thing*."

"You and Tom were caught in a raid—"

"Snogging in a doorway! I should be ashamed of myself, I suppose." Yet Lily knew she wasn't.

"Do you think it will be soon?" she asked. "The invasion?"

"Who knows." Sophie still sounded disgusted, and so very tired. "Who bloody knows."

*

As February gave way to March and then April, a sense of expectation silently built but was not rewarded. The winter had felt long and dark and cold; February had been far colder than expected, and on the eighteenth of the month the British cruiser *Penelope* was torpedoed by a German submarine as it was returning to Anzio, with a loss of four hundred lives. Miss Challis hired another girl to help in the Casualties Section.

Yet, despite the losses—some of the worst of the war—hope began to unfurl, a tattered flag blowing in a determined breeze. In March, the border with Northern Ireland was closed, causing people to wonder why. Then, in the middle of March, General Eisenhower moved his entire headquarters out of London, and again whispers reigned—all rumor with no reality and no reward.

Every night, the Mathers huddled around the wireless, longing to hear anything other than the list of losses and the variable victories, wanting to hear John Snagge's sonorous voice tell them that planes were flying over the Channel towards France, but it didn't happen. Nearly five years on and everyone was still waiting.

Throughout those long months of lurching into spring, Tom wrote to Sophie sporadically, claiming he wasn't "much of one for letters"; Matthew wrote not at all, which Lily tried not to take to heart.

"Perhaps he isn't much of one for writing, either," Sophie said, all sympathy now that she felt somewhat secure in Tom's affections.

Lily gave a small, pinched smile. She did not think Matthew's silence was due to lack of ability.

Then, in early April, Sophie received a letter from Tom asking if he and Matthew could visit while they were on leave. The weather was warm but dull, and they suggested going to the cinema; *Bees in Paradise* was playing, and was meant to be, according to Tom, "a real gas".

Sophie was in an immediate flurry, ripping out seams of an old dress in order to freshen it up with a bit of bright ribbon, while Lily's old anxieties about the pigeons in Matthew's shed rose up. For the last few months, she'd managed mostly to quash them; while he certainly wasn't out of mind, the potential dangers he presented had been. But now she was going to see him, and she had no idea what he was, never mind how she felt about him, or how he felt about her.

On one gray afternoon in early April, the two GIs appeared at the door of the house in Holmside Road, familiar yet strange in their uniforms—Tom's brash smile, Matthew's quiet containment. They hadn't changed at all.

Sophie chatted all the way to the Underground, her voice full of laughter, her manner a bit frantic as she linked arms with Tom and sauntered ahead. Lily gave Matthew a strained smile; this parade to the Tube station felt as awkward as that walk across the Common back in January when they'd first met, which saddened her, because surely they should be better than this by now, on easier terms, at least.

Then Matthew reached over and touched her arm. "How are you?" he asked quietly, as if he really wanted to know the answer, as if it mattered.

"I'm all right. It's been so long." She didn't know whether she meant waiting for the invasion, or waiting for him. Perhaps both.

"It has," he agreed. "I read about the *Mahratta*, and I thought of you."

Lily's throat closed. "Only sixteen survivors," she whispered. And over two hundred letters to type.

Matthew nodded. "I wonder how you bear it. To only deal with the horror of war, and none of the hope."

"Is there hope, in war?"

He nodded, the movement swift and sure. "There has to be. A belief, a faith that one day this will all be over, and the evil of fascism will be forever wiped from the world."

He spoke with such bitterness, such ferocity, that Lily nearly stumbled in her step. He *couldn't* be a spy, she thought yet again, filled with buoyant relief. *Unless he was simply trying to gain her trust.* Her thoughts forever circled.

"People are starting to hope now, I think," she said. "You hear things."

Matthew nodded again, solemnly this time. "Yes," he said simply, and that was enough.

"Come on, you two!" Sophie called back to them. "Or we'll miss the film."

The film was atrocious—a ridiculous comedy filled with scantily clad women inhabiting a mysterious island where men were as good as drones, used only for breeding. Lily couldn't help but flinch at the crude baseness of it, although, next to her, Sophie hooted with laughter and Tom made appreciative guffaws.

Matthew's expression was rigid, and Lily suspected he found the absurdity of it all as excruciating as she did, the wide-eyed women with their exaggerated moues and the buffoonish soldiers bumbling around… it was the grossest parody of what they all knew, making a joke of what was their painful reality, and all for a few cheap laughs.

Back outside, Tom suggested they all get a drink, and they ended up drinking beer in a shabby pub near Piccadilly, a far cry from champagne at The Berkeley. Sophie squeezed in on the banquette next to Tom, his arm wrapped around her, while Matthew and Lily sat in chairs.

The mood of the city was both dour and expectant; the evenings were light and warm, and everyone was straining for news that still hadn't come, and Lily felt that same push-pull here with Matthew, half of her clamoring to demand he tell her who he was, while the other half stayed meekly silent.

"Will you get any more leave?" she asked in a low voice after several minutes of silence. Tom and Sophie were wrapped up in themselves, her head on his shoulder, making the situation all the more awkward.

"I don't know." Matthew spread his hands in apology. "They don't tell us much, I'm afraid."

"It must be soon, though, surely."

"One hopes."

Lily caught a bead of condensation on the side of her glass with her finger. "Will you write to me?" she asked, feeling bold for saying as much as that.

"Do you want me to?"

Lily looked up in surprise and Matthew gave that lovely quirk of a smile.

"It's only, sometimes it seems..." He paused, and Lily leapt in clumsily.

"I don't... that is... I would like it very much if you wrote to me. I should have said before."

"Good. I'm glad."

He touched her hand briefly with her own, barely a brush, and yet it was enough.

Lily smiled and looked down, afraid that the expression on her face would be too much for Matthew to see.

An hour later, they were heading towards the Underground station when Tom broke away from Sophie to stumble towards them, a glazed but happy look on his face.

"Look." His gaze was somewhere between the two of them, so Lily couldn't tell which one of them he was addressing. "Sophie and I, we're going to find somewhere. Can you make your own way back?"

"Sophie!" Lily couldn't keep from calling for her sister, her voice sharpening.

Tom put a large, clumsy hand on her shoulder, a heavy weight she wanted to shrug off.

"I care about her," he said, his tone the sloppily earnest one of a drunk. "I do. I'm going to marry her, you know."

Lily stepped back, angry now. "You barely know her, and you're leaving. Sophie—"

Sophie was leaning against a hoarding, a cigarette to her lips, refusing to look at her.

"She's a grown-up," Tom insisted. "She can make her own decisions."

"Then let Lily talk to her," Matthew said quietly.

"Go home, Lily," Sophie called out, sounding tired. "Just go home. I'm fine."

Lily watched in silent outrage as Tom turned and went back to Sophie, slipping an arm around her waist. Together, both of them stumbling a bit, they disappeared into the darkness, to who only knew where. A hotel? A dark alley?

"I'm sorry," Matthew said quietly.

Lily pulled her coat more tightly around her, though the evening was warm.

"There's nothing to be sorry for." She shouldn't feel this desolate. Sophie was simply living her life. And if Tom did marry her, it would be all right in the end, she supposed. "What is going to happen?" she wondered out loud, realizing she wasn't asking only about Sophie and Tom. "What is going to happen to all of us?"

Realization, sudden and swift, clutched her by the throat, made it hard to breathe. Tom and Matthew would be in France soon, or maybe Belgium, parachuting behind enemy lines, risking their lives. Nothing was certain, not one single thing. All they had was this moment, and Sophie at least had taken it.

She turned back to Matthew, who was watching her with the quiet intensity she'd come to know—and like. "I thought you were a German spy," she blurted.

Matthew's expression, strangely, did not change, and he didn't answer.

"Are you?" she demanded, feeling both desperate and foolish.

"A German spy?" He did not sound as surprised, as incredulous, as she would have hoped. "No."

Lily shook her head slowly. "But…"

"Why did you think I was?"

"The pigeons. I saw them in your shed. There was a message in German…"

"You went in the shed?" He looked bemused, almost impressed, which confused Lily all the more.

"What are you?" she asked, a bit desperately. "Who are you?"

Matthew stared at her, a long, steady look that made her afraid even as it made her hope. She waited, her handbag clutched to her chest, her heart starting to thud.

"I'm a Jew," he finally said quietly.

Lily stared. "A *Jew*."

"A German Jew. I emigrated to America in 1938, after Kristallnacht." He waited, while Lily's mind raced.

Kristallnacht… it had been in the newspapers, but she'd only been fifteen at the time. She couldn't remember exactly what it had all been about, and she felt a sudden rush of shame at her ignorance.

"I'm sorry," she whispered. "I don't know—"

"The night of the broken glass. Jewish businesses were ransacked or destroyed by the Nazis. Jewish synagogues were burned. Jewish men were arrested. And for all of this the Jews were blamed and fined a billion marks." He spoke flatly, matter-of-factly, yet, for the first time, Lily could hear the German accent he'd been trying so hard to hide. "My father was beaten to death in the office below our home."

"*Matthew…*" Lily gulped in horror.

"My mother hid me. I was seventeen, and she was afraid I'd be taken to a concentration camp, like so many others. They were looking, asking for me."

Lily's mouth opened and closed. She couldn't manage a word.

"I left the next day. I went to stay with my uncle in Munich, and when things calmed down—or seemed to—he arranged my visa and transport on a Spanish merchant ship to America, so I could start a new life. I knew English from school, and I took classes when I arrived. I didn't want to be German any longer."

"I'm so sorry." Lily had no other words. Tears swam in her eyes and she blinked, causing them to spill down her cheeks. She felt as if she didn't have the right to cry; Matthew looked stony.

"I joined the army in 1942, because I wanted to fight the Nazis. I've wanted nothing more. I'm no spy, Lily."

"I know you aren't," she choked. "Of course not."

"But you were right to be suspicious. I'm not... like Tom."

"What do you mean?"

"I can't say more than that. I was trained separately from him, and I have separate orders. But, trust me, I hate the Nazis more than you do."

She stared at him—his fierce eyes, his hands clenched into fists at his side from the force of his emotion. "I believe you," she said softly. "I believe it all."

In retrospect, Lily couldn't be sure what happened next. Did she step towards him, or did Matthew reach for her? It seemed to happen seamlessly, all at once, so that his arms were around her and his lips were on hers—her very first kiss.

She closed her eyes as she reveled in the moment—the hard press of his lips, like a seal, and his arms tight around her, as if he were fusing her to himself. She knew the kiss was goodbye, for however long. Maybe forever, and yet in that moment she was still filled with hope and even joy.

Someone nearby catcalled, and Matthew stepped away from her. "I'll write to you," he said. "And will you—"

"I'll write to you."

"Write—yes." That crooked smile. "But also... will you wait?"

Wait? The enormity of his question felt like a wave crashing over her, pulling her under. *Wait... for him?* "Yes," Lily said. "*Yes.*"

"Even though I'm Jewish?"

"I don't care about that."

"Your mother will."

"I don't care." She spoke with fierce certainty, but Matthew didn't look convinced.

"There will be time to talk of such things," he said, but Lily wondered if there would be. "It's getting late. Your mother will be worried." He took her arm and led her down the steps to the station. There was no chance for them to say anything further as they moved with the crowds onto the noisy train.

In front of the little house on Holmside Road, Matthew kissed her again, brief and hard, and then he said goodbye. It happened so quickly, Lily felt as if she could have blinked and missed it; suddenly he was walking away from her, his head down, and she was tottering down the path to her front door, her head spinning. Everything had changed.

Five weeks later, Lily and Sophie woke up in the middle of the night to the loud, insistent drone of planes flying overhead, but strangely no air raid siren, making it seem silent, when it was anything but.

Heedless of the danger, Sophie ran to the window and undid the blackout curtains, throwing open the window to the balmy June night.

"*Sophie,*" Lily protested, although she knew it would do no good. Since the night she'd walked off with Tom and had only returned in mid-afternoon, she'd been like a different person, remote, preoccupied, as if she were already somewhere else, waiting for her real life to begin.

But then Lily felt as if she were somewhere else as well, her mind consumed by the letters that came from Matthew, two or three times a week, revealing nothing yet saying everything, because they were from him to her, and he wanted to write—even if it was simply about what he ate in the canteen, or the color of the sky on a May morning.

"Lily, *look*." Sophie gestured to the night sky, now streaked with light.

Lily hurried to the window, her mouth opening soundlessly as she stared at the dozens of planes moving purposefully across the midnight canvas of the night sky, like arrows pointing east. *So many…*

"What…" she began, but of course she knew. The invasion was happening at last.

"It's beginning," Sophie said, and she sounded triumphant. "It's finally beginning."

PART TWO

CHAPTER FIFTEEN

June 6, 1944

Matthew sat hunched over, his elbows braced on his knees, on one of the metal seats set in facing rows along the length of the C-47 plane as it moved steadily towards the Channel.

He was wearing seventy pounds of equipment—a parachute on his back, and another strapped to his chest; a gas mask tied to one leg, and a small hoe for digging foxholes attached to the other. From his belt hung a first-aid kit, a bayonet, a trench knife, and two fragmentation hand grenades, along with extra ammunition. He had another grenade in his musette bag, along with all of his personal gear, as well as his most important possession: a bundle of letters from Lily. His shoulders ached and his stomach felt as if he'd swallowed a stone whole.

Next to him, another paratrooper of the 508th was cracking his knuckles and chewing gum with grim determination. Across from him, a whey-faced boy of no more than nineteen had been sick down his front. Whether that was from nerves or the motion of the plane which had been flying in circles waiting for other planes to join up, Matthew didn't know. Further down his row, Tom Reese sat, his face set in grim lines. Matthew didn't meet his eye.

The last twenty-four hours had felt utterly surreal, as if none of it was actually happening, or, if it was, he was merely an observer to someone's else drama. He'd felt this way before, back in Fraustadt in 1938, when stormtroopers had broken into his father's office, smashing glass and hurling papers and books to the floor with looks of naked, savage glee on their faces.

Matthew had stood, transfixed, on the stairs from their flat above, while his father, clad in a dressing gown and slippers, had strode through the mess, demanding that the soldiers stop their needless destruction and leave the premises. For such unthinkable folly, he'd been kicked in the stomach by a stormtrooper's jackboot, and when he'd fallen to the floor, they had continued their savagery, kicking and beating him, while Matthew had watched, his mind and body both frozen with terror, unable to comprehend that this was actually happening, that it already had.

After a few terrifying minutes, or perhaps just seconds, his mother had urged him back up the stairs, her face gaunt, her eyes filled with mute horror. "They will come for you next," she'd hissed as they'd crept towards the kitchen. "You're seventeen, practically a man."

And so, man that he hadn't been, he'd spent the night hidden in a cupboard, his knees up to his chin, his body aching, his mind both numb and blank, before learning the next morning that his father was dead.

Just after dawn, his mother had handed him a parcel of food and another of clothes, with the best of her jewelry sewn into the hem of a pair of trousers. She'd hugged him tightly, and his sister Gertie had clung to him, while his little brothers Franz and Arno had stared silently. Then a man he'd never seen before had come to the door, urging him to leave all he'd known and follow him he didn't even know where.

He'd spent the next nine months moving from house to house, a parade of nights spent in attics or sheds or understair cupboards, until he'd made it to his uncle's in Munich and then to Spain and then to America, the whole process an endless, exhausting fight for freedom, a blur in his mind now, of kindly faces and anxious eyes, what food could be spared bolted quickly, days and nights passing as if the same.

Yesterday, while they'd all been kicking their heels outside an air hangar in Leicestershire, knowing the invasion was imminent, he'd felt the same sort of separation of self; they'd been told, after bad weather the night before had kept them grounded, that they would fly that evening, and then be dropped ten miles inland on the Cotentin Peninsula of Normandy. If the sea assault failed, there would be no rescue for the men stuck deep behind enemy lines.

But Matthew was used to that sort of hopelessness.

He'd become used to it after Kristallnacht, when the reality of what was happening in his home country finally penetrated his arrogant, teenaged naivety. He was the son of an accountant, a German before he was a Jew, proud, like the rest of his family, of his Prussian heritage, his father having served in the First World War. He'd thought those things had mattered. He'd believed, so ridiculously, so wrongly, that stormtroopers didn't come for the likes of him and his family, good Germans with proper pedigree and education, who had fought in wars and spoke several languages, patriots rather than religious zealots.

He thought they came for the Jews who spoke Polish and wore yarmulkes and muttered in their pidgin languages of German and Hebrew. Not that those were deserving of such treatment—of course they weren't, but still, he'd thought back then, they were different. Perhaps a bit too different. And so Matthew had somehow convinced himself he and his family were safe.

He'd had plenty of opportunity to learn that he wasn't in the years since then. Plenty of time to look back on his arrogant folly, when the Nuremberg Laws had passed in 1935, and somehow he still hadn't thought it mattered. Yes, he'd had to go to a different school, one only for Jews, but he had friends there, and, for the most part, people were still kind; his old math teachers had apologized to him, tearfully, when he'd seen him in the street.

And yes, he was no longer allowed to marry a non-Jew, not that he'd even been thinking about girls at that point. His father could have only Jewish customers, but somehow he accepted even that; money turned tight, but they had enough and it would all surely pass. Hitler had to go out of favor, because no thinking German could support such craven idiocy for long. Or so his father had said.

The C-47 stopped circling and began to straighten out. In the eerie red light that was meant to accustom them to night vision, Matthew looked out and saw that a flotilla of planes had joined them as they made for France, gliding like steel ghosts through a night sky. There would be no turning back.

As they'd been loaded onto the plane less than an hour before, the mood of joking camaraderie that had prevailed during the forty-eight hours—and really, months and even years—of waiting had become suddenly somber. Hours ago, they'd been using British money for their poker games, throwing dice, cracking jokes, but now everyone fell silent as they took their seats and a recorded message from General Eisenhower, meant for all Allied forces, was played.

"You are about to embark upon the Great Crusade, towards which we have striven these many months. The eyes of the world are upon you. The hopes and prayers of liberty-loving people everywhere march with you. In company with our brave Allies and brothers-in-arms on other fronts, you will bring about the destruction of the German war machine, the elimination of Nazi tyranny over oppressed peoples of Europe, and security for ourselves in a free world. Your task will not be an easy one. Your enemy is well trained, well equipped, and battle-hardened. We will accept nothing less than full victory. Good luck! And let us all beseech the blessing of Almighty God upon this great and noble undertaking."

The import of his words, of what they were doing, was impossible to comprehend, as if someone was playing a massive joke and they were the punchline. These pale-faced men hunched over in their seats, burdened by their own equipment, were, quite literally, tasked to save the world. It was absurd. It was impossible.

It was happening.

Matthew glanced around at the grim faces of his comrades, bluish in the weird light, the rattling of the plane and the drone of its engine making speech impossible, not that anyone was inclined to talk. What were they thinking? How many of them would survive? Matthew knew the odds weren't good. There was every likelihood that they wouldn't even make it to France—their plane would be hit by antiaircraft fire before the drop and they would plummet to their fiery deaths, their war over before it had really begun.

He prayed—and it had been a long time since he had prayed—that that wouldn't happen. He wanted—*needed* a chance to go back to Germany. To find his family, and to seek justice for his father's death. And then return to Lily…

"Up!"

As one, the men rose from their seats, their movements lumbered by their heavy and bulky equipment.

"Equipment check!"

Each man checked the static line of the man in front of him to make sure it was securely attached before jumping, so their parachutes would open properly. If they didn't, it was just one more way to die.

Matthew craned his head to look out the wide-open exit door, and something in him jolted in ridiculous surprise when he saw the clouds of smoke and orange lights from the tracer fire. It looked eerily beautiful, until he watched, incredulous, as a plane nearby suddenly exploded in a fireball and pirouetted gracefully towards the sea. Behind him, a man muttered something that sounded like a prayer, or maybe he'd just said "Jesus".

The plane shuddered beneath them, and someone cried out and then fell silent, ashamed. The air was full of crackling, thick with smoke, and still Matthew had trouble believing any of it was happening, even as the plane shuddered again, and then jerked like a living thing. It took him a stunned moment to realize they'd been hit.

The jumpmaster cursed as the plane started to lurch like a drunk beneath their boots, and the men staggered, grabbing onto each other to stay upright, no one meeting anyone's eyes, afraid of what they might see there.

Time seemed to have slowed down and sped up all at once, and Matthew heard a roaring in his ears—whether it was the sound of the battle now raging all around them or simply the rush of his own beating blood, he didn't know.

The plane continued to twist and turn, writhing like an animal, and one of the men crossed himself, muttering the Hail Mary in a strong Brooklyn accent. Matthew wondered, in a distanced, disinterested sort of way, if this was actually the end. He might be dying, and he wasn't even *sure*.

The jumpmaster shouted for them to pay attention, and then he began to push the equipment bags out the door, a jumpsuited Santa with his sacks of crucial toys. Then, as Matthew watched, the first man went, stepping straight out into air, like a magic trick. They'd all had to complete at least five jumps during training, but those seemed like child's play compared to this. The sky was full of gunfire and smoke. They were parachuting not into a muddy English field or a bayou in Louisiana, but enemy territory. Matthew might be dead in five minutes, maybe less.

He shuffled forward as one by one the men stepped out into the air and disappeared. His moment was coming, and it made him think of Lily, her letters tucked away in his pack. He hadn't seen her since that night by the Underground, when she'd told him she'd thought he was a German spy because of those ridiculous pigeons, and then he'd kissed her. When his whole world had shifted on its axis, and he'd realized he needed to survive this war, not just for his family, but for himself—and Lily.

Although the 82nd had been kicking their heels for the better part of May, they hadn't been granted leave, and so Matthew had had to content himself with letters. He did not consider himself an emotional man, and any tender feeling he might have nurtured had been suppressed for the sake of his situation.

No one had cared what he'd felt when he'd been one of a hundred blank-eyed refugees packed in the cargo hold of a Spanish freighter. And no one had cared when he'd washed up on the shores of New York, having to convince a bored immigration inspector that he wasn't a drain on the American people or their economy.

When the US had declared war in 1941, Matthew had found himself in the surprising position of being classified as an enemy alien, and once again no one had cared that he was a Jew, not a Nazi. When he'd first enlisted, after his basic training, he'd been regarded with suspicion; after just three months, he'd been rounded up with a dozen other German-born Jews and sent to an internment camp in Illinois, where they'd been subjected to hard labor without any explanation.

Eventually he'd discovered he'd been sent there because a German spy had been caught off the coast of Canada whose contact had the same last name as he did. He'd realized then that in Germany he'd been made to be a Jew first; in America he was just German.

After nearly a year of such treatment, he had, without explanation, been ordered to Camp Ritchie in Maryland, where, thanks to his knowledge of German, he'd been earmarked for the course in Interrogation of Prisoners of War. He'd changed his name to a gentile one, not wanting the same mistake to happen twice, and now he was here, about to jump, Lily's letters in his pocket the only thing anchoring him to this earth anymore.

Dear Matthew, I'm no good at writing letters; I don't know what to say except that I think of you often. So often…

Someone jabbed Matthew in the back and he realized he was next. He stepped to the edge of the plane, its floor tilting under him, nearly making him stagger right out the door. Beneath him, by the light of the tracer fire, he could see the fields of France spread out in a patchwork of dark greens, punctuated by thick swathes of pine forests. The sky was so full of sound, Matthew had somehow tuned it out, and it felt weirdly and utterly silent as the jumpmaster gave his order, and without a thought but obedience, Matthew stepped out of the plane.

For a second or two, but what felt like an eternity compressed into a moment, he simply fell, windmilling and whirling through the air that rushed by him in a cool, surging stream. Then he felt the painful, breath-catching jerk as his parachute opened like a flower above him. His training took over and he pulled the risers to reduce oscillation as he stopped falling and simply began to float, the sensation strangely gentle in a world that was exploding savagely all around him.

When he blinked the darkened world into focus, he saw another paratrooper floating down in the distance, too far away to call to him or even to wave. The planes that had filled the sky were now far above, a separate, fiery universe as he continued to spiral downwards, entering a dark, silent, dangerous world.

The ground began to rush up to meet him and he saw he was going to land in a field, utterly exposed. He dropped to the ground, hitting it hard; he let out a grunt as he came to a stand and unhooked himself from the parachute before quickly bundling it up. He looked around but could see no one; the only sound was his breathing, loud and ragged. He needed to find cover.

Fumbling for his compass, Matthew checked it and then set off to the east, where he believed their planned meeting point to be. His mind felt cold and clear and as weirdly detached as when he'd been about to jump, but his heart was hammering hard enough to hurt, and he could still hear his own breathing, as if he were gasping for air.

Every nerve and sense was on high, tautened alert, and yet part of him felt as if he were hovering above this scene, idly wondering what might happen next. Would a German sniper blow his head off? Would he step on a mine and be torn to pieces? He had an absurd urge to laugh, and he wondered if it was shock—or hysteria.

He stayed silent, moving steadily across the field, towards a cluster of pine trees that provided the only possible shelter. Once under their covering branches, he released a shaky, pent-up breath and the tension banding across his shoulders and clenching his jaw relaxed, if only a little.

As he stood there, surveying the darkened scene, he realized there was nowhere safe, not from here, all the way through a war-torn Europe, to Fraustadt. He was utterly alone, wandering around the French countryside like some sort of drunk tourist, yet in the uniform of the enemy. He couldn't see another soul, which was both a relief and a worry. No soldiers of any description—but no friends, either.

Where were the rest of the 82nd, not to mention the other divisions, who had parachuted down with him? The wind must have blown everyone off course.

Matthew had no idea where he was, or how close he was to safety, or the enemy. With no alternative but to keep going, he kept to the trees as he began to make his way east. After about twenty tense minutes of skulking along the ridge of pines, he came to a road.

He dropped to his belly at the sound of a car engine, and then watched with that same sense of unreality as a Jeep with four German soldiers in it came and went. He recognized their uniforms, as part of his training had been to learn the emblems and insignia of every single division in the German army, to help with his interrogative abilities. Yet to actually *see* living and breathing German soldiers wearing those gray greatcoats—*four* of them—made him shake his head in wonder. Again he fought that unwise urge to laugh.

He waited another ten minutes, as several motorcycles with German riders passed. Another ten minutes, as sweat trickled from under his helmet and down his back, and then finally a further ten before he felt safe enough to dart, crouched, across the road.

On the other side of the track, he let out another shaky breath. The unfamiliar landscape stretched away endlessly in the dark.

He walked another half-hour, searching for someone, something, *anything* that looked familiar, that would mean he wasn't alone. He halted on the edge of a clearing, some instinct making him go still even before he saw the three soldiers standing by a mounted machine gun, smoking.

How to pass them? He didn't trust his own ability to take them all out, and standing there, he realized he'd never killed a man. He'd never actually *hurt* anyone before, and yet he had two grenades dangling from his belt, another in his pack.

He must have made some movement, some sound, without realizing, for one of the soldiers looked up, sniffing the air like a wolf as he dropped his cigarette and ground it beneath his jackboot.

"*Wer ist da?*" he called. "*Zeigen Sie ich!*" *Show yourself.* Matthew stayed still, every muscle quivering with tension, with expectation. "*Zeigen Sie ich!*" the man called again, louder this time, his voice more strident.

"*Unteroffizier auf Patrouille,*" Matthew called out before he could think through his response. It was as if some instinct were taking over, possessing his mind, but as soon as he said the words, he knew they were wrong. A corporal on patrol would not be alone.

Kate Hewitt

Sure enough, the man started walking towards the sound of his voice, his pistol now drawn.

"*Zeigen Sie ich*," he said for a third time, and he didn't sound friendly.

It couldn't end like this, all because of a stupid mistake. Matthew fumbled at his belt, his hands curling around one of the grenades.

The man kept walking, the other two coming up behind him, pistols drawn as well. Three against one.

Matthew pulled the safety ring and hurled the grenade towards the men.

He didn't wait to see whether the grenade had hit the intended target; he tore through the woods, his heart feeling as if it could beat right out of his chest. He heard the crack of a pistol and he jerked instinctively even though he realized after a few tense seconds that he hadn't been hit.

He kept running, clawing at the undergrowth as he barreled through the forest, his panting breaths tearing at his chest, everything in him rearing up, wild.

He heard footsteps behind him, too close, too fast, and he whirled around, his hand on his pistol, only to stumble back in shock at the sight of Tom Reese chasing him, his face spattered with mud, the whites of his eyes almost glowing as he stared at him.

"What the *hell*…" Tom choked out and Matthew saw he was clutching his knife. He knocked it out of his hand with one sharp movement, borne of instinct rather than intention.

"Why were you chasing me?" he demanded.

"Why were you speaking *German*?"

Matthew stared at him; he felt as if his mind had gone very cold and clear, that first fog of fear and disbelief dissolving completely as his breathing slowed. He wasn't being chased. He wasn't going to die. Not right now, at any rate. "We're not safe here," he said shortly. "Those Nazis were following me."

"*I* was following you. I heard you—"

"Why didn't you make yourself known?"

"Because there was a damned German right there!" Tom stooped to pick up his knife.

Matthew stared at him coldly.

"Let's walk." He turned and started striding through the woods, conscious that if his grenade hadn't met the intended target, the Germans were not far behind him. Were they still looking for him? Had the sea assault started?

The sky was lightening to pale gray, streaked with pink. The whole world might have changed forever, and he was stuck in a pine forest with Tom Reese.

"Who *are* you?" Tom demanded hoarsely.

"You know who I am."

"But you spoke German—"

"I am German."

Tom made a choking sound.

"I'm a Jew," Matthew explained shortly. "I emigrated to the US in '38. I was trained and brought here to interrogate German soldiers for military intelligence."

"What? But…" Tom sputtered as he shook his head. "Why did you never tell me? Or anyone?"

"Because of the reaction you just had."

"Why should I believe you?" Tom asked, sounding belligerent, and Matthew sighed. Another reason he had kept his identity unknown. Those born in Germany had been advised to by their instructing officers. People were suspicious, and stupid.

"Because I was just shot at by three German soldiers," he answered. "And I threw a grenade at them."

"Even so—"

"Don't believe me, then," Matthew cut across him. "But we're going to be gutted like two fish out here if we don't keep moving and find the rest of our platoon. Let's keep walking, Lieutenant."

Silently, looking aggrieved and still suspicious, Tom fell into step beside him. It was one of those absurd twists of fate that Tom Reese, of all people, should be the first man he found here. Despite the time they'd spent together in London, Matthew didn't think Tom would call him his friend, and nor would he call him his.

When he'd first encountered him on the ship over, Matthew had seen the advantages of aligning himself with Tom's obvious Americanness. He was an utterly open book, simple, really, in his brash way. To Matthew, Tom Reese seemed entirely American—blond, brawny, with his loud laugh and wide smile, and an "aw shucks" manner that charmed some and annoyed others. If Matthew stayed in his shadow, his own otherness might be noticed but not questioned.

But he and Tom had never been natural allies. Tom didn't understand him and had, on some level, always distrusted him, while Matthew had struggled with a weary disdain for Tom's easy shallowness, sometimes swallowed by a shameful envy for the simplicity of his life—a farm in Minnesota, parents who were a bit taciturn and stern, an older brother who had outshone Tom on too many occasions. Such little problems; to Matthew, worrying about such things felt like a luxury, but he knew that wasn't fair.

Still, he and Tom had never truly been close, no matter their relationship with Sophie and Lily, who were as different from each other as they were. Yet now they were here, and at least for the immediate future they had to work together. Their very lives were at risk.

"Is West like you?" Tom asked after about fifteen minutes of walking in silence, the only sound the rustle of their footsteps on the fallen pine needles.

"Yes." Guy West was another Ritchie's boy, as they were known, having gone through the training at Camp Ritchie in Maryland to become interrogators of prisoners of war.

"Are there any more?"

"Not in our unit, not that I know, but across the whole army? Thousands."

"Why do you keep yourselves so secretive?" Tom demanded. "Make everyone suspicious? You both seemed pretty off to me, you know. I told Sophie so, and she agreed."

"We don't mean to." Matthew felt suddenly incredibly weary. It was early morning, and he hadn't slept in thirty-six hours. His muscles ached, his jaw pulsed with pain from clenching it, and they were no nearer finding the rest of their platoon. They might be miles away. They might never make it there.

"It's damned strange," Tom said in the tone of someone making a pronouncement, and Matthew simply shrugged. He had no answers to satisfy him. They kept walking.

An hour later, both of them becoming hot and sweaty under a rising, boiling sun, they heard voices and ducked into a hedge before they realized it was women—two tired-looking women with kerchiefs over their white hair. Matthew decided to take a risk, and stepped out into the road, his hands in the air, explaining in clumsy, schoolboy French who they were.

The women exclaimed over them, throwing up their hands and then kissing their cheeks, before they told them what the next village was, and consulting his map, Matthew realized they'd been dropped nearly twenty miles off course. Who knew where all the others were?

They walked all day, seeing no one, not a German, not a French villager, and not an American paratrooper. It started to feel as if they were the only soldiers who had been dropped into France, the only people left alive. Maybe all the Germans had packed up and gone away. Maybe all the Allies had been killed.

All day neither of them spoke; Matthew was too tired and Tom had lapsed into a sullen silence, shooting him darkly suspicious looks that Matthew supposed he was meant to take note of. Did

Tom still not believe him? The idea was ludicrous—and pointless, because they were alone.

That night, they slept in a barn, taking turns to keep watch until, from sheer exhaustion, they both fell asleep against a bale of hay.

They woke to another pinkish dawn, the only sound the lowing of cows, as peaceful a morning as one could possibly wish. The sea assault must have happened by now. Had it been a success? Were their troops pouring into France even in this very moment? In the still silence of a summer's morning, golden sunlight filtering through the cracks in the wooden planks of the barn, it was impossible to imagine.

As they were making to leave, a farmer came into the barn, seeming remarkably unsurprised at the sight of them. He gave them a craggy smile, along with a slice of bread with fresh butter and a cup of warm milk, before sending them on their way.

They walked for two more days, sheltering the next night in another barn, another farmer granting them food and kindness, before they finally heard the strangely welcome sound of shelling in the distance. Both of them came to a halt, the whistle and thud of bombs both familiar and strange. This was finally real.

"They did it," Tom said, his voice somehow managing to sound both wondering and flat. "They came."

"We need to be careful," Matthew replied. They'd been walking along a narrow, dirt road, the isolation they'd experienced over the last forty-eight hours lulling them into a certainly false sense of safety that was now obliterated by the sounds in the distance, the reality of war.

"They're miles away," Tom scoffed, taking a cigarette out of a pack in his breast pocket.

"Don't," Matthew said, but Tom just raised his eyebrows and stuck the cigarette between his lips.

Matthew wasn't sure what happened next—a flash of something in his peripheral vision, a prickling on the back of his neck—but before he even knew what he was doing, he grabbed Tom hard by the shoulder and hurled him flat onto the ground. A crack sounded and a bullet lodged into the pine tree Tom had been leaning against, right where his head would have been.

"*Halt!*" The German voice was distinct and far too close.

Flat on his stomach, Tom stared at Matthew with wide, terrified eyes. Matthew stared back, that cold sense of clarity taking over him once more.

Slowly, as silently as possible, he reached for his pistol. He heard someone walking through the long grass towards them and he propped himself up on one elbow, saw the German soldier frowning as he continued towards them. He was alone, God only knew why, his pistol drawn as he scanned the field in front of him. Matthew took aim and shot.

The soldier staggered and fell; Matthew had aimed for his chest. Next to him, Tom swore quietly. Matthew rose and checked the man was dead; he stared down at his sightless eyes and wondered, only for a second, who he was. Did he have a wife? A sister? Would they receive a letter like the ones Lily typed?

He turned away, only to see Tom standing there, staring.

"You saved my life," he said, but his voice was full of fear.

CHAPTER SIXTEEN

ABBY

"Why are you looking so down in the dumps?" Shannon gave Abby a smiling glance as she poured them both glasses of wine.

"I'm not," Abby said automatically, simply because she was so used to saying she was fine. And she *was* fine. Mostly. It wasn't as if she and Simon had actually been dating, or anything even close to that. But she hadn't heard from him in three days, since she'd walked away from him in the orchard after what had definitely been an argument, and the whole thing made her feel anxious and unhappy.

She'd watched from the living room window, Bailey at her side, as he'd climbed into his car and headed back down the drive. It had felt weirdly anticlimactic, a simple driving away, when part of her had wanted to howl with rage and sorrow in a way she never had before. How had they come to this?

"Something's going on," Shannon said as she tucked her feet up under her legs and took a long swallow of wine. Abby had come over for one of their every-so-often get-togethers at Shannon's little rowhouse in town, for wine and Netflix and a general catch-up on life. It was pretty much the extent of Abby's social life, and she hadn't minded that until now. Until Simon Elliot had walked into her life and stirred everything up, made a turbulent mess of her calm emotions. "Is it about your Brit?"

"He's not mine."

"Oh?" Shannon raised her eyebrows. "That sounds ominous. What's happened?"

Abby hesitated, and then, with a sigh, she decided to come clean. Shannon would ferret it out of her, anyway, and it might feel good to tell her at least a little bit of what had happened.

Abby didn't go into too many details, although Shannon wanted them; she just gave the basics—the picnic by Lake Geneva, the kiss, his visit a couple of days later, their argument.

"He's insisting on digging all this stuff up, even though I asked him not to," she finished, shaking her head before she downed the last of her wine. "And he claims he's doing it for my sake—I mean, how patronizing is that?" Shannon didn't answer, and Abby stared at her, her eyes narrowed. "Don't tell me you agree with him."

"No, not exactly," Shannon said slowly. "But come on, Abby. Don't you think he has something of a point?"

"No, I don't."

Shannon sighed. "I know your relationship with your dad is off limits—"

"What is that supposed to mean?"

"You don't like to talk about it—"

"There's nothing to talk about, Shannon." Abby knew how prickly she sounded. How prickly she *felt*. Why on earth was her best friend coming over all sanctimonious, acting all I-know-better-than-you now? That was not the response she'd wanted at all.

"Okay, I'm sorry." Shannon rested her elbows on her knees as she gave Abby an earnest look. "I know this is upsetting you, but I do feel as if I've got to say something."

"Of course you do," Abby muttered. She'd always taken Shannon's gentle nudges to have more of a social life in her stride. Yes, she probably should get out more. Date more. Live a little. But whatever her friend intended to say next felt like something else entirely.

"Look, Abby, I know your mom and brother's deaths… that was hard."

Hard? Hard was a math test, or a tricky work situation, or maybe a chronic health problem. Her mother and brother's death, her *family's* death, had not been hard. Abby bit her lip to keep from saying something she'd regret.

"Sorry, maybe that didn't come out right," Shannon said, seeming to read Abby's thoughts, as she always did. "It was more than hard. Way more. I do get that."

Abby forced a nod, even though she knew her friend couldn't, not completely.

"It's just, it's been fifteen years, Abby. And I'm not saying you should be over it by now or something. I'm really not. But sometimes it feels like you're living like a—like a hostage."

"A *hostage?*" Abby managed a dry huff of laughter. "You're sounding a bit melodramatic. Anyway, that's not how it is at all."

"Are you sure about that?" Shannon met Abby's scoffing gaze with a steady, sympathetic challenge she couldn't stand. She'd wanted an easy night of wine and *Gilmore Girls*. Why did her friend have to nail her like this? She felt exposed, and she hated that. She shouldn't even feel that way, because Shannon didn't understand at all, even if she thought she did.

"I don't even know what that's supposed to mean," Abby dismissed with a shrug.

Shannon took a deep breath and Abby knew to brace herself. She had a horrible feeling that fifteen years of papering over the cracks wasn't going to cut it anymore. Not that she would have considered it that, all this time. She'd been *fine*. Really, she'd been fine. And their friendship had been fine. They didn't need this kind of heart-to-heart, no soul-searching required.

When she'd decided not to go to college, Shannon had been understanding. Abby needed to be there for her dad. Of course she did. They'd got together on Shannon's breaks, and, for the most part, it had been fine. Abby was accepting that Shannon had made new friends, went to Fort Lauderdale or Vail with them, started living her own life. Meanwhile, Abby had gotten on with the orchard, the shop, finding a way to live her life, too, even if it wasn't quite as exciting as Shannon's.

A distance had opened between them then—natural, under-standable, but still a little sad. But when Shannon's job in Chicago had gone bust and she'd returned to Ashford to set up as a private, small-town accountant, Abby had felt like she was getting her best friend back.

The years that had already happened had served as a bridge from the past to the present, so there had been no need to discuss all the water under it—the car accident, Abby's choice to stay home, Shannon's life that had flamed out, the serious boyfriend she'd left behind. And as the years in Ashford had passed with nothing more than Netflix, wine, and the occasional blind date, Abby had been perfectly satisfied with that. But now, looking at Shannon's resolute expression, she had a horrible feeling everything was about to change, or that maybe it already had.

"Okay," Shannon said. "I'm just going to say this—"

Abby let out a sigh, knowing better than to tell her not to. She reached for the open bottle on the coffee table between them and sloshed more wine into her glass.

"The thing is, Abby," Shannon said, speaking hesitantly but with determination, "I understood why you chose not to go to college. I really did. You needed to be there for your dad, and while I was sad for you, I supported your decision."

"I know you did." Abby lowered her gaze as she took a sip of wine.

"But you know, at some point, I thought you'd do something else. Take some night classes, or think about moving to a city."

"I like working at the orchard, Shannon," Abby cut across her. "Even if you don't think I do."

"I know that," Shannon insisted. "I might have had my doubts at first, but I get that now."

"So what's the problem?" Not that she really wanted to know.

"It's just…" Shannon looked uncharacteristically uncertain. "There's a part of you that seems as if you don't want to be happy," she said in a rush. "Almost as if you don't think you deserve to be happy. And I get that you may have survivor's guilt. I understand that—"

"You *get* a lot," Abby said with acid in her voice that made Shannon blink. "Really, you've missed your calling. You should be a therapist."

"Sorry," Shannon said after a moment. "I'm probably coming across as patronizing—"

"You think?" Abby couldn't keep the bitterness from spilling out. She didn't need Shannon as well as Simon coming over all analytical, treating her like some sad specimen to be examined, understood, helped. "Look, I don't tell you what I think is wrong with your life," she continued, hurt fueling words she knew she'd regret later. "I don't question why you came running back to Ashford when you could have got another job in the city. I don't ask you if you're being *held hostage* because you're living in a small town and you date about as much as I do. Why can my life go under the microscope, but yours can't?"

Shannon was silent for a moment, absorbing everything Abby had said, until guilt, her usual companion, rushed in.

"I'm sorry," Abby muttered. "I shouldn't have said all that."

"No," Shannon cut across her, using a diffident tone that meant she was hurt but trying not to be. "We're best friends. You have every right."

That made Abby feel even worse. "I don't want to fight with you," she pleaded. "Can we just turn on *Gilmore Girls* and forget all of this?"

Shannon looked tempted, but Abby knew her friend well enough to know she wouldn't back down. "No, we can't. Not if we're really best friends. Let's have this out, Abby."

"There's nothing to *have out*—"

"I came running back to Ashford because my confidence was knocked," Shannon cut across her. "Really knocked, more than I ever let on, because I was too proud. I was the one who had my life together, right?" She gave a twisted smile. "I really thought I was all that, up and coming, high flyer, you name it, and then when the redundancies started coming, I was the first name on the list, before the most recent hires even, the college grads who had barely started. I couldn't believe it. I realized I must have been crap at my job." She took a quick breath, continuing on before Abby could interject with another groveling apology. "You're right, I could have got a job in Chicago, I could have sent my resumé out to umpteen firms, but I realized something about myself—I realized I'd rather be a big fish in a small pond than the other way around. And so I came home."

Abby felt terrible now, wretched with misery at hurting her friend, and all because she'd been hurting. "Shannon, I'm sorry—"

"And as for the dating, or lack thereof? The truth was, I thought Mike would follow me. We'd been dating for three years. I was hoping he'd propose, we'd settle in Ashford, have a couple of kids, the minivan, the picket fence. Moving back here was my passive-aggressive way of giving him an ultimatum, and he didn't bite. When I lost my job, I lost him, too." Shannon looked down at her wineglass while Abby stared at her, appalled.

"*Shannon*. Why didn't you tell me any of this before?"

"Because, in my pride, I thought I was the friend who had it all together. And I didn't want you feeling sorry for me. But I'm telling you now, because… well, because I want to be honest. And I want you to be honest."

So that was how it worked. Abby swallowed, knowing that no matter what her friend had shared, she wasn't ready to have a similar bloodletting, but Shannon was clearly waiting for one.

"You're right," she finally said at last. "My relationship with my dad is complicated. He can be difficult, but that's because he's sad."

"But you're not responsible—"

"For his happiness. No." Abby nodded. No, she wasn't responsible for her father's happiness, but she had been for his sorrow. His grief. And no matter how much she talked it out—she'd had a couple years of therapy in her mid-twenties—or rationalized it in her own head, no matter how much she understood intellectually that it was a trucker asleep at the wheel who was at fault for her mother and brother's death and not her, her heart and her gut told her otherwise—every single day. Every single moment. And she knew her father felt the same way.

But she'd never admitted to Shannon how or why she was to blame, and she couldn't bear to now. She knew—at least she hoped—that Shannon wouldn't judge her; if anything, her friend would feel pity. So much pity. But Abby didn't think she could stand that, either. She'd had enough of it already. And so she stayed silent, because that was what she always did, and she wasn't ready, or able, to change now.

"So do you think Simon is justified in doing this research?" she asked, and Shannon sighed, leaning back against the sofa, accepting, thank goodness, that Abby wasn't going to share anymore. "Because it concerns his family too?"

"Maybe he could have been more respectful, but it's not as if it really matters, does it? It happened so long ago. Even if your grandfather did something truly shocking, which I doubt he did…"

"It matters to my dad."

"But that's your dad, Abby," Shannon said gently. "Not you. If you take your father out of the equation for a moment, does it matter to you?"

Abby simply stared at her. She'd never taken her father out of the equation, not once in fifteen years.

"Are you curious about this Matthew whoever and why your grandfather might have ended up with his medal? And, more importantly, do you want this thing that happened in the past, whatever it is, to come between you and Simon, or draw you closer together?"

"I'm not sure there is a 'me and Simon', not really."

"There still could be."

"He lives in England—"

"That's a whole separate issue."

Abby let out a heavy sigh. "I don't know what I want," she admitted. "I'm curious, it's true, and I… I like Simon." That felt like a confession, a big one, for her. "But my dad." Three little words that meant so much, that had guided so much of her life. *But my dad.* She thought of the look of anger on her father's face and then, far worse, the look of weary resignation. "This matters to him. A lot. I don't know why, and I think he even knows it shouldn't, but it still does."

"It's not like Simon is running to the papers—"

"He's thinking of writing a book."

"But he hasn't written it yet. And maybe it would actually be better for your father—and for you—to find out whatever this thing is. Secrets are usually not good or healthy, especially in a family."

And I'm so very tired of secrets. The realization, as obvious as it surely was, felt strangely groundbreaking. Revelatory in a way that had her sitting back and shaking her head slowly. She didn't want any more secrets. She didn't want to keep them; she didn't want to stay silent about yet another thing in her life, or someone's else life. And she didn't want to throw away the promise of something—*someone*—good in her life, no matter how fleeting or uncertain that relationship might be, for yet another secret, and one that wasn't even hers.

"You're right," Abby said at last, smiling a little tiredly. "Thank you for saying so. And thank you for putting up with all my crap. I'm sorry I'm not a better friend."

"You're the best friend." Shannon smiled and reached for the bottle to top up their glasses. "Now, I think it is finally time to put on *Gilmore Girls*."

Two hours later, Abby was walking the mile and a half home through a sultry summer darkness, the country road back to Willow Tree lit only by the stars and a full, silver disc of a moon. Silvery light gilded the fields as she walked, the air balmy and still.

She felt a tangled mix of sadness and hope; even though she hadn't told Shannon much, the whole conversation had rocked a door in her heart right off its hinges. Whether she chose to nail it shut once more or pry it open even more remained to be seen.

Back at Willow Tree, the house was cloaked in quiet, the only light coming from the one on the top of the stove. Her father always left it on when she was out at night, just as her mother had. Traditions carried on, a little reminder of the love and care she knew both her parents had felt for her—and still did.

Her father still loved her. Abby didn't doubt that. She never had, except for in her very darkest moments, right after the accident, when they'd both been frozen in shocked grief and terrible silence.

With a shuddery sigh, Abby flicked off the stove light, so only moonlight lit her way upstairs, the steps creaking under her soft footsteps. She passed her father's bedroom, and then the guest one, and was about to turn into her own when the fourth bedroom's door, as firmly shut as always, caught her eye.

Abby hesitated, and then, feeling a little bit as if she were existing outside herself, observing her actions, she walked to the door and quietly turned the knob. It swung open easily, surprising her. Surely after all these years it should be stuck, squeak in protest?

But when she stepped inside her brother's room, she knew immediately that her father had been in there. All the surfaces were free of dust, everything neat and tidy, far tidier than Luke had ever kept it. The room didn't smell stale, a tragic time capsule. It smelled like lemon polish.

Her father must have come in here on his own, maybe many times, to have a private moment of grief he'd never even told her about. The thought brought a strange comfort, as well as an intense sadness. They weren't able to share even this.

Abby ran her hand along the top of the dresser, smiling faintly at the sight of Luke's soccer trophies lined up there. He'd loved soccer and piano equally, although he was much better at the latter. All the trophies were for most improved or just participating, but Luke had been proud of them all.

Luke. A shaft of grief, as fresh as ever, pierced her so deeply she nearly doubled over. Did it ever get easier? Did it ever stop taking you by surprise, leaving you winded and reeling? Even now, fifteen years later, she felt as if Luke could bound into the room with his lopsided smile and his messy hair and ask her if she wanted to play Monopoly. She could hear her mother's laughing voice floating up the stairs, full of warmth.

Okay, but if there are arguments I'm throwing it out!

Another sigh escaped her, this one sounding alarmingly close to a sob. She hadn't cried in ages, hadn't let herself. It had been years, perhaps, since she'd let herself weep, although she'd certainly shed enough tears in the weeks after her mother's and brother's deaths; she'd felt like a dried-out husk, hollowed out and empty inside, with nothing more to give, and yet somehow she and her father had had to go on and on and on.

As she stood there in her brother's darkened bedroom, Abby knew she wasn't ready to cry now, just as she knew if she did weep, it would not just be for her brother and mother, but for the relationship with her father that had been so less than it could have been. She could feel the emotion building inside her like water rising, a storm about to break, and she willed it back. One day maybe, if she was strong—or was it weak?—enough, but not now.

Right now, she wanted to feel hope. Frail, fledgling thing that it might be, tattered and desperate, barely there, poking up from the barren soil. She still wanted to feel it. She could almost grasp it with her fingertips, could see it just out of reach, and she longed for more.

She wanted to move on past the sorrowful stasis her life had become, without her even fully realizing it. Months and years had passed when she'd told herself she was happy, or at least happy enough, not even questioning the lie. Yet now she recognized it for what it was, and she wanted something else. But was that Simon? Did he fit into the reconfigured picture of her life at all, or was he just a passing fancy, someone she might recall one day with a faint smile, a wondering "what if"? Abby had no idea, or whether she'd ever be able to find out.

The next morning, her father was drinking coffee by the kitchen sink when Abby came into the room. He looked up, his hooded gaze lifting and dropping again in the matter of a second as he nodded his usual greeting. He was already dressed for a day spent in the orchard and barn, his gnarled fingers wrapped around a mug of coffee, an empty cereal bowl in the sink.

"Dad." Abby took a deep breath, let it buoy her faltering courage. "I went into Luke's room last night."

Her father didn't move, hadn't been moving in the first place, but somehow it seemed as if he went even stiller.

"I saw how clean it was, everything dusted," Abby continued, trying to pitch her voice both gentle and determined. She had a feeling she'd failed; it was wobbling all over the place. "It looked nice. Have—have you been going in there?"

Her father didn't answer and Abby made herself continue.

"It's only… I didn't know. The door was always closed, but I would have… I would have gone in too." She trailed off, realizing she didn't actually know where she was going with this. She just wanted her father to say something, *anything*, to bridge the yawning space that had been there since the accident, even if Abby had acted like it hadn't been. Even if she had done her best to step over it as if it didn't matter, as if it wasn't the huge gulf she knew it had been all along.

"Not that often," he said, his voice giving nothing away. "Just once in a while."

Abby nodded slowly, at a loss for her words. "I wish I'd known," she finally said, and too late she realized she sounded reproachful.

Her father finished his coffee and put the cup in the sink.

"I'll be out in the barn," he said, and then he was gone, striding out the back door, the screen door slapping against the wood frame like a rebuke.

Was it ever going to change? Was he? *Was she?*

Abby stood in the center of the empty kitchen, her mind drifting despondently over old conversations, so many tired moments like this one.

She didn't know how long she stood there, staring into space, the sun slanting across the floor even as her mind felt as if it were in a fog. Her phone buzzed and she took it out of her pocket, saw, with a flicker of trepidation, that it was Simon.

"Hey." His voice was warm yet hesitant. "I hope you don't mind me ringing."

"No, I don't mind."

"I should have called before, I know. I wanted to. I just didn't know what to say."

Abby closed her eyes. "I didn't, either," she said. "I still don't."

"Are you angry with me?" Simon sounded as if the question cost him; here, perhaps, was the man who had been considered emotionally unavailable. When it wasn't all easy chat and light flirting, musings about the distant past rather than the painful present, conversation was hard. For both of them.

"I don't know," Abby admitted. "I feel like I don't know anything anymore."

"That's better than a 'hell yes', I suppose," Simon said with an uncertain laugh.

"Yes, I guess it is."

They were both quiet, the only sound their breathing, a give and take, a silent exchange. It felt like a weirdly intimate moment, and yet Abby didn't understand it at all. What did Simon want? What did *she* want? She had no idea why he'd called.

"Look, I know what you said the other day and I respect it," he finally said. "I'm not going to write a book or dig up your family secrets and wave them about for all and sundry to see. I don't want to do that. I don't want to hurt you, Abby. I hope you believe me about that."

"But?" she said after a moment, because there so obviously was one.

"But I've found some things out, and I think you deserve to know what they are. At least, you deserve the right to decide if you want to know." He paused while Abby tried to think of something to say. "Whatever your choice, Abby, I will respect it."

"Will you?" She gazed out the window at the backyard, its colors seeming muted under a humid, gray sky that pressed down on the earth.

"Yes, I will."

Simon was silent, waiting for her verdict, and Abby wondered what he wanted her to say. She felt so *tired*—tired of it all. Tired of her father's silence, of tiptoeing across the painful cracks of their relationship, of trying to be happy when something in her wanted to weep and weep and yet never could. She hadn't even realized just how tired she'd been, until Simon.

Until Simon.

Maybe he was little more than a stranger, yet he was already important, if just for that—except, of course, it wasn't just for that. She'd been backing away from life for the last fifteen years. Maybe now it was finally time to stop.

"All right," she said, her voice heavy with the weight of her words. "Tell me what you've found out."

CHAPTER SEVENTEEN

Normandy, France

June 1944

"He's ready for you, Lawson."

Matthew flicked his cigarette onto the road and ground it beneath his boot, the acrid smell of the tobacco still stinging his nostrils. He hadn't smoked a single cigarette in his life until two days ago, when he and Tom had finally joined up with a raggedy section of the 508th, everyone milling about the battered buildings of an abandoned village, soldiers seeming both dazed and impatient. The assault had started, and yet there was nothing to do.

The jump, Matthew had discovered, had gone rather disastrously wrong. Most of the men had been dropped miles from the right place, and many of them were still stumbling around alone in the fields and forests of France, if they hadn't been killed or captured. Meanwhile, the sea assault had gone ahead, with massive casualties but tattered success, and yet now that they were actually in France, it felt like the next step hadn't been planned.

Matthew knew the 508th's main objective had been to capture Sainte-Mère-Église, secure crossings of the Merderet River, and establish a defensive line north of Neuville-au-Plain. Whether any of that would happen now was in serious question. He suspected the main objective of all the regiments was simply to assemble together and figure out what the hell they were doing.

But none of that concerned him now; although there had been several exchanges of fire, Matthew hadn't been involved in any of them. He was deemed too valuable to be lost to a stray bullet or hidden landmine. He was one of the few people in the Allied army who knew German, and who could get military intelligence from one of the hundreds of captured soldiers now in their charge.

Straightening his shoulders and narrowing his eyes against the glare of the midday sun, he walked towards the empty bar where the soldier he was to interrogate had been brought. No one knew anything about him except he was of low rank, the equivalent of a private, and he seemed terrified.

Unconsciously, Matthew clenched and unclenched his fists as he stood before the wooden door leading into the pub. This would be his first real interrogation, so different from the many practice ones he'd done back at Camp Ritchie, when the "prisoner" had been his instructor or a fellow student, simply pretending to be a German soldier, acting either surly or scared. Even though Matthew had taken it all with the utmost seriousness, he knew now it had never truly felt real.

Not like this, when a latent fury was coursing through him, and he willed it into something colder and more solid. There was no room for emotion here. He'd been told that many times over the course of his training, and he knew it now.

He opened the door and stepped inside.

The bar was dim, a few tables scattered around, most of the chairs broken, everything covered with dust. Whoever had been patron of this place had left long ago.

Matthew blinked to adjust himself to the gloom and then saw the man sitting at a table in the center of the dusty room. He stared at Matthew uncertainly, his eyes wide. Matthew regarded him back coolly.

The man was young, no more than a kid, maybe nineteen or twenty. Blue eyes blinked at him rapidly and his blond hair was cut short.

Matthew reached into his jacket pocket.

"*Zigarette?*" he asked casually, proffering the pack, and the man blinked at him.

"*D-d-danke... ja,*" he stammered, and took one of the cigarettes from the pack. He put it between his lips as Matthew leaned forward with his lighter. "*Danke,*" he murmured again, and drew deeply on the cigarette. Matthew remained silent and the boy eyed him with obvious curiosity. "Are you German?" he asked, speaking his native tongue.

"I am," Matthew said after a moment. He'd been advised to use discretion when telling POWs he was German, for if he were captured himself, he could be executed by his captors for, ironically, being a deserter of the Germany army, not to mention a Jew.

The man raised his eyebrows. "How did you end up there, while I am here?" He gestured to his seat.

"I emigrated to America in 1938, after stormtroopers beat my father to death," he answered shortly. A wave of sudden, unexpected rage rose up in him, threatening to engulf him, but Matthew forced it down.

The boy's eyes widened. "You are Jewish?"

"Yes." It was reckless, perhaps, to admit as much, but Matthew knew he couldn't have kept himself from it. He *wanted* this man—this paltry, pathetic little tool of the Fuhrer, a tiny cog in the vast machinery of the Nazi party—to know who he was. What he was.

If he expected some sort of jibe or barbed retort, he did not get one. The man let out a defeated sigh as he flicked some ash from the tip of his cigarette. "What is it you wish to know?"

Matthew masked his surprise with a cool look. In his training, he'd learned the four methods of interrogation, from building rapport to playing on fear, and how to use each of them effectively to gain information from a prisoner, often without him even realizing he'd given it. This fatigued compliance was not something he'd ever expected. The instructors who had pretended to be prisoners during his training had surely never given it. Was it some sort of trick?

Matthew reached for a chair and sat down opposite the man. "What is it you wish to tell me?"

The man shrugged. "I don't know how much I know. I'm just an *Obersoldat*. But I am tired of this damned war, and I want to go home. We're going to lose anyway." He drew deeply on his cigarette as he gazed at Matthew with a deadened defiance.

Matthew stared back evenly. The rage he'd felt a moment before had trickled away, replaced with a weary numbness. "What were you doing before you were captured?" he asked.

"I was laying mines along the road to Sainte-Mère-Église."

Matthew kept his expression neutral as he asked in a diffident voice, as if it didn't matter very much, "Would you be able to show me where they are?"

The man shrugged and dropped his cigarette. "If you like."

Fifteen minutes later, pistol in hand, Matthew was following the soldier along the road, accompanied by a lieutenant and a private who walked along warily, rifles at the ready.

"Here," the man said with a shrug, as he pointed out the place where a mine had been buried. "And here. And here. And here."

By the time they returned to the village several hours later, over fifty mines had been discovered and, thanks to the help of the German *Obersoldat*, dismantled. Matthew felt a weird mix of exultation and fury; what might have happened if those mines hadn't been dismantled? And the *Obersoldat* had seemed almost indifferent to it all, to the lives he had saved, or those that might have been lost. He just wanted the war to end, so he could go home.

"There's another one for you, Lawson." Matthew turned around at the sound of the voice, and then he nodded and headed back to the dusty bar with its broken chairs—and another German prisoner.

This one, he saw, was completely different to the first. He was sitting up straight in the chair, his military bearing evident, shoulders thrown back, chin poised at a haughty angle. Matthew took in the insignia on his uniform—he was a Wehrmacht *Ober-leutnant*, with an impressive Knight's Cross on his tunic, granted when fighting in the Afrika Korps. A seasoned soldier, then, who would not volunteer information when offered a cigarette.

As Matthew approached, the man's eyes narrowed and his lips twisted in scorn, even though Matthew hadn't said a word.

"Name?" he asked shortly, in German.

"Hahn, Dieter."

"Rank?"

"Oberleutnant." The single word rang out proudly.

"Serial number?"

The man gave it.

Matthew stood in front of him, surveying him coolly. He could not bring himself to act out the camaraderie he'd first intended on, and he felt instinctively Dieter Hahn would mock it, anyway. Instead, he relied on a silence that spun out several minutes until finally Hahn broke it.

"You are German." It wasn't quite a question.

"Yes, and a Jew." Again he could not keep himself from saying it. He watched impassively as the man spat on the floor.

"You left," Hahn stated, a sneer in the words.

"Isn't that what you wanted?" Matthew didn't know how it had become so personal so quickly; he knew it wasn't meant to be. He and the other German-born Jews had been coached again and again not to make their interrogations emotional. They needed information, not justice.

Hahn turned his head, as if dismissing him. "This is your revenge, I suppose."

"No." Matthew kept his voice even. "This is my job. But justice will come, *Oberleutnant*. It is only a matter of time." Hahn did not reply. "There are fifty thousand German soldiers in cages on the beaches of Normandy." That was the estimate that had been given, at any rate. "And many more are surrendering every day. Your time has come and gone."

Hahn turned to stare at Matthew with cold blue eyes. "*Das ist mir Wurscht,*" he said, his lips twisting cynically.

Matthew let out a huff of humorless laughter as he acknowledged the other man's deliberate barb. *That is sausage to me*—an idiom to express his complete and utter disinterest in what Matthew had said. Hahn had said it as one German to another, and yet Matthew knew this man thought him less than human, less than the mud caking his fine leather boots.

"That may be," he answered. "But your defiance will not change the outcome of this war, of that we can both be very sure."

Hahn gave a regal nod, unmoved. "Then let it be so."

Matthew stared at Hahn, with his air of cool, indifferent acceptance, in frustration and a growing fury, directed as much at himself as the man before him. He had not found out one damned thing from this man. He'd failed as an interrogator in order to pursue his own emotion-driven agenda. How could he have been so childish?

"Where is the rest of your regiment?" he asked abruptly.

Hahn just smiled coldly and shook his head.

"How many tanks are left on the Cotentin peninsula?"

Another shake, along with a small, knowing smile.

"Where is your commanding officer?"

This time a shrug.

Matthew clenched his fists. This was going badly. Very badly. "Do you realize you will be tried for war crimes?" he demanded.

For the first time the man looked the tiniest bit uncertain. Shaken. But it was only for a second, like a shadow in his eyes, and then his expression hardened all the more.

"Let it be so," he said quietly, and Matthew knew he'd lost him for good.

He turned on his heel and strode out of the room, slamming the door behind him. A private, guarding the door with a rifle and a cigarette, stood to attention.

"Return him to his quarters," Matthew snapped, and kept walking.

Back in his quarters, an abandoned house he shared with Guy West, his fury had abated, leaving only a scathing self-loathing that coated him like a slick oil.

Only his second interrogation and he'd lost it. What was *wrong* with him? He was good at his job. At least, he could be good at his job. Matthew knew he could. Back at Camp Ritchie in Maryland, he'd been applauded for his cool head, his clear thinking. His instructing officers had appreciated his careful reserve, the way he kept his own counsel, gave nothing away, not even to friends. Yet in the space of a few minutes he'd shed all that like some deadened skin, and emerged raw and red and vulnerable, clothed only in naked emotion. He could not let that happen again. He would not, for the sake of this war. For the sake of his family.

The door to the house opened and Guy came in, his dark hair pushed back from a high forehead, his eyes narrowing as he caught sight of Matthew standing in the middle of the dusty room; the only furniture was a mattress of straw ticking and a broken chair.

Sometimes Matthew wondered what the French people thought, being taken over a second time, the battles raging all around their villages, homes, and farms. Then he saw some remnant of the Nazi occupation—a tattered flag, a blood-spattered wall—and he knew they had to be grateful. They certainly seemed grateful, when he caught sight of their haggard faces split into smiles of both relief and joy. The end was in sight.

"What happened?" Guy asked in German. "The man was useless?"

Matthew shrugged. "I was useless."

Guy lit a cigarette and passed one over that Matthew took silently. They smoked without speaking for several minutes. "It happens," Guy said at last.

"It shouldn't."

Matthew had met Guy on the boat over; they'd trained separately at Camp Ritchie, and although they saw in each other shared pain and a kindred spirit, neither of them had spoken much of their families or former lives in Germany. The only thing Matthew knew about Guy was that his father was a tailor and he was from Berlin. They'd all emigrated to America in 1936. They were all safe.

Guy shrugged. "There is much that shouldn't happen in this war."

"He wasn't even that bad." Another wave of self-loathing rolled over Matthew. "Just an arrogant bastard, nothing more."

"Then remember that for next time." Guy gave him a brief smile, a humorless twisting of lips in a face marked by weariness. "He probably wouldn't have given you anything, anyway. Arrogant bastards usually don't."

That evening, by the light of a smoking oil lamp, Matthew tried to write Lily. He hadn't written her since the day before he'd dropped down in that muddy field a fortnight ago, although it felt like an age, a lifetime lived in days and weeks, sometimes in minutes.

He raked a hand through his hair, his eyes gritty with fatigue, his body grimy with both mud and sweat; he hadn't had a proper wash since Leicestershire. Although vague rumors had begun circulating that the 508th might be shipped back to England on leave sometime in the next few weeks, Matthew could barely imagine it; England felt like another universe.

And while part of him relished the thought of clean sheets, a hot, or at least a warm, bath, and, most of all, *Lily*, part of him didn't want to go. Here in Normandy, as the Allies pressed forward, he was closer to finding his family, or at least finding out what had happened to them. Leaving felt like defeat, a personal one he couldn't stand.

For a moment, Matthew looked up from his blank page, his gaze unfocused. He wasn't naïve. He knew it was likely at least some of his family members had died in the war—from bombing, illness, starvation, or simply being killed. It was more than likely.

Rumors, most too vague to be trusted or believed, had started drifting through the rest of the world like vapors of smoke— stories of Jews rounded up in ghettoes, denied basic food, water, and clothing, living in virtual prisons.

Then, later, there had been stories of Jews being shipped east on trains, to populate Poland, or even somewhere more distant. When Matthew had first enlisted, a story had broken in the US newspapers that Jews in Russia and Lithuania were being sum- marily executed. While the stories had chilled him, they'd always brought a treacherous, shameful relief.

At least it's not German Jews, Matthew had thought, utterly ashamed of his thinking, yet unable to keep himself from it. *They wouldn't do that to German Jews*. Then he remembered the look of savage glee on the stormtrooper's face as he'd kicked his father to death.

Now a shudder ran through him at the prospect of what might—or might not—await him back in Fraustadt. Had his mother been clever enough to hide Gertie? She'd been such a tiny thing, with her dark eyes and hair. Such a tiny, little slip of a girl, although she'd be sixteen now, practically a woman. Where was she? What had happened to her, to all of them?

He thought of Franz and Arno, mere boys, just twelve and fourteen when Matthew had left, six years ago. They were young men now. Young Jewish men in a country that had chosen to despise them.

Matthew glanced down at the blank page again, and wrote *Dear Lily*.

He stopped, unable to think what to say next. In the months of their letter writing, neither had ever said very much. Lily had taken him through her days, expressing shy pleasure at small moments—a crocus poking through the shattered bricks of a bombed-out building, a seaman who had been missing, presumed dead, only to be found alive hanging on some wreckage—and Matthew had done his best to communicate about his life, although both the secrecy and monotony had made it difficult.

In the end, though, he didn't think it mattered. Lily could have written about anything at all and he still would have eagerly devoured her words. Her gentleness shone through even the most mundane of letters, and that was what had drawn him to her in the first place. Sophie's alluring boldness and charming manner had put Lily's quiet nature into stark relief; Tom had called her mousy, but Matthew recognized her for what she was. *Kind*.

Now he pictured her—her brown eyes as soft as pansies, her light brown hair curling about her small, homely face. He could see her slightly crooked front tooth and the freckles on her nose that he didn't think she liked. He remembered how sweet her kiss had been, hesitant and yielding all at once.

How could he tell her about any of this? *When I interrogated a man today, I felt as if I could throttle him with my bare hands. I saw a dead German lying in a field and I thought—"Good". I want to go home, but I don't think such a place exists anymore, anywhere. I know this war will end one day, but I'm afraid it never will for me.*

With one hand, Matthew crumpled the nearly blank page into a ball and tossed it onto the floor. Then, by the light of the oil lamp, with its greasy smoke curling upwards towards the ceiling, he smoked silently until the flame had gone down, sputtered out, and then was dark.

CHAPTER EIGHTEEN

July 1944

The beach was a scar. It had been over four weeks since the D-Day landings, and the twisted metal skeletons of wrecked tanks and Jeeps were still strewn across the grimy sands of Utah Beach. Matthew gazed out at the litter of abandoned equipment and vehicles, and then at the metal cages that zigzagged across the hills and held thousands of German prisoners. Here were the vestiges of victory, the price of war. He looked at it all and he did not know whether to feel triumphant or defeated.

He'd been rattling in the back of a truck for several hours, across ravaged countryside towards the beaches that had borne the brunt of the assault, and then back to England. The rumors had been true, and the 508th were being shipped back to be refreshed and restocked. From the two thousand that had dropped into France just over a month ago, only a thousand remained.

In the last few weeks, as the 508th had reorganized and continued operations to secure the peninsula, Matthew had interrogated dozens more prisoners, most of them tripping over their words in their eagerness to be helpful to the Allies. It had become painfully clear to the Axis forces that they were losing, and the average German soldier wanted only to go home.

One medic had drawn Matthew a map of all of Normandy, with the positions of German forces and weaponry. Another officer had been able to give approximate numbers of all the troops positioned in northern France. While Matthew was glad of the information, it hadn't assuaged the sense of vengeance he'd felt burning through him when he let it. At least he'd learned to hide the strength of his feeling; he'd never lost his composure with another POW the way he had with Hahn. He'd never written Lily, either.

Now he glanced at all the prisoners in their cages waiting to be processed and he wondered who they were. His countrymen, certainly, and some might be former school mates, friends, neighbors. How many of the blond, blue-eyed boys he'd gone to the gymnasium with had ended up as Nazis? Where were they now—here?

At least this distant curiosity was better than the rage he'd first struggled with, and that he knew others had felt. He'd heard stories, over the last few weeks, of revenge enacted by his fellow soldiers. A division of paratroopers had massacred thirty captured Wehrmacht officers in an abandoned village. A private had shot two Germans in the head after they'd surrendered, and no one had said a word.

Matthew had heard such stories, and he'd felt pity for both the soldier and the captive, the killer and the killed. War was grim, grimmer than he even realized, or wanted to think about, or write to Lily.

And yet he wanted, *needed*, to go back to England and see Lily, and yet he was afraid to do so. Afraid of what she might see in him, what was surely growing in him like a canker.

The beach was strangely quiet, almost peaceful, as Matthew walked across it towards the tank landing ship that was taking the 508th to Southampton. He'd been given five days' leave and he intended to spend them in London, before he had to report back to duty in Nottingham.

He had no idea what the rest of the war held for him, if he would be put on active duty in England, interrogating prisoners of war there, or if he would go with the 508th back to France, into Germany and the end of the war. Sometimes he wasn't even sure what he wanted, and then he felt a curdling rush of shame that he could have been conflicted for a moment. He had to get back to Fraustadt. He had to find his family.

London felt like a battered paradise when Matthew stepped off the train and into a rainy summer's evening. The sky was a dull pewter with intermittent drizzle, and everything looked tired and dirty and gray, but he could breathe easily as he walked down the street, grateful for the strange silence of a place that was not being constantly shelled, except he soon found out it was.

In the month since D-Day, London had been hit worse than ever before; the Germans had begun launching V-1 rockets, buzz bombs known as doodlebugs that moved so quickly that anti-aircraft guns couldn't be mobilized in time and people often weren't able to take cover.

Thousands of bombs had been dropped on London alone in the last five weeks, and it showed. The city looked worn down to the bone. With a clench of true fear, Matthew wondered if Lily had stayed safe.

He checked into a small, rather shabby hotel near Piccadilly, reveling in a few inches of tepid bath water and a cup of tea the color of dishwater as if these were great luxuries. He went to Rainbow Corner for a hamburger and a beer, and then fell into bed and slept for sixteen hours straight, waking at midday to watery sunlight and a sense of unreality that he was no longer in France.

It wasn't until that evening that he took the Tube to Clapham, feeling unaccountably nervous as to what reception he might have. He hadn't alerted Lily to the fact that he was returning to England, or that he had leave; he hadn't been able to bring himself to write her at all, but now he regretted his reticence. What if she couldn't get any time off? What if she wasn't even there? What if—and this was surely the worst of all—she no longer felt the way he did?

Yet how *did* he feel?

Sometimes he wasn't sure he knew.

As he emerged from the Underground near Clapham Common, the rain had cleared, revealing a pale blue sky, the sun still bright above, even though it was nearing seven o'clock. The Common seemed peaceful, people strolling in the sunshine, enjoying the balmy weather, the respite from their troubles.

Matthew had just turned the corner when he felt a prickling along his skin, an instinctive awareness, followed by a whistling sound he knew well, although it was usually accompanied by the distinctive wail of the air-raid sirens.

With a sound like a thunderclap, smoke billowed up in the next street over, and it felt as if the very ground beneath his feet had rocked. The sirens started up, and the people near him began dodging for cover.

Matthew whirled around, looking for shelter as another doodlebug landed another street over, and smoke clogged his lungs. He stumbled towards a doorway, one arm thrown above his head.

He could hear the thunder of the bombs falling, just as he had before with Lily, and he closed his eyes tight against it all, half-wishing he was back in France. Then, after what could have been a minute or an hour, the all-clear sounded.

Matthew straightened, lowering his arm as he blinked in a world that seemed muted, the air full of smoke and grit, the sound of police and ambulance sirens starting up.

"*Matthew!*"

He whirled towards the sound of his name, and, calling out again, Lily came, half-running, half-stumbling towards him.

There was dust and grit in her hair and mud on her cheek, but she was safe and whole and in his arms, her slight frame shuddering against him as he pressed his lips to her hair.

"I thought you were a ghost," she choked out. "Or I was… I thought I must have died. I'd just come out of the Tube when it happened."

"We're both alive," he assured her as he kissed her forehead. Now that she was here, in his arms, he knew he'd been simply waiting these last five weeks to see her. To hold her. "We're both very much alive."

She eased back to study his face, her eyes wide, her expression serious, her voice full of wonder. "How did you come to be here? How can you be back?"

"I'm on leave. I'm sorry I wasn't able to tell you—"

"I didn't expect letters, not with everything." Even though Tom had written Sophie, or so he'd told Matthew once, when they'd come across each other in the canteen. They'd continued to avoid each other otherwise, Tom looking at Matthew with wary distrust whenever he saw him. "I knew you wouldn't," Lily continued quietly. "I understood." And even though he hadn't said a word about why he hadn't written, Matthew felt that she did.

"You're safe?" he asked. "Your family?"

"Yes, all safe. Not even a crack in a windowpane."

"Thank God."

"Yes," she said. "Thank God."

They were quiet for a moment, holding each other in their arms, and then Matthew let go and they started walking towards Holmside Road.

"Has it been very bad?" Lily asked, and even though Matthew knew she understood, he shook his head. He didn't want to talk about Normandy, or the interrogations, or any of it.

He reached for her hand and they walked silently towards her home, slowing as they came to a building that had been hit directly, reduced to little more than rubble and broken beams, with several people huddled around.

"Can you help?" a man called, his voice hoarse with anxiety. "We need someone small."

Lily stopped, squeezing Matthew's hand tightly. "Someone small," she repeated, as if to herself.

"To go down there." A soot-faced man nodded towards a deep crater that had opened up in the middle of what had once been a house, a house just like Lily's. "There's a man stuck down there, he's in a bad way. He needs help."

Matthew glanced at Lily; her face was pale, her chin tilted upwards. "How bad?" he asked.

"I don't think there's much hope," a man in a dark suit said quietly as he stepped forward. He held the battered leather medical bag of a doctor. "But I have some chloroform. We could ease his pain, at least. Surely that is our Christian duty."

It was only then that Matthew became aware of the piteous groaning coming from the dark pit; it sounded like a wounded animal, inhuman and awful, and he had an absurd urge to cover his ears.

"But it's too small a space for any of us," the man finished with a nod towards Lily. "But I think you'd do, Miss, if you weren't too scared. You look small enough."

"I'm not scared." Lily's voice trembled and her gaze darted towards the darkened hole. In one of her letters, Matthew recalled, she'd written about how much she hated small spaces.

He took a step towards the house and saw just how narrow the hole was, barely big enough for Lily to fit her shoulders through. It was like a tunnel into hell.

"She can't go down there," he said, sounding angry. What they were asking was outrageous, yet Lily was already undoing her buttons.

"I can," she said. "But not with my jacket on."

"Attagirl," the man said approvingly, and the doctor began to prepare the chloroform, while Matthew watched helplessly. He did not want Lily to go down into that pit where such horrible moans were coming from, a place where he could neither protect nor comfort her, yet he knew she would not even think of refusing. She was gentle, yes, she always had been, but she was also strong. Brave, just as he'd told her she was. Here was the proof.

Lily's face was pale with determination as she slipped her jacket off and handed it to Matthew.

"How will she get down there?" he asked, still sounding strident. "It's too small for a ladder."

The man grimaced in apology. "We'll have to lower her down by her ankles."

"What!" Matthew shook his head. "I wouldn't even ask a soldier back in Normandy to do something like that."

"We're not in Normandy," the man replied grimly.

Lily laid a hand on Matthew's sleeve. "I'll do it," she said, and there was a note of quiet certainty in her voice that made Matthew feel ashamed.

He nodded and stepped back.

"I'm sorry, Miss," the man crouching by the hole said, "I think you'll have to take your dress off, as well. It's going to be awfully tight down there, and we wouldn't want your clothes catching on a bit of rubble and bringing the whole thing down."

Matthew opened his mouth and then closed it as Lily began to undo the buttons of her dress, while the men respectfully looked away. He took it from her; she was so pale and slight in nothing but her slip, freckles dusting her shoulders, the hollow of her throat making her seem even more vulnerable. A breath of wind could blow her away.

"How do I do it?" she asked, and the doctor explained about the chloroform, how she should put a few drops on a cotton mask and hold it as close to the man's face as she could, while trying not to breathe it in herself. She would have to grip the torch between her teeth.

Matthew longed to protest, but one glance at Lily's tense body, bristling with determination, kept him silent. He watched helplessly as she clenched the torch between her teeth and two men held her by her thighs to lower her down into the ghastly hole. He could not imagine what she was enduring.

The next few minutes were an endless torture, worse than any Matthew had experienced in his five weeks in Normandy. He could hear the horrible moans coming from the hole, and then suddenly they stopped.

Lily called out, and the men hauled her by the ankles.

She spat out the torch, her whole body trembling as she began to retch helplessly.

Matthew caught her in his arms as her body convulsed again and again.

"I'm sorry," she choked out. "His face… the *smell*…"

One of the men patted her clumsily on the shoulder. "There's nothing to be sorry for. You did brilliantly, love."

Still Lily continued to retch, doubled over, tears streaming from her eyes as she shook her head. "There's nothing to be done for him," she finally managed. "His *face*…"

"Don't think of it," Matthew said, and she looked up at him, her eyes wide and dark as tears continued to stream down her cheeks.

"I have to," she said. "Can't you see that? That man… he's every sailor I've written a letter for." A shudder went through her. "And that hole… it was as if I was in a submarine, as if I were going down into my nightmares, the things I try so hard not to see."

"*Lily.*" Her name broke from him and she buried her head in his shoulder.

"I'm glad I was able to help," she said fiercely. "I'm *glad.*" Her body convulsed again and he wrapped his arms around her more tightly. He didn't think he could have loved her more.

"Let's get you home," he said. "You need brandy and tea, and in that order." She nodded and began to dress, her fingers trembling so badly as she tried to do her buttons that Matthew stayed her hand and did them himself.

She looked up at him as he did the last one by her collar, and a tear slipped down her cheek. He caught it with his thumb as he leaned his forehead against hers, closing his eyes.

"I must smell terrible," she said in a shaky voice.

"I don't care."

She did, and he didn't; he wanted only to stay there with her, to imbue her with his strength as she gave him her own. But they couldn't stay; there was nothing more for them to do, as the doctor tended the wounded he could help and the man and his friends began clearing rubble. The man in the hole might already be dead.

With his arm around her shoulders and her head nestled against him, Matthew drew Lily away from the wreckage and they resumed walking towards the safety of Holmside Road.

As they turned onto the road, Matthew stiffened and Lily looked up, drawing her breath in sharply as she saw the rubble in the street, neighbors milling around aimlessly, looking woebegone and lost, as smoke spiraled into a darkening sky.

"No," she whispered. "*No.*"

"Lily—" Matthew tried to catch her hand, but she shrugged him off as she started running down the street, heedless of the wreckage strewn about.

Matthew chased after her, knowing before he came to the smoking ruin what had happened.

A V-1 rocket had hit the house directly, so there was nothing left but a gaping hole, a mess of bricks and broken plaster. Matthew could not make out a single thing that had been left intact.

Lily stood in front of her home, her fists clenching and unclenching.

"Was anyone home?" Matthew asked a neighbor quietly; the woman stared at him with shocked eyes.

"I don't know," she said. "Carol's usually home at this time. Richard, too." She let out a choked cry and shook her head, her fist to her mouth.

Matthew reached towards Lily as an ambulance turned onto the street.

"Lily," he said quietly. "Lily. Love. There's nothing you can do here."

"Don't say that!" Her voice rose savagely. "There must be. I helped that man. There must be something I can do." A sob erupted from her then, and then another, and Lily fell to her knees on the pavement as Matthew put his arms around her and she wept.

CHAPTER NINETEEN

ABBY

Abby watched the car come up the dusty drive, just as it had done three weeks ago, only this time she was getting in it and driving three hundred and fifty miles to Minneapolis.

Simon hadn't told her much on the phone, only that he'd found another man from the 82nd Airborne, Guy Wessel, who now lived in a nursing home outside Minneapolis and remembered Matthew Lawson very well.

"He said he'd talk to us. We might not find any answers, but he's not too far away and I thought it was worth a chance."

And so Abby had impulsively, recklessly, agreed to accompany Simon. She wasn't even certain why; whoever Matthew Lawson was, whatever he'd done, it surely wasn't going to affect her own life all that much.

Except, of course, it was, because her father was going to be furious, and worse, hurt. And maybe, Abby realized, that was why she was going, at least in part. Because she needed finally to live her own life; she needed to stop making everything she did an apology, hostage to her father's feelings. And she needed her father to understand that.

She'd left a note for him on the kitchen table, propped between the salt and pepper shakers, and a tuna casserole in the fridge. She'd felt both exultant and terrified as she'd closed the front door behind her, a bag in hand. It was too far to go and come back in one day, and so Simon had suggested they stay in a hotel near the nursing home, separate rooms, of course. Abby had flushed at that, and made no reply.

Now Simon stepped out of the car, smiling in greeting, even though Abby saw an uncertainty in his eyes. She had no idea how things really stood between them, and she had a feeling he didn't, either. A kiss, an argument, two continents.

She pushed the thoughts away, not wanting them to take over.

"Hey." She came down the steps and Simon took her bag.

"I'm glad you decided to come with me."

"I am, too." Abby gave him a brief smile as he stowed her bag in the back and she slipped into the passenger seat.

"How did your dad take the news?" Simon asked as he climbed into the driver's side and then started back down the drive, leaving the farmhouse behind. Under the pallid sky, it looked empty and old, the paint peeling off its weathered clapboard. Abby gave it a fleeting look before twisting back around in her seat.

"I don't know. I left a note. Told him I walked Bailey." Simon raised his eyebrows and she shrugged. "I didn't want to get into it with him, to be honest, and I probably would have changed my mind."

"And you didn't want to do that?"

"No." She took a quick, steadying breath. "We might not find anything out, and what we find out might not be important at all, but… I feel like I've been stagnating. I don't want to, anymore. So this is my big moment of liberation." She gave him a quick, teasing smile, trying to make light of the moment. "Kind of pathetic, isn't it?"

"Not at all." Simon reached over and touched her hand briefly, barely more than a brush. "Not at all," he said again quietly.

They drove in silence down the country road Abby knew so well, the country road where Luke and her mother had lost their lives, although she hadn't seen it happen. She didn't want to think about it now. Then they were turning onto route 12, and then I-94 towards Minneapolis, cutting northwest across Wisconsin, leaving everything familiar behind.

"Tell me about this guy," Abby said as the fields flashed by and she relaxed back into her seat. Willow Tree Orchards was far behind her now.

"His name is literally Guy," Simon answered with a laugh. "Guy Wessel. He was in the 508th with both Lawson and your grandfather, part of the 82nd Airborne."

"Is that all you know?"

"I know Guy seemed quite close to Matthew Lawson. He spoke about him fondly, or at least it seemed so, in his Facebook message, and he's happy for us to come and see him so he can tell us what he knows."

"But he might not know anything. Or at least, not much." Abby felt both a needling sense of disappointment and a flicker of relief. Maybe it would be easier, if they weren't able to find anything out. *Don't worry, Dad, there's nothing there.*

Except, by her father's own admission, there was.

"He might not," Simon agreed. "And then that might be it. A dead end."

"If so, it might be for the best."

"It might." He didn't sound convinced.

"You're going back soon, aren't you?" Abby asked. It was early August, with the heat and humidity to prove it, the damp skies and stifling nights, the sudden thunderstorms. "You've already been here for nearly a month."

"My ticket is for this Wednesday. I have to get back for exam results."

Just a few days away. Had he even been going to tell her he was leaving so soon?

Abby didn't reply as she looked out the window at the familiar scenery—fields and an occasional barn, weathered billboards advertising everything from Mars Cheese Castle to one of the country's biggest dollar stores.

"What is it with Wisconsin and cheese?" Simon asked after a few minutes had passed, nodding towards a billboard with a photo of a rather tacky "cheese castle", complete with a crenelated turret.

"Wisconsin is the number-one cheese-producing state in America," Abby told him with a smile. "It produces a quarter of the country's cheese."

"Do you learn that in school?"

"We recite it along with the Pledge of Allegiance." Abby laughed at the expression on Simon's face. "I'm joking. It's just something you know if you live here."

"And yet your family produces apples."

"Dairy farming is big business. Most of the farms are huge, with thousands of cows. And, in any case, my dad said his father wanted to go into crop production. His family were beef farmers in Minnesota, and he didn't like it." She paused. "Maybe that's the reason he left Minnesota, and didn't stay in touch. No big mystery."

"But you never met them."

"No, but they were older even for grandparents... surely lots of people don't meet their grandparents?" She considered this for a moment before admitting, "But I suppose I always got the sense that there had been some sort of break."

"It makes you wonder if it's all connected somehow—my grandmother, your grandfather, the medals, Minnesota. Or am I just trying to tie everything up with a neat bow?"

"I don't know." Abby rolled the thought over in her mind. Matthew Lawson's medal... Tom Reese leaving his family behind him... even her own father's reticence. "That would be nice and simple, I suppose," she said.

"Or very complicated."

"Yes, true."

"We don't need to keep talking about it, though. We'll learn what's what soon enough." He glanced at her. "If you'd rather talk about something else?"

"Like what?"

"Like about these amazing billboards." Simon gestured to one they'd just passed. "Paul Bunyan's Cook Shanty! That looks incredible. Do you think we can go there for lunch?"

"Only if you're hungry. It's the next exit."

"Done." Simon glanced in the rearview mirror as he moved into the right lane. "Fantastic. 'Wisconsin's Favorite Restaurant'. You must know what to recommend."

Abby laughed. "I've never been there in my life."

"What!" Simon gave her a comically shocked expression. "I can't believe it. You don't even know what you've been missing out on."

"I guess I'll find out."

Abby was still smiling as they turned into the parking lot of the restaurant. Built like an enormous log cabin, with a huge statue of an axe-wielding Paul Bunyan and large signs promising all you could eat, as well as lumberjack meals—whatever they were—the restaurant looked as if it would fulfill all Simon's expectations and more.

The interior was just as over the top, with wooden walls, checked tablecloths, and everything oversized.

"I love it," Simon said fervently. "I absolutely love it. I feel like saying 'howdy'. Would that be too much?"

"Definitely. Especially in a British accent."

A smiling waitress led them to a table near the window; it was only half past eleven but there were a few diners determinedly plowing through what Abby surmised were lumberjack break-fasts—pancakes, eggs, sausages and fried ham, hash browns, and a basket of sugary donuts. Abby had never seen so much food on a single table.

"This is going to be amazing," Simon said, and she laughed and shook her head.

"I would think most British people would find this sort of thing a bit corny," she said. "But you love it."

"I do," he agreed solemnly. "Every bit of it. There is absolutely nothing like this back in the UK." He glanced down at the menu. "Now, obviously, we are both going to have to order the lumberjack platters."

"I was thinking of getting a salad—"

"Absolutely not."

She laughed and shook her head. "Seriously?"

"Seriously. Lumberjack lunch or bust."

Abby looked at the description of the lumberjack platter—two kinds of meat, mashed potatoes, two vegetables, plus the shanty's homemade lumberjack bread, whatever that was. "I'll burst," she told him. "But fine."

"That's settled, then." Simon looked so pleased that Abby couldn't help but laugh again. He made her so *happy*, she realized, just being with him. His enthusiasm was catching.

"How do you do it?" she blurted, and Simon raised his eyebrows. "How do you find pleasure in such small things? And—seem so pleased by everything? How can you be so *happy*?"

A veil dropped over Simon's eyes briefly, making Abby wish she hadn't asked, and yet she still wanted to know. "You mean, because of things that have happened before?" he asked after a moment, his tone cautiously neutral.

"Your divorce?" She hadn't actually been thinking about that, but now that he'd mentioned it she knew she wanted to know. "Yes, I suppose that's part of it. I just meant generally, but, yes. That, too."

Simon looked down as he needlessly rearranged his knife and fork. Abby waited. She hadn't meant to mention his divorce, but she wasn't sorry they'd arrived at that point.

"I suppose it's a choice I make," he said slowly. "But sometimes it feels like slapping plasters on gaping wounds. Sometimes... I feel like a hypocrite." He looked up with a lopsided smile, his eyes shadowed. "I made a mess of things once before."

"Why do you blame yourself so much?" Abby asked, knowing he could ask the question right back at her, and she was definitely not ready to answer.

But he didn't deflect; he stayed silent, considering her question, and then he answered it. "Because I think I am to blame," he said starkly. "My mother... I know I mentioned before how up and down she was, but I think I downplayed it to you, to most people, because..." He let out a breath. "Well, because it seems like the actions of a little boy to blame your mother for the way you are."

"But?" Abby prompted softly.

"But my mother made my life feel like a roller coaster, and I really don't like them. They make me feel sick." His eyes glinted briefly with humor before turning serious once more. "Although she never had a diagnosis, I think she must have been bipolar. There were a lot of highs and even more lows, and I never knew which I was going to get at any given moment."

"What about your sisters? Did they have the same experience?"

"Somewhat, I think, although not as severe. They're quite a bit older than me, and they'd all flown the nest when my mother's symptoms really started to show, so I was the only one home. Which makes me sound very woe-is-me, I realize. Which is part of the reason I don't talk about it."

Abby could certainly understand about not talking about things, for whatever reason. "What about your dad?"

Simon shrugged. "I think he just felt that was how she was. He loved the highs and he checked out a bit during the lows. Not... not terribly. Really, I had—*have*—a great family." His lips twisted. "Especially from the outside."

Abby nodded slowly. She was glad he'd told her, but she also felt troubled. She didn't know what this meant—if anything—for them. If there even was a them. Did sharing secrets bring you closer, or draw you even farther apart?

The waitress came to take their orders—two lumberjack platters with all the fixings—and when she'd gone again, Abby sensed Simon wanting to move the conversation on, but she wasn't quite ready for him to.

"What about your marriage?" she asked before he could change the topic to something safer. "You talked about your mother, but I don't even know your wife—ex-wife's—name."

"Sara." He paused, as if he was going to say something more, but then didn't. "I mentioned my mother because I think it affected how I was with Sara. Sara wasn't—*isn't*—bipolar, in the least. But I more or less acted as if she was." He sighed. "She would get upset about something, and I simply shut down. She'd tell me she was angry, and I couldn't deal with it. At all. And that was hard for her. The trouble was, I didn't know how to change, or even if I wanted to. I didn't like confrontation. Still don't." He gave her a game smile. "Can you tell?"

"Yes, although you probably can tell I don't like it, either." Abby hesitated, the question, the very obvious question, on the tip of her tongue, waiting to be said, yet she was afraid to go there. But wasn't she trying to change, as well? "And now?" she made herself ask. "How do you feel about it all now?"

SIMON

Simon stared at Abby, the way her anxious gaze scanned his face as she bit her lip. This conversation was almost as hard for her as it was for him, although maybe not, because for him it felt like peeling back a layer of skin—although hadn't she said that before, when talking about her family? It wasn't easy for either of them.

He knew it shouldn't be that bad, not really. He should be able to talk about these things. He was a grown man. He'd tried therapy—briefly, but still. He knew what his issues were, at least, and yet even now he felt like clawing at something, crying out, or maybe just his usual, making a joke. Making a big deal of the stupid lumberjack platters because that was so much easier than making a big deal about this. And he hadn't even told her about Maggie yet.

He should, he knew that. The longer he left it, the worse it became, a yawning ignorance on her part, a gross deception on his. And yet still he held back, because he didn't want Abby to see him differently. Wonder what kind of man he was. This was bad enough.

"I'm trying," he said at last. "And I've been trying. Hence this conversation."

"Thank you," Abby said quietly, and Simon couldn't keep from letting out a little sigh of relief. She sounded as if she was going to leave it.

"Do you think Sophie might have had similar issues to your mother?" Abby asked after a moment. "You said she was like her, with the highs and lows, didn't you? What if it was something like that that contributed to whatever happened between her and my grandfather? She said she hoped he'd forgive her, you mentioned?"

"Yes… I never thought of that, but you may be right."

"Tell me about her. Sophie."

Simon smiled and shrugged. "I wish there was more I could tell you. I didn't see her all that often, but I have some vague memories. She argued with my mother once, I don't know what about, but we left in a hurry. Sometimes she seemed… discontented, I suppose. She tried to hide it, I think, but she made me feel uneasy. She could also be charming, though. She had a wonderful laugh—throaty and real."

Abby sat with her chin in her hand. With her dark hair soft about her shoulders, Simon thought she looked as lovely as a painting. He wished he could tell her something of how he felt, but it sounded sentimental and stupid and, in any case, he didn't even know what was going on between them. They'd kissed twice, but they'd also argued, and he was beginning to wonder if he'd already been friend-zoned. Maybe that would be no bad thing.

Then again, maybe it would.

"It sounds like she was a very interesting person. I wonder if Guy Wessel will have anything to say about her, as well."

"Perhaps, even if just from what Matthew Lawson or your grandad might have mentioned." Simon shrugged. "Maybe not, though. This really could be a wild goose chase of the first order."

"I know." Abby smiled self-consciously. "I don't mind."

Something warm and welcome bloomed in Simon's chest at that, and at the hesitant but hopeful look on her face, which made him feel like letting out some sort of ridiculous primal roar. He didn't know how Abby felt, not exactly, but the look on her face was enough. "I don't either," he said.

The waitress came bearing their lumberjack platters, which really were enormous.

"We can put what we don't eat in doggie bags and have it for dinner," Abby suggested a bit doubtfully. "There's no way I'm going to eat even a third of this."

"But you can try," Simon declared. "It's practically your duty."

She laughed and shook her head, and they both started eating. Outside, the sky was still pressing down on the earth, everything limp and colorless from an August day's humidity, and yet Simon felt as if the world was turning to Technicolor. Something was expanding in his chest, taking over his body, making him smile. Grin.

Maybe they wouldn't learn a thing from Guy Wessel. Maybe nothing would happen between him and Abby. But right here, right now, he felt as if he could live in this moment, and it would be enough.

CHAPTER TWENTY

London

July 1944

There had been nothing to save from the rubble of the house on Holmside Road, nothing useful or precious, not a single keepsake to remember the many happy years in that home.

In the days after the bombing, Lily withdrew into herself, like an animal seeking self-protection, curling inward, while Sophie became hardened, the appealing gloss worn off her veneer, leaving her brittle and determined, the humor and charm that had once softened her seeming to have vanished completely.

Richard Mather had not been home when the V-1 had hit, which was, at least, a mercy. Moments after Lily had run towards the house, he'd come haring down the street, shouting his wife's name uselessly.

Matthew had watched as the Mathers stood in front of their ruined house, praying that by some miracle Carol hadn't been inside it. But there'd been so little warning, and when Lily had run to look, the Anderson shelter had been empty. Rescue workers had pulled her broken body from the wreckage as Sophie turned onto Holmside Road, Lily utterly silent as Richard let out an anguished cry.

In the aftermath, no one knew what to do. When it had been someone else, there was tea to brew and blankets to find and comfort to give. Now, other people were pressing cups of tea into their hands, and finding them clothes and blankets, murmuring sympathies and shaking their heads. Lily had looked blankly at the cup she was cradling as if she didn't know what it was.

"Where will we sleep?" she'd asked no one in particular, as if it was a matter of only passing interest.

Neighbors up and down the street had offered spare rooms, settees, and more blankets than they knew what to do with, but Matthew knew the Mathers could hardly spend the rest of the war on someone's sofa.

The next day, instead of walking with Lily in Regent's Park or going to the cinema, holding hands and talking about nothing, he queued with her for a clothing grant, and then helped to look for accommodation for the family.

The government, Matthew discovered, was near to useless in providing anything behind the barest of essentials; there were simply too many people in similar situations, too many homes and lives wrecked for them even to try to make much of a difference.

Eventually, after three days of the Mathers sleeping in a neighbor's sitting room, they found a set of rooms in Stockwell, a far cry from the cozy comfort of the house on Holmside Road, but just about adequate.

There was a small bedroom for Sophie and Lily, and a front room where Richard could sleep, along with a tap and a gas ring so they could make their own meals and wash. The toilet was outside, at the bottom of a muddy strip of garden. The whole place smelled of boiled vegetables and soiled nappies, and everyone living there seemed grim-faced and sullen, but it was all there was.

"It will do," Lily said firmly, while Sophie simply curled her lip as she looked around the two shabby rooms with peeling linoleum floors and plaster flaking off the walls. "Mother would have been able to make this place a home," Lily added as Sophie walked off. "She was brilliant that way. It's up to us to carry on as best as we can." And with a purposeful air, her lips trembling only a little, she reached for the little tin teapot they'd been given with a box of other secondhand household items and placed it on the table. This was home, Matthew realized with both affection and pride, because she would make it so.

"Let me take you all out to Rainbow Corner tonight," Matthew suggested later. He didn't know if he could get them in, with so many GIs on leave, but he would do his best. "For a slap-up meal. It's the least I can do."

"Why not?" Sophie answered with a toss of her head, a hard glitter in her eyes. "Might as well get a meal while I can."

Richard cried off, insisting he was fine on his own and wouldn't spoil their fun—although Matthew wondered how much fun they could have, considering the circumstance. He knew Tom had been granted leave after his ended, and he hoped he'd be able to provide some comfort to Sophie, although she seemed indifferent to the prospect. Nothing seemed to matter much anymore.

This was what war did to you, Matthew thought, in the end. After all the fury and fear and the desperate, wild hope, it made you stop caring, and in its own way that was worse than anything that had gone before.

That evening, the crowd at Rainbow Corner seemed both determined and jubilant, a far cry from the dour mood of the little group who filed into the foyer of the former Lyons Corner House on Piccadilly.

"Haven't you heard?" an airman at the bar asked Matthew, who shook his head. "They tried to kill Hitler. His own men. A bomb or something in a suitcase."

Matthew's heart felt as if it were lurching towards his throat. "They didn't succeed?"

"Nah, he's got the luck of the devil, that bastard." The man tossed back half his beer in one gulp. "But his own men trying to kill him? Even they want to be shot of it all. It won't be long now. It can't be."

But any amount of time was too long, Matthew thought as he waited for their drinks. He glanced back at Lily and Sophie, standing apart from the jostle of GIs, Lily looking pensive and Sophie with her hand holding her jacket closed at the throat, her gaze darting here and there.

Matthew thanked the bartender and took the drinks back through the crowd.

"It's like a party in here," Lily remarked with a wan smile. "What are they celebrating?"

Matthew hesitated and then answered, "Some Nazis tried to assassinate Hitler, apparently. It's been on the wireless."

"What!" Lily's eyes widened. "Did they—"

"They obviously didn't," Sophie cut in sharply. "Succeed, that is." She threw back her drink—straight vermouth—in one abrupt movement. "Otherwise there really would be a party." The bitterness in her tone was unmistakable. She thrust her empty glass towards Matthew. "Another?"

"Sophie," Lily said quietly.

Sophie raised her eyebrows in challenge. "What is there left to do but to drink?"

Matthew took her glass and made his way back to the bar.

Sophie continued to drink steadily through the evening, despite Lily's gentle reprimands. Matthew thought of refusing her requests for more drinks, but he suspected Sophie would just ask another GI, who would be all too willing to oblige. At least he was able to ask the bartender to water them down, but at the rate she was going that hardly mattered.

As the evening wore on, Sophie became louder and wilder, gesticulating with her arms, her bitter laugh like a bird cry, while

Lily grew more anxious. It was hardly the respite from their troubles that Matthew had intended it to be, and conversation came in desperate fits and starts, with Lily doing her best to talk normally, until halfway through their steaks. While Lily was telling him about the WI effort to collect rosehips to make syrup for children, Sophie slammed her glass down so hard on the table, they all jumped.

"Oh, shut *up*, Lily," she said in a voice that now carried through the whole dining room; a hundred GIs and their dates had fallen silent. Sophie pushed back from the table, standing up as she raked her hands through her hair, causing it to tumble from its French roll. "Just shut up," she repeated, loud enough for everyone to hear. "What is the point?"

"Sophie, please," Lily said quietly.

"What is the point?" Sophie repeated, her voice rising to something between a snarl and a wail. "What's the *point*?" She gazed around the dining room, pinning people in their places with her contemptuous gaze. "You're all sitting here guzzling your beer and sawing at your steaks, and I'm asking you, what's the bloody point? Of any of it? If I were a man—my God, if I were a man—I wouldn't be here, sitting back and relaxing. I'd be out there, shooting every damn German I could in the head. I'd be winning this war, I tell you, not typing a bloody letter or knitting some poor sod socks."

"Give that girl a gun," someone called out, and a titter ran through the room.

It wasn't malicious, Matthew knew. It was meant kindly, a way to defuse the awful moment. He saw pity in people's faces, but he knew Sophie didn't see it, and he thought that was perhaps a good thing.

"Damn the whole lazy lot of you," she cried, and then she stumbled from the room, with Lily lurching up after her.

Matthew threw some bills on the table before he hurried after them, catching up with them on the pavement outside. A light drizzle was falling, beading in their hair, and Lily's arms were around Sophie as her sister sobbed as if she'd been split right in half.

"I'll get a cab," Matthew murmured.

A queue of hopeful entrants to Rainbow Corner watched the scene play out with a weary sort of curiosity that soon slouched into indifference. There had been too many similar scenes already; every street corner had become a stage for someone else's tragedy.

Thankfully they didn't have to bear the strangers' apathetic scrutiny for very long. A cab came, and Matthew ushered the sisters into it.

Back at the set of rooms the Mathers now called home, Matthew stood in the kitchen with Richard, both of them silent, as Lily helped a now alarmingly docile Sophie to bed. It was as if the fight had drained right out of her, her face and hair both pale, her expression deadened. She said not a word as Lily ushered her into the bedroom, and Richard watched them with tired eyes.

"Carol would have known what to do," he murmured. "She always knew how to handle Sophie, God bless her." With a shake of his head, he reached for his newspaper. They no longer had a wireless.

After a few moments, Matthew excused himself and went to wait outside in the hall. Even though the older man wasn't unfriendly, Matthew felt as if he were intruding into an intimate family moment. Out in the hallway, he could hear a baby crying upstairs and there was a persistent smell of boiled cabbage and drains. He waited, unsure if Lily would come out or not, and yet not wanting to leave.

After about twenty minutes of uncertainty, the door opened and Lily stood there, her dress rumpled, her smile tired.

"I was hoping you'd have waited," she said quietly and then she stepped closer to Matthew, and he put his arms around her, a matter of instinct rather than decision.

Lily leaned her forehead against his shoulder and closed her eyes. Neither of them spoke. There felt like nothing to say, and yet a lifetime of conversations seemed to pass through the air between them, questions asked and answered, understanding given and taken in the mere drawing of their breaths.

"She'll be all right," Lily said after a few moments. "She just needs to sleep."

"I'm leaving tomorrow." He had to say it, even though he didn't want to. "I've got to report to Nottingham by four o'clock."

Lily nodded, her eyes still closed, the top of her head brushing his chin.

"May I see you before I go? During your lunch hour, perhaps?" He knew Lily had already been given all the leave she was likely to get for her mother's death.

"Yes, of course." She opened her eyes and leaned back to look at him. "Where will you go, from Nottingham?"

"I don't know."

"You don't know, or can't say?" She didn't sound reproachful, just tired.

"I really don't know. Maybe up to some POW camps in the north. Maybe back to Europe."

Lily nodded slowly. "Do you think it will be over soon? I can't even imagine it anymore, what it would be like to not be at war."

"It will." Matthew spoke with conviction, because he had to. "The Germans are surrendering in thousands. They *want* the war to be over. It can't be long now."

"If everyone wants it over, why isn't it?" Lily said sadly. "Can one man really have so much power, to keep half the world in thrall?"

"It appears so." Matthew heard the thrum of tension in his voice, and knew Lily heard it, too. He'd been feeling so weary these past few days, but now the old rage licked at him again, firing his insides, making his fists clench even as he held Lily to him.

She laid one hand against his cheek, her skin pale and cool. "Don't," she said softly, and then with her other hand she reached down and unclenched his fingers.

*

At noon the next day, they met at a Lyons Corner House near the station and drank cups of well-stewed tea, their knees touching under the table, his kitbag at their feet.

"How is she?" Matthew asked of Sophie, and Lily sighed.

"She went to work. She seemed determined, but I feel there's so much she doesn't tell me." She glanced out the window, at a muted London going about their weary business. "We used to be so close. Perhaps when Tom visits, it will lift her spirits. If anything can—" She glanced back at him. "Have you seen much of him, over there?"

"A bit." After those three endless days tramping through fields, searching for their unit, Matthew had spent very little time with Tom Reese, which was how he suspected they both preferred it. "He told me he's been writing Sophie."

"Yes, quite a lot. They've even talked of getting married, although I don't know if that is just because of the war. When things seem so uncertain, people make rash promises." She looked away, blushing a little.

Matthew tried to think of something to say, and found he couldn't.

"Do you want to go back?" Lily asked after a moment, as she lifted her cup to her lips and then put it back down without drinking from it. "Are you—I know it sounds strange, but are you hoping to?"

"Yes." Now that the possibility lay before him, Matthew knew he wanted it quite desperately. "I need to find out what happened to my family."

"Gertie," Lily said, her gaze flickering over his face. "And your brothers?"

"Franz and Arno."

A look of surprise flashed across her features as he said their names. "Your name isn't really Matthew, is it? Or Lawson. Of course it isn't. It can't be."

He smiled wryly. "My name is Matthaus. The German form." He hadn't said it in such a long time.

"And your last name? I can't believe I don't know it." She shook her head, looking troubled by the thought, as if it actually meant anything.

"You know *me*, Lily," he said, and reached for her hand across the table. Even though they'd spent so little time together, even though they'd said so little to one another, he knew it was true. She knew him, just as he knew her, a deep knowing that needed no words, no idle conversation or chitchat to prove it.

"Will you tell me what your surname is?"

He paused and then said, "Weiss. I am Matthaus Weiss." It sounded strange on his tongue.

"Matthaus," she repeated wonderingly, and then let out a little laugh. "Matthaus Weiss. It suits you."

"Does it? I'm not sure I feel like that man anymore."

Lily squeezed his hand. "It will come back."

"What will?"

"The person you were. Your sense of self, I suppose. You might not feel it now, but he's still there. Matthaus." She gave him a small, teasing smile, an effort. "Can I call you that now?"

He smiled back, just a little. "If you want."

"Do you want me to?" She looked at him seriously.

"Yes," he said, but he wondered if he did. If he was Matthaus Weiss, he was even more of a foreigner, an alien, a Jew. Was that man someone Lily could contemplate spending her life with? Had she even thought that far ahead?

And yet maybe she would never have to. The war wasn't over yet, for either of them. Right now he was simply spinning dreams.

Anything could happen. The thought made him squeeze Lily's hand. Another V-1 rocket… if he went back to France…

"Then I will call you that," Lily said. "Matthaus Weiss." She nodded, seeming satisfied. "I like it."

"Good." Already time was slipping away, like pearls off a string, precious and fragile, and so very fleeting. His train was due to leave in fifteen minutes. Matthew slipped his hand from hers and she nodded in understanding.

"Is it time?"

"Yes, I'm afraid so."

Matthew paid for their barely drunk teas and slung his kitbag over his shoulder while Lily gathered her coat and handbag. A thousand scenes like this were being played out up and down the country, so familiar they were becoming trite, but they still garnered a sympathetic smile from the tired waitress at the till.

"Take care of yourselves," she said, a command, and they both nodded like children who had to obey. If only they could.

They walked in silence towards the station, joining the stream of men in uniform and the women who were accompanying them, a parade of sacrifice and duty. With every step, Matthew had the urge to both hang back and break into a run; he wanted Lily to walk away quickly, and he wanted her to take his hand.

Everything felt impossible—the 508th waiting in Nottingham, the war in Normandy. His family in Fraustadt, or not. And Lily here, in a set of shabby rooms, her mother dead, and he'd never even told her he loved her. He couldn't say the words now. It didn't feel fair. It would be a conjurer's trick, magic words that meant nothing, considering their situation. He might never see her again. Considering the 508th's casualties so far, it was all too likely. The last thing he wanted to do was bind her to a broken promise.

And yet if he didn't say them, she might never know. That seemed impossible too, a burden neither of them should have to bear, the unbearable ignorance of it, to journey on into the unknown without that sure and certain knowledge that pulsed inside of him.

They wound their way through the crowded station, people surging forth, a sense of brittle expectation crackling in the air like static as a train whistle blew, and another let out an impatient breath of steam.

His train was already there, GIs striding up and down the platform, laughing, smoking, catcalling, kissing their girls, all trying to cram as much of their lives as they could into a matter of minutes.

Lily turned to Matthew, an uncertain smile making her mouth waver.

"I'll write," she said.

"As will I—"

"You don't have to. I know it must be hard."

"I want to."

She nodded, and Matthew hitched his bag more firmly over his shoulder. Now was the moment.

A soldier walking past them bumped into Lily and she stumbled slightly. Matthew reached for her arm to steady her, and then he drew her to him and kissed her softly on the lips. She yielded beneath him, and as he closed his eyes, he let the world fall away for a moment. He knew it would all come rushing back again—the noise and the duty and the fear—but for now, for this, he allowed himself to feel a burgeoning sense of promise, a fragile and yet certain hope.

He opened his eyes as she smiled up at him, and the words came naturally, as essential and elemental as breathing. "I love you."

Her eyes widened, and her smile curved deeper. She laid one hand on his cheek, her skin soft and cool. "And I love you," she returned simply. Suddenly it had become easy.

A whistle blew. Matthew kissed her again and then, as he stepped back, Lily gave a little wave.

"Goodbye," she said, and he boarded the train.

CHAPTER TWENTY-ONE

Nijmegen, The Netherlands

September 1944

"Let me tell you what I know."

Matthew gazed at the anxious Wehrmacht soldier sat forward on a chair in a room in an abandoned monastery by the Waal River and did not reply.

Three days ago, after cooling their heels in Nottingham for six weeks, paratroopers of the 82nd Airborne Division had been dropped over Nijmegen, with an order to secure the bridges across the Waal and Maas rivers immediately, to prevent the Germans from blocking the Allies' relentless push into Germany.

The jump, made on a sunny day in mid-September, had gone well, with all but two of the planes reaching their target areas. Matthew had landed with a dozen others in a muddy potato field, the sky full of planes and parachutes, the drone of engines filling the air and thrumming through his chest.

The nearby antiaircraft guns did not release a single shot as the sky darkened with the relentless force of the Allies' assault. The artillerymen had their hands up in surrender as the paratroopers landed, and Matthew began his interrogations that evening, in this abandoned monastery overlooking the medieval city of Nijmegen, the 508th fighting in its streets towards the bridge over the Waal River.

Interrogations had become, for the most part, ludicrously easy—soldiers babbling in their eagerness to reveal what they knew, and to be considered helpful to the onslaught of Allies. Matthew struggled against a complicated disdain for men who so quickly abandoned the cause they'd fought for, even as he knew how evil that cause truly was, and was convinced with the utmost certainty they were doing the right thing, if not always for the right reason.

Yet many of the conscripted soldiers, he'd come to discover, were not actually Nazis. Many weren't even Germans. They were desperate Poles, disaffected Communists, dissenters and free thinkers and undesirables of any sort who had all been forced to fight under the swastika banner. While many were volunteering information simply because they wanted to save their own skins, others did so out of a genuine desire to help the Allied cause.

Since the Allied forces had dropped down into the Netherlands, the Germans were surrendering in droves, entire units and battalions at a time, hurling their guns to the ground and their hands up into the air, so the Allies were struggling to find places to contain them. It hadn't taken long to realize this part of the Netherlands had been a neglected corner of the Nazis' war strategy, and was populated with units of barely trained soldiers who had been forced, often under great duress, to march and to fight.

It was Matthew's job to ask them questions, note their information, and sift through the useless chaff to find the all-important grains of wheat. He'd become both assured and hardened in his interrogation manner, refusing to be moved by a Communist weeping that he'd never wanted to fight, or an eighteen-year-old recruit shaking so much he couldn't even hold the cigarette Matthew always proffered.

Matthew knew he was playing a role, whether it was soothing confidant or disdainful officer; whether he was thanking a penitent private or dismissing the information an officer offered as unimportant even when it was actually crucial. Never, ever giving the game away—for that's what it was, a game, and yet one on which they were all gambling their lives.

That afternoon, Guy Wessel had gone with another team to attempt to convince a nearby German unit to surrender, a job considered now to be a veritable stroll in the park. Matthew was here in the monastery with a soldier who had promised to tell him whatever he liked.

The trouble, Matthew had discovered, was that what the man told him could just as easily be a lie. He had to sift the truth from the wished-for; frightened soldiers would sometimes pretend they had more knowledge in order to be helpful, which wasn't, of course, helpful at all, especially when they plucked numbers and positions out of the air.

"What is it you think I wish to know?" he inquired of the man, his hands in his pockets as he leaned against the curved arch of the monastery's window.

The man shrugged. "Numbers of guns? Troops?" His eyes darted to the right and left, and then back again. "I know there are explosives all along the Waal bridge—"

"We have already secured that bridge," Matthew told him. Even though it had come at a bloody cost, with two hundred lives lost as they'd fought their way up the steep riverbanks, straight into gunfire, three days after they'd been meant to secure it.

The soldier shrugged again, looking defeated now, with no more to offer. "Do you have a cigarette?" He looked hopefully at Matthew's pocket.

"No, I'm sorry. I do not." The man didn't know anything more. Matthew had done dozens, even hundreds, of interrogations by this point, and he had learned to tell when a prisoner was out of information. He nodded towards the GI waiting by the door. "Take him back, Private."

Alone in the drafty room, Matthew lit a cigarette as he looked out over the embattled streets of Nijmegen. Despite the many disaffected soldiers so willing to surrender, others were determined to fight to the last man and nothing was going quite to plan. Every time another life was lost, on some nameless alleyway in a city no one had heard of, Matthew wondered why this war had to keep going on and on—and what would happen when it finally ended.

What would happen to a shattered Europe, and what would happen to his family, and to him? Were his mother and brothers and sister hiding away somewhere, frightened but safe? Had they found a place of protection? Or could they be in one of the camps he'd heard murmurs about—somewhere in the east, a place for prisoners? If they were in a camp, Matthew told himself they would at least be safe there. He knew the conditions would be hard, but they would be far from the fighting.

"Ah, here you are."

Matthew turned to see Tom Reese surveying him coolly. His uniform was splattered with mud, his hair ruffled as he raked one hand through it. Matthew hadn't seen Tom since they'd dropped into the Netherlands, and he hadn't spoken to him when they'd both been in Nottingham waiting for their orders, after they'd been granted their separate leaves to London. There was enough to do, and enough men in their battalion, to make interaction far from a necessity, especially since it seemed it was something neither of them particularly wanted.

"Were you looking for me?" he asked.

"We just came back from the Volksgrenadier lines."

Matthew raised his eyebrows. "Did they surrender?"

Tom let out a harsh laugh. "No, they damned well didn't. The regiment had been relieved a couple of days ago, it turns out." His lips twisted. "By Waffen-SS troops. We barely got away with our lives."

"They've sent in the SS?" Matthew assimilated that information into the store of knowledge he already had. "So they're not just giving up, then."

Tom gave another humorless laugh. "Hell, no. They'll fight to the last man. At least the true Nazis will. They're real believers, those bastards. They're not stepping down anytime soon." He paused, taking a step into the empty room. "Smoke?"

Wordlessly, Matthew handed him his pack of cigarettes.

"I ought to tell you," Tom said as Matthew lit his cigarette, "Sophie and I are engaged."

He regarded Matthew with a faint smile, his eyebrows slightly raised as he waited for a response.

"Congratulations," Matthew said.

"I'll tell you something else, Lawson," Tom added as he drew on his cigarette. "I don't like you."

Matthew cocked his head.

"But it's not because you're a Jew."

"Oh?" He wondered if Tom was aware of how much that seemingly innocuous statement revealed.

"No, it isn't." Tom managed to sound magnanimous. "To be perfectly honest, it's because you've never liked me."

Matthew stiffened at that, and then he inclined his head in acknowledgment. It was true, after all, in the main.

"You've judged me from the beginning," Tom continued with a rather boyish determination, sounding more like a hurt child than a hardened soldier. "I don't know what you are, where you come from exactly, but I know you've thought I was some stupid yokel fresh from the farm, wet behind the ears, finger itching on the trigger."

"Those were not my exact views," Matthew returned dryly. "I am from a small town in Germany, as it happens." Fraustadt was a market town, nothing more. "I am as much of a 'yokel' as you are."

"What have you thought, then?" Tom asked, sounding tired rather than belligerent. "Because you've looked down on me, Lawson. I know you have."

Matthew sighed. He did not wish to enumerate the ways he'd found Tom—and a hundred or more men like him—disappointing. He knew it revealed something in him, as much as in the men whose lives could seem so petty and small—and why shouldn't they be? Most of them hadn't suffered very much at all. They had a certain right, or at least a leniency, to be a bit small-minded.

He knew he could not explain how Tom's brashness, his foolish bravado, his silly swagger and his blustering certainty that he knew what he was talking about, irritated and angered him in increasing measures, as much as he tried to blank it all out. He could not tell this truculent man-child that he had no idea about anything, because Matthew knew that wasn't fair.

Tom had fought for four months. He'd seen his fair share of battles, of violence—more than Matthew had, now that he was kept behind the front lines for interrogations.

"It doesn't matter," he said, even as it occurred to him that perhaps he and Tom Reese were nothing more than products of their separate upbringings; that Reese could not help being who he was, just as Matthew could not prevent it, either. They'd both been brought to this moment, so why should they hate each other for it? And he didn't hate Tom anyway; he didn't feel enough for that.

"Well, it matters to me," Tom answered, his voice rising. "Sophie and I will be getting married. And if you have any intentions towards that mousy sister of hers—"

"Don't," Matthew said quietly. There was no menace in his voice, but Tom's eyes widened for a second and he shrugged.

"Maybe you don't have any intentions, then." The sneer in his voice made Matthew's become more lethal. Maybe he hated him, after all.

"My intentions towards Lily are none of your concern."

"They are if we are to be brothers-in-law."

Matthew was silent. Amazingly, this rather unappealing possibility had never even occurred to him. Perhaps because he didn't know whether either he or Tom, never mind Sophie or Lily, would make it to the end of the war. Or perhaps because Sophie and Lily were so entirely different in their natures, that he occasionally somehow managed to forget they were sisters. He did not relish the idea of being brother-in-law to Tom Reese, but neither could he credit it as a real possibility now.

"Let's make it to the end of the war," he said. "And then we shall see."

Tom set his jaw. "It won't be long now, and I for one intend to stay alive."

"As we all do, I'm sure."

Tom shook his head, his expression turning grimly purposeful. From outside, they could hear the steady sound of shells falling, like a hard rain. Matthew had become so accustomed to the noise that he found it was silence that was now strange.

"I can tell you this," Tom said. "I'm not going to die in some godforsaken foxhole or on some damned bridge I've never heard of, just months before Hitler finally decides to call it quits."

"You may not have a choice," Matthew pointed out mildly. "Although I am sure you will do your best, as will every other man, to stay alive."

Tom looked as if he wanted to say more, but then he didn't. He gave an angry jerk of his head as he flicked his cigarette out the window. "You're needed, by the way," he said as he turned to leave. "We captured some stupid sod wandering around, claiming to be a deserter. He's lucky we got to him before his own damned army did."

*

What became known as Operation Market Garden—the securing of the way into Germany from the Netherlands—turned quickly into a disaster for the Allies, with the British Airborne losing three-quarters of their troops as the Germans became the aggressors once more in a conflict that seemed to stretch on forever.

The 82nd, having succeeded in holding the bridges, were ordered to stay in and around Nijmegen, which was still being shelled, for over a month. Already eight hundred men had been lost.

Matthew had plenty of prisoners to interrogate, and was kept occupied finding out as much as he could about the Wehrmacht's troop movements and artillery positions. By mid-November, the 508th were relieved by Canadian troops, and sent to Camp Sissonne, a former Wehrmacht base in France, for several weeks, to restock and recover, and wait for their promised Christmas leave to a newly liberated Paris.

In the canteen of the base, the walls decorated with remarkably unfunny German cartoons and drawings, Matthew sat with a bottle of beer at his elbow as he gazed down at the blank sheet of paper in front of him. He wanted to write Lily—he'd promised to write her, after all, although since returning to the front, he'd had neither the words nor the will. Now his head ached with all the things he didn't want to say.

He didn't want to tell her about the SS officer he'd interrogated who had spat in his face, or the sight of his fellow soldiers climbing on their hands and knees up the side of the Waal River, straight into gunfire. He couldn't tell her about the hopelessness he felt that infected him like a poison, seeping through his blood and making him wonder what the point of it all was, if anything would ever get better, if he would find his family, or even, after so many years of war and devastation, he wanted to. He certainly wouldn't tell her about the fury he felt, and how he didn't know if it was worse than the indifference, as he veered wildly and wearily between the two.

He rested his head on his hand, and thought perhaps he would just tell her how tired he was.

Dear Lily, he wrote after a few moments of contemplation. *I am writing you from a safe place, which feels like a great luxury. When I go outside, it is silent, and the only light comes from the stars in the sky. I look up at them and I think of you seeing them as well, and I hope you think of me. It feels like the only thing to hold onto in these dark days, which I know we both hope and pray will soon be over. Although I am afraid of what I will discover when they are over, whether I will find my family, or learn of their fate.*

I know I have told you of dear Gertie, but I have not said much of my brothers. Arno is the older one, and he is twenty now. He was like me when we were children, quiet and studious, but he also had a bent for mischief. Once, while playing a game, he locked poor Arno in a cupboard and then forgot about him there—he went off to play outside and no one heard Arno for hours. My mother was furious, but Arno got his own back—he poured a bucket of cold water all over Franz while he was sleeping. I look back on those childish pranks and think my mother must have despaired of us, but I remember her as full of laughter. She knew we loved each other, even if we did not always show it.

Matthew put his pen down as the memories came over him like a mist, engulfing him with both longing and sorrow. He pictured the four of them—the three scuffling boys and little Gertie watching their antics from the side—and wondered how any of them could have imagined what would happen to their family, to their lives, that comfortable home, full of love and light and warmth, shot straight through with grief and loss and misery.

He thought of his father, a serious look on his face as he listened to whatever childish complaint was brought to him, determined to give whatever slight it was a fair hearing. He'd been a man who had believed in justice, and that the German people had an inherent sense of it.

How wrong he'd been.

Matthew was just putting his pen to paper again when a duty officer rushed into the half-full canteen.

"Everyone to report to their quarters immediately!"

"What's going on?" someone called out. "Is it an airborne operation?"

"Infantry," the man replied shortly, and everyone began to hurry out of the canteen.

Matthew stuffed his unfinished letter in his pocket.

It was clear from the charged atmosphere that something big was about to happen—or already had. Orders were given to leave dress uniform and anything unnecessary at the base, and ammunition and rations were distributed.

Matthew caught sight of the grimly determined looks on his fellow soldiers' faces, and knew they were all thinking the same thing. They were going back into it. There would be no Christmas leave to Paris.

By dawn, they were being loaded into open-backed trucks and heading northwest, towards the Belgian border with Germany.

They were silent as they rode in rattling trucks towards Ardennes, for thirteen bone-jarring hours. The day grew colder, snow beginning to blanket the ground, a soft whiteness at odds with the violence that surely awaited. They'd been told very little, only that the Germans had broken through into Belgium.

At Werbomont, along the Bastogne–Liege line, the 82nd fanned out to take up defensive positions, while Matthew went on to find the headquarters of the operation, and see if he was needed to conduct interrogations.

As he rode along the line with a stern-faced driver, looking for the headquarters, Matthew saw sights that chilled him right through to his weary bones. Army men not trained for combat—

clerks and cooks who were used to pencils or spoons—were holding defensive positions, reading the instruction manuals of weaponry they'd never even looked at before, their faces gaunt and pale with panic. The situation was more desperate than he'd ever seen it, and yet they were meant to be winning the war. They clearly weren't winning this.

The situation was even more alarming when he finally found the headquarters in an old farmhouse, its steep roof thickly blanketed with snow. As he came in, he saw three officers in a flurry of angry panic, arguing over a battered map and the positions of Allied regiments on it.

Matthew took in the scene with a plunging sense of icy fear. These men were in command, but they did not look it. Their voices were high and taut with fear, and they seemed at a loss as to how to proceed. Matthew couldn't even tell who was in charge, but he took a steadying breath and approached the most senior officer, a colonel.

"Sir," he said, and saluted. "I'm with the 82nd Airborne—"

The colonel's bushy eyebrows snapped together as he registered Matthew's accent. Having spoken German so often in the last weeks and months, it had become more pronounced, although it hadn't mattered as the men in his regiment now knew who he was. They even joked about it, while Matthew smiled faintly on.

"The 82nd Airborne?" the colonel repeated incredulously. "Then why do you sound like a damned German?"

"I'm with the IPW," Matthew explained as calmly as he could, although the officer's eyes were wild. "That is, the Interrogation of Prisoners of War—" He fell silent as the colonel withdrew his pistol and cocked it two inches from his head. The other two officers simply watched, wide-eyed, bemused.

"That's interesting, son," the colonel said in a voice that belied that statement. "But we've had reports of Germans impersonating American soldiers, so why the hell should I believe you?"

CHAPTER TWENTY-TWO

ABBY

Oak Bluffs was a pleasant "Senior Living" facility on the outskirts of Minneapolis, overlooking the wide winding path of the Minnesota River.

"Guy Wessel lives in his own apartment," Simon explained as he pulled into a parking lot by a series of single-floor buildings. "Which is pretty amazing at his age."

"How old is he?"

"Ninety-seven. He joined up in 1942, as soon as he turned eighteen." He shot her a quick smile. "But that's all I know, really. That, and that he knew Matthew Lawson, and called him a friend."

"We'll know a lot more soon," Abby answered. "Hopefully."

The last few hours of driving had been easy and companionable, relaxed rather than intense after their conversation at the cook shanty. It was as if something had loosened between them, or perhaps just in Abby herself—a tangled knot whose complicated strands were just beginning to separate and reveal themselves.

It had been so very pleasant to simply *be* with someone, without heavy conversation or the need to skirt serious issues. Abby had switched her phone off, not wanting to worry about calls from her father, asking where she was, or texts from Shannon, seeing how she was. Right now she was with Simon, and she was absolutely fine.

The car parked, Simon paused for a moment as he glanced at her with his wonderfully crooked smile. "Are you ready to do this?"

"Yes." Abby wasn't sure if she actually thought—or hoped—Guy Wessel would have information for them or not. It wasn't even about that, she was beginning to realize, not really. Coming to Minneapolis with Simon wasn't even about Tom Reese or Sophie Mather. It was about her stepping out of her carefully constructed comfort zone, which hadn't been all that comfortable, in the end. It was about daring to do something different for once, and then daring to see where it might lead.

"Let's go, then," Simon said with a smile, and Abby nodded.

They both got out of the car and Simon started looking for number six, Guy Wessel's apartment. A few minutes later, as they walked along a pleasant path lined by rhododendron bushes, they found it, and he pressed the doorbell.

"Coming," a surprisingly strong voice called out from within. "Just takes me a minute."

Abby and Simon exchanged curious smiles and then, a few moments later, the door was unlocked and opened and a man stood there, white-haired and stooped over, his face as wrinkled as a walnut, his dark eyes full of both warmth and acuity.

"Well, well," he said as, with the help of a cane, he shuffled back a step. "Come in."

The apartment was small, with a spare, military neatness, a living room with a kitchenette and a bedroom and bathroom down a small hall.

Guy led them to one of two sofas underneath a picture window and gestured for them to sit down before he gently eased himself into a chair opposite, lying his cane to one side and resting his hands on his knees as he appraised them each in turn.

"So you must be Simon," he said, before turning to Abby. "But I don't know your name, miss."

"Abby Reese," she supplied with a smile. "I'm the grand-daughter of Tom Reese."

"Ah." The man nodded, the single syllable seeming to possess a wealth of meaning that made Abby suddenly feel nervous. What if she did find something out here? She hadn't actually expected anything more than an old man's vague recollections of someone she didn't even know, but what if Guy Wessel had something specific to say, not just about Matthew Lawson, but about her own grandfather? Her own life? Looking at his sharp eyes, his kindly if rather knowing smile, she had a sudden, uneasy feeling he might.

Guy turned back to Simon with an air of expectancy. "So you, young man, were asking about Matthew Lawson, as he was known."

"Was known?" Simon raised questioning eyebrows. "It's the only name I've heard."

"Well, it wasn't his real name, of course." Guy looked between the pair of them. "But I guess you didn't get that far in your research?" he surmised with a slight smugness that made Abby smile. Here was a man who was enjoying having—and telling—a secret.

"The only thing we know about Matthew Lawson," Simon said with a self-deprecating smile, "is that he was in the 82nd Airborne, and he received a Distinguished Service Cross for acts of bravery in May 1945, which came into the possession of Abby's grandfather, Tom Reese."

"Ah," Guy said again, sounding unsurprised, and Abby felt a frisson of apprehension ripple through her.

"What do you know about him?" she asked.

"About your grandfather? Not very much at all, I'm afraid. Not as much as you do, I'm sure. I only talked to him a handful of times, if that. We didn't move in the same circles, as it were, even though we were both in the 508th."

"Oh." Abby wasn't sure whether she felt disappointed or not.

"But Matthew Lawson, I knew quite a bit," Guy continued. "If I can say that. We were Ritchie Boys together."

Abby stared at him, her gaze as blank as Simon's seemed.

"Ritchie Boys?" Simon repeated.

"You haven't heard of us, I see." Guy almost sounded pleased; here was another secret he could share. "Amazing how few people know our story, even now."

"What is your story?" Abby asked.

Guy settled back into his seat, readying to tell the tale. "Ritchie Boys were part of an American covert operation in the Second World War. We trained at Camp Ritchie—hence the name—in the art of interrogation and psychological warfare. After D-Day, we were brought in to question prisoners of war on the front lines."

"Wow." Simon looked impressed. "That's quite a job. Was there a reason you were chosen particularly for that task?"

"There certainly was." Guy laughed. "We were chosen because we were German."

Abby and Simon both stared, trying to make sense of that information.

"German," Simon repeated slowly, shaking his head. "I don't—"

"German Jews," Guy clarified. "Not all of us were, to be sure, although we were all German speakers, which was why we were chosen. But a good few of us were emigrants, refugees from the war, or before it. I left Germany in '36, Matthew—or really, Matthaus—in '38. I was lucky, my family came with me." He paused, the corners of his mouth drooping down like a basset hound's as he shook his head slowly. "Matthaus wasn't so lucky."

"Matthaus? That was his German name?"

"Yes, Matthaus Weiss. He took the name Lawson because it sounded less German. Less Jewish. I changed Wessel to West. As much as I'd like to say otherwise, that sort of thing mattered.

More than once we had a pistol waved in our faces as we were accused of being spies. Many of the German-born Ritchie Boys did the same."

"And you were both part of the 82nd Airborne in this capacity… as Ritchie Boys?"

"Yes, we parachuted into Normandy the night before D-Day. Nearly got ourselves killed." Guy smiled in nostalgic remembrance. "I don't think I've ever been as terrified as the moment I landed in an apple orchard and realized there was a nest of Germans not a hundred feet from me."

Abby gasped and Simon leaned forward. "What did you do?"

"Ran like hell," Guy said with a chuckle. "Like any other sane fool, I should think. They fired, of course, but they missed. Matthew had a similar experience, as I recall. Threw a grenade behind him and kept running."

"Wow." It was hard to imagine this wrinkled, wispy-haired man running like hell, never mind parachuting into enemy territory or interrogating Nazis.

"And Matthew—Matthaus?" Simon continued. "You were friends?"

"Of a sort, yes, certainly. We were the only Ritchie Boys in the 508th, although some others came and went. We had a lot of freedom to move between units. But I don't know how well I could say I *knew* Matthew. He was always a quiet one. Kept to himself, even with me. Neither of us wanted to talk about our old lives, or all we'd lost. No one did. It simply wasn't the done thing back then. You just shut your mouth and got on with it."

"But you worked together? As… interrogators?"

"Oh, yes. It was quite a job, let me tell you." Guy crossed one leg over the other, seeming to enjoy himself. "We did all sorts of things. You'd think we were crazy now, but it was wild and fun and sobering and terrifying all at once. Ritchie Boys were able to move between battalions and regiments, up to the front lines and back, here and there and everywhere, answering to hardly anyone, to get the results we needed." He let out a raspy chuckle. "We lent our hand to all kinds of crazy things. I remember in London they had us writing fake messages in German and sending them to Europe by carrier pigeon, hoping the Nazis would think they were from their own spies. As far as I know it didn't work." He shook his head, smiling. "And then there was a time, right near the end of the war, when I dressed up as a Russian officer and we threatened a Nazi or two that they'd be sent to the Gulag if they didn't cooperate. They were scared of that more than anything." Guy gave another snort of laughter. "Matthew would threaten that he was going to bring in Commissar Karkozy. They didn't believe us until I marched in, with my fur hat and my big coat and some medals we'd taken off some Soviets—I knew a little Russian back then, but the truth is I made half of it up, and they almost always believed the whole thing." He laughed again, and Abby found herself smiling at the bizarre image—Guy dressed up like a Russian, Matthew threatening the Gulag. It was funny and horrible and hard to believe it had actually happened, and yet it had.

"That sounds like an amazing story," Simon said with a chuckle. He looked impressed. "You must have so many to tell."

"Not many people to listen to them, these days." Guy's smile faltered and he let out a weary sigh.

At ninety-seven, Abby supposed, there wouldn't be too many people left who shared your memories, or even cared about them. It had to be lonely, growing so old.

"We'd like to listen to them," Simon assured him. "But first, can I ask, do you know about Matthaus Weiss' Distinguished Service Cross? He received it in May 1945. Were you there then? Do you know what he received it for?"

Guy's smiled slipped right off his face then, and he looked away, suddenly seeming reluctant to impart any more information.

Simon glanced at Abby, and she shrugged, frowning. After the older man's genial recollections, this felt like something else entirely, a memory he didn't want to recall, never mind share. A ghost was in the room with them, drifting silently.

"Ye-es," Guy finally said slowly. "I know what he received it for. But you have to understand something. My family got out."

The words seemed to hang in the air before falling into the stillness, creating ripples.

Simon shifted in his seat. "What—what are you saying, exactly?"

Guy looked at him bleakly. "What do you think I'm saying, son? Matthew was a Jew, the same as me. His family were Jews. He left his mother and a couple of brothers and sisters—I can't remember how many, but a fair few—back in Germany. His father had already died, that I remember. Beaten to death during Kristallnacht. Matthew's mother hid him in a cupboard and he escaped the next day."

Abby let out a soft gasp of horror. She'd heard of such things, of course; she'd studied the Holocaust in history class and read novels about it and seen *Schindler's List*; she'd been to the museum in DC and had watched documentaries about survivors, and yet, even so, she'd never heard or felt it as starkly as that, the reality of it right there in the room with them.

Guy nodded somberly, accepting their reactions. "You couldn't imagine how it was, now. We couldn't even imagine it back then. We'd heard things, of course. Rumors. Whispers. Just a bit here and there—trains going east, ghettoes put up, stories of dark things that no one really liked to say or even think about. We didn't credit any of it, not really. We couldn't. Because to believe it…" He shook his head slowly. "It was simply too terrible to think about. Even though Matthew and I both saw some terrible things before we left Germany before the war, we still hoped it wouldn't get as bad as that. That it couldn't."

"I can understand that," Abby said quietly. She paused, before continuing hesitantly, "So Matthew's family…"

"They'd been left behind in some little town in what was part of Germany but is now Poland—Posen, the province was, although I can't remember the name of the town. He got out—took him months of hiding and finally getting passage on a Spanish freighter to America. He didn't talk about it much at all, but I know it ate at him, especially as we got closer to Germany, and then right into the heart of it all. He wanted to find out what had happened to his family. It drove him more than anything else." He paused, his face seeming to have collapsed in on itself in sadness. "And then… then we came to Wobbelin."

There was a note of finality to Guy's voice that Abby didn't understand.

"I haven't heard of that," Simon said and Guy let out a gusty sigh that seemed to come from the depths of his weary being.

"We'd been through a lot by then. The drop into Normandy, the disaster of the Waal bridge, the horror of Ardennes—the Battle of the Bulge as they called it later—and then that final push into Germany. The war was almost over, we were so sure, it was as if we could taste it. Abandoned Panzers, artillery and ammunition just left in rusty heaps on the side of a road, Dutch and then even German villagers welcoming us with open arms, kissing us on our cheeks. One hundred and fifty thousand German soldiers surrendered in a single morning. We saw them going by in droves, trying to escape the Soviets. They were more frightened of the Soviets than us. We knew it was only a matter of time, and not much at that."

"So… Wobbelin?" Simon let the words hang in the air, a question, an admission of ignorance. Abby had never heard the name before either.

Guy's hand trembled as he covered his eyes briefly, and Abby reached out and touched his other hand lightly, a gesture of comfort she felt compelled to give. He dropped his hand from his eyes and gave her a kindly, watery smile. "I didn't go to see it. I... I couldn't. Three miles away and we could *smell* the place." He gave a little shudder. "That was bad enough. You just knew... and yet you didn't. You couldn't. You could never imagine. Never guess."

"It was a concentration camp," Simon surmised softly.

Guy nodded. "Matthew was determined to see it for himself. A couple of them went. Intelligence officers. They had to. But Matthew..." He shook his head. "He wanted answers, and I'm sorry to say he found some of them there. He wasn't the same, after. He didn't say a word of it to me, not one word, but he wasn't the same. I remember he came back into the camp and it was as if he was... as if he was blind. He didn't look anyone in the eye, just walked straight past everyone as if they didn't exist, right to the canteen and got himself a shot of whiskey. Downed it in one go, and then another, and no one stopped him. I went to ask him how he was, but he didn't answer. He didn't even look at me. And, to my shame, I let him be. Looking back, I wish I hadn't, but I was scared." Guy hung his head, the shame he still felt like a shroud over him. "I didn't want to know. I didn't want to hear. Of course I did, we had to, later. A few days later, we had a funeral service for everyone who died there. We made the townspeople dig the graves. They'd known all along, of course, and had done nothing." He swallowed. "So many graves... I'd seen a lot in the war, but I'd never seen anything like that. I remember, one of the Nazi officers was smoking while the chaplain gave his address. And Matthew—" He stopped.

Simon leaned forward. "And Matthew?"

"He took out his pistol and pressed it to the man's forehead. That wasn't as much of a shock as it might sound—tempers ran high and those Nazi officers were right bastards." He shot Abby an apologetic smile. "Sorry, miss."

"Don't be," she answered. "They were that and more."

"We were tough with them. Too tough sometimes, but still. You couldn't help but feel they deserved it. But that time… I was standing near him, and I saw his finger tremble on the trigger. I realized he wasn't just doing it for show, a fit of temper, nothing more—he was really struggling. He wanted to kill that arrogant SOB. I couldn't blame him, but I also knew he couldn't do it. I told him to back off, and Matthew looked at me then like I was the one he wanted to shoot in the head. For a second I actually thought he might, but then he put away his pistol and the Nazi stamped out his cigarette, thank God. I don't know what would have happened if he hadn't."

"My goodness." Abby could picture it all, as clear as a photograph, or a film. She could *feel* the tension, and she had an urge to shiver.

"I've never even heard of Wobbelin, I'm ashamed to admit," Simon said quietly.

Guy nodded in understanding. "It wasn't one of the big ones, like Auschwitz or Dachau. They'd only set it up a couple of months before, as a—well, as a holding pen, as awful as that sounds. Bringing the survivors of the other camps to one place. They were trying to get rid of the evidence, by that point, of what they'd done." His face twisted with remembered bitterness and even hatred. "They might have acted as if they had all the answers, their damned Final Solution, but they *knew* how evil they were, and they tried to hide it from the rest of the world, damn them to hell and back."

Abby swallowed. Her throat felt thick and tears pricked her eyes, and she wasn't quite sure why. She'd heard horrible stories before, and yet this only felt far more personal, far more real. She wasn't related to Matthaus Weiss; she'd barely heard of him, had only seen the one photograph, in front of the Mathers' house. And yet she felt almost unbearably moved by Guy's story, by Matthew's anguish.

"So did Matthew find out what happened to his family?" Simon asked after a moment. "Had they been in the camps?"

Guy shook his head. "I never found out about that. He never told me, and the truth is, we barely spoke after that terrible day, the day of the funeral. He was angry at first, and then everything was happening all at once—Hitler killed himself, and then the Germans were surrendering, and Matthew was seconded somewhere else quite quickly, to interrogate some Nazis. I'm sorry to say I never saw him again. None of the Ritchie Boys kept in touch, as far as I know. It just wasn't done. We'd had a different war than everyone else, being both Germans and Jews." He smiled sadly. "I wish we had stayed in touch. It's good talking about these things—good, but hard."

"So you don't know what happened to Matthew after the war? If he came back to America, or...?"

Guy shook his head. "I don't know a thing."

"What about Tom Reese?"

"Tom Reese..." Guy scratched his chin thoughtfully. "Like I said, I wasn't friends with him, although he and Matthew stuck together a bit. They were dating a pair of sisters, as I recall. British girls."

"Sisters?" Simon perked up at that. "Do you mean Sophie and Lily Mather? My grandmother is Sophie.'"

"Those may have been their names. I'm afraid I didn't pay close attention, and Matthew didn't tell me about his love life, or anything else. But even so, I could tell he was awful sweet on her."

"And Tom and Sophie?" Abby asked after a moment. "Do you know what happened to them?"

Guy shook his head. "Tom was wounded in Ardennes, I know that much. Shot in the leg. He was shipped back to England and saw the last days of war out in a military hospital in London. Matthew told me about it, but he seemed quite tight-lipped about the whole thing. I always got the sense there might have been a bit of bad blood between them, but I never got to the bottom of it, not that I asked." He smiled apologetically at them both. "I'm sorry I don't have more to tell you. You probably thought I did, inviting you to come all this way, but the truth is no one wants to talk about those days anymore. I was so glad someone took an interest."

"We're so glad we came," Simon assured him, and Abby murmured the same. "You didn't actually say what Matthew Weiss received his Cross for—do you remember specifically?"

"He interrogated some Nazi officers," Guy said slowly, his tone heavy with sadness. "Thoroughly nasty characters, I'm sure. I heard from someone else that he'd got some information out of them about the camps. It couldn't have been easy, in any respect, especially after seeing Wobbelin."

"Thank you," Simon said quietly. He glanced at Abby, his eyes dark with imagined sorrow. No, it couldn't have been easy.

They stayed for another hour, looking over Guy's photo albums and hearing more about his life both during the war and after. He'd married a woman he'd met after the war, a nurse, and they'd lived in Minneapolis for their whole marriage, until she'd died fifteen years ago. They hadn't been able to have children.

"I feel as if I've lived a whole life in a matter of hours," Abby said as they walked back to the car. It was already dusk, the air humid and warm, and as thick as a blanket. "I'm exhausted, but my mind is spinning."

"Mine too." Simon blew out a breath. "It's all so incredible. I'm still taking it in." He jangled his keys. "We can check into the hotel and order room service, unless you feel like going out?"

"No, that sounds perfect. I really am tired."

They were both quiet, lost in their thoughts, during the short drive to the hotel. After they'd checked into their separate rooms, Abby joined Simon in his and he called down for room service.

It felt odd, and also intimate, to be sitting cross-legged on his bed while he asked her if she wanted anchovies in her Caesar salad. She made a face.

"Definitely not."

"I had a feeling…" Simon murmured, his eyes glinting, and then he finished the order. "So." He tossed his phone on top of the bureau as he gave Abby an appraising look. "The food should be here in about fifteen minutes. What did you think about Guy? Everything he said, now that you've had a bit of time to process it?"

She blew out a breath. "Honestly, I don't know. It's so much more than I expected. It felt so real—I mean, it *was* real. I know that. Such unbelievable devastation and tragedy, and yet you can forget about it, sort of, until you realize it actually happened to someone. Someone's life was changed forever." She let out a frustrated laugh. "I know I'm not making sense."

"You are."

"I feel sad, and somehow ashamed by it, too. I'm not sure why. It's just so hard to believe people are capable of such evil."

"I know. It's a terrible stain on humanity." Simon's face was drawn in sorrowful, pensive lines. "You want to believe all Nazis were inhuman monsters, but they were people like us. They had wives and children and slept and laughed and all the rest. How could they have done such terrible, terrible things? How could anyone?"

"I don't know, but it scares me, that someone could. We're all only one step away from savagery."

"An appalling thought, really." Simon sighed and shook his head. "What do you think the bad blood was between your grandfather and Matthew Weiss?"

"Honestly, I have no idea." Her head still felt as if it was spinning from everything Guy had said; she couldn't grab hold of any of it.

"And so they must have been dating my grandmother and my great-aunt. Funny to think of that. I suppose neither relationship worked out."

"You said you never met Lily?"

"No, not that I can recall. But I feel like I would have heard, if she'd married a German Jew whose family might have been killed in the Holocaust. That's kind of a big thing, isn't it? If I had cousins, I would have known, surely?"

"Second cousins, wouldn't they be? And he was American by then."

"Yes, but even so." Simon shook his head. "It's just a lot to never have even heard of. I suppose we could find out what happened to Matthaus Weiss. Do some digging, now that we have his real name, although I imagine there are a lot of Weisses out there, and we wouldn't be able to go by his army experience since he used a different name."

"Isn't it funny," Abby said slowly. "That we started wondering about Sophie Mather and Tom Reese, and now the real mystery is about Lily and Matthew, people we didn't even know existed. At least I didn't."

"Of course, we still don't know what happened between Tom and Sophie."

"I think my father does," Abby said quietly.

Simon raised his eyebrows, waiting.

"He doesn't want to tell me, as you know, so Tom must have done something to be ashamed of. Something during the war, maybe. I think he knows the whole story, or at least most of it."

"And this thing, whatever it is, might have been the source of the bad blood between him and Matthew?" Simon surmised.

"Perhaps." Abby glanced away, her mind reeling through everything Guy had said—and everything he hadn't that she couldn't keep herself from imagining. The camp... the smell of it, he'd said, from three miles away... it was so unbearably awful.

How had Matthew been able to walk out of that camp, knowing his family might have experienced something similar? How had he been able to cope with that information, to go on? "I hope Lily and Matthew ended up together," Abby said suddenly, her voice turning fierce. "I hope they had children and dogs and a lovely, lovely house. I hope they were happy. Really happy."

Simon cocked his head, his gaze sweeping over her like a searchlight. He could tell, she knew, that there was a personal undercurrent to her words, a throb of feeling that had less to do with Matthew and Lily, and more to do with herself. "Do you?" he said quietly.

"Yes." Abby swallowed, more of a gulp. "Because no one should be in thrall to their past, to whatever happened, no matter how awful." Tears rose behind her eyes, in her throat, and she pushed it all back. "You should be able to find a way to go on... to forgive yourself... to be happy. Somehow."

Abby hugged her knees to her chest as Simon sat on the edge of the bed. "Why," he asked, "do I get the feeling we're not talking about the past anymore? At least not about Matthew or Lily."

"We're not," Abby agreed, the words catching in her throat. She hadn't expected to make it personal, because she never did, and yet some part of her acknowledged the rightness of the moment, and how everything—from meeting to Simon, to finding the medal, to coming here—had been leading to this. A confession. An absolution. Both were necessary.

"Abby." Simon reached for her hand.

She stared at her knees, willing herself not to blink.

"Let me tell you something," she said softly, and Simon threaded his fingers through hers.

CHAPTER TWENTY-THREE

December 1944

The colonel reminded Matthew of a mad dog. With the pistol pointed in his face, he felt himself go quiet and cold inside, a familiar blankness that stole over him like a freezing mist, keeping out fear, leaving only needed certainty.

"Well?" The colonel demanded. "Who the hell are you?"

"I'm not a spy."

"Says you—"

"I'm a German, and a Jew." How many times would he have to say it? These things that made him who he was, that for some meant he was utterly worthless, no more than rubbish to be rid of, and yet right now they could be his salvation. "I trained at Camp Ritchie in Maryland—"

"I've never heard of it."

"It was a covert operation." Matthew kept the edge from his voice, as the colonel's gun was still just a couple of inches from his face. Surely the man wasn't going to actually shoot him. And yet Matthew had heard of the private who had shot a captured German in the head, just because he could. This man was a colonel. "They trained us to be interrogators of prisoners of war, because we speak German, and we know the customs and culture. I'm here to interrogate, not spy. If I were a spy, why would I come straight into headquarters? I'd have to be an idiot."

The man stared at him for a long moment, his hand steady on his gun, not wavering a millimeter. The other two officers simply watched, waiting. One of them winked at Matthew, which he didn't find particularly comforting. He wondered if they would even care if he was shot in the head. He was German. He'd said so himself. Maybe that was all that mattered.

Then, finally, thankfully, the colonel lowered his pistol. "You'd better be here to fight," he stated flatly. "We'll be damned lucky if we're not taken prisoners ourselves."

Matthew released a pent-up breath slowly, so no one could hear the needed exhalation. "What's the situation?" he asked when he trusted his voice to sound level. His legs felt weak. He'd been afraid, even if he hadn't let himself feel it in the moment.

"The situation?" the colonel repeated in exasperation, panic giving his words a ragged edge. "Just about the worst snafu I've ever seen."

Matthew kept his expression neutral as he listened to the senior officer describe the current crisis of events. On what had been thought to be a sleepy front in Belgium, used to train raw recruits, the Wehrmacht had poured in masses of artillery, tanks, and hundreds of thousands of troops, including Waffen-SS units.

The entire center of the VIII Corps had collapsed as the German army pushed the Allies westward, and the 82nd Airborne had been called to hold defensive positions and attempt to push the Germans back towards Germany.

"We've got everyone who knows how to pull a trigger out there," the colonel said. "And everyone who doesn't. We need every last man if we're going to hold the line."

"Where do you want me to go?" Over the last few months, Matthew had done precious little fighting, as he was considered too valuable to be wasted on a front line. But clearly this was a different situation entirely, and part of him was more than ready to do his part. To pull a trigger.

Ten minutes later, he was walking through a pine forest, the ground thickly blanketed with snow, towards a battalion's machine gun company. It would have been a peaceful scene, save for the traces of light arcing the sky and the thunder of guns like a stampede in the distance. God only knew what was happening. Matthew felt removed from it all, even as his heart thudded harder.

He called out his name and rank as he approached the machine gun positioned at the crest of hill, throwing himself on the ground next to a grimy-faced sergeant. "What's happening?" he asked.

"We're getting the shit kicked out of us," the sergeant replied with a grim laugh. "It's been a God-awful couple of days, let me tell you."

"And now?" Matthew asked as he pressed closer to the frozen ground, the chill penetrating right through his uniform, and narrowed his eyes. The hill was cloaked in darkness, and the booming in the distance could have come from a fairground rather than a battle scene.

"They're coming. Can't you hear them?" He cocked his head towards the distant sound. "We're meant to hold this position no matter what, but you should see these bastards when they start coming. They're *crazy*. We've been pushed back, but we've got to hold now, or else. So the higher-ups say." He shook his head. "If this is their last-ditch effort, it's a helluva one."

"All right, then," Matthew said. His heart had slowed to steady thuds, each one a deep throb in his chest. Even with the artillery fire cracking through the air, there was a strange stillness to the scene. It had started to snow again, big, soft flakes like something out of a fairy tale.

"Lawson. You keep showing up like a bad penny."

Matthew lifted his head from the ground to see Tom Reese crouching by the machine gun, a weary smile on his face. He almost seemed glad to see him.

"I could say the same of you." Of course he would bump into Reese along the whole of the Bastogne–Liege line. They seemed destined to see the war out together, for better or for worse.

"I thought you didn't fight." There was a note of something like envy in Tom's voice as he glanced at the sergeant Matthew had just been talking to. "He's a German."

"What the hell are you talking about?" The sergeant sounded disbelieving rather than suspicious, which gratified Matthew a little.

"I'm a German refugee, a Jew," he explained tiredly, the words all too familiar. "My brief is usually to interrogate prisoners of war, but everyone is needed at the front right now."

"I've heard about you guys," the sergeant said. He looked impressed. "That's a job and a half, I bet. Some of these Krauts are tough customers." He grimaced. "Sorry. You're one too, of course."

Matthew shrugged him aside. He didn't feel German. He didn't feel anything.

They lapsed into silence, huddled on the hills, bellies flat on the frozen ground, as the snow continued to fall. Tom had turned back to the machine gun he was manning, and they were all quiet and watchful.

Moments passed, perhaps hours. No one spoke; muscles tensed and ached as they waited, the softness of the snow at odds with the pistols in their hands, the tracer fire in the sky. Matthew started to feel sleepy, despite the clench of his jaw, the fact that he couldn't feel his toes.

And then they came. Fireworks lit up the sky as signal flares went off, and in the ensuing, eerie yellow glow, Waffen-SS troops began to charge up the hill, scrambling in the snow, shouting loudly to encourage one another on. Matthew was transfixed by the manic look on their faces, the way they ran straight towards enemy fire without a single misstep.

"Start shooting, for fuck's sake!" the sergeant shouted and Tom got behind the machine gun as everyone else began to fire.

Some of the soldiers fell, scarlet staining the snow, and yet others kept coming, undeterred, undismayed by their fallen comrades, pressing forward with determined zeal.

Bullets zinged past Matthew as he pressed deeper into the earth and took aim. There was a ringing in his ears and a coldness in his chest that had nothing to do with the snow beneath him. Tom was swinging the machine gun wildly, a look of wild terror on his face. No matter how many fell, still more came, shouting, shooting, an endless, undulating wave of manic hostility.

They were all going to be killed, Matthew thought numbly. There were too many of them; they couldn't shoot them fast enough. They would be overrun, perhaps in minutes. They would be cut down right here in the snow. He reloaded and took aim again, the air around him full of smoke and sound, light and fire.

"They're never going to stop," Tom cried. "They're going to kill us!"

"That's the idea, isn't it," the sergeant returned grimly. "Us or them."

"We can't," Tom insisted. His voice was high and thin. "I'm not going to die here, damn it."

"Keep shooting that fucking gun, then!"

But the machine gun fire had stopped, even as the onslaught of soldiers continued. Matthew twisted around to see Tom stumbling away from the great gun. For an instant their gazes met, and Matthew saw something terrified yet resolute in the other man's eyes. Then Tom turned and started running, sprinting in the snow, away from the battle.

Matthew's mind felt cold and clear as he watched Tom run away, abandoning his position as well as his comrades. In that single, sharp moment he thought of Sophie, and how she might hate Tom for this. He thought of Lily, who might understand.

And he thought of himself, and how he'd never liked Tom Reese much, but how he was signing his own death warrant by the U.S. Army if he deserted.

Even so, there was no conscious decision, no weighing in his mind, no *what if* or *should I*. He simply leveled his pistol and shot, a single bullet fired into the darkness. Tom fell.

"They're going to overtake us, damn it!" someone shouted.

Matthew scrambled towards the machine gun, a piece of equipment he'd never actually used before. His fingers curved around handles, the freezing metal seeming to burn.

The SS troops were coming closer; he could see the whites of their eyes, their faces twisted in a grimace of something that looked disturbingly like joy. They were crazed, possessed, almost as if they were oblivious to the hail of bullets, or even welcomed it.

"I have command!" he called out hoarsely. "I have command! Do not leave your positions!"

Then Matthew aimed and fired.

CHAPTER TWENTY-FOUR

Ludwigslust, Germany

April 1945

The 82nd Airborne crossed the Elbe on the last day of April, after months of shelling and fighting, a relentless, bloody push into Germany. As the snow melted and the world came to life again, trees and flowers budding into blossom under an indifferent blue sky, as if it were any other spring, Matthew entered his homeland for the first time in seven years, coming face to face with a destroyed Germany, its cities and towns devastated by Allied bombs, its people by starvation and loss, its culture and its hope by over a decade of Nazi rule.

Hundreds and even thousands of soldiers were surrendering every day, arms up in the air, faces gaunt, resigned yet also hopeful. The war was over all but in name, and yet still people were dying. Soldiers. Civilians. Jews.

Three days before the 82nd crossed the Elbe, a reconnaissance patrol was sent across by cover of night in small, flat-bottomed boats; all but two were lost to enemy fire. It felt even more pointless, to make it this far, knowing that peace was finally imminent, only to die in a futile exercise, just days before Hitler himself committed suicide.

Every day, there was another soldier for Matthew to interrogate—desperate conscripts, arrogant officers, broken men, terrified soldiers. Some gabbled in their eagerness to be helpful, while others remained icily aloof, infuriatingly disdainful to the very end.

Still, there were odd moments of humor amidst the unrelenting grimness—when Guy came up with the idea of posing as Commissar Karkozy, Matthew had felt a spark of amusement at his friend's absurd get-up, the absolute farce of the thing, although mostly he felt too weary to laugh or even smile. He wondered if he had either in him anymore, and then told himself he had to, for Lily's sake. He held onto his humanity so he could return to her. It was that stark, that simple.

It had been four long months since what had become known as the Battle of the Bulge had been fought in Ardennes, where Matthew had shot Tom Reese as he'd tried to desert, and then taken command himself. They'd managed to hold off the SS assault throughout the night and retain their position, something that had garnered him a promotion to master sergeant.

As for Tom, Matthew hadn't known whether he'd actually killed him or not until after the battle. Tom had been taken by orderlies to the nearest field hospital, and Matthew had visited him there as a matter of duty rather than desire, knowing he needed to see him face to face. Tom had been shot in the thigh, a deep but non-threatening wound that would have him see out the war recuperation back in England before being demobbed.

"You *shot* me," Tom had stated flatly, when they were alone, the poor sufferer next to him, with a bad head wound, thankfully lost to unconsciousness. "I can't believe you actually shot me. I didn't think you had it in you."

"I'm sorry," Matthew had said, and wondered if he meant it. In the moment he wasn't sure what he'd been thinking, or what had prompted him to fire. "But you were deserting. You could have been court-martialed for cowardice in the face of the enemy and sentenced to prison, if not death."

"So you were saving me?" Tom had sounded disbelieving. He'd glanced away, a closed look coming over his face. "You could still tell them, if you wanted. You've never liked me, anyway. Maybe this is what you've hoped for all along."

Matthew had shifted where he stood. Outside, the sky was slate gray, intermittently offering an icy, unforgiving drizzle. His boots were constantly wet, and he couldn't remember what it felt like to be either full or warm. "I don't hate you," he'd said after a moment.

Tom had turned back to him with a huff of laughter. "That's something, I guess. I don't hate you, either, for what it's worth."

"I'm glad," Matthew had answered, deciding he meant it. Tom gave a small smile, and he'd smiled back. It seemed absurd that they might find some point of sympathy in this after everything, and yet perhaps they had.

After a second, Tom's smile had faded and he'd looked away. "I thought we were all going to die, you know." Color had suffused his face as he kept his gaze averted. "Those SS guys were crazy… *crazy*. Shouting the way they did, and how they just kept running at us… they would have killed us all, Lawson. Did you *see* them?"

"I did."

"It looked completely hopeless," Tom had said in a low voice. "You *know* it did. They would have mowed us down."

Matthew had said nothing. What could he say? How could he possibly offer Tom the absolution he seemed to crave? The sergeant who'd been next to him had taken a bullet in the head. Three others had been critically wounded, not including Tom. And yet they'd held the position.

"I wasn't thinking straight," Tom had confessed. "I wasn't thinking at all. I couldn't…" He'd lapsed into silence, shaking his head. "Why *did* you shoot me?" he'd finally asked. "You could have just let me go. Let me face the consequences, be imprisoned or worse. Maybe they would have had me shot. Maybe they still will."

"You don't deserve that, after everything you've been through." It might have been an act of mercy to have shot Tom in the leg, but Matthew knew he could have easily missed. What if he'd killed him, or wounded him terribly? What *had* he been thinking in that moment? Matthew wasn't sure he could even remember. He recalled standing in the snow, and how cold he'd felt inside, as if something hard and elemental was taking over his soul.

He didn't want it to, he fought against it, but with every passing day he remained in this war, every sneering SS officer he looked in the face, every corpse he gazed at, unmoved, by the side of the road, he felt it close another inch over him. He wanted to have something left to offer Lily, but some days he didn't know if he would.

Looking at Tom, his leg swathed in thick bandages, his expression close to despairing, Matthew had felt no compassion at all, not so much as a flicker of pity, even though he knew he should. "I won't say anything," he'd said, because that was what he suspected Tom wanted to hear, and he knew he could promise at least that much.

"Well, the war's over for me." There was no disguising the relief in Tom's voice. The push into Germany would continue, taking months and many lives, and yet Tom would not fight again, and he was glad. Perhaps, if Matthew were in the same position, he would feel likewise. He knew there was nothing more to say but goodbye. He'd walked out of the field hospital without looking back.

Now, as April turned to May, the end of the war was perhaps only days away, here in the pretty town of Ludwigslust, fifty miles east of the Elbe. On Eisenhower's orders, the 82nd Airborne had been told to push forward as fast as possible, to keep the Soviets from gaining any more territory than they had to. The war was changing shape, the German army collapsing, to be replaced by another, more insidious enemy, yet that battle was one Matthew had no wish to fight.

He wanted to go home, even though he no longer knew where that was. He wanted to find his family, even though he wasn't sure he could. Both prospects filled him with despair, and so he tried not to think at all, and welcomed that cold hardness even as he fought against it, for Lily's sake. Always for Lily.

While the other GIs were daydreaming about huge steaks and grateful girls back in America, Matthew's future felt like a disturbing blankness, a yawning emptiness of uncertainty. He'd had no letters from Lily in over a month, and he hadn't written any, either, since he'd been dropped into the Netherlands. It hurt to think of her at all, even as he tried to cling to some shred of hope that there could be a future for them, somehow. Somewhere. When this was finally, really over, when he could see a future emerging from the dust and death of war.

In the stately palace in Ludwigslust, General Gavin was poised to accept the surrender of a hundred and fifty thousand men. Hitler had killed himself, the government was collapsing. There was nothing left to fight for. Finally, finally the fight could truly end.

Matthew worked on the translation of the surrender documents, feeling strangely distant from it all as he watched the largest ever surrender of soldiers, artillery, and equipment completed in the formal drawing room of the palace.

Afterwards, he walked outside into the bright spring sunlight and tried to summon some emotion—satisfaction, if not joy, or at least relief. He felt nothing. He didn't know when he'd stopped feeling, when that part of him that wept and laughed, wondered and hoped, had become so deadened he could not remember when it—or he—had been alive. He prayed there was still a flicker left, buried deep, waiting to be breathed back to life.

A jeep pulled up in front of the palace, kicking up clouds of dust. Matthew watched silently as an intelligence officer he knew by name—Jamison—jumped out, his expression tense.

"We've had reports of a camp about three miles away," he stated starkly. "Wobbelin. We might need you for your German. Depending…" He stopped, but Matthew could fill it in himself. Depending on what they found.

Matthew dropped the cigarette he'd barely smoked and ground it under his heel. "I'll come."

As he climbed into the jeep next to another officer, he realized he had no idea what to expect. They'd all heard, vaguely, about the camps that had been discovered as the Allies pushed east. Other units had liberated a few, but details hadn't been forthcoming. In any case, he'd known about such camps before the war, political prisons like Dachau. Someone in Fraustadt, a suspected Communist, had been taken there. He'd emerged four months later quiet and haggard, and no one had asked him any questions.

Matthew was prepared for the conditions to be brutal, food and water and decent clothing all sparing, but something in Jamison's face made him wonder if it might be worse. Yet how much worse could it be, than beating and starvation and unjust imprisonment? What else could they possibly find?

As they took the narrow road out of Ludwigslust towards Wobbelin, the smell accosted them first. It rolled over them on a warm spring breeze, and it was like nothing Matthew had ever breathed in before. It smelled of something dreadfully dead, and yet also horribly alive. It held the sickly-sweetish tinge of decay, along with the terrible odor of sweat and feces, and another, charred smell he couldn't and didn't want to identify. It stung his nostrils and coated the back of his throat, and as they continued down the track, he fought the urge to gag, his stomach roiling.

At one point, Jamison cut the engine, squinting through the trees as he covered his mouth and nose with his handkerchief. "My God," he said, his voice muffled. "What the hell is causing that stench?"

They found out just a few minutes later, when the zigzag of the high razor-topped fences surrounding the camp came into view above the trees, sunlight glinting off wire.

The gates were already opened, and another army jeep was parked in front. The smell was so thick, Matthew fought the urge to be sick; it felt like a miasma, palpable, visible, blanketing them with its utter awfulness.

He blinked in the bright spring sunlight as he gazed at the entrance of the camp, trying to take in what he was seeing and yet unable to. It was as if his brain had ceased to function, the images in front of him impossible to translate into fact or reason.

"My God," Jamison said again, softly. All three of them stared in mute, shocked horror at the devastation that lay before them. They had no other words.

The camp was made of a dozen or so long, low buildings, little more than cattle sheds, and stacked outside of them were bodies. At first, Matthew could not believe they were real, actual human beings stacked like lumber, arms and legs poking out like matchsticks. Some already snapped off and littered the ground like broken twigs.

He'd seen dead bodies before, of course, many times. After Ardennes, he'd crept from corpse to corpse, searching for any information hidden in dead soldiers' pockets. He'd thought he was used to the look of a dead man—the glassy-eyed stare, the slack limbs, the bluish tinge, the inevitable stiffening. Even the unavoidable gore—gaping wounds, body parts blown off, heads no longer whole. He thought he'd seen it all.

Yet he'd never seen this.

Slowly, dazed as if in a horrible dream, he climbed out of the jeep. Jamison and the other officer followed, each one walking slowly, mouths agape, arms futilely covering their faces to ward off the terrible smell.

As they approached the gates of the camp, a few wraithlike figures stumbled towards them, arms outstretched, skin stretched so tightly over their bones they looked like living skeletons, like something out of a horror film with Boris Karloff, the kind you'd laugh at for being so ridiculous, and yet Matthew had never, ever been as far from laughing as he was now.

He was filled with a mute, overwhelming horror, a terrible incredulity that kept his mind frozen in place, his body too as the figures stumbled towards him. They wore striped uniforms, ragged and dirty; on each was a Star of David. As he stared at them, he realized they were speaking, their voices so hoarse he was barely able to hear them.

"Essen… essen… hast du etwas zu essen?"

Food. They were asking for food.

Matthew fumbled through his pockets, desperate to give them something, but he didn't have so much as a stick of gum. Then one of the poor wretches saw his pack of cigarettes and motioned to it with a clawlike hand. Matthew thrust the pack at the man, heedless, only to watch in shock as he unrolled the paper and began stuffing the tobacco straight into his mouth.

"What…" The word exhaled from Jamison as he shook his head slowly. He'd found a dry piece of ration biscuit in his pocket and he handed it to one of the prisoners, who began to gulp it so fast he choked. All three of them watched, horrified, as the man began clutching his throat before falling to the ground, twitching and moaning. "I only gave him a biscuit," Jamison cried, falling to his knees in front of the man. "Please…"

"Don't give them food." A hassled-looking medic came running towards them, snatching the half of a Hershey bar the other officer had been about to offer. "It will kill them. Their bodies won't be able to take anything solid."

"My God." Jamison covered his mouth with one hand. "I'm so sorry."

"You weren't to know. How could you know?"

For a second they were all silent as they contemplated the depth of the horror around them, and the evil that had caused it.

Matthew looked around at the starved beings who were utterly desperate for food they were unable to eat, one further injustice that had been wreaked upon them. They were *human beings*, people who had once loved and laughed and lived, and yet they seemed like ghosts now, barely alive, their humanity stolen from them. He could not take it in.

"What…" He cleared his throat, the words rasping it raw. "What happened here?"

"They've been liquidating the camps," the medic said. "Sending them all here, to get rid of the evidence. Trying to kill them all, by the looks of it."

"Camps?" Matthew stared at him in blank shock. Somehow he had made himself assume this was an anomaly, the only one, a horror only they had stumbled upon. Surely it had to be, and yet of course it wasn't. "You mean… there are more like this?"

The medic nodded somberly. "Dozens, at least, some much bigger than this one. Much worse."

"*Worse*…" How could anything be worse than this? "They were for political prisoners," he whispered to himself, as if even now he could convince himself of a truth. "Before the war. The camps… they weren't like this." He thought of what he'd been imagining—beatings, hunger, yes, yes, of *course*, but this was something else entirely. Something he could not conceive of, even as he looked at it, as he made himself take it all in.

He half-walked, half-stumbled away from the others, needing to see it all for himself, although already everything was emblazoned on his brain. He would never forget. He would never be able to.

He walked slowly through the camp, staring in mute, dazed incredulity at the bodies lying discarded in piles; he realized some of those stacked so carelessly were actually alive, yet too weak to move. Hoarsely, he called for a medic to help, and together they gently moved a man from a pile of corpses to a ragged blanket on the ground. His body felt like a bundle of brittle twigs, and his eyes were glassy and unseeing even as his chest rose and fell in barely visible breaths.

Near another building, Matthew saw a pool of quicklime that he didn't want to think about; he turned his head away from several inmates who crouched around a dead horse, eating its raw innards in frenzied desperation.

How could this be? How could anyone have allowed this, caused it—*exulted* in it? The questions raced through Matthew's mind with no answers, and despite all he saw, he still found he could feel no emotion. It was all too big to contemplate, too horrific to possibly comprehend. The flicker of humanity he'd been holding onto, for Lily's sake, blew out. There was nothing left. He felt as if he were suspended in space, as if he no longer walked the earth like a normal man, and never would again.

A man came stumbling towards him, his face covered in sores, his stubbled head crawling with lice. He could have been twenty or eighty; it was impossible to tell. He held his arms out towards Matthew, his liberator, as he wept.

"*Danke*," he said as he fell into his arms. Matthew embraced him, heedless of his filth and stench. "*Danke*," the man said as he rested his head on Matthew's shoulder. "*Danke, danke.*"

Matthew patted his back gently, uselessly. He had no words, no thoughts, nothing. "I am a Jew," he heard himself saying, the words coming as if from outside himself, a fact he had to reveal and claim, now more than ever. "*Ich bin ein Jude.*" He could have been here. *He* could be this man he held in his arms, and, far more frighteningly, his brothers could. His mother. *Gertie…*

The man looked up at him; he had no teeth, and his breath was foul, everything about him unbearably repulsive and pitiable. Once he might have been a man of standing—an accountant like Matthew's father, a lawyer, a doctor, a violinist. Once he might have lived in Warsaw, or Berlin, or Vienna, or Fraustadt, in an apartment with velvet curtains and hardwood floors, Mozart on the gramophone. Now he was little more than a wraith, a skeleton, barely alive. *How could this be?*

"*Danke, Jude,*" the man said as he wept on Matthew's shoulder, two men joined in this moment, this tragedy. "*Danke, Jude.*"

CHAPTER TWENTY-FIVE

ABBY

Abby looked down at Simon's fingers laced with hers. Where to begin? How to start? Simon squeezed her fingers, an encouragement as well as a comfort, and she took a steadying breath.

"This feels a bit melodramatic," she said, "considering we've just heard the most harrowing story about war, and concentration camps, and all the rest." She trailed off, shaking her head. Her own small, sad story felt so pathetic in comparison, unworthy of such an emotional confession. Compared to Matthew Weiss, she had nothing to complain about.

"You're hardly being melodramatic," Simon told her gently. "Just honest, I think?" His hand remained warm wrapped around hers. "Are you going to tell me about your mother and brother's accident?"

Her lips trembled as she forced them upwards. "How did you know?"

He offered her a sad smile. "What else could it be?"

"It's that obvious, huh?" She meant to sound joking, but already she felt near tears, every emotion skating so precariously close to the surface. She didn't want to cry. Not yet, before she'd even said anything. Maybe not ever.

"I wouldn't say it's obvious. But I think—I hope—I've come to know you, and this is the big thing in your life you don't like to talk about."

She sighed, a raggedy sound. "Yes. Does everyone have a big thing, do you think?"

"Maybe not as big, but then it's not a competition, is it? There are no medals for who's experienced the worst tragedy, none that anyone would want. And this… this is your story, Abby. If you want to tell it to me."

"The thing is," Abby said slowly, staring down at their joined hands, "I already know what you're going to say. You're going to tell me it wasn't my fault, that I need to forgive myself, that I need to let the past go and move on. And I *know* all that." She looked up, managing a watery smile. "I had therapy, you know. Not a lot, but some. I've tried to work through my feelings of guilt Sort of, anyway."

"I believe you."

"Do you?" Abby withdrew her hand from Simon's and wrapped her arms around her tucked-up knees, holding herself together. "Because I'm not sure I believe myself."

He remained silent, sympathetic, waiting.

"Okay," Abby said after a few moments. "This is how it happened. My brother had a piano lesson on Saturday mornings. It was a ten-minute drive away. Luke loved piano… he played all the time. Anyway…" She blew out a breath as the image of Luke sitting at the old piano, shaggy head bent towards the keys as he let his fingers ripple over them, filling the house with music, flitted through her mind. "That morning—it was April of my senior year—my mom wasn't feeling well. She had some kind of flu, headache, stuffy nose, maybe a fever. She usually drove him, but I was seventeen, I had my license. Sometimes I did it, if I was needed." She stopped then, and Simon nodded, encouraging.

"Okay."

"But I didn't want to that morning." Saying just that much had the memories rushing back, so Abby could see it unwinding like a reel of sepia-tinted film in her head: her mother at the kitchen table with a cup of coffee and a couple of ibuprofen, looking exhausted; Abby, in the doorway, hands on her hips, anger flaring at the seeming injustice of her mother's weary request. *I have plans, Mom. You know Jason and I are going to Milwaukee, to shop for college. We've had it planned for weeks. Can't Dad do it?*

Her mother's tiny sigh and tired smile. Yes, she'd known Abby had plans. *I'm sorry, sweetheart. I wouldn't ask if I felt better…*

Fine. A single word hurled like an insult. She'd grabbed the keys off the counter, making sure they jangled angrily in her hand, an accusation. *I'll do it.* The voice of a manipulative martyr, still hoping to be excused.

And she was. Her mother rose from the table and held her hand out, smiling wearily, utterly unfooled by Abby's theatrics. *It's all right, sweetie. Give me the keys.*

For a second Abby had hesitated. She'd felt guilty for her petulant outburst, and she could see how unwell her mother looked, even though she didn't want to. *I really will do it, Mom…* Uncertain, though. Craving reassurance. Still wanting an out even though she knew she shouldn't take it.

Her mother's smile had been both tired and tender. Understanding, sympathetic even. Her hand was still stretched out.

"Abby."

She blinked Simon's concerned face into focus.

"I gave her the keys," she whispered. "I knew I shouldn't have, but I did."

A frown creased his forehead as he studied her face as if looking for clues. "Why shouldn't you have?"

She realized she'd been replaying it all in her head, but she hadn't told Simon any of it. And so she did, in halting, haunted sentences, jumbled thoughts forming into a sobering whole. "She was sick… Luke's piano… I had plans with my boyfriend… I knew I should have driven him." Her throat thickened and she shook her head, unable to say any more.

"So she drove your brother to his piano lesson," Simon surmised quietly. "And they were hit by a trucker who had fallen asleep at the wheel."

"We don't actually know that," Abby felt compelled to point out, her voice sharpening like a lawyer's. "It was just what the police decided must have happened, because it was a head-on collision on a straight road, on a perfectly sunny spring morning, but there's no way to tell what really happened. Maybe the trucker didn't fall asleep. Maybe my mother did, or maybe she felt so sick she swerved into the opposite lane…"

Simon pursed his lips. "Who told you that?"

She blinked at him, startled. "No one."

"Exactly."

"Still, it's true," she persisted. It felt like a point of honor somehow. "They did say they could never know for sure."

"Even so, there seems like a most likely outcome, which was what the police described." Simon was silent for a moment. "But you blame yourself."

"Wouldn't you?" It was a challenge.

"Yes," Simon said, surprising her, *hurting* her, "I probably would."

Abby sagged back against the pillows, shocked, gratified, and deeply wounded by his response all at once. If he'd said anything else, it wouldn't have been honest. But to admit it, to as good as say she was *right* to feel guilty… that felt worse.

"Abby." Simon tugged her hands from her knees where she'd locked her fingers tightly together. "That doesn't mean it's the right thing to think or feel. I'm just empathizing with you. I understand, at least as much as I can, considering I haven't lived it, why you feel guilty. Why this has haunted you for so long."

"I'm not *haunted*." Now she sounded huffy.

"Tormented, then? Tortured? Troubled?"

"Why don't you get a thesaurus out while you're at it?"

"Actually, I've got one on my phone." He smiled sadly. "I'm sorry. I'm not trying to make light of things. Tell me to shut up if you need to."

"Shut up."

He looked startled, and she let out a wavery little laugh.

"Not really. I just couldn't resist."

"Oh, Abby." He leaned forward until their foreheads were touching, their breaths mingling.

Abby closed her eyes, squeezed them shut tight, but a tear stupidly slipped out anyway.

"It's not as if I've wanted this to wreck my life," she told him in a suffocated whisper. "You know I've actually done my best to forgive and heal and all the rest of it. I really have, but I guess it wasn't very much."

"I know."

"And it's not as if I haven't been happy," she felt compelled to say, although she knew that in saying it at all, she was indicating the opposite. "I really do like working at Willow Tree. And my dad…" She stopped then, because she did not know how to begin to explain her dad, even to herself.

Simon eased back, forcing Abby to open her eyes and stare at him unhappily. He was going to ask questions, and she wasn't sure she was ready for them.

"What about your dad?"

Abby shrugged, opened her mouth, closed it again. A tug-of-war was taking place in her head. "He blames me," she said at last, and then she felt guilty for saying even that.

Simon's eyebrows rose. "He doesn't…"

"He does. At least, he did. After." Another memory reel spun out: her father in the hallway, a policeman in the kitchen, Abby blurting out her guilt, seeking absolution even then. *She asked me to drive her… I should have been there…* The look on his face; she'd felt as if she were watching him age in seconds. *Oh Abby, what have you done?*

Six little words that had absolutely felled her. Six words she had never been able to forget. He'd turned away from her then, talked to the policeman in a monotone. Abby had hovered in the kitchen doorway; she had no real memory of that conversation, or even that whole afternoon, except her father's silence.

After the policeman had left, her father had walked past as if she didn't exist. He hadn't so much as turned his head. Abby had stood there, feeling as if she were the ghost, rather than her mother or Luke, and then she'd gone up to her bedroom and curled up on her bed, hugging a pillow to her chest, sobbing silently until she'd felt as if she'd been turned inside out.

"He didn't speak to me for a week," she told Simon matter-of-factly. "While we were getting ready for the funeral, accepting a million casseroles, people in and out of the house all the time. He didn't say a single word to me."

Simon looked torn; he wanted to comfort her but he'd met her father. "He was grieving," he said at last.

"Yes. I know. And after a week, after the funeral, when everyone had gone back to their homes and it was just the two of us, he spoke to me. Well, I spoke first. I said I wouldn't go to college, I'd stay and help, and he just said 'All right'. That was it." She shrugged, amazed that the memory could still hurt so much, all these years later. The finality of that moment, of realizing this, and only this, was what her future was going to look like, and it was no more than she deserved. "And then we carried on as we have been ever since." She held up a hand to stem the response she expected him to give. "Look, I know it's dysfunctional, okay? But it's a functioning dysfunction, if I can put it that way. My dad was never a chatterbox, and so it didn't feel all that different. We've talked about the farm and the weather—"

"The weather?"

"I just mean, it's been normal," she clarified. "Mostly. Sometimes."

"Which is it?"

"A bit of both." Abby sighed, grateful that the threat of tears seemed to have passed. Maybe she wouldn't cry, after all. "It hasn't been great, I can admit that, but it hasn't been terrible, either. At least, not all the time. Not even a lot of the time." She caught Simon's eye, jolted by the look of utter, sorrowful sympathy on his face, and somehow it made the thin veneer of matter-of-fact acceptance she'd just about managed to cover herself with crack right through. "It has...," she began, but her voice wobbled all over the place. And then, to her own amazement and shock, she was crying—not a few trickly tears to dab from the corner of her eye, but from-the-gut sobs she was horrified to hear coming from herself—and even more so that she couldn't stop.

"Abby," Simon said, and then his arms were around her, her head against his chest, and still the sobs kept coming, right from the bottom of her, deep down, the ones he hadn't even realized she'd been suppressing.

But I've cried, she thought, even as she continued to soak Simon's shirt right through. *I cried so much, back at the beginning.*

But she hadn't cried like this—in someone's arms, offering her comfort, understanding her pain, giving her the acceptance and understanding she had never found before, not in fifteen years of both suppressing and searching. Before, she'd always cried alone, and she realized now that it wasn't the same thing at all.

"I'm disgusting," she choked out after what could have been five minutes or an hour. "I'm all snotty."

"I don't care." There was a smile in Simon's voice, even though his tone was serious.

"You should." Urgh, she really was gross. Abby wiped her eyes and felt her nose running, but she didn't really want to wipe that, at least not without a tissue. Simon was going to have to change his shirt.

"Here." He scooted off the bed and went to the bathroom, returning with a bunch of scrunched-up toilet paper.

Abby managed a wobbly laugh.

"Thank you," she said, taking it, and then she blew her nose heartily.

A silence stretched between them, and she didn't know how to fill it.

"I didn't realize I was going to cry that much," she said eventually. She felt empty now, but not in a bad way. Exhausted, too. "I thought maybe a few artful tears, you know, glassy eyes, a hitch in my voice, that sort of thing. All very dignified."

Simon shook his head, smiling. "Nope."

"Nope," Abby agreed. She felt absolutely spent, as if she'd run a marathon. She stared down at the balled tissue in her hand. "What now?" she asked eventually. "Is this where you tell me I need to forgive myself?"

"No, because you already know that."

She sighed. "Yes, I do."

"If you want me to tell you something, then it would be to talk to your father. Honestly."

"I've tried," Abby said, although she knew she hadn't. Not properly. "It's hard."

"I'm sure it is."

She glanced at him uncertainly. "So have I freaked you out, Mr. Emotionally Unavailable?" she made herself ask. "Or is this removed enough from your life that it's not making you uncomfortable?"

SIMON

Simon would have laughed, except it all cut a little too close to the bone. "You haven't freaked me out," he said, but Abby wasn't fooled.

"But?"

Simon hesitated. All the while he'd held her in his arms, longing to give her comfort, he'd painfully felt his own shortcomings. His own silences. Because if Abby was going to lay herself bare for him, then surely he had to do the same?

But was now really the time? This was about Abby—her grief, her past, her problem. Not his. And yet even as the thought flickered through him, Simon knew it was a cowardly cop-out.

"But you've made me feel that I should be as honest with you as you've been with me," he said with a heavy sigh. Even now he didn't want to do it. He knew it might change things between them, and not for the better.

Abby's reddened, swollen eyes widened. "What do you mean?"

"For fifteen years you've struggled with guilt and regret over one moment," Simon explained slowly, "one decision you made in an instant that you wished you'd done differently. I'm the opposite. I've had fifteen years of moments, of decisions I wished I done differently."

"Do you mean your divorce?"

"No," Simon answered, and it almost, but not quite, felt like a relief. "I'm talking about my daughter."

CHAPTER TWENTY-SIX

Boizenburg, June 1945

"Captain to see you, Lawson."

Matthew gave a terse nod as he turned from the window and its view of the pretty main square of the town of Boizenburg, on the banks of the Elbe, thirty miles west of Ludwigslust.

After the war had officially ended, after Wobbelin, he'd been assigned to this small military government office to round up and interrogate local Nazis, some of whom desperately denied their involvement, others who, in their terror or defeat, were all too eager to help.

Matthew felt absolutely nothing for any of them—not pity, not hatred, not even disdain. Something had frozen hard and solid inside him and would not be shifted, which at least made interrogation rather easy.

There was no question of him losing control; he would not be moved by anything these wretched men said—not by their clear-eyed arrogance or their pathetic sniveling; not their recitation of unimaginably evil facts without a shred of emotion or their absurd denials of even knowing about the camps they'd already been identified as running. There had been a camp right in Boizenburg, until the very end of the war.

Before being posted here, Matthew had been granted three days' leave to return to Fraustadt, to find what he could of his family.

It hadn't been an easy journey, for the country was in complete chaos, soldiers everywhere, of every stripe, fraternizing, arguing, and enjoying what paltry pleasures a conquered Germany could offer them.

Matthew had heard stories, and seen things too—soldiers breaking into homes, taking what they liked, including the women. He'd heard of the suicides of high-ranking Nazis, and how Berlin, along with the whole country, would be carved up like a Christmas goose. He found he didn't care about any of it; he couldn't, because to let in so much as a flicker of feeling was to acknowledge the utter, awful vastness seething beneath, and to do that was unthinkable. Unbearable. Impossible. He needed to stay cold.

Fraustadt and the surrounding area had been occupied by the Soviets since February, and so he'd had to ask, bluster, cajole, and sometimes bribe, his way back home. He owed particular gratitude to a sympathetic Soviet officer who spoke German, respected Matthew's uniform, and allowed him passage on a military transport all the way to Dresden.

When he'd finally arrived in Fraustadt, he saw the town was remarkably preserved, and he was reminded of his childhood with a ferocity he forced himself to suppress. As he'd walked the street, looking for familiar faces, no one seemed to want to meet his eye. The house where he'd been born, where his father had been kicked to death, and where he'd been spirited away in the gray dawn like a thief, had stood abandoned and empty.

When he'd knocked on neighbors' doors and explained who he was, they shook their heads, gazes skating away, a look of fear on their faces. Perhaps it was his uniform.

"We don't know anything," one woman, he couldn't remember her name, had said piteously. "Your mother left years ago… before…"

Before. Such a terrible word. Before the Jews were rounded up like cattle, before they were herded onto trains, before they were sent to their deaths in ways it was nearly impossible to comprehend.

Already, just days after the war, details of the death camps had begun to filter through military channels. Matthew had heard about Auschwitz, and Majdanek, and Treblinka, about Dachau and Ravensbruck and Bergen-Belsen, among others. So many others.

He'd read matter-of-fact reports, and heard low, horror-struck voices describe scenes like those he'd seen at Wobbelin, and even worse.

He'd heard how prisoners were told they were merely on a transit stop, to rest and wash, before they went on to a labor camp. How they were made to strip and taken into a chamber that looked like a shower but in fact became a tomb. He'd heard it all, and he had accepted it and understood it even as he refused to let it affect him. He couldn't.

All he learned in Fraustadt was that his mother had left with his brothers and sister before the worst, maybe in 1941. No one could quite remember, or perhaps they didn't want to.

It gave him not quite hope, but the approximation of it, to know that they hadn't been deported, at least not then. His mother was smart, he reminded himself; she'd got him out, after all, and he knew she'd been squirreling away valuables for years. Before he'd left, before he'd run away like a child, she'd promised him they would all get out.

"Don't worry, *mausi*," she'd said, using an endearment he hadn't heard since he'd been a little boy. "I'll keep them safe. I know what to do."

He'd believed her. He'd believed her for her sake, and for Franz's and Arno's, as well as for dear little Gertie's, but most of all he'd believed it for his, because he could never have gone as he had if he hadn't taken his mother at her word, if he hadn't looked into her brown eyes and seen the sincerity, accepted the firmness of her tone, her smile. *We'll be all right. I promise.*

In mid-May, when Matthew finally left Fraustadt, and any answers, behind him, he wondered if he should have taken his mother at her word, or if she'd simply been saying what she'd known he'd needed to hear.

"Sergeant Lawson." Captain Betts, the officer in charge of this small military governance in Boizenburg, was a kindly man who had come over on D-Day, unlike the new recruits who had plenty of military intelligence training but no combat action, and had just been shipped in after V-E Day for the cleanup job.

Matthew had little time for any of them, although he tried to hide his visceral disdain for their know-it-all attitudes, their buoyant sense of confidence without any experience, like children on a holiday. They talked more of going to Paris than what the Nazis had done. He liked Captain Betts well enough, at least.

"Sir." His tone was neutral as he saluted.

Betts looked at him unhappily. "Sergeant, I'm afraid I've discovered something I believe you should see."

Matthew kept his face expressionless. "Sir?"

"I took the liberty, after you returned from Fraustadt, to ask some higher-ups about your family."

Matthew tensed, a stillness stealing through his body that left him unable even to breathe.

"Weiss," Betts said, as if asking a question, and Matthew forced a nod. "The Nazis destroyed many of their records, and looking for a name is like looking for a needle in a haystack. I don't think we'll ever know everyone who..." He paused to clear his throat. "But I found this." He pushed a piece of paper towards Matthew; it was a mimeograph of a typed list of names.

When Matthew took a step closer, he saw it was a deportation list, and the names of his mother, brothers, and sister were all on it. It was dated October 1942.

"From Dresden," Betts said quietly. "To Treblinka."

Matthew's head jerked up as he looked at his senior officer, his rapid blinking the only sign that he understood what the man was telling him. Treblinka... one of the extermination camps that had been destroyed by the Nazis, a desperate cover-up of their unbearable evil. A place utterly without hope.

"I'm sorry," Betts said.

"You know what happened?"

"Your mother and sister died upon arrival. Cause of death was noted as heart failure."

"They were gassed." He spoke flatly, unemotionally. "And my brothers?"

"They were transferred to Auschwitz, after the uprising at Treblinka. They died in August 1944, the same way."

Matthew nodded slowly, saying nothing. He felt as if nothing in him was working properly—muscles, lungs, heart. It was all mechanical, a series of contractions and jerks that only just kept him alive.

Betts cleared his throat. "I am sorry, Lawson. Weiss, I should say. I'm really very sorry to give you this news." A pause, as if he expected something from Matthew, some sort of response or emotion, but he had nothing to give. "Take the rest of the day off," Betts said at last.

Matthew shook his head. "I'm fine."

"Take it off," he repeated firmly. "You need it. I'll see you here at eight hundred hours, sharp, tomorrow."

Outside the military headquarters housed in the Rathaus, or town hall, Matthew didn't know what to do. People walked down the street; the sun was shining. Boizenburg had escaped the worst of the bombing, despite a shipbuilder's right in the town, and the summery scene was disconcertingly pleasant: a child holding her mother's hand, her steps light and skipping; two women gossiping. One of them laughed.

He took a few steps towards the center of the square, and then stopped. He did not know where to go. He felt as if he were both shrinking and expanding, the world coming in and out of focus, so he could see with extraordinary clarity in one moment, and then only a troubling blur the next.

A cold cattle car rattling east... He'd heard that they'd had to scrape the ice from the sides because they were so thirsty. And when it had stopped at the gates of Treblinka, with its fake timetables and its big clock, the grossest, most evil parody of a rail station...

An SS guard, smoking, indifferent. "Take off your things. We'll hold your valuables for you." Almost kind, in his reassurances, perhaps, knowing what was next. Had his mother known? His brothers? Franz and Arno would have been taken somewhere else with the other healthy young men and women, to work, often to death. But *Mutti*... and Gertie... dear, little Gertie with her black button eyes and her curly hair...

Matthew closed his eyes, fighting the images that came anyway. Gertie unbuttoning her dress, carefully folding it. She'd always been so neat with her things. Mutti, her hand on her daughter's shoulder, a comforting weight.

His mother had not been an unintelligent woman. She must have known what was going to happen. Did she try to comfort Gertie? Or did she jolly her along, take part in the horrible pretense because it was better than having her only daughter, just twelve years old, facing such unimaginable fear?

Matthew squeezed his eyes shut tighter, hard enough to hurt, yet he could not block it out. *Don't worry, mausi. There's nothing to be afraid of. Think of it, we will finally get nice and clean after all this time...*

A sound escaped him, like an animal in its death throes. He started striding down the street, faster and faster, until he broke into a run. He did not know where he was going, only that he could never run fast enough.

*

At eight o'clock the next morning, Matthew reported for duty. Despite Betts' doubts, he assured his commanding officer he was fit and ready for service, his voice as flat and unemotional as ever.

Half a dozen low-ranking Nazi officers had been rounded up the night before, and were waiting in their cells to be interrogated. Some of them had been involved in running the camp in Boizenburg, one of the small Neuengamme subcamps. Without a flicker of an eyelid or a tremor of emotion, Matthew assured Betts once more he was fine and perfectly capable of conducting interrogations as necessary.

And he *was* fine; his head felt remarkably clear as he read the brief and then came into the room where a prisoner waited, a short, red-faced man in a cheap suit, doing his best to look composed. Matthew had interrogated dozens of men like this— men who had been shoemakers or butchers before the war, and who had become puffed up by their own importance, their SS status, only to then tremble and stammer in fear when they were cornered, attempting denials, and then absurd justifications, and finally squealing for mercy. *Mercy.* The idea was an insult.

"*Guten morgen.*" He kept his tone civil, which gave the odious little man a flicker of hope. He had squinty eyes like a pig, and a wide, wet mouth.

"*Guten morgen.*"

Matthew leaned against a desk and folded his arms, keeping the man's gaze as the silence spun out. The man licked his lips, his gaze darting nervously around the room.

"I don't know anything," he finally said. "I told them before, you've got the wrong man."

Matthew's expression did not change. "You are *SS-Unterscharführer* Heinrich Henck," he stated, "director of camp labor for Boizenburg, a subcamp of the Neuengamme concentration camp."

"My name is Henck, but I did not have that position. I was never in the SS. I never even knew about the camp." The man's chin quivered.

"You were seen. You have been identified."

"By one woman?" Clearly Henck was aware of the source of their information: a near-hysterical woman who had seen him on the street, a loaf of bread tucked under his arm. "She is clearly demented."

"No."

"She's mistaken me, then." He straightened. "How can I be SS? I'm an accountant." Like Matthew's own father. "Besides, I don't have that tattoo they all have—"

"The blood type tattoo?" Usually on the underside of the left arm, near the armpit. A status symbol as well as a practical sign, in case they were wounded and needed a blood transfusion. "Not every SS has it," Matthew returned coolly, "especially those who were drafted in at the end of the war."

Henck deflated slightly, before he puffed up again. "It's my word against hers, that of an unstable woman—"

"There are others." They hadn't found them yet, but they would. There were survivors, as well as other camp personnel, who would rat this little man out. Matthew was sure of it.

"Who are they, then?" Henck asked, thrusting his chest out, a moment of bravado.

Matthew smiled. "It doesn't matter."

Henck stared at him in wary confusion. "What is that supposed to mean? You are meant to be the law, now, aren't you?"

"Do you really wish to talk about the law?" Matthew lit a cigarette and blew the smoke out in a steady, contemplative stream. "At Boizenburg, you were in charge of implementing the directive *Vernichtung durch Arbeit*." Extermination through labor. One of the survivors of Neuengamme had told them as much as he could. Ten- to twelve-hour days of forced labor under unimaginable conditions, little food, arbitrary beatings and other cruel punishments. Even though it hadn't been a death camp like Auschwitz or Treblinka, it was estimated that half of the inmates there had died.

"I don't know what you're talking about," Henck said firmly.

They continued for another hour, Matthew remaining calm and controlled, Henck veering wildly between determined denials and blustery bravado, even as his story began to change. Yes, all right, he'd known about the camp, of course he had, but he'd never *been*. Then: he might have been once, very well, who could remember? He didn't keep track of every place he went. He wasn't aware of what was going on there, who had been? Well, yes, everyone knew it was something. But no one could possibly *realize…*

His forehead was shiny with sweat, the armpits of his shirt dark and damp. He kept glancing at Matthew's cigarette with a look of naked longing.

And then he began to break. A single slip, made when he was tired.

"You should question someone important," he said crossly, thoughtlessly, after Matthew had asked him a dozen questions in a row, rapid-fire. "Someone like Pauly. He was in charge of the whole thing. Or what about that lunatic, Trzebinski?"

Matthew merely raised his eyebrows.

"I've heard of them," Henck blustered quickly. "Everyone has. Their names were bandied about."

Silence, as he sweated. Matthew smoked.

"Look," Henck finally said, and his voice broke along with his resolve. "I wasn't anyone important. I was second in command of the labor, not even the *Unterscharführer*. She had that wrong, you know. I was just obeying orders. That's all I did." Another long, uneasy pause. "I'll tell you what I know," Henck said, wheedling now. "I can be helpful. I can give you names. But you must realize I didn't make any decisions. I just carried them out. There are so many others you could—"

"Who was Trzebinski?" Matthew asked as if it were a matter of passing interest. "Why did you call him a lunatic?"

"He was the camp doctor, although one would hardly call him that. It wasn't as if he made anyone better." A slight guffaw, quickly suppressed.

Matthew eyed him coldly. "You called him a lunatic."

Henck shrugged, caught between discomfort and indifference, battling a cautious hope that information might be the way out for him. "He did experiments on some of the prisoners. I never saw. I just heard." He gave a little shiver as he grimaced. "It didn't seem right to me," he added with an absurd self-righteousness. "I never thought anyone should do *that* sort of thing."

"Experiments," Matthew said tonelessly, and waited.

"All sorts. Like I said, I never saw. But… all sorts." Another self-conscious shiver, as if his discomfort somehow united them. "You heard things. Injections, prisoners made to stay in ice water until they'd died… I know he took twenty children, some as young as six, from one of the extermination camps, for experiments with tuberculosis. When he was finished with them, he had them hung in the basement of the Bullenhuser Damm school." This was recited matter-of-factly, with no shiver, no moue of disgust. The man wasn't bothered at all.

Matthew stared at him without any emotion. *When he was finished with them.* He stubbed out his cigarette.

"I've been here for hours," Henck said plaintively. "I need to relieve myself."

Matthew gestured to the door. The hallway and bathroom were guarded; Henck could not escape. He rose from his chair, straightening his cuffs as he gave Matthew a pointed look down his nose.

"At the end of the day," he said with a sniff, "they were only Jews."

Matthew did not reply. Alone in the room, he smoked another cigarette and tried to keep his mind empty. *Don't think of it. Don't think at all.*

Twenty children, perhaps like Gertie. Perhaps Gertie. As young as six. *When he was finished with them.*

A perfunctory knock on the door thankfully startled him out of his thoughts. "Hey, Lawson, where's your prisoner?"

He turned to see Cardenas, one of the new military intelligence recruits, standing in the doorway, chewing a wad of gum.

"Relieving himself," he said shortly. "But I'm done for now. I'll do the paperwork and he can be returned to his cell."

Cardenas raised his eyebrows. "How long has he been in there? Because you know some SS bigwig killed himself yesterday, while he was supposed to be taking a piss? Betts was spitting bullets. The bastard cut his wrists while he was on the john."

Betts hadn't told him any of that. Matthew stared at Cardenas for several seconds. Then he strode out of the room, down the corridor to the toilets. A new fury was building in him, rising like a tidal wave, or perhaps an avalanche, overtaking any thought. It had been there all along, of course, but Matthew had always controlled it, kept it down. He'd had to, for his own sake. His own sanity. Now he felt it unleash, a wild and uncontained thing, overwhelming him with its intensity.

He threw open the door to the toilets. "Henck, you fucker," he demanded, "where are you?"

He pushed open the door of the first stall—empty. The second was locked and Matthew kicked it in, so full of rage now he could barely take in the sight before him—Henck hunched over on the toilet, his trousers about his ankles.

The Nazi looked up, startled, as the door swung open. And before Matthew even knew what he was doing, before he could so much as think, he had his hand around the man's throat.

Oh, but it felt good to have his hands there. To squeeze hard. It felt so very satisfying, so very *right*, to watch Henck's eyes bulge and his face go red as his pudgy little hands clawed uselessly at Matthew's own. He was going to kill him, and he was *glad*. He wanted it to happen; he welcomed it.

"Lawson, don't kill the bastard!" A hard hand on his shoulder threw Matthew back, and he fell against the doorway of the stall as Henck doubled over, choking and gasping for air. "We want him alive, not dead," Cardenas reminded him matter-of-factly, seemingly unperturbed by the grim scene that had just played out. "They're no good to us dead. Not before they've all sung like canaries."

But I wanted him dead, Matthew thought as he stared at Henck's reddened face, his fingermarks livid on the man's throat. *I needed him dead. I still do. And I want to be the one to kill him, to get revenge.*

The former SS *Unterscharführer*, he saw, had pissed all over the floor.

The next day, he received his Distinguished Service Cross, given by Captain Betts with an understanding smile.

CHAPTER TWENTY-SEVEN

ABBY

Abby watched the fields blur by as Simon drove across Wisconsin under a hazy sky, back towards Ashford. They'd been in the car for several hours already, and neither of them had said much at all. Abby didn't know what there was to say; her head felt full, her heart empty. It was a strange sensation.

Last night, when Simon had said the words "my daughter", she'd simply stared. They'd bounced off her brain, not making sense, because he looked so sorrowful, so *resigned*, and she didn't understand why, just as she didn't understand how he could possibly have a daughter he hadn't told her about.

Except he did, obviously he did, and she realized she shouldn't feel surprised—never mind betrayed—by it, because surely this was just another reminder that they really didn't know each other well at all.

"Your daughter," she'd finally said, testing the words out, feeling their strength, and Simon had nodded, more of a hanging of his head than anything else.

"Yes."

"Tell me."

And so he had, as haltingly as she'd told her own tale of complicated grief, about his divorce, which hadn't been as simple as he'd made it out to be, because there had been—there still *was*—a child involved, a little girl.

"Maggie," Simon had said, with an ache in his voice.

"How old is she?"

"Twelve."

"And when you separated...?"

"Five."

Abby was silent, absorbing these unexpected revelations, unsure what to make of any of it. Somehow it changed things, and yet she couldn't even articulate why or how. "Why didn't you mention her before?" she had asked finally.

"Because I felt guilty," Simon had said. He'd looked wretched, and she had wanted to comfort him, yet somehow she couldn't, even though he'd comforted her. He'd put his arms around her, he'd held her while she'd cried. And yet somehow she couldn't do the same; she had leaned back against the headboard, her arms around her knees.

"Guilty?" she'd repeated after a moment. "Of what?"

"Of failing my family." He'd paused, each word drawn out of him like a poison, with both reluctance and healing. "Of... of being a bad father."

"Why... why would you feel that way?" Asking the questions felt like edging through the dark, tiptoeing, not sure what she might bump into. "What happened?"

Simon was silent, his gaze moving despondently around the bland room as if looking for answers he knew he wouldn't find. "Nothing *happened*," he'd said at last. "There's no big moment I can point to and say 'that's when I should have done x' or something like that. I wish there was. If there had been, I hope to God I would have done it."

"Then..." She had stared at him, confused. "I don't understand, Simon. I think... I think I feel a bit like you must have, when you knew there was this big thing I hadn't told you about, and you kept coming up against it like a brick wall I pretended wasn't there. What happened with your daughter? With... Maggie? Because something did, obviously."

"Well." He had shifted on the bed, trying to look composed and practical when Abby suspected he possessed as deep a wound, a grief, as she did, or almost. "Sara had sole custody, for a start. It didn't feel quite like that at the time—I didn't just sign away my rights to my child. But I was the one who moved out—Sara asked me to—and it just seemed like the right thing for Maggie to stay in her family home, with the parent who had been at home with her the most. Sara was a stay-at-home mum for four years, while I'd worked. And I told myself I still had summer holidays and the rest of it. We agreed on—well, visitation is the wrong word, because I was more than a visitor. At least at the start. But I'd have Maggie for weekend afternoons—we both agreed she should sleep in her own bed every night—and Sara had her the rest of the time. That's how it began."

Which sounded both depressing and ominous. Abby didn't reply, just waited, as Simon once had for her to organize her thoughts, explain her regret.

"It happened gradually," he had resumed quietly. "So gradually I almost didn't realize, except I think at least part of me did." He'd looked down, seeming unable to meet her eye. "I just didn't want to acknowledge it."

"What happened?"

"I spent less time with Maggie. I—I wasn't a proper father to her." He'd swallowed audibly, his throat working. "Not that I would have seen it like that. But I didn't like having her in my flat—she didn't like it. It wasn't familiar, I didn't have the right toys or food even if I tried to... basically, it wasn't home. I wasn't Mummy. So I started taking her out to places she'd like, soft play places or McDonald's on a Sunday afternoon because she had ballet on Saturday, and she wanted Sara to take her to that." He'd sighed. "It was always something. I felt like I had to fit in around a busy schedule, someone else's life, and I hated that. And, you know, there's nothing more depressing than a half-empty McDonald's with a bunch of single dads and their glum kids struggling to have a conversation over a greasy burger and some cold fries." He gave himself a shake as if to rid himself of the memory. "I know I most likely sound like I'm complaining. Or doing the whole poor-me act. And, looking back, I wish I'd tried harder. Made it work somehow. Maybe if I'd had a nicer flat, or I'd insisted on having the whole weekend from the beginning... but I was trying to be reasonable, and to do what seemed like the best for Maggie, even if it didn't feel like it was the best for me." He'd looked up at her then, resolute, wretched. "So my time with Maggie started slipping. Missed weekends, because she was busy. A birthday party. A special outing. There always seemed to be some reason, and I was willing to accept it."

"That's understandable," Abby had murmured. She could see how it would happen, a gradual wearing away, the erosion of a relationship without the realization of the crumbling. Her relationship with her father had been transformed in an instant; Simon's with his daughter had changed infinitesimally, yet irrevocably, over time. Yet, despite the differences, the result seemed to be the same—terrible, endless regret.

"I took her on holiday when she was six," he had resumed, "to one of those all-inclusive places in Spain, and frankly it was a disaster. I wish it hadn't been—you don't know how much I wish that!—but by then it felt like it was already too late for us. There were rules and routines I didn't know well enough. I didn't tuck her into bed the way she liked. I couldn't do her hair in pigtails properly. There were a thousand moments like that." He'd swallowed again, gripping his hands together tightly, knuckles bony and white. A deep breath, a careful exhalation. "So while you only have one moment, Abby, I have more than I can count. More than I can remember. And I know none of them are as significant as yours, not even close, but the result is I barely see or talk to my daughter now." He looked away, his mouth tightening, his usually laughing eyes full of self-recrimination.

Despite everything he'd already said, this had surprised her. Shocked her, in a prickly, uncomfortable way. "Why don't you? I mean, barely is…" Bad. But she didn't want to say it.

"Oh, it's not quite as cut and dried as that." He had forced his lips stiffly upwards, all easy, affable charm gone now, something vulnerable and pulsatingly painful revealed. "You know, neither of us would say it quite so bluntly. And there's nothing *hostile* between us, although sometimes I actually wish there was. At least that would mean there was something to work out, rather than just this—this weary indifference on Maggie's part." He'd sighed, a long, drawn-out sound of surrender. "Sara met someone when Maggie was seven. Pete. Very nice guy. Very solid. Very genuine." He spoke flatly, without any bitterness, but Abby could tell it cost him. "And a great father figure, of course. The more he was involved in Maggie's life, the less I needed to be. Not that anyone said that, or even implied it. But Sara and I had agreed that Maggie could make her own choices, that her happiness was paramount. And, time and time again, first just once in a while, then more often, she chose Pete. Which I understood—I really did. She wanted to go to Pete's take-your-daughter-to-work day. Pete was the one who taught her to ride a bike." His face had contorted, then evened out, expressionless. "I became this… this extraneous appendage, like some awkward uncle who won't leave the party. And I let it happen."

And there was the poisonous root of the guilt—*I let it happen.* Just as she had. And sitting there on the bed with her knees tucked up to her chest and tears still dried on her cheeks, Abby had realized she and Simon weren't that different, after all. What did it matter if it had been one moment or a million? The result was the same—a choice you hadn't realized you were making, a consequence you could have never foreseen. And a life of crippling regret as you insisted you'd forgiven yourself even as you knew you never would.

"It all sounds incredibly difficult," she had said at last, hating how careful her voice sounded, but not knowing how else to respond.

Simon had given a grimace of self-disgust. "Oh, who I am kidding? Here I am, painting myself to you like some absurd victim. It all just *happened* to me. That's not true, Abby. That's just not true."

She had blinked at the self-loathing in his voice, like an acid coating his words. "What do you mean?"

"I mean I didn't just let it happen without realizing. I realized. I saw it unfold. And I allowed it, because frankly it felt like shit to be sidelined, and I'd rather just choose to fade out myself. When I came here to America, I didn't even tell Maggie until I was on the plane. Three weeks of summer holidays, we could have done something together, but I knew she wouldn't want to, and so I chose to check out. As I have been for years. *That's* the truth. That's the truth I can't forgive myself for, and yet I keep doing it." He had finished with a sound of self-disgust, a full stop to his recriminations.

"So don't," Abby had said simply. Gently.

He'd blinked at her. "Don't…?"

"You'd say the same to me, wouldn't you? Don't do it anymore. Stop feeling guilty. Stop blaming yourself. There's no point in it, even if you have something to be guilty about. You can't change the past, only the future, so choose a different path. All those lines worthy of a meme or to be on a mug. Come *on*, Simon. It doesn't have to be this way, just because it has in the past."

A tiny smile had quirked the lines of his mouth. "I wasn't expecting you to say all that."

"I don't know if I was, either," Abby had admitted. "But we're not so different, you know. We've both let the past predict our future. We've let moments define us, whether it's one or one hundred, and they don't have to. We don't have to let them. I finally get that, thanks to you. So you need to get it, too. You've helped me, Simon. Let me help you."

"Thank you," he had said. He'd stared at her for a long moment, and then wordlessly he'd leaned across the expanse of floral-patterned bedspread and wrapped his hand around the back of her head, drawing her to him. Their lips had touched softly, as if in slow motion, a press, a promise. It wasn't a passionate kiss; it felt like something more important than that.

Abby drew away first. "You're leaving in a few days." She spoke matter-of-factly.

"I know."

Neither of them had said anything for a few moments. Simon's fingers were still threaded through her hair.

"I've never told anyone what I've told you. I've never let myself," he'd admitted.

"I never have, either."

More silence that they breathed in, letting it relax them.

"Let's not talk about us now," Abby had said finally. "If there even is an us—"

"There is."

His quiet assurance had made her smile. "Really, we should be thinking about Matthew and Lily. Do you think you can find out what happened to them?"

"I can try."

Their food had arrived then, and they ate in surprisingly relaxed affability, considering all the revelations they'd had, all the emotional outpouring that had been going on. Afterwards, they watched a silly movie, Simon's arm around her shoulders, her head nestled against him, and at eleven Abby had finally decided to go to bed. Simon had kissed her at the door like a gentleman. It felt like the best evening she could remember having in a long, long time.

And now they were here, quiet and thoughtful, in a car speeding towards home, towards her father, towards Simon's departure. Towards the beginning of the rest of their lives. Except Abby had no idea if those would be intertwined or not.

The farmhouse looked tired and faded under a humid sky when Simon dropped her off. He'd offered to stay, but Abby knew she needed to talk to her father alone.

"But I'll see you?" Simon pressed, sounding both determined and anxious. "I don't leave till Wednesday."

"You'll see me," Abby promised him, silently thinking, *even if it is only to say goodbye.*

Inside, everything was quiet and empty-feeling. Abby put her bag by the front door and headed for the kitchen, starting in surprise when she saw her father slumped at the kitchen table, a photograph in his hand, Bailey at his feet, her tail thumping at Abby's arrival.

"Dad?"

"Did you find out?" He sounded resigned, as resigned as Simon had, talking about his daughter.

"Find out what?"

"About my father. Tom Reese."

She realized she hadn't given her grandfather much of a thought at all, once she'd discovered Matthew and Lily. "No, I didn't. Not really, anyway. We found more out about Matthew Lawson, actually." But she didn't think her father cared much about that. "What is it, Dad?" she asked gently, with a courage and a compassion she knew she hadn't possessed before. Seeing him looking so weary and defeated, she ached to put her arms around him, but she couldn't remember the last time they'd hugged. "What are you trying to keep from me? Because, whatever it is, it doesn't matter to me. I promise you it doesn't."

"My father was a coward." The words were barely audible, yet still distinct. "He told me all about it before he died. It had haunted him for years—ever since it happened, I think. Wrecked his life, in some ways."

Gingerly, Abby pulled out a chair next to her father and sat down. Bailey put her head on her knee. "Since what happened?" she asked.

"Since he deserted." David looked up at her bleakly, his face drawn into haggard lines of sorrowful acceptance. "He ran away from the battle. Ardennes, when the SS kept coming in waves. Not that that's any excuse. He was shot as he was fleeing the scene, leaving his comrades to fall, and they did." He drew a heavy breath. "Shot by his fellow soldier."

Abby's mouth dropped open; she knew what—who—he was going to say before he did.

"By Matthew Lawson."

"Matthaus Weiss," she said softly, and David frowned.

"Who?"

"It doesn't matter. I'll explain later. Is that why he gave Grandad his medal?"

"Part of it, maybe. My father was engaged to Sophie Mather—"

"You knew—"

"So you found that out, did you?" He didn't sound sour, just accepting.

"We guessed."

"They were engaged, right at the end of the war. My father loved her. Spoke about her beauty and her fire, how spunky she was." David sighed heavily. "He went back to London to recuperate after he was wounded. The knowledge of what he'd done was eating him up. Day after day, he couldn't think about anything else. Couldn't eat, even. Sometimes he felt as if he couldn't breathe, just thinking about that moment. That choice…" The pain in her father's voice, the memory, made Abby certain he wasn't just talking about his father, about Tom Reese's regret, but something far closer to home. Closer to their own painfully fractured relationship. "Eventually, he couldn't keep it to himself. He told Sophie, hoping she'd understand. Needing her to forgive him."

"But she didn't," Abby whispered. It was all starting to make sense, in a terrible way.

"No, she didn't. He told me she was furious with him. She'd lost her mother to a V-1 rocket, and she'd waited out the war, longing to do something herself, or so my father said. When he told her, she called him a coward. She threw her engagement ring in his face and said she never wanted to see him again."

After hearing so much about the tempestuous Sophie, Abby found she could picture the scene all too well. "And yet he gave her his Purple Heart—?"

"As a keepsake, to remember him by. He hated having to let her go. I don't think he blamed her, but she broke his heart. He never told another soul, not till his deathbed, when he told me, a confession he felt he had to make."

"Oh, Dad." Abby rested her hand over her father's gnarled one. It was the closest she could remember them being in years. "I'm so sorry."

David wiped his eyes, and then he shook his head. "Don't be sorry about that. It was years ago. Lifetimes. It doesn't matter anymore. I've always known that."

"Then…" *Why did you fight so hard to keep me from knowing it?* Considering her father's state, Abby couldn't make herself say the words.

"It's me I'm crying for," David admitted in a choked voice. "Me and you. It's my guilt, not my father's, that's eating me up, just as it did him. I'm as much of a coward as he was, and I haven't been able to stand you knowing, even as I've been afraid you've known all along."

Shock blazed through her like a single, pure flame, right down to the tips of her toes, leaving her immobile, speechless. She'd never, ever expected her father to say something like that. She'd returned from Minneapolis hoping and praying she would be brave enough to say *something*, to begin to bridge this chasm between them that they'd both always pretended wasn't there, but she'd never expected her father to be the first one to speak.

"Dad…" She licked her lips, unable to say more. Even that was hard enough. She didn't know how she felt, whether she was happy or sad, hurt or relieved. Everything was jumbled up, a tangle of emotions.

David shook his head. "I did it all wrong, Abby, after they died. I went about it all wrong. I was a coward."

Tears stung her eyes, tears she hadn't thought she'd had left. She'd cried so much last night, wept herself right out, and yet these were different. These weren't tears of grief, they were ones of emotion, and even of hope. "You didn't," she whispered.

"I did." He sounded fierce now, a remnant of the gruff man she'd always known—and loved. "I did. I shut you out, I blamed you. I know I did."

Oh, but that was hard to take, even though she'd been expecting it. Had known it. "You had a right to," she made herself say, even though each word felt like drawing a razor across her soul.

"No, I didn't, Abby. I never did." David spoke staunchly. "You were seventeen." He paused, struggling to rein in emotions he'd never showed her before. "I was in the barn." He looked up at her with bleak, reddened eyes, their hands still clasped on the table. "I didn't have anything all that important to do, just the usual work, and I knew about your trip to Milwaukee."

Abby shook her head, although she didn't deny what he'd said. She'd known he was in the barn, or the orchard, somewhere, busy, always busy. Yet she'd never blamed him. Never even thought of doing it, not for a second. Yet, she realized in wonder, he'd been blaming himself, all these years.

"It wasn't your fault," she whispered. Her lips felt stiff, her tongue thick.

"It wasn't yours, either. I shouldn't have acted the way I did, but it was—it was as if I didn't know how to be. Like someone had taken my leg off, or half my heart. I just didn't know how to be anymore, Abby."

Tears leaked from his eyes and trickled down his craggy cheeks. He glanced down at the photo, and that was when Abby saw it wasn't a picture of her grandfather, as she'd assumed, but of them—the four of them, a family, the last photo they'd had taken, the Easter before Luke and her mom had died. Everyone was smiling in it; Luke needed a haircut.

"Oh, Dad." She put her arms around him, breathed in the scent of him—apples and leather and old-fashioned aftershave. Her dad. *Her dad.*

"Forgive me, sweetheart." He hadn't called her that in fifteen years. "Forgive me."

"Of course I do." It was as easy as that, and yet Abby knew it wasn't. You couldn't simply sweep fifteen years of hard history under the carpet and then walk over it, all smooth and neat, normality restored. Life was messier and more complicated than that. They were. Still, this was a start, a second chance, something she'd never expected to have.

David eased back, his mouth working its way into a smile before he wiped at his eyes, embarrassed, gruff again. Bailey trotted over to him and put her head on his knee, tail thumping on the floor. He rested one hand on the dog's head as he looked at Abby. "I'm not sure why you digging into my father's past brought out my own. Maybe I was scared you'd see a connection between us. Maybe I'm just used to having secrets."

"So am I," Abby said softly. "But I'm glad this has all been brought out into the light."

"So am I." He slapped his thighs and rose from the chair as Bailey circled him. "I should get on, check things."

It was five o'clock in the evening, but Abby didn't protest. He needed a moment. She did, as well.

Her father gave her a nod that for once didn't feel like a terse dismissal, but an acceptance, almost as good as a hug. Abby nodded back, a beginning.

She didn't know how long she sat at the table, staring into space, trying to make sense of the jigsaw of memories, of emotions, and only able to leave it a jumbled mess, a piece found there, another one slotted in. Her grandfather. Her father. Her mother and Luke. Simon...

At some point, her phone buzzed. She slid it out, and saw it was a text from Simon.

I've found Matthew Weiss.

CHAPTER TWENTY-EIGHT

ABBY

"He married my great-aunt!"

Simon sounded almost giddy with the knowledge, so much so that Abby had to laugh.

"What? Really?" They were sitting in Simon's little cottage, his laptop on the table between them, as the afternoon sunshine poured in, the day after Abby had returned from Minneapolis. The relentless humidity had finally broken, if not the heat. The colors had returned, under a blazing blue sky—the shimmer of the lake, the verdant green of the grass, thanks to the rain overnight. The world in Technicolor, once more.

"Yes, it's crazy, isn't it? I was searching online, looking up every Matthew Weiss from here to Timbuktu, and getting nowhere. Do you how many Matthew Weisses there are?"

"I have no idea," she confessed with a laugh.

"Well, neither do I, but a lot. So then I decided to talk to my sister, the one who loves all the genealogy stuff?"

"Eleanor."

Simon smiled. "That's right. And, on a desperate hunch, I asked her what she knew about Lily. Not much, as it turned out, and she never met her either, but she had a bunch of certificates in a file—my grandmother had kept them, a whole load of dusty papers that didn't seem all that interesting. But one of them was a marriage certificate between Lily Mather and Matthaus Weiss, New York City, 1946."

"They married," Abby said, a grin spreading across her face. "They stayed together."

"They must have emigrated, which is why I suppose I didn't hear about them as a child. It's too bad, considering I spent a year in Philadelphia, but I suppose my grandmother and my great-aunt must have been virtually estranged by then."

"So you could have found out about Matthew all along." Abby shook her head. "He was right there, waiting for you."

"But I wouldn't have been able to find out all the things we know now."

And that she knew, as well. Abby hadn't yet had a chance to tell Simon about her grandfather, or, more crucially, her dad. So many things had happened—some seventy years ago, some yesterday. So many important, life-changing things, and she was still trying to come to terms with all of it.

"I wouldn't have connected Tom Reese to Matthew Lawson, for one," Simon continued. "Isn't it strange? This whole story, from one medal to another, Germany and back, has led us right back home. To family."

And that was a good place to be. This morning, Abby and her father had eaten breakfast together—mostly in silence, but he'd poured her coffee and he'd asked her about her plans for the day. Small steps, those first halting, stumbling ones as they learned how to walk. How to be.

"So do you think they really had their happily-ever-after?" Abby asked, a bit wistfully. "Do you know if they had children? You'd have second cousins…"

"I do," Simon said. "Three. I actually found Lily on Facebook. Look." He typed a few words into the search bar and then pushed the laptop over so Abby could see the screen.

It was Lily Weiss' Facebook page, now a memorial. She scrolled through, smiling a bit at the photos of a small, white-haired woman surrounded by grandchildren; another one of her with Matthew, both of them wrinkled and frail, but with big smiles.

"I can't believe that's actually *them*."

"They lived in Albany," Simon told her. "He worked as an accountant. She was a schoolteacher. And they were part of a charity that fostered Jewish children, refugees from the camps. They had over twenty live with them at various stages, over the years."

"You found all this out on Facebook?"

"They link to a website." He grinned. "They sound as if they were kind of incredible, if I'm honest. I wish I could have known them."

"It's a shame Lily and Sophie drifted so far apart."

"It is. But knowing how high-strung my grandmother could be, and the distance..." He shrugged. "I can understand how it happens."

Abby thought of Maggie, and nodded. Yes, it could happen all too easily.

"Lily died only two years ago, sadly," Simon continued, and Abby let out a soft sound of distress, even though she supposed it should have been expected. "I didn't know about it at the time. My grandmother must have, though—she had her marriage certificate, after all. She must have received some of Lily's things after she'd died."

"Wow." Abby shook her head slowly. "It's so much to take in. You could meet your second cousins! Where do they live?"

"All in America, as far as I can tell. One in New York, another one in Seattle. It's so *weird*." He let out a little laugh. "I have family I didn't even know about."

"I suppose I do too, if I consider Tom Reese's family that we never met... those grandparents, that whole branch of my relatives."

Simon raised his eyebrows. "You sound like you know something."

"I do," Abby said. "But I'm not sure how important it is, in the end."

"Tell me?"

And so she did, sharing the secrets that no longer needed to be kept about Tom Reese's cowardice, and Sophie's tempestuous declaration, and how it had ended between them, with Sophie keeping Tom's medal as a keepsake.

"Wow," Simon said when she had finished. "Wow."

"If Sophie hadn't broken it off, or if she'd changed her mind, we would have been related," Abby said with a little smile. "Or really, I suppose, I'd never have been born."

"I don't like to think of that." He reached for her hand, threading his fingers through hers one by one, a deliberate act.

Abby's heart caught in her chest, like someone had thrown it at a wall. She didn't know what was coming, didn't even know what she wanted to hear. *I really like you, but… It's been fun, hasn't it?* Or maybe just *I'm sorry I have to go so soon.*

"Abby."

She made herself look at him and smile. "Yes."

"I don't want this to end here."

Surprised by his certainty, she could only stare for a moment as she tried to collect her scattered thoughts. "But you live in England," she finally managed. "And my life—my life still is at Willow Tree." Even if she was only just starting to imagine that it might not be always. Or at least not *just*. But that was too far into the future to think about now, or to pin hazy hopes on it.

"I know. I'm not saying it will be easy."

"What are you saying, then?"

"I don't know." He let out a little laugh, endearing in its uncertainty. "I'm saying I want to see you again. You could visit me in Cambridge. Meet Maggie."

Surprised, she eased back a little. "You want me to meet Maggie?"

"Maybe. I called her last night. I've been WhatsApping her this whole time, but she's never responded. But I realized that's a bit like cheating, the coward's way out, to just send a text. So I rang and she answered and we talked for twenty awkward and rather excruciating minutes, but in the end it was okay. I think. Sort of?" He gave her a lopsided smile, pain shining in his eyes. None of this was easy. That was why it hadn't happened before. "I spoke to Sara, too, about stepping up a bit more. She liked the idea."

"That's wonderful, Simon."

"And us?" He prompted. "If you think there could be an us, even if just one day?"

She stared down at their joined hands, her mind doing somersaults. "I don't know," she said slowly.

Simon wilted a little, although he tried to rally. "I understand."

"It's not that I don't want to," she explained. "It's not that at all. It's just…" Things still felt fragile with her dad. And Willow Tree was her home. And even though she was trying, trying so hard, to make changes in her life, could she really do this? Did she want to risk what she'd only just started to have for something neither of them was ready to name? "I don't even have a passport."

"It's quite easy to get one. Just fill out a form."

She smiled at that. "You know what I mean."

"Yes, I do."

What if she went to Cambridge, and whatever they'd shared here didn't transfer? What if she came for a week or even two, and they remained awkward strangers the whole time, exchanging rather shamefaced smiles as they realized they really didn't have anything in common after all, and it had just been one of those intense holiday things?

"Just think about it," Simon said, and squeezed her hand.

SIMON

He left three days later, three glorious days he'd spent with Abby, on the farm, in town, and even another memorable lumberjack platter at the cook shanty. The last night, they'd had dinner with David, and Simon was gratified that the old man actually made an effort. It was awkward rather than easy, but it was the attempt that was important.

But none of it still felt settled as he said his goodbyes on the weathered porch where he'd first made her acquaintance, what felt like a lifetime ago, when he'd seen the pain in her eyes and wondered at it. Three short and yet endless weeks. He couldn't believe he was already going back, even as he felt he'd been here for ages.

"This doesn't have to be goodbye," she reminded him as she nervously tucked her hair behind her ears, Bailey sitting loyally by her feet. "Not a final one, anyway. We can just say 'see you later', and give a wave."

"I don't want to give a wave."

"You know what I mean—" Abby was cut off as he kissed her, pulling her close, reveling in the feel of her against him. Her eyes closed and his did too, and the kiss went on, a wish and a keepsake, and hopefully more than that. A promise.

He wanted to tell her that he was falling in love with her, that he didn't think he'd ever get tired of holding her like this, but he suspected those were the kinds of sentiments he didn't think either of them were ready for. The last few weeks had been wonderful and intense and yet also fragile.

He understood Abby's reticence about committing to some sort of future; part of him felt it too, and yet he still wanted to try. Try *hard*. For once in his life he didn't want to back away, hands in the air, deciding it was all just a little too intense, a bit too much for him. For once he wanted to give a relationship everything he had, even if it hurt. Even if it didn't work out, although he hoped it would.

"You're going to miss your plane," Abby said when he finally let her go, his head spinning, and, he suspected, hers too.

"Would that be a terrible thing?"

"Yes, it would, because Maggie is waiting for you." She gave him an encouraging smile, the firm look of a teacher with a wayward pupil, although her eyes were dancing.

"Not at the airport. I could call her and tell her I'd got held up."

"You don't want to do that, Simon." Her voice was gentle, her eyes full of warmth.

"No, I don't." He smiled and stepped back, even though he didn't want to. It really was time to go.

As he climbed in the car, he marveled again at how much had changed in such a short time. It was as if he was seeing the entire world through a different lens, and every few seconds he'd startle himself with the unexpected perspective. *How strange*, he thought, not for the first time, *that so much has changed, and all because of people who will never know how they've affected me. Helped me. Helped us.*

One last wave, and then he was starting the car, a cloud of dust kicking up as he drove down the dirt track, Abby waving in his rearview mirror. He kept her in his vision as long as he could, wanting to imprint her there, determined to believe he would see her again, even though they'd made no promises.

Sometimes you just had to trust. To accept, to forgive, and finally, to hope.

Holding onto his smile, Simon turned onto the main road that headed south to Chicago.

ABBY

The house was dim and quiet as Abby went back inside, breathing in the peaceful stillness. Sorrow tugged at her even as a smile came to her lips. There really was so much to be thankful for.

She walked slowly back to the kitchen, savoring all the familiar sights—the grandfather clock, the photo of her grandparents, the dried roses in a vase that had been there since she was a child. *Home*.

As she stood in the doorway, for a second she could see her mother standing at the stove, humming under her breath, giving her one of her quick, distracted smiles. *Everything okay, sweetheart?*

Yes, Abby thought. *Yes, actually, Mom, everything is okay.*

With a smile still on her lips, she took out her phone and typed in a search for airline tickets to London.

EPILOGUE

He stands on the cracked pavement in front of the block of flats—dilapidated, nondescript, but he knows the building so well. He has been dreaming of being here, of mounting these weathered steps, for the last year and a half.

For the last half-hour, he has simply been standing there in the cold, braving the icy drizzle of a wet January afternoon, unsure if he can bring himself to ring the bell. If he can face her—and, more importantly, if she can face him.

He has been back in London for nearly a week, finally a free man. He has filed all his reports, handed in his uniform, been given his suit of civilian clothes and a small grant to see him through, for a little while at least.

He saw Tom Reese as well, at the army headquarters, both of them being demobbed. They did an almost comical double take at the sight of one another, and then gave surprised and sheepish smiles. Just as he'd thought all those months ago, they were seeing the war out together.

Tom had loitered while he'd filled out his forms, and then, to his surprise, he'd asked him to go for a drink. He'd agreed, and they'd spent fifteen minutes somberly sipping watery pints before Tom had finally spoken.

"Sophie broke it off, because of what I did. I told her, in the end. I couldn't bear her not knowing, not if we were going to marry."

"I'm sorry." The words were inadequate, but he realized he meant them. He'd known Tom had loved her.

"She was so angry. And disappointed too, which was worse. She threw my ring back at my face and shouted at me that she thought I was a better man than that." Tom's voice had choked. "I thought I was, too."

"It was only one moment," he said quietly. "Surely we are all allowed those."

Tom shook his head. "It was a moment that cost men their lives. I can't forgive myself that. Abruzzo? The sergeant next to you? He took a bullet in his arm for me at the Waal." His face twisted. "And I as good as killed him."

"No," Matthew said quietly. "The Nazis killed him."

"But they might not have, if I'd kept my position." Tom released a shuddering breath. "It's something I'll have to live with for the rest of my life. I know that. At least I wasn't court-martialed, thanks to you." He gazed down, unseeing, at his pint. "I gave Sophie my Purple Heart. I want her to have something to remember me by, and maybe—maybe to make her see I wasn't always a coward."

The aching regret in his voice made Matthew reach for the medal that had been heavy in his pocket since he'd taken off his uniform. He hadn't known what to do with it; he certainly didn't want it. Not after Henck. Not after he'd realized what he too was capable of. He'd had six months with the wretched thing pinned to his chest, a constant reminder of his failure. "I want you to have this," he said, and offered the Distinguished Service Cross to Tom, who blinked down at it in surprise.

"What… I didn't know… why were you given it?"

"For an interrogation I did, after V-E Day." The words burned in his chest, along with the knowledge. "It doesn't matter."

Tom was quiet as he ran one finger over its crenelated edge. "And why would you give it to me?"

"You fought more than I did." As he said the words, he realized how true they were. "Six months of hard fighting." Tom had been among those to climb up the banks of the Waal, straight into enemy fire. He'd fought through the streets of Nijmegen, had been there for the horrendous surprise attacks at the start of Ardennes. Somehow, in the midst of it all, Matthew had forgotten all that. Now he remembered.

"It's yours," Tom said.

"No," Matthew answered, meaning it. "It's yours." He didn't want it. And Tom deserved something for his courage. He realized he didn't blame Tom for a moment of madness—hadn't he had one, as well? Weren't they both as guilty and as innocent as the other?

Tom's fingers closed around the medal. He looked strangely moved, a throb of emotion in his voice as he spoke. "Thank you."

The rain has drenched his overcoat and hat. A woman next door keeps coming to the grimy window and shooting him suspicious looks from behind some dingy net curtains. Without his uniform, he is nothing more than a vagrant, just one more hollow-eyed man who wanders through the city, looking as lost as he feels. Is this all that is to become of them?

He should ring the bell. He wants to. He has lifted his hand more than once, only to have it fall back limply to his side each time. What if she sees the emptiness in him? What does he have to offer her now? And yet he longs to see her. He longs for it with a desperation and an urgency that he thought he hadn't had it in him any more to feel, but he realizes now, to both his gratitude and terror, that he does.

The last six months he has discovered more than he has ever wanted to know—about his country, about the camps, about the fate of his family, and about who he is, or at least who he could be. The knowledge has transformed him, as surely as Jekyll into Hyde. Even if no one else sees it, he knows he always will.

And yet... there is Lily. There has always been Lily, the hope of her waiting for him, believing in him. But believing in the man he was, or the one he is afraid of becoming? Could she possibly be waiting for him as he is now?

And then the decision is taken out of his hands. The door opens, and she is there. He blinks and then drinks her in—those soft brown eyes, the gently curling hair. There is a streak of premature gray by her temple now. Her dress is worn and frayed, and she looks tired, but she is smiling, if just a little.

"I was waiting for you to come in," she says. "But then I decided I wouldn't wait any longer."

"Lily." He can't say any more.

He can't tell her of all the things he's seen and felt and done. Of war, and Wobbelin, and the smug face of Henck, the matter-of-fact descriptions given in the Nuremberg trials that made him feel as if his soul could claw its way out of his body.

He can't tell her about how he feels as if he has lost himself, forgotten something essential and elemental that everyone else takes for granted. A heart, perhaps? Maybe a soul.

He can't tell her any of that, at least not yet, even though, as he looks at her, he realizes he will one day, he will want to, and she will understand. She will accept and forgive.

And even in this moment, when he has said nothing but her name, she understands already, and he doesn't have to speak another word.

Lily steps forward, and then her arms are around him, drawing him in, like a tender mother with a child, but also a woman to the man she loves. His head rests on her breast and his shoulders shake, as, for the first time since he can remember, he weeps.

He is home.

A LETTER FROM KATE

I want to say a huge thank you for choosing to read *Into the Darkest Day*. If you did enjoy it, and want to keep up to date with all my latest releases, just sign up at the following link. Your email address will never be shared and you can unsubscribe at any time.

www.bookouture.com/kate-hewitt

When my editor first asked me to write a book set during the Second World War, I stumbled across the Ritchie Boys while researching ideas, and was immediately transfixed by their powerful story—Jewish refugees who returned to Germany to face those who had once tormented them. I owe a huge debt of gratitude and knowledge to two authors and their books about the Ritchie Boys—*The Ritchie Boys* by Bruce Henderson, and *Witness to the Storm* by Werner Angress, the personal memoir of a former Ritchie Boy from Berlin. I highly recommend both books for their powerful stories.

At the heart of my novel is the question of whether a moment should define us, and I hope as a reader you are encouraged that, no matter what the circumstances, forgiveness and healing can be found. Although I like to write about hard and often tragic situations, I do believe that redemption can be found in the midst of, and even through, suffering, as it was for Abby and Simon and Lily and Matthew.

I hope you loved *Into the Darkest Day* and if you did I would be very grateful if you could write a review. I'd love to hear what you think, and it makes such a difference helping new readers to discover one of my books for the first time.

I love hearing from my readers – you can get in touch on my Facebook page, through Twitter, Goodreads or my website.

Thanks,
Kate

 katehewittauthor

 @katehewitt1

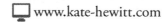 www.kate-hewitt.com

ACKNOWLEDGEMENTS

I must admit it was a bit daunting to start *Into the Darkest Day*, as I was writing a historical genre I'd never tried before. The research alone felt like enough to overwhelm me, and so I have many people and books to thank for helping me with facts and inspiring me with true stories. Thank you to Bruce Henderson, Werner Angress, Virginia Nicholson, Megan Westley, and many others for their books of impeccable research. Thank you also to the staff at the Imperial War Museum who answered some of my questions and directed me to appropriate books and exhibits. Thank you also to my dear husband Cliff, whose WW2 expertise helped me thrash out some issues, especially concerning battles and armies. Now I know the difference between a platoon and a battalion! It was also fun, if sometimes harrowing, to watch *Band of Brothers* with you.

I also must thank my old friend Greg Evans, to whom this novel is dedicated. He contacted me out of the blue a few years ago, to tell me a true story he'd heard that he thought would make a good novel, about an American GI and a British woman who had a wartime romance, and how he gave her his Purple Heart medal, and then how, years later, his family didn't want it back. That's all Greg knew, but it was enough to spark this story, so thank you, Greg, for the initial idea!

I also want to thank the Bookouture team who are all so amazing and generous with their time and expertise. Firstly, my lovely editor Isobel, who was so understanding when I went through a time of personal tragedy in the midst of this novel. Thank you for your patience! Thank you also to Kim and Noelle, who are so unfailingly wonderful with their marketing efforts, as well as Alex H, Alex C, Leodora, Peta, Radhika, and many others whose time and talents invested in this book I'm not even aware of! I wouldn't want to be with any other publisher.

Lastly, thank you to my family and friends who have supported my writing in so many ways—to Jenna, who is always patient and willing to listen to me brainstorm or moan, and to my non-writing friends who always gamely ask what I'm working on—Jo, Cat, Amanda, Jane, Julie, Abby, Georgie, as well as many others. Thank you finally to my wonderful family—Cliff, Caroline, Ellen, Teddy, Anna, and Charlotte—yes, I've named you all this time! Are you all amazing or what? As Grandad would have said, Does a chicken have lips? Love you!